LAST MAN STANDING

LAST MAN
STANDING

RICHARD HOLLAND

Troubador Publishing Ltd
Unit E2 Airfield Business Park,
Harrison Road, Market Harborough,
Leicestershire LE16 7UL
Tel: 0116 279 2299
Email: books@troubador.co.uk
Web: www.troubador.co.uk

ISBN 978-1-80514-358-1

British Library Cataloguing in Publication Data.
A catalogue record for this book is available from the British Library.

Printed and bound in Great Britain by 4edge Limited
Typeset in 11pt Garamond Pro by Troubador Publishing Ltd, Leicester, UK

For Nicky, Dominic, Betty & Welford.

For Bernie. I miss your company while I write.

With thanks to Andy and to Laura for your diligence, and to
Lucy for your brilliance and creativity.

And for Alex. I miss you so much. You will always be with me

x

PROLOGUE

It had been a glorious summer. Long, hot and carefree. The sort of summer your grandparents talked about fondly, and in the past tense. As if heatwaves had only ever happened in the seventies. Parks had been packed with children; families had spent time together for long glorious days and warm afternoons eating ice cream from Mr Whippy, or one of the many other vendors doing a tidy trade across the city. The sun seemed to hang endlessly in the sky, pubs were rammed with revellers and the warm aroma of barbecues permeated the air.

The Spice Girls had just released *Wannabe*, the Fugees were on top of the singles charts and Britpop was exploding. Oasis versus Blur was at its peak, and the UK rave and garage scenes were in full swing. The Prodigy had hit the mainstream, *The Fat of the Land* was sitting proudly at the top of the album charts, and weekends for those coming of age were spent in run-down nightclubs on sticky floors, with Sunday mornings spent waking up in unknown places and with little knowledge of how you got there. Nights of hedonism were enjoyed and forgotten in the same breath. The best of days.

iPhones were still a generation away, and there was the

freedom to experiment freely without having pictures, videos and live streams of what you did to hold you back, or to judge you in years to come. Job applications and job interviews of the future couldn't be tainted by the events of a Friday night a decade before. Teenage years forever documented, waiting to hold a thirty-year-old to account for something the seventeen-year-old version did, or said.

The last truly free generation.

Only Belfast was different. The summer had been memorable for many parts of its fragmented society, and for its student base and a generation too wrapped up in their own lives, but for wider society there was more than just the sunshine and the music. The football and the nights out. For the everyday man on the street, there was an undertone of menace. A toxic element to the cultural mix. Ever-present and with an edge to the mood. The Troubles.

Daily life hid a level of fear. Catholics and Protestants lived in close proximity in the literal sense, but a world apart in another. The IRA and dissident gangs ruled the streets, and even with the sun up, you knew which streets to walk down, which ones to avoid and which pubs and shops you were *allowed* to go into. The social order. One you didn't break, with reprisals and beatings for those who dared to, those who stepped out of line or those who simply forgot.

Peace lines defied their name and provided a cold and stark barrier. Six metres high in places, with brickwork, shards of metal and barbed wire combining to create an industrial barrier, separating those of differing views living yards from one another. Back gardens, garages and beliefs divided in a very literal sense. Metal gates pegged open during the day to allow traffic to flow through the numerous districts and territories;

van drivers, milk floats and bin men allowed to do their jobs unchallenged, but closed at night, with the police able to enforce the division and reduce the likelihood of it all just kicking off. To prevent something bubbling over in the most fragile of environments. Even on a quiet night, the odd petrol bomb could easily be tossed over, to smash and burn out in an empty street. If you were lucky. Everybody was being kept on their toes.

A variety of murals were painted onto the rendered blockwork at the end of terraced streets and on walls leading into alleyways, shining in the light. Colourful and striking images, brought to life in vibrant graffiti. Their artistic integrity, primary colours and cartoon styles masking the ruthless division within the communities in which they stand. Thirty kilometres of walls dividing a modest-sized capital city, a modern-day Berlin. Streets separated in the most brutal and physical of ways.

The summer in Belfast had been as good as the rest of the UK, in meteorological terms at least. The rest of the year had been littered with attacks, assaults and cold-blooded killings. It was business as usual, with the odd spike. The odd reminder of how life worked on these streets. Three glorious days of sun followed by a shooting. Reminding you. Keeping you in check. Evenings could be filled with joy as much as they could fear, and even during the summer knowing where to be, and where not to be, had become a dangerous game of cat and mouse.

The year had been so bright in cultural and sporting terms, but if you peeled back a layer and looked with a different lens, you'd find the London Docklands bombing in February, which had claimed the lives of two civilians and injured thirty-nine others. And in June, just prior to a Euro '96 match at Old

Trafford, the Manchester bombing took place, destroying large parts of the city centre and injuring over 200 people. Glass, metal and shrapnel had rained down from the Arndale, leaving the frame of the Corporation Street bridge hanging symbolically broken across the shattered causeway. The violence and the targets were escalating and had reached the mainland.

The damage was extensive and the ambition of the terrorists was becoming more brazen.

CHAPTER 1

BELFAST, JUNE 1996

It was just before 3pm when Chris Wilson checked his digital Casio watch. Within minutes, the school bell had ended the day, and the class of exuberant teenagers had thrashed the double doors of the school wide open, bursting out into the June sunshine.

It was only a short walk home, and as he unlocked the front door and entered the three-bed semi, he shouted for his parents but found neither of them at home. His dad was rarely home at the best of times, and something had been going on at work. More recently, his mum had become just as irregular. He checked for both of them again before using the opportunity to sneak a couple of chocolate bars into his rucksack. As he was doing so, his phone rang. A Nokia 3210 with a clip-on cover. A style everybody at the school had. In '96, if you didn't have a Nokia, you simply weren't with the 'in-crowd'. It was the phone of choice.

It was a school friend, Alex Delaney. Somebody he'd known through the back end of primary school, and into secondary.

His dad was always defensive and wouldn't welcome Alex into the house. He'd said that he just didn't trust him, and seemed to not care much for his dad either, but Chris liked his sense of humour. He was popular in the school, he'd befriended Chris and they'd got on.

"You're coming to this one, right?"

Chris tried to hide the apprehension in his voice, asking Alex how he knew there was a demonstration happening, and what it was about.

He didn't like to get involved in these things. Hated it. He'd been to a couple, but fighting usually broke out before the police waded in to disperse any troublemakers. Somebody always got hurt, that was guaranteed, and his parents would definitely disapprove. It was dangerous. It was stupid. Nothing good would come of it. It was a sure-fire way to get into trouble. To get hurt.

The teenager in Chris Wilson was measured. More measured than almost all of his peers. But the nagging in the pit of his stomach was digging from the inside. He'd decided to not go to a house party a week ago, when seemingly everybody else had. Hadn't fancied it. He had an assignment to write and some revision to catch up on, but he didn't want to get neck-deep in some stupid shit that would most likely get out of hand. Didn't want to feel compelled to get drunk and feel vulnerable. Didn't want to be in the position of being exposed to drugs and having to say no. To be the strong one, but look weak. And it had kicked off. He thought it would. Staying home that night had been the right choice.

He'd also said no to another recent party, as well as an official demonstration, and despite his apprehensions, he was aware that saying no would come to a point where being asked

2

and declining would morph into not being asked at all. The pressures on a teenager wanting to do the right things but being expected to do otherwise. To be seen. To fit in.

Keep saying no and even his close friends would become distant, to the point that neither could recall the last party they went to together. The point at which friendships start to untangle. The point at which somebody in a circle starts to leave it. Those points we all have where we see someone for the last time without knowing it. A friend. A loved one. A parent.

Alex ignored the silence. "You're home alone, aren't you? I'll be outside yours around eight, and you'd fucking better be there!"

Chris grunted an answer, but it was a 'yes'. He probably should go. Even if he went for a bit. Show his face and then sneak home after an hour if the mood got bad.

His dad would likely be working so no need to worry about him, and he could tell his mum he was going out with Alex and another friend, just for a couple of hours. At most. A little white lie that nobody would ever need to know about. He wouldn't be expected to drink too much tonight, and there was unlikely to be any drugs. Crack a few jokes and walk the streets. Enjoy the bravado and feel part of something. Part of the gang. One of the lads. Either way, he'd be back at home and in bed by 10pm at the latest.

The best of both worlds.

It was just past eight when Chris Wilson saw Alex Delaney sitting on a wall opposite the house. He was drinking a beer and immediately passed one to Chris, who reluctantly took it. Alex slapped him on the back and headed up the street. It was a longer walk than Chris was expecting, and the apprehension grew as they got closer to an area he knew to be one of conflict. The sunshine of the afternoon had been replaced with a cloudier evening that was beginning to match the tension in the air.

Two more of Alex's friends had joined them as they reached the back of a group of people protesting. It was several hundred strong. The chanting was angry, and growing in volume. Fists were raised and the protestors lurched forward a yard or two, closing the gap with a large line of police officers who were patrolling the opposite side of the street. Alex finished his bottle of Beck's and launched it confrontationally towards the police. It smashed on the floor in front of them and the crowd cheered, lurching forward again and taunting those behind the tight formation of riot shields.

Chris pulled his hood up and took a step back. He didn't like the mood already and felt vulnerable. Exposed. More bottles were thrown and the cheering grew. Baiting the police. Inviting them. A piece of brick smashing into one of their shields proved the final straw and the police line charged. Batons were drawn and those protestors inviting the conflict were now shielding themselves with their bare arms. Crushed between a charging police line and several hundred of their own.

The first petrol bomb was thrown in retaliation, landing just behind the police line and bursting into flames in the street. An officer stepped backwards, off balance and quickly realised that his right leg was engulfed in flames. The crowd erupted and the intensity soared.

Backup arrived and the first of the tear gas was fired towards the crowd, whizzing and hissing its way into the melee. One pellet landed near Chris, who lurched backwards, covering his eyes and nose as best he could, but the gas was seeping in. He could feel it. Could taste it. Alex dragged him away and pulled

4

him down a small street close by. He was laughing, relishing the confrontation.

Chris coughed. His eyes were stinging. Alex picked half a brick up and held it in his right hand. Desperate to be involved, his adrenaline was coursing. He raised the brick to throw it, but with no obvious target, he dropped it in front of him. He grabbed Chris, who could see that Alex had his phone in his other hand. He tried to talk but coughed again; his vision was blurry and his throat sore.

Some of the crowd ran past and away from the front line. Chris tried to follow them but felt Alex grab his top, pulling him roughly to one side and down an adjacent street.

"We're going… the wro…" Chris coughed. The words didn't come. Alex pulled him and he fell forward, picking himself up before lurching forward again.

He knew it was the wrong way, knew the street kinked right and looped back up to where the police would be able to head off those trying to escape. If the police headed down this street in numbers, they could cut off and counterattack the crowd. Alex pulled him violently as his eyes continued to sting and his throat burned. He allowed Alex to pull him. He didn't know why. His cough got worse. His eyes were weeping, his breathing heavy.

Then suddenly Alex stopped pulling. Chris sensed a number of officers running down the street and past him. He fell to his knees by the side of the road with his hands in the air defensively, still coughing. He felt for the kerb but found a car. He leant against it and waited. Blinking heavily and trying to catch his breath. There was now a heavy police presence in the street, and Chris sensed somebody close to him. He mouthed "Alex" but somehow knew that it wasn't.

He sensed the danger, and even though he was certain he was surrounded by the police, a feeling in his gut told him he wasn't safe. Digging and nagging away in the pit of his stomach. The noise of the mob was distant now, and Chris wanted to speak to his parents. Wanted to hug his mum. Wanted to apologise to his dad.

But before he could reach for his phone, the large bomb that had been planted in the Ford Sierra he was leaning against detonated.

CHAPTER 2

PRESENT DAY – LEICESTER

DCI Rob Rhone was sitting in his office. His mood was relaxed, more so than it had been in recent weeks. He sat in his chair, in smart trousers and a comfy blue shirt. One that was neat but older. One of his favourites, with the sleeves rolled up, and a well-worn watch on his left wrist. The leather strap was soft and furrowed to the edges, and it went well with a brand-new pair of chestnut brown brogues. He'd been unconvinced he was ready to get away with them, having only recently turned fifty, but they felt good and he was happy with the look.

He flicked his head to see the autumn rain falling outside, tapping gently on the window as it fell, before looking at the new addition to his office wall; a canvas print of his two boys at the King Power Stadium, taken before the Southampton game last February. He'd had it printed by an online retailer who was now emailing daily to ask if he wanted a mug or a mouse mat. He'd been meaning to opt out of the emails.

He looked at another picture on his desk. A small but precious one. His younger sister Emily who was fighting her own battles from a hospice not five miles away. It was a photo from a family barbecue. They were off guard, laughing raucously at one another and enjoying the sunshine. Enjoying life. He touched her face caringly, knowing that he'd see her again later. It had become a well-trodden path. He smiled in frustration; she deserved so much better from life.

Rob's team were busy, although the office itself felt quiet, with most out working active cases. The monthly reports that had landed this morning were showing Rob that Leicestershire was making progress in the fight against crime, with consistent monthly reductions in the key areas measured and reported to the police commissioner, town hall and to anybody who asked for it through a freedom of information request. All areas that mattered most – violent crime, rape, robbery, murder and drug crime – had all shown reductions and had been in consistent decline for three months, offering the force a positive position and some breathing space after a choppy 2022.

The surrounding counties had all shown mixed progress in their own battles, and different conversations would be happening across the varying forces. Northamptonshire had made progress in some areas but had seen a relapse in violent crime. Derbyshire had seen a steady increase across all areas, and would be the one getting it in the neck this month. The area of focus.

Nottinghamshire remained red. Its drug, violent crime and street violence on the fringes of the city contributed to a consistently low score. Rutland, Lincolnshire and Warwickshire were mixed and had been RAG'd as green, orange and orange respectively, with Leicestershire the only other force in green alongside neighbouring Rutland.

He sat back and sighed, out of relief more than anything

else. He shouldn't get too much grief for the results. He wasn't expecting a pat on the back, that didn't come too often, but Rob was at a point in his career where not getting a wave of grief and a month's worth of pressure was sufficient to know he was doing a number of things well. That the right steps were being taken to the satisfaction of the governors and, hopefully, the governed.

He had a conference call scheduled with the Chief Constable, Laura Mathers, later in the day to go through the numbers and to decide on the plan of action for the coming weeks. Where resources were needed, where they weren't and to identify areas where more was expected. Laura Mathers had settled well into her new role, having been promoted from ACC following the fallout of the recent murders. Murders that all had been pleased to file away following a torrid investigation. One that would haunt the hierarchy and those involved for the foreseeable future.

Chief Constable David Parker had paid the price. Taken one for the team. After a long and distinguished career, the recent murders had been enough for the public and the press to demand a head. The changes could have been wholesale, more sweeping, but the powers that be had decided that David Parker's 'retirement' after a lengthy career had been sufficient. Rob had his suspicions that Parker's stock had been falling anyway. He didn't know his actual age but he must have been touching sixty, and he'd grown older as the hierarchies and the decision makers driving the change had become younger. They wanted new ideas, fresh ways of thinking and constant evolution. Parker wasn't it, but he'd overseen the force through diverse and divisive periods. Miners' strikes, Premier League football and increasing immigration had all been navigated with David Parker in uniform or in charge. He was an old head. Wise.

But the force was becoming something different, and Parker's time had run out. His tenure would have been close to a natural conclusion anyway, but with Emma Sharpe's murderous spree and the national press scrutinising the force, Parker had fallen on his sword. The timing hadn't been great for him, and those with the authority to force him from his position had taken the opportunity to do so. The press and the public had seemed satisfied with the outcome, and Parker himself must have known that his goose was cooked. He'd even been afforded the dignity to resign, a move reserved for those respected servants as opposed to those who had been forced from office in disgrace Nixon-esque style, but David Parker's service had been sufficient to give him the opportunity to leave with his head high. Or high enough. It certainly wasn't out of the back door on a Friday afternoon.

The power struggle had started well before Parker left. Those in a position to make a grab for it had been wrangling; conversations had happened behind closed doors and late at night. The position was senior, influential, and didn't come around too often. It was a position that had been fought over by the ambitious, the driven and those looking to further their careers for the next political cycle.

The ACCs of Northamptonshire and Derbyshire had both been in the mix. Rob had heard that on the grapevine, but he'd backed Mathers during the murder investigation and had nailed his colours to her mast. Both of them had circumvented David Parker's authority as the murder investigation unravelled, and maybe they'd subconsciously undermined his authority. Shown him as the one not in touch, the one without his finger on the pulse, but their decision-making had been for the benefit of the investigation and for the right reasons. In their eyes at least.

Rob was comfortable; Parker would have done the same thing. He was astute. He knew the game; he'd been playing it for long enough. You don't become a chief constable without knowing that sacrifices have to be made. When people either fall under the bus or need to fall for the benefit of the force. Rob had seen many officers come and go. Some for the right reasons, others not so much, but there were many whose careers had been brought to an abrupt end by David Parker.

Mathers had been the front runner, and Rob had rooted for her to land it. She knew the force, she knew Rob, and she'd be ideally placed to provide change and stability in one. She'd ticked a number of boxes for those making the decisions, both in terms of her political views and alignment to County Hall. She was also smart, energetic, and had an elegance that would no doubt have played in her favour. The number of female chief constables nationwide remains imbalanced, and her gender would have also been to her benefit should the voting have been tight.

A new chief would have meant change; perhaps even Mathers herself would have been asked to move on. Rob had wanted her to be appointed, for entirely selfish and holistic reasons, and had been delighted when her appointment was confirmed. It had been Mathers herself who had told Rob. One to one and face to face, something he'd taken as a massive positive. He was close to her, and backing her had proved to be a wise career move. The next three to five years would now be broadly planned out, and Rob would be able to continue his efforts with solid backing and without having to impress a new chief constable. Without having to change tack or adapt his style to a newcomer. An unknown.

Good result.

CHAPTER 3

David Cramer's day was going well. It was a warm autumn afternoon, and he'd spent much of it in his garden. A long narrow space belonging to a 1930s semi in suburbia. A bay-fronted property with a wide block paved driveway, and a garden with a neat hedgerow to the rear that had taken significant time and commitment to achieve. Flower beds that had spent years reaching a level of maturity, with bullseye-straight borders which were perfectly trimmed and with contrasts of colour and texture that the *Ground Force* team would be proud of.

A shed at the bottom of the garden sat with a single door propped open, with a fork leaning against it to stop it moving in the breeze. Its three prongs stabbing into the ground, which was still hard after a better-than-average English summer. Rainfall had been infrequent and the summer sun had baked and scorched the garden, with some of the neighbours' lawns showing bare patches and cracks that he'd managed to avoid by consistent watering. Even with the inevitable hosepipe ban, David Cramer had hoarded hundreds of litres of water in butts hidden from sight behind his shed, in a nook protected by a wooden trellis entwined with climbing plants. He was well accustomed to planning ahead. To being resourceful.

At sixty-seven, Cramer was in good health and had a level of fitness a man a decade his junior would be happy with. A fitness and strength that he maintained through regular walks, occasional jogging and early-morning visits to his local gym; a chain with modern kit and a dirt-cheap monthly fee. The locality made for a pleasant drive up the A47 towards King's Lynn, with the gym situated on his side of town. Easy access at the time of the day he started.

He continued to potter around his garden, picking up a metal watering can – traditional design and in British racing green – and splashing a good dose of water across a bright bed of dahlias.

A tall figure, his shadow long and his tan reflecting a man enjoying retirement. He wore a smart but ageing shirt, turned up at the cuffs, and open by two or three buttons to the breastbone, showing off a tuft of silver chest hair against his tanned skin. His mid-length salt and pepper hair flowed, and his face looked clean after his morning shave. A force of habit; a daily wet shave. Something that was simply part of his routine given his life of military service and the importance of discipline in his profession.

He checked the watch worn loosely on his left wrist, flicking it around to see the time and deciding that a coffee was in order, and contemplating whether to have it with a piece of lemon drizzle cake that had been dropped round by a friendly neighbour.

He swept some soil back into a bed from a patio area with an old broom, the patio still bathed in sun and a likely option for the coffee break. An old cast-iron patio set sitting on worn flagstones, the metal in desperate need of some repair and love. The rust patches woven in against fading black Hammerite paint. He'd considered replacing it; it was never something he liked that much, never fully warmed to. Only his wife had loved it. Loved sitting there in the afternoon in the sun. An orange juice in the morning, a coffee in the afternoon or a crafty cigarette in the evening. Always the same of the two chairs, facing the same direction. Enjoying the same view.

He walked into his kitchen, flicking the kettle on before running his hands under the tap. He threw a heaped spoonful of sugar into his favourite garden cup, and an equally heaped spoonful of his favourite Columbian blend. The warm smell of the coffee granules was still something he enjoyed. A comfort, and something reassuring that still heartily satisfied his senses.

He stepped out of the French doors whilst the noise of the kettle escalated towards boiling point, standing on a small step he'd put down for his wife, when mobility had become harder and the deep step from the back door had become too much.

Three years now. It was always the little things he recalled fondly. The way she sat in the garden, the knife she liked to use to spread her toast. The step. The ring of a mug she left on a wooden shelf. Always without a coaster. Every time, he told her it would leave a mark, but she just smiled and left it there all the same. He was now oddly glad that it had, the mark a reminder, and something that made him smile every time he saw it. Keeping her memory alive.

He walked back out into the garden holding the steaming mug, the sun behind a cloud but still warm, the birds still vocal against a quiet backdrop of country life.

They'd retired to Guyhirn, a small village on the A47 just outside of Wisbech in Norfolk. Quiet, quaint and rural. As they had little in the way of ties, it had presented itself at the right time and offered the perfect 'out' for a couple looking to slow down. To leave everything behind.

There was a lot that had needed leaving behind.

A property they'd been able to move straight into as cash buyers, with ample space, garages and land. Enough to keep David busy, and enough for Mary to settle into community life as a local volunteer. The isolation had proved perfect, a large plot of land for both of them to enjoy. The fields had been ideal for Mary to walk the dogs when she and they were still alive. Hours of joy in fields picturesque enough to belong in a lifestyle magazine. Days to live for, and sufficient to suppress memories of the past. For an hour or two.

He wandered through his kitchen and into his hallway, looking curiously at the front door mat where a solitary newspaper lay. He picked it up, his brow furrowed. He didn't have newspapers delivered, and if the mood ever took him, he'd walk to the local shop and buy one, along with a packet of biscuits to have with a coffee in the garden. Chocolate digestives, or custard creams. He groaned as he bent down to pick it up. It must be a new freebie, and the sign on the glass of the front door deterring cold callers and free papers had clearly been ignored. He thought he'd heard the postman but there was nothing underneath. No gas bill, no letter from his sister. Nothing. Just the newspaper. He looked at it, then laid it on the worktop as he walked back into the kitchen. It had saved him a wander today, and it could always help to keep tabs on what was happening locally. He'd become less involved with the wider community as a widower but still liked to see the good, the bad and the ugly rounded up from the locale.

He'd skip past the stuff on local thieves and break-ins

and find solace in the primary school children excelling, the elderly raising funds for the NHS and in another of his passions; sport.

Rugby union and cricket were his preferred choices, but he'd sit and watch rugby league on a quiet weekend, or even tune in to the more obscure sports. Golf, American football, darts.

He flicked from the back page and was pleased to see a report on rugby union, as the Eastern Counties Cup had started. He'd missed rugby through the summer and was always pleased when the Norfolk league got fully underway. The standards in the London North East three division were good, and he'd go several times a year and stand on the touchline, idling away a couple of hours. Making small talk with strangers about the scrum going backwards, the hooker who couldn't throw a straight line out, or the loud opposition scrum-half who needed taking down a peg or two.

He was delighted to see they'd made it through to the next round with a hard fought 36-28 victory over Leicester Lions at Ely. The Lions were not a team he was familiar with, and they played their rugby in a different division. The report showed a tough battle and had a team photo of the victorious Norfolk first XV, with torn shirts and muddy, smiling faces.

It also called out one of the opposition back row; Martin King who had been named player of the match despite being on the losing side. His picture was a smiling portrait with his medal around his neck, but the smile was no doubt for the camera after a losing cause. There was a thin trail of blood seeping out from a wound just above his left eye, showing the scars of the battle.

David Cramer looked at the photo and squinted. He looked again.

He leant forward to neutralise the light of the sun and failed. He snatched the paper and walked into the kitchen, to a corner with the least daylight, rummaging and grabbing a magnifying glass from a drawer, before slamming it back shut. His relaxed demeanour had flicked like a switch. His senses raised.

He looked at the image again in dull light. His gut wrenching, he felt sick. He knew what he'd seen but was denying it in his own mind. Anger started to flow. A pure anger. A rage that coursed violently through his veins.

He looked again. Martin King was a face he recognised. It may have been muddy, sweaty and a little bloodstained, it may have aged by a decade or two, but it was unmistakably him.

The features, the jawline, the eyes. He'd been about twenty miles away only last Saturday. Smiling in a losing cause. Carefree, enjoying life.

Not all of the past had stayed behind.

CHAPTER 4

The dust had just about settled following the series of murders carried out by Emma Sharpe. Their old colleague. Their old friend. In reality, the shadow cast over the force would linger for years to come. For generations to come. Processes and protocols would change, everybody would be under a microscope, and life within Leicestershire Police would be irrevocably different. It already felt different.

Everybody was already feeling sorry for the next wave of recruits whose personal lives, marriages, affairs, social media presence and children would be raked over in minute detail by a force desperate to protect its reputation. To stop a repeat.

Jack had recovered after the assault, with no long-term effects seeming to impact him after being drugged, aside from the odd pain in the neck. Especially first thing in the morning. It was now seemingly appropriate to take the piss, with comments around 'getting it in the neck' making a daily appearance.

Jack had just been unlucky. Been in the right place at the wrong time. Trusted somebody who maybe hadn't fully earned it. Or earned it and lost it.

A life lesson learnt in the worst possible way. A colleague who'd taken advantage of Jack, and who had injected drugs into his system. Incapacitating him in order to murder a suspect. A witness. Jack had lain unconscious yards from where the murder had happened, which had embarrassed the wider force if not Jack himself. Even the brass seemed to have been protective about it, showing care and compassion and affording him some time off to recuperate. It was right. It wouldn't have happened in the nineties; he'd have been shunned, or possibly even sacked, but looking after your employees, especially those of public service, was now the expected standard.

Jack wouldn't make the same mistake again. The trust brought about by his youth had been shattered. His character hardened by the experience, inwardly if not outwardly. That would come in time. An abruptness. A wall. A complete lack of trust which would take any new relationship much longer to achieve stability, and to a more fragile degree. Accept nothing, question everything, trust no one.

There was something 'coming of age' about the experience, professionally and personally. Jack was still as smartly dressed as ever, still looked catalogue ready in the right suit. Today's was light grey, a fitted jacket and skinny trousers with smart, polished black shoes. A dark blue shirt with an open collar could have made him look like an estate agent from nearby Belvoir Street; only the face and demeanour told you very clearly that he wasn't. His hair was slightly longer but still perfectly groomed. Fair and swept back, with a stubble length that complemented it. There was something more *masculine* now. Not in appearance, just in how he carried himself. Walked. Looked at you.

Nicky and Jen had looked after Jack since he'd joined the

team as a DC. Had him under their wing. He was still there, the bond stronger than ever along with the desire to look after one another. A great quality brought about by something awful.

Nicky and Jen were both business as usual. They'd had to give statements for the inquiry but were as polished as ever. Stick to the story was always the plan, but when the story is also the gospel truth, it reduces the complexity. Reduces the chance of an anomaly, which a prosecutor, lawyer or journalist would love. A contradiction. To be picked at like a scab until the starting point and the truth become so distorted that you wondered how you ended up where you did.

Jen was busy and was glad of it. Something to focus on, something new and different. Even the details of a rape case were a welcome distraction. Something she oddly enjoyed. She was vying for a suspect who was well known to the police. He was even more well known to Jen, and she was out for him. She loved the opportunity to take down somebody who thought he was above the law. Above women.

Jen was working out of a large community station on the outskirts of town; an old police building on the Narborough Road. Barely a mile from Fosse Park and with good office space. The vibe was more laid back than Lodge House, plus there was ample parking. She sat back with her hands behind her head, lifting one to wave at a colleague as they walked past the open door, their shoes clicking on the old tiled floor. She had picked her favourite black skinny jeans and flat black slip-on shoes. A comfy option for a day behind the desk. A knitted grey jumper completed the look, along with a red and black cheque scarf that was still being worn, having not yet found its way to the coat stand. The office was old and chilly and it was keeping her warm. Her dark hair was loose and flowing nicely;

it hadn't changed colour for a few weeks now and was elegantly long and stylish.

Her demeanour was serious. There was a softness to her character. A warmness and a kindness reserved for those who earned it. For those she let in. But her day face was not one to be messed with. She enjoyed life in the force, didn't take shit from anybody and could be quick and harsh in rebuking anyone who tried.

Her phone rang. Becky Ryan. She picked it up with a smile. "Hey, Becky! How are you?"

"I'm good, Jennifer! How are you?"

"Pretty good, ta. Keeping my head down and getting on with things."

"What happened last night? Didn't you have a date?"

"No, I sacked it off. Wasn't in the mood. Went for a walk instead."

"Which one was he? The tall weird guy or the short fetish one?"

"The tall weird one."

"Was he Bumble or Tinder?"

"Tinder. I need to give Bumble more of a go, but I'm just not feeling it right now. Humanity is barely filling me with much joy. How's your love life?"

"Up and down."

They both laughed at the innuendo. A puerile moment that made them both smile, and which brought an end to the small talk.

"Want some news on your man?"

Jen perked up. It was good news and would allow progress of an investigation that meant so much to Jen. An individual who she'd been gunning for. One that had got to her. Got under her skin. Some crimes can leave you feeling oddly passive, some are just procedural, and a few, just a rare few, can crawl under your skin and manifest into an ingrained feeling of anger. Of hatred. Becky knew how much Jen hated anybody who took advantage of the vulnerable, the old, the disabled or the infirm, but she reserved a special level of hatred for those who sought to commit violent crime against women. Taking her responsibility to protect those in need, and to enforce those laws to the fullest extent. Somebody had to, and Jen relished it.

"What have you got for me? Something useful, I hope!"

"Depends on what he's given you so far. If he's saying there was consent, then maybe not as much as we'd like, but we've found and matched trace DNA from the items you provided. The underwear and the skirt both have traces of semen on them, and we've also found a couple of hairs for good measure. The follicles are intact so there's absolutely no wiggle room. We've also been able to match a mark on the victim's neck to his right hand, so he's used enough force to bruise her and we can directly link that injury to him."

"I love you, Becky Ryan."

"Does that help?"

"It sure does. He's a fucking idiot, and he's arrogant too. He'd denied any sexual contact at all. Maybe he was cocky enough to think we wouldn't find anything or that he'd done enough to get away with it, so he's going to need to change his story as a bare minimum. He may even go no comment, but I think we'll be able to charge him with what you've got. I'll do it personally once I've spoken to the CPS, and I will savour it greatly."

"Glad to be of service, Miss James."

"Fancy a drink later?"

"What day is it?"

"Does it matter?"

They both laughed.

"Is Nicky up for it?"

"I haven't asked yet but reckon she'll be a yes when I tell her the news."

"Jack?"

"He may do, I'll ask him but he's fifty-fifty."

"I'll come for one, Jen!"

"Meet you in the Orange Tree at half six? We'll just have a couple!"

Becky hung up. She was looking forward to seeing the girls, and she hadn't had a hangover for a while.

CHAPTER 5

It was a dark miserable night. Bleak. The sort of evening devoid of hope. An invisible sky pouring rain relentlessly on everything in its path, with large puddles formed on uneven ground and lashing through lights on the eaves of nearby warehouses.

Deserted.

Frog Island had stood tall in the inner city for decades. It had been a workplace, an industrial giant and a place to socialise for generations. Factories, engineering units and cotton mills through the industrial boom made the area central to the city. A railway station and the canal weaving through its heart only made it more attractive to the merchants and the entrepreneurs, bringing raw materials, goods and people as the cyclical moth-like nature of humanity peaked during the seventies and eighties.

An economic boom had preceded the birth of globalisation, before the crash that had enveloped a generation who had seen it start to fall.

It now stood, a shadow of its former self. Abandoned. Forty years had passed. Forty years of decline and negligence. Glass was broken or missing from windows entirely. Roof panels were missing or had collapsed completely. Graffiti was spattered on the walls and litter blew across an abandoned yard.

Bored youths, drug dealers and society's outcasts had now come to use the darker corners recreationally, replacing the captains of industry, engineers and narrow boats that had gone before them. A total role reversal. An area of popularity, employment and wealth was now derelict and desperate.

It was in many ways reflective of life. Representing the fragility of it all. The temporary nature.

I walked across what resembled an old loading yard. An open space. The ground uneven, gravelly underfoot. My path staggered and weaved deftly to avoid the puddles and piles of litter. I looked around at the array of buildings, sheds and storage areas. There is very little natural light, the odd warehouse across the canal providing a flicker from a security fitting. A Kirkby and West milk distribution depot is still operating, with the quiet hum of forklift trucks audible in the background.

This is not a good place to be.

The city centre is only a mile or so in front of me but feels like a thousand. The solidarity and dereliction of it all.

I walk towards a larger warehouse, my hands firmly in my coat pockets, my head tucked down in a vain attempt to avoid the rain. The loading bay in front of me is level with the height of my chest. Its dark timbers are soaked, with weeds crawling through the gaps and clinging to life.

I find a concrete staircase to the side of two of the bays, where lorries would have once parked and goods would have been shuttled on and off their beds. I can envisage men in flat caps laughing and joking, or sitting on the edge for a smoke or a sandwich.

At the top of the stairs to the bay are two large sliding

timber doors that are padlocked shut, with the rot on the edge of the wood providing a slit to look through. Even large enough to get a hand through.

I'm carrying a torch but I don't want to alert or frighten anything, or anybody who may be holed up in there. Rats, of the human or rodent variety.

My training may come in useful. That itself feels like a lifetime ago, but if I need to, I'll defend myself. Or more.

I carry on walking, turn a corner of the warehouse and am greeted with a smaller door. A fire exit. An ornate black railing frames the corner, with rain dripping steadily onto the concrete below. The years and abandonment have eroded the edges, causing rust and more decay.

I'm wearing gloves. Black leather gloves which aren't protecting me from the cold in the way I expected when I bought them.

I reach the edge of the door. There's no visible padlock. With a gentle ease and a squeak, the door shudders ajar. I look down, half expecting something to crawl out. It doesn't.

I peer round, looking in. My eyes flicker, adjusting to the light, which is somehow darker.

My conscience rises up as a potential moment gets closer. I swallow hard. My intentions are not good. They're actually pretty fucked up. It wouldn't be the first time I've taken a life, but it still goes against everything I've ever known or been taught. Against my own values. It's a means to an end, though, which I've managed to justify to myself.

Life has had a way of changing those values. Testing, twisting and morphing them until they're barely recognisable as the values they once were. As who I once was.

I've thought about this for a while. Dismissing the idea at

first, but the notion had been planted. Manifesting and growing itself over months as my desire to act grew, exponentially, until it became my only focus. An obsession.

My hands are back in my pockets, with my right hand holding the butt of my gun firmly. I flick the safety catch off with my index finger. It's good to go. So am I.

I close my eyes. What the fuck am I doing.

I need a cadaver. A cold dead body.

Breaking into a mortuary was an option. Just too hard and too obvious. And noticeable.

Exhumation was in my mind for about ten seconds before that was dispatched. Way too messy. Time-consuming and high risk. And just grim. Creating my own dead body seemed the most reasonable option. It did at the time.

The prospect of shooting a homeless man dead had seemed abhorrent to start with. Yet here I am scouring the streets in the dead of night looking for an unwilling volunteer.

I feel rain land on the back of my neck and trickle downwards, causing me to shiver. My body shakes and I pull my hood up tighter, desperate to stop any further ingress of rain or cold.

The hole in the roof responsible for the ingress of rainfall allows a flash of light to streak across my face; my eyes readjust once more. I look up at it, a floodlight from a neighbouring cement works on the corner of Swan Street and the edge of the Fosse Park recreation ground provides the shadows amongst the darkness. A powerful beam from the last of the industry still operating on this land, clinging on for its own life.

I can see a collection of belongings further up the warehouse. My senses heighten. A sleeping bag, some bottles. A pillow. It's tucked under an internal bay that looks like an old workbench area, where men would have once stood hammering, welding or machining.

I walk slowly towards the bag; there's no movement. At this point, I'm unaware if the bag itself is abandoned. It looks dry. The old workstation and the patchwork roof overhead are providing some protection to the area. I consider firing a bullet through the bag to take the risk out. It seems cowardly and I wince at my own idea but raise the gun out of my pocket anyway.

I look around; the homeless have a habit of gathering in numbers. It was one of my concerns about this option. Finding three, four or more gathered together round a burning oil drum in the depths of night. The stereotype is clear in my mind.

There is no obvious company, and with the view I have from twenty yards away I'm not sure whether I'm the only heartbeat in the warehouse. I walk sideways to get a full view of the sleeping bag, which has blankets and other paraphernalia surrounding it. I can't see any motion. I can't see any feet, but the bag has an inflated quality to it as if there's something inside. My inner self asks me if I know what I'm doing, tells me I can walk away now and just go home.

My resolution and my reason for doing this shout more loudly. My desire for vengeance screams. There's a rusty metal road pin on the ground. It's about three feet long with an S shape bent into one end and a spike on the other. It's camouflaged against the concrete but becomes visible on the floor as I step closer to the sleeping bag.

I pick it up; there's still no motion in front of me and I'm convinced it's empty, but it just doesn't look like it.

I'm four feet away; the gun in my right hand is relaxed and by my side. I raise my left hand with the metal pin and point it towards the dark blue fabric. It's rolled over, tightly so, and I think I can see the top of a head peering out from the cocoon. Dark gnarly tight-knit hair with some grey strands becomes clearer as my angle changes and a strand of light reflects across the figure inside.

I grip the gun firmly but my senses and instincts are more relaxed than they should be. The nerves I had twenty feet back have subsided. I reach out with the metal rod, the spike pointing at me and the hook down. I feed it into the bag by the neckline and start to pull the fabric gently down, away from what emerges as a full head of hair. An ear becomes visible against pale skin.

I should be nervous. I should be twitching. I'm not.

What I'd started to suspect is becoming apparent. The skin is pale. Ghostly white. Veins in his cheeks are clear blue and offset against the flesh. The eye I can see is open. Staring. And the bloated nature of the body now explains the bulging sleeping bag I first saw.

I set out this evening to source a dead body.

I've found one.

CHAPTER 6

Lancaster Road Fire Station sits beautifully in an old part of the inner city. Flanked by the Medical College and the Attenborough Arts centre to the north and east side, the beautiful and ornate De Montfort Hall and gardens to the south, with Nelson Mandela Park sitting alongside Welford Road Stadium to the west.

The station is a large robust brick building, with a wide frontage and shiny black hardwood doors for six appliances, and wing extensions to the building either side. The second-floor houses officers, sleeping quarters and mess rooms, with a central balcony providing structural symmetry. A large painted Leicestershire crest is attached to the wrought-iron balcony, with the roofline above incorporating a white stone plinth and a gold dragon sitting proudly atop it.

The architecture is completed with a white stone clock tower, four small individual balconies and a black and white Roman numeral clock face to each side, with a brass flag pole climbing into the sky. A Union Jack flutters in the gentle autumn breeze.

The building is majestic, looking reassuringly like a fire

station and highly visible, providing an assault on the senses at every call-out; with appliances roaring across the courtyard and out onto Lancaster Road since its opening in 1927.

Blue watch were on duty for the evening shift, having arrived several hours earlier under watch commander Paul Shorter, a larger-than-life character with a broad Essex twang and a face that smiled. Loud, confident and with a brilliant sense of humour, but a true leader in the literal heat of battle. Experienced, dependable and trusted by his team.

The early part of the evening shift had been quiet; a couple of shouts and a precautionary after a fire alarm had gone off at a local supermarket. A Morrisons store on Freemen's Common. The store had been evacuated but with the building surrounded by major roads into the city and sharing land with an Odeon cinema, Mecca bingo, several pubs and a number of popular restaurant chains, the people count would be both high and dense. It had turned out that the fault had been in the alarm system, and Paul and blue watch had ended up chatting and high-fiving a few excitable kids outside the cinema before making the short journey back to base.

Dusk had set in, the temperature was above average for early September, but the nights were drawing in and the temperature would deteriorate quickly in the coming hours. Spirits were high amongst the team; they'd returned to the station and stripped back to their navy blue t-shirts, deciding whether a snack was in order alongside a coffee.

Jane Downey was a new firefighter to the team, and had proven herself to be a popular member of the crew having moved down to the Midlands from Wigan. Her broad accent and northern charm had endeared her to the largely male workforce, but her brilliant sense of humour and ability to bake had made her instantly popular.

"What have we got, Jane?" harked one of the lads.

"Fuck all for you!" came the response.

The room erupted in cheers with the unlucky victim bundled into a headlock. His hair rubbed and ruffled in triumph following the put-down, and with a few light missiles thrown at him for good measure. A screwed-up piece of paper bounced off his forehead.

"Any of those choccy muffins left from yesterday, Jane?" asked a hopeful Paul Shorter.

"There may be one for the watch commander," Jane replied, smiling as she walked over to a cupboard.

More jeers came from the team, this time aimed at the favouritism being shown. Jane raised a middle finger high in the air as she opened a cupboard, pulling out two large dotty cake tins with fifteen or so muffins in.

"At least one each, lads!" she declared loudly.

The jeers turned back to cheers as one of the team went to fill the kettle up. Tea and muffins was a favourite amongst blue watch, who took a tea and cake break seriously.

The alarm rang loudly and the jeers returned as the crew leapt to their feet and headed quickly towards the primary engine, known affectionately as Cherry.

"Where are we going, boss?"

"Soar Lane, it's off Great Central Street and Frog Island."

"I know it. It's less than ten minutes away. There's not a lot down there, though. What have we got?"

In the back of the fire engine, the crew were still pulling on jackets and readying themselves for the ensuing fire. Arms were being stretched into coats in a confined space, with a team used to working with one another jostling into gear, each knowing each other's ways and adjusting, like a dance, only with less elegance and the occasional elbow to the head.

Paul Shorter turned, his position in the passenger seat forcing him to look over his right shoulder to see the team. His driver sat next to him. Focused. Staring intently ahead. An experienced and dependable firefighter, and the best driver Paul had ever worked with.

"Car fire, boys, that's all, but reports are that it's raging, so we'll need to be careful and work from a distance. Fuel tank may have gone already, but we'll know once we see it."

The adrenaline and the buzz in the cab made the Essex wide boy in him pour out in his voice, something he normally played down in the station, but in the heat of battle the twang and the shape of the words reverted to home.

The engine exited smoothly off Vaughan Way and headed at speed down towards the top of Great Central Street, slowing for the bend as the one-way system kicked in. Cars stopped to allow safe passage, with the blue lights and bull horn giving road users ample warning to clear the way. Eyes flicked gently to the left and right, watching out for anybody vulnerable, ignorant or just too engrossed to be aware of a twenty-tonne fire engine hurtling in their general direction. Shovel hands delicately gripped the wheel. Anticipating, ready to make any necessary adjustments as the wagon glided towards her destination.

The land was mostly derelict. Frog Island had been in decline and was preparing itself for a rebirth. Expensive flats and a waterfront area were yet to be started despite the glossy billboards and promise of a better life. Leicester's docklands were still to materialise.

Soar Lane was a dead-end street going on to something of a no-man's-land. An area between a long run of terraces on Tudor Road and the River Soar running parallel, with the patch of land in between known locally as Tudor Road Rec, but more formally as the Rally.

The smoke could be seen against the night sky as the engine passed an abandoned garage and swung left into Soar Lane, with the vehicle not yet visible due to a kink in the road and a small humpback bridge separating Cherry from the blaze.

"I'll stop on this side of the bridge, guv. Unless she's well over the other side."

Paul's driver had only ever got an engine stuck once. All part of life's experience and never to be repeated. He'd long since mastered his craft, knew where it could go, where it couldn't, and he treated his fire engine better than his own car. It was his office. His domain.

The car became visible as the crew chewed up the last hundred or so yards, the burning vehicle just the other side of the bridge and providing neat access.

"I'll stop here and get her as sideways as I can. It'll help with the hoses."

"Top man, not too close. The police may already be here."

The engine was parked neatly and deliberately with the in-cab camera pointing squarely at the burning car, to capture the event and any evidence that may be required by the police. Paul, Jane and two other experienced firefighters had already exited the vehicle.

Shutters were sliding and hoses whizzing as they unreeled, and the slick operation fell into place. A car fire on waste ground was pretty easy as far as they go. No risk of spreading, nobody about, and with the fuel tank clearly having already exploded, it was a formality. The crackling orange flames and thick black smoke were still doing their best to put up a fight; the plastic, fabric and fuel were all going up in a thick black smog, but with water raining down from multiple hoses, the fire soon fell into line.

"Vauxhall Astra," Jane shouted across, "or what's left of one."

The shell of the Astra sat as the last of the flames was exhausted and the billowing smoke was replaced by a wisp as the water took the heat away. The metal fully exposed with no way of establishing the colour or registration, with the engine block providing the best chance of identifying the car once the heat had dissipated.

The glass had gone; a shell remained as Jane Downey continued to hose the vehicle down lightly, to cool the metal and the area around it.

As she walked to the rear of the vehicle, pointing away from the bridge, she could see that the boot had become ajar, the locking mechanism having melted away and eased open by an inch or two.

"Guv, the boot's popped!" shouted Jane as water pooled around the rubberless tyres of the burnt-out shell. The steel rims were exposed and bare.

"Take a look!" Shorter shouted, "see if there's anything in there."

She walked slowly towards the vehicle as the area around the car continued to be showered with cold water. Heat still radiated and her cheeks turned a shade of pink as she got within touching distance. She started to ease the boot open with a length of pole with a hook on the end. The metal twisted and warped by the heat, she used some force to slowly prise the boot, which started to move with a defiant creak. Almost complaining, groaning as it moved a foot or so. Not fully open, but enough to see clearly inside.

"Guv!" she shouted, stepping back away from the heat.

Shorter walked around the shell as the flow of water was slowed, before stopping it altogether.

The two stood side by side as the outline of a blackened body lay clearly visible in the boot of the car.

"Shit."

Paul reached for the radio on his jacket and looked back at the engine.

"Call Nicky Green at Serious Crime and tell her we need her on the rec. We've got a body in here, mate."

CHAPTER 7

"Bowery! Where are you?" Nicky shouted playfully, still conscious of any fragility that may exist in DC Jack Bowery. She didn't want to change the nature of a relationship which had blossomed and was fully functional, before Jack's assault and subsequent period of recuperation.

"I'm here, Green," retorted Jack, playfully, and with a wry smile, which Nicky matched.

"Fancy a dead body in a burnt-out car?"

"I thought you'd never ask."

They both smiled. Nicky took a gulp from her coffee cup. The caffeine provided a burst of energy as she pulled on an overcoat, a smart black trench coat with the bottom sitting neatly just above the knee. Dark grey formal trousers and black shoes with a slight heel completed a more formal look than Nicky had intended when she'd got dressed that morning. The coat had been a late decision in the hall, with the grey clouds and threatening sky peering in through her front door. Pulling her long blonde hair back into a simple ponytail was an equally late decision, with her tortoiseshell Ray-Ban specs framing her face.

Jack looked down at her shoes, which weren't new but had a tidy shine to them.

"I thought you said it was a car fire," he said, dryly.

"I have spare shoes in my car, Jack. For all occasions!"

"Oh yeah, what else have you got in there?"

"Bits and bobs, Jack, just the norm."

"I haven't fully figured out what normal is yet, Nic!"

Nicky's car boot had evolved down the years, from her days in uniform when options were limited and you just improvised, through the years of new kit, bolt croppers, extendable batons and pepper spray. Her experience now saw a boot with multiple emergency shoes, a crowbar, several coats, a pop-up warning triangle, a box of blue nitrile gloves, a couple of white paper crime scene suits and a plethora of supermarket shopping bags. A pair of emergency flip flops lay to one side that were used for post gigs or summer nights.

Evening was well settled as the two left the station, the air cool and with a tinge of damp. The sky was dark and the clouds threatening, but there'd been no rain for a day or two now. Nicky looked up and wondered how much Paul Shorter would have been grateful for some rain across town. Just a bit, to cool the scene down.

Seatbelts were secured as Nicky started the car and pulled out of the underground car park, taking the short one-way loop on Campbell Street before merging onto the busy A594. She traversed four lanes immediately before the road split, and headed right onto Tigers Way. The train station filled the rear-view mirror as she settled back into her seat.

"How are you feeling, Jack?"

"Pretty good, glad to be back and just want to get on with stuff, y'know. Just want things to be normal."

"They are normal. It just might not feel like it for a while."

"The lads downstairs seem happy to dish out the shit, but I guess I'm flavour of the month until somebody else takes centre stage."

"You know all the people who matter have your back, don't you?"

Jack smiled and looked across at Nicky. She caught him in her peripheral view, but with the road busy and late-evening commuters weaving their way home she was unable to look back. She smiled anyway. Jack knew the people he was close to were in his corner, and was quickly learning that anybody else was superficial. With the conversation close to a natural conclusion, he changed tack.

"So how do you know Paul Shorter?"

"We go way back, me and Paul, have known each other for years. I've been to far too many house fires and car accidents and found his beaming mug outside the place. Pubs too! Got to know each other over the years and we speak outside of work. He's the first person I call if I need anything at all on fires, there's nothing he doesn't know, and I'm the first person he calls if we ever need to get involved, or if he just needs to pick my brain."

Nicky's network was vast. Diverse too, and Jack was gaining invaluable experience by spending time in her circle, becoming acquainted with a wide range of skilled and knowledgeable people, all happy to share information with an experienced and respected officer.

A key part of the job was asking questions, always had been. Gathering and gaining information was central to any copper worth their salt. But *who* you asked, and *how*, that really sorted the wheat from the chaff. The knowledge, the people skills. The soft ones as well as the hard ones, and having people willing to pass information to you, or withhold it for you in the right places, was gold dust to a senior DS.

"What else do we know, Nicky?"

"Not a lot at the minute. The car was reported on fire just before 7pm. Paul's team were on site by 7.15pm and we got the call at 7.43pm. All seemed like a simple car abandonment until they got a look inside the boot."

Jack had organised uniform before they'd left, his instructions clear and delivered more abruptly than usual. They should be there already, taking care of the scene and any dog walkers or locals trying to get a close-up, or a Facebook-worthy photo of the burnt-out shell.

Jack was a dog lover but without actually owning one. Single life and the hours were not conducive to having a dog. Making a commitment to them. Plus, he'd already encountered far too many dog walkers who had stumbled across a body, a suicide or something that they could never unsee. A twenty-minute walk that would change their life forever. He didn't know what the odds were of finding a body with your dog, but he was unlucky. It was always a dog walker. He was happy for now with regular stories of Nicky's dachshunds – Harry and Marv – and newly adopted rescue puppy Betty, who were keeping her and her husband entertained. The pictures were aplenty on Instagram, including a recent one of Marv running around the house with a toilet roll, ripping it to shreds.

"We'll suit up when we get there, Jack," Nicky offered, with the destination now less than five minutes away. "I've got a couple of decent white suits in the boot. There's one in your size." There was a wink in Nicky's voice and Jack smiled again.

"Becky and Rob?"

"I sent her a text before we left, saying we'd call her when we get there. I'll call Rob later too. He knows where we are so I'll update him later. It depends what we find."

The car slowed as it passed a pub. The Ship Inn. It was boarded up, hadn't served a pint in years by the looks of it and was in none too salubrious surroundings. The road split into three. There was a fenced-off building plot to the left wrapped with metal site construction fencing, with whatever used to sit there on full view. Reduced to a pile of rubble and red brick, with a solitary outbuilding not yet having had the same bulldozer treatment.

The blue lights of the fire engine came into view as the car climbed a short incline to face the wagon and a marked police car, which had been parked to one side. Nicky and Jack got out. Nicky didn't immediately recognise the driver, who was still sitting behind the wheel of the fire engine, but he lifted a hand to acknowledge her.

The uniforms had started to put up a barrier, easier on this side of the bridge with the road narrowing and the vehicles parked there blocking the path. Almost a natural dead end. They'd gone to the far side where the roadway turned from asphalt to gravel and spread out, leading onto the recreation ground and much harder to block access on a popular public right of way.

Jack was pleased to see that the uniforms had done a good job; they'd used streetlights, a steel railing and a shiny black bollard to give a broad perimeter, which had already attracted some kids on bikes on the other side. Sitting with their mobile phones out.

Nicky looked at Jack. He was dressed more smartly than she'd noticed when they left the station. A grey suit, white shirt and a red tie. His shoes were black and nearly as shiny as hers, and his black overcoat made him look more like a lawyer than a police officer.

"Are *you* ready for this?" Nicky asked, playfully, looking down at his shoes as they crossed the bridge and headed towards the car. The firm click of asphalt being slowly replaced with the crunch of gravel and ash.

"Nicky! How are you, darlin'?"

"Good evening, Paul."

Pleasantries were exchanged. A hug was usual, but with Paul in full gear and with a film of ash on his brow, a nod sufficed. Nicky introduced Jack and Paul to one another, with Paul removing a glove to offer a warm and slightly sweaty hand, which Jack shook.

"I know I said call me anytime, but a café would have been preferable."

Jane waved and mouthed a 'hi' to Nicky as she walked back from the burnt-out shell, which was still simmering. The two had met several times before, and with Nicky's reputation as an excellent baker having reached the fire station, the two had got to know each other. Nicky looked over towards the car, with white steam licking its way across the vehicle and peeling away gently as the cooling process continued.

Nicky and Jack had put their pale blue gloves on, wanting to get an initial look before making some calls and suiting up as the evening continued its march into full-blown nightfall. It was now dark, with the last of the daylight having drifted away. Paul walked with them, explaining the sequence of events as they got within a few feet. They stopped, looking down at the ground. A grey slushy mixture of ash and water. Paul walked straight into it, standard fare for him and his riggers. With his hands gloved and using a short metal staff, he prized the car boot a little more ajar than they'd been able to twenty minutes ago, the metal hinges creaking as it gave another couple of inches.

Nicky and Jack bent down to take a look inside, with Paul shining a torch into the cavity.

Nicky caught a glimpse of what was inside and, without moving, said: "We're going to need a team."

CHAPTER 8

The cordon had been widened and more patrol cars had arrived within fifteen minutes of Jack making the call, with cars now blocking the turning into the adjacent Swan Street, and a small team of uniforms positioning themselves across the recreation ground. Those who had drawn the short straws would be asking teenagers, park walkers and society's outliers what they'd seen. The odds of decent information were slim on that side of the bridge, unlike the chances of abuse from gangs on bikes who'd already heard of the find, with Messenger, Snapchat and WhatsApp spreading the message like a disease.

Nicky took a piece of gum from a packet and started to chew hard on it, focusing the mind and taking some of the taste of the smoke away. Of burning rubber, metal and plastic. She offered a piece to Jack, who took one. Paul Shorter declined.

Nicky had made the call to Dr Becky Ryan, who'd been at home when she picked up. She may have been hoping for an invitation to a pub or an impromptu meal out, but she got neither. She'd been cooking a stir fry, having been to the gym, with the hiss of the pan audible on the call, along with the sound of her own barking dog, Louis, who was equally eager to tuck into his evening meal.

Nicky had spelled out the scene to Becky, who had immediately notified the on-call forensics team for the evening. It was possible they were tucking into chocolate muffins, following the fire crew with their love of food, but they were about to be invited to the party. An initial team who would start their evening's work sifting through the wreckage of an Astra, which would no doubt do its best to hang on to its grisly secrets.

Becky would come to the scene later or, worst case, first thing tomorrow morning following an already lengthy day. The forensics team was more populous than it was just a few months back, with Becky now well settled in her role, having built strong relationships with a county hall seemingly happy to invest in forensic science.

It was less than half an hour before the first of two forensic science vans arrived, the first a white marked Peugeot Partner with 'Forensic Services' written on the side. The second was also a Peugeot but was unmarked. Nicky clocked the '22 plate and guessed the two people inside it were as new as the van. Faces she didn't recognise in a van not yet marked as one of authority.

Two men climbed out of the marked van and headed straight for Nicky and Jack. She knew both; one was nearing retirement and was an unflappable and measured character. The other was younger but equally measured and had a cheerful and friendly face. The four walked as she explained the nature of the scene, which was now a bustling hive of emergency services roughly numbering twenty. Police, fire brigade and forensic services were now sharing the scene and would be jostling into the night, but with the fire crew coming to the end of their role. Forensics would be here through the night, with the police supporting. Nicky and Jack would be here for a couple of hours before retiring, picking back up tomorrow with Becky and an investigative team.

The four forensics officers were speaking with Paul Shorter and setting up lights and a small area to work from, discussing cooling times and the dangers of the scene. Shards of twisted metal as well as the cooling would all present hazards, but with the car holding a body, the team were keen to safely extract it. To start their work. To start to offer dignity to a life denied it at the end.

The post-mortem would confirm it, but to the naked eye this was already ranking pretty highly on the grisly scale.

The scene had established order; Jack was having a discussion with the two new forensics guys who were to-ing and fro-ing from their van, keen to get stuck in. Keen to be seen to be doing a good job. Making an impression. Jack was introducing himself and telling them what he expected. What the police needed and what Becky would expect.

The site lights were starting to do their job. Industrial tripod lights placed around the vehicle with their heads pointing at it, adding desperately needed light which would take over from the headlights of the fire engine that were currently on full beam, and which would provide forensics the light to work with throughout the night.

Nicky was keeping an eye on Jack. His style was firm but fair and it delivered a message they may have already had, but there was never any harm in backing that message up.

Forensics were starting their work. Their painstaking work which Nicky had more than an appreciation for. Their attention to the finest of details. Their patience. Paul's team were preparing to help with the forced opening of the boot and the removal of the body, all of which would be transported locally for full investigation. The body would go to Becky at Leicester Royal Infirmary, with the car going to an unmarked police facility. Photography was well underway from one of the team, and lights had now been fully erected. The area around the car had a sense of illumination; a ball of light surrounded by darkness.

Jack had sent a message to Jen, to let her know where they were and what they were dealing with. What they'd all be dealing with tomorrow. He'd resisted sending a picture. It felt indecent with the body in situ, although she'd probably see a version of it on Facebook in the coming hours. Blurry footage from a hundred yards back, with teenagers talking inaudibly in the background as the fire had burned.

It took Paul's team ten or fifteen minutes to loosen and cut through the sections of metal left intact, or welded together by the white hot heat of the blaze. To free the section of the boot acting as a coffin lid.

Nicky and Jack were standing ten yards back, directly behind the car and with hands in coat pockets. Keen to see what they were dealing with. Who they were dealing with. A man. A woman. Although both were pessimistic about finding that out tonight. Bodies in fires never fared well, especially in the tight proximity of a car fire. The heat was focused and intense. Even house fires had a way of distorting a body and taking it way beyond any form of recognition. Where all the usual indicators had burned away. Tattoos. Piercings. Scars. Rings. All gone, usually leaving a dentist to do the honours on behalf of the force. To provide the victim with a name, which could often take a day or two given the complexity of the scene and the sensitivity of the situation.

Jane Downey eased the boot from one side as it creaked and groaned. Her crowbar forcing its way in and easing the bare metal further ajar. She took a step closer and at arm's length patted the top of the boot with a heavily gloved right hand. She patted it again as the heat failed to pass through the industrial-strength glove, then two or three times more just to make sure. Nodding to confirm that the heat was no longer a match for her heavy duty PPE. Paul Shorter stepped forward to match Jane's position. Symmetrical in their approach.

Jack and Nicky took a step forward, checking the ground beneath their feet as they did so. Eight feet or so back, waiting patiently for what was to come.

Paul took a small step forward, the heat still abundant enough to cause both firefighters to perspire. Their heavy duty jackets protecting them but doing little to help to shed body heat. Jane looked towards Paul. He nodded and the two put some force into the lift for the first time. The metal section creaked and cracked, providing a final loud groan as it gave up the fight and the section came free. She checked with Paul again. He nodded once more and they lifted it clear, walking sideways until the car was no longer between them. They laid the metal section down on the floor, close to two of the forensics guys who had prepared a large blue sheet for the piece to go on.

One of them stepped forward and shone a light into the open boot as Nicky and Jack peered in, with the two of them looking to see the immediate intricacies of the coming hours. Of their night.

Jack stepped closer still, but he was unable to combat the

immense heat that was still emanating from the shell. His eyes watered and he relented back a yard.

Nicky could see what looked like melted black plastic. A twisted mess but the shape was unmistakably human. Mostly anyway. Nicky looked at it one way, then tilted her head. The legs seemed to be visible as a shape, with the blackness and debris making it hard to work out size.

Jack was desperate to get a proper look but stayed put. He wasn't in the required forensic attire, and the level of the heat just wasn't something he was used to. He'd also given more than a thought for his shoes.

The two forensics guys started to look closely at some of the wrapping to get a first glance, but to them the nature of the situation was already screaming.

Nicky and Jack could both see the tragic outline of a body. It looked to have been wrapped in something polymer based which had melted in the heat, binding the victim in further. A contorted mess cradling the lifeless body of the victim within. Almost like a mummification.

The light and the angle afforded them a better view as shapes became slightly clearer.

Nobody uttered a word, whilst the horror of the situation screamed violently over the silence.

CHAPTER 9

Dr Becky Ryan sat back in her office and took a large gulp from her coffee cup. A reusable Starbucks mug with bamboo green print on the side and a matching rubber cap. A macchiato picked up on the way in, from a local drive-thru before parking up at Leicester Royal Infirmary ahead of another early start.

She'd walked in as dawn was breaking outside. The early-morning sun shining through the stands at Welford Road Stadium opposite the car park, casting long shadows across the building. Glistening off the metal window frames and flashing a blinding reflection in the glass.

She switched the lights on in the main office as she'd buzzed herself in with her access pass. They'd whirred and flickered as they always did first thing. Waking up slowly like a human being. Stirring first, a groan and a stretch before finally springing to life. Almost complaining about the time of day in the process.

She'd slung a smart black handbag on a chair in her office and hung her stylish jacket on a hook behind the door, switching a lamp and a monitor on as she sat at her desk. She'd had the emails and scene photographs from both Nicky and the members of her team who had attended the scene last night. Multiple PDF's and messages which started to land after Nicky and Jack had arrived at the scene, with the frequency of her phone vibrations doing more than enough to tell her she'd be busy, even without the details. She'd spoken to Nicky after the boot had been cracked and knew what today would entail.

Her evening until that point had been quiet, email interruptions aside. An hour in the gym had followed an HIIT class with some weights and kettlebells, which had served its purpose. Burnt off some energy, physically and mentally, as she ignored the emails buzzing on her smartwatch, catching a glance from the instructor in the process. She'd built up a nice sweat before a relaxing evening in front of the TV with a stir fry and a G&T. There'd been a bottle of white wine in the fridge, but she'd fancied a gin. It was only Tuesday, and she might need the wine once the charred body on her to-do list had been dealt with.

She'd sat down with her meal and switched Netflix on in the background, picking something easy whilst looking at the images and a file on a MacBook Air. An old and slightly battered model but religiously reliable and one which she carried everywhere. Between mouthfuls and with *White Collar* talking to itself in the background, she'd twisted and squinted as Nicky had done, trying to pick out parts of the photographs but failing to do so. The shadows and the darkness proving too hard to navigate, with the artificial light blurring the images. Any detail at all was impossible to pick out, but she'd got the gist from what she could see and from her phone call with Nicky.

She'd sent a message to say hi to Rob, which had turned into a social chat on WhatsApp about plans for the weekend, an update on his kids and whether he'd been to the new Italian on Granby Street.

She stretched her arms in her chair, waking herself up before the subject of the photos would come before her for the first time. The body had been removed from the car boot by her team in the small hours and transported across town. It was the first show of decency it had seen since long before death.

As she supped on her coffee, she started to prepare herself for the post-mortem. The body was lying on a stainless-steel table within the mortuary. A white sheet afforded some dignity, but the black plastic sheet that the remains were lying on, and which was overhanging the table, told Becky that her morning's work was going to be difficult. That and several boxes containing the smaller remains that had been recovered, and that were no longer attached to the corpse.

Becky's team was imminent and she wanted to be ready to go. She'd told Nicky the post-mortem would be first thing and she meant it. Her department was in a good place and able to be flexible; the emerging team were well organised and skilled, and relationships with the wider judicial authorities were building nicely. Becky took pride in providing an exceptional service and was able to react and adapt quickly, knowing other forces and forensic teams either couldn't, or wouldn't, without political force.

Becky had changed into her formal white disposable clothing, which was a stark contrast to her usual stylish appearance. She was still wearing a smartwatch on her left wrist. She ran her hands through her sleek black hair, stroking it behind her ears, pulling it into a neat ponytail with a hair band, which was also on her left wrist. It was longer than normal but as sleek and elegant as ever. She pulled the hair band, tightening the ponytail in the process before checking the CCTV on her monitor. Nicky was due. Jack would also be here within the hour.

Two of her colleagues had arrived in the meantime, leaving her alone but finalising the preparations for the difficult job ahead. Becky emerged with her scrubs on, heading into the pathology suite, towards a shiny steel trolley which sat in the middle of a row of three identical gurneys in the centre of the forensic examination suite. The remains were still covered in a white sheet. Nicky had arrived and walked into the viewing gallery, waving a 'hi' with her left hand whilst nursing her own coffee with her right. A caramel latte.

Becky switched on the comms links to the gallery and told Nicky she looked tired. Her long blonde hair was also tied back, she was smartly dressed and her light makeup was giving her a fresher look than her eyes were able to.

"Five hours," Nicky proclaimed, holding her coffee cup aloft.

Nicky and Jack had called it a night after gauging what was inevitably to become a full-blown murder investigation. The scene had been fully secured. The fire crew had been able to leave, allowing the police and forensics to work through the night on recovering evidence and, more importantly, the body.

"Where's the car, Becky?"

"It's in the unit at Enderby. We'll have a go with that later, but we wanted to spend the morning with our John Doe."

"It's a man then?"

"We think so. Poor bastard."

Jack arrived, walking in coffee-less and with an equally tired face, the bags visible under young eyes.

"I'm used to nine hours," he declared, arms spread wide in exasperation, and without having visited Starbucks.

"I'm going to grab a brew. Anyone else?" Jack looked at those in the suite. Becky declined, with the other forensic guys giving nods or negatives, before he headed off to a canteen, hoping the milk in the fridge was fresh and the sugar pot was full.

He returned with a steaming mug of tea, still wearing his coat. A smart beige mac that contrasted well with his blue suit. The early chill of the morning had stayed with him, and the mediocre heating in the suite was doing little to warm him up.

"What can we expect, Becky?" asked Nicky. She was vastly experienced, but other than a couple of non-suspicious house fires, none of which she'd been lead officer in, her experience of burns victims was thankfully limited.

Becky looked perplexed, before looking at the body, which was still covered with a white sheet. She looked up at Nicky.

"This could be considerably more difficult than you're expecting…"

Nicky looked perturbed, but the forensic team hadn't yet disclosed a key factor to the body which had been unclear from the scene. From inside the boot. The body had been heavily wrapped and in poor light very little else was visible. One of Becky's assistants peeled back the white cotton sheet to reveal the body, lying tragically on the table. Becky pulled the overhead microphone down and formally recorded the date and time to start proceedings.

Nicky looked at the corpse, then looked at Jack.

"Where's the head?"

"There isn't one," replied Becky.

"What do you mean, there's no head?"

"I mean it wasn't there. On the body or in the car."

It was Jack's turn to look perplexed. Nicky looked pissed off.

She'd put her coffee down and had already pulled her iPhone out. Rob was about to get an early message that wouldn't start his day well. She looked at the body further, now knowing the body had been decapitated at some stage. She looked at the limbs. The ends of them.

"There's no hands or feet either?" Nicky asked, but she could see it. The question was rhetorical. The bones of the ulna and fibula were visible, ending abruptly at the wrists and ankles.

"And they're missing too?"

Becky nodded.

"Are we likely to be able to identify a cause of death?" Nicky asked, pessimistically.

"We'll do the best we can," Becky promised, "but it's always a tough ask when the body's been burned this badly as well as dismembered. Although, if I'm honest, it's the first time I've come across both at the same time."

"Are we likely to learn much, Becky?" asked Jack.

"Not sure at this stage. We should be able to assess the parts of the internal organs that did survive, we'll run all the normal tests on the heart and stomach, and we'll know from the lungs whether he was alive when he went into the boot or not. We'll also be able to guesstimate age from the bone composition, and match DNA, should there be an owner in the system."

"And if there isn't?"

"Then it's time for some old-school policing!" Becky smiled. Her comment was tongue in cheek, but she was acutely aware of the difficulties that already existed for Nicky and Jack. All had become reliant on DNA. Its neatness, its accuracy. Rarely did a case, or a body, hold so many questions and so few answers. Establishing the 'who' was always a priority, and was always the conduit to the wider investigation. Their John Doe currently didn't have a name, a head or a next of kin.

"Will you be able to tell if the hands and feet were removed before death?" asked Jack. Hopeful for something.

"Yes, we should be able to tell from the trace blood, even with the body in this state, so we'll know just how bad this guy's end of life got."

Jack sighed. He was still cold. He took a sip of his tea; it was bitter. He knew he'd put sugar in but had forgotten to stir it. He swilled it, taking another bitter mouthful, knowing the last one would give an injection of sweetness.

"There is some good news from our initial work, though," Becky offered.

Nicky looked up and waited. Becky turned to the back of the room, which had a long worktop-type surface running along the back wall. It was as steel and as sterile as the rest of the suite. She picked up a jar. A small glass jar with a screw cap.

She held it up to the light and shook it gently. Nicky and Jack strained to see what was inside. The contents rattled against the sides. A small single and hard item chinked on the glass.

"We did find a tooth."

CHAPTER 10

It was a crisp autumn morning. A Tuesday in September. The time of year when leaves were starting to fall from trees, creating a beautiful hue of browns, oranges and reds. The sun was up but not offering a great deal of heat in the early morning, and even by lunchtime any warmth would be a token offering. The air was cool and the temperature was unlikely to hit double figures, and if it did, it wouldn't feel like it.

Rob tossed a tea bag into his blue Leicester City mug and waited for the kettle to boil. It was at the end of the main office in a little kitchenette; a cheap white kettle with a green PAT test sticker on it that was out of date. He poured the water over the tea bag; the steam flooded the small area and steamed his glasses. He enjoyed the warmth.

He pulled his iPhone from his pocket and opened WhatsApp. He saw his sister Emily's face on her profile and smiled.

Need anything for later? x, he typed. She replied immediately.

Some of those cakes we had yesterday! Viennese whirls, or the other Kipling ones you liked. Or both! x

I'll get both :) I should be with you by 6 tonight x

He got a big thumbs-up and a big heart. It matched hers.

He headed back to his office and held his brew in both hands. The burn emanating through the cup was doing a better job of warming him than a forty-year-old heating system and a poorly insulated building.

He looked at his inbox, which was in a reasonable state. An email invitation appeared from Laura Mathers under the heading *Management brief – ES.* He sipped the still-steaming brew and sighed inside. It was internal speak for the ongoing situation following the five murders, which had caused a monumental storm for those in the police force and in local government. The inquiries were ongoing, David Parker was history and many questions were still being asked as to the vetting process for police recruits, both locally and nationally. The *Daily Mail* had run with a story about how the police could not be trusted under the headline 'Killers in Blue', and went on to report that up to 2,000 corrupt police officers were serving nationwide and were suspected of tipping off criminals, stealing, fabricating evidence and using their powers to procure money and sex. The picture on the front page was of Lodge House, with a faded and tatty Leicestershire flag hanging limply outside. That was a bad day.

He accepted the invitation.

Jen walked into the office and, for no particular reason, was surprised to see it so empty. She waved a 'hi' at Rob, checking for her own mug which had vanished from her desk, possibly at the hands of the cleaners who swept the office and banished any remaining crockery to the dishwasher. It was quietly whirring away in the kitchen area where Rob had made his drink. She headed off to locate her mug and make herself a drink.

As she returned to her desk with her coffee, Rob waved her into his office.

"How are you, Jen?" asked Rob, with sincerity in his voice.

"I'm okay, thanks, how are you?"

"Only okay?"

Jen looked perplexed.

"No, I'm doing fine. Just trying to keep busy and put things behind us."

"But you're feeling okay?"

"I'm fine, thank you for checking," Jen replied, equally sincere. Her relationship with Rob was strong. There was a trust and a bond that went beyond simple colleagues.

"Tell me about *him*," asked Rob.

Rob had spoken to Becky. He knew the rape case was progressing well, and he had already assured Laura Mathers that a conviction was highly likely. The evidence was strong and the news was welcome to the team. The CPS had approved the charges and he'd been remanded into custody, much to Jen's satisfaction.

The *him* had become an unspoken word. An unspoken name. Jen despised hearing his name and had taken to referring to the man charged in simple terms. To remove his name. To dehumanise him. It was no less than he'd done to his victims. Jen and Nicky had embraced the stance of Jacinda Ardern, the New Zealand prime minister who had refused to use the name of a terrorist in public, instead focusing on the victims. Their families. Their memories.

"You've done a good job, Jen. An important job."

"Is it enough, though?"

"Why do you say that?"

"I enjoyed charging him. It felt good. I knew he would be remanded and I can look his victims square in the eye and tell them he's going down. But there was still such anger in his face, a defiance in his eyes."

"He'll go down for it, Jen, you know he will, and you'll have done the work. You'll get the credit. Mathers knows how much work you've put in already."

Jen smiled. It was a nice thing to hear, but she wasn't doing it for career points, or to look good. She sipped from her mug; a natural pause fell between them.

"Have you spoken to Nicky?" Rob asked, to change the subject.

"I have. The body in the car?"

"Yep, the body in the car."

"Do we know who it is?"

"Not yet, Becky's still working on it."

"Can I help?"

"Possibly. Depends how much it fans out." Rob opened a folder on his laptop and spun it round so Jen could see it. Nicky had uploaded an initial report which she'd add to, as well as a selection of photographs which had been taken at the scene. A large number were in the Google file under the heading 'Tudor Road Rec – Operation Unicorn'.

Jen leant down to look as Rob flicked through the images. Dozens of images taken of the car and the immediate area, including some closer images of the body through the prised-open bonnet. The light quality moved as the angle of the pictures changed, and improved as the tripod lights from Becky's team had been erected around the forlorn-looking Astra. The latter images were more useful and showed the tragic detail of a body left to burn. Blackened. Defenceless.

"That's a sad end to a life," Jen commented. Rob's silence agreed.

"Man or a woman?"

"We think it's a man, but there's a lot we don't know. We're hoping to find out more tomorrow. Will you be about?" Rob asked Jen.

"Yes, I'll be in here. I was planning on having an office day anyway."

"Could you spare an hour to sit in on the session? I'd welcome your input."

Jen smiled inside. Her eyes smiled too. She felt happy at the inclusion.

"I'd like that. It'll make a welcome change."

"Then I will ping you the details and we can catch up tomorrow with the team."

Jen smiled and thanked Rob, heading back to her desk with a spring in her step.

CHAPTER 11

The weather was holding, and Wednesday was emerging into a crisp dry autumn morning as daylight broke over Leicester. There was a calm breeze that wasn't bringing a chill with it, and a blue cloudless sky. Leaves fluttered across the streets and people were walking calmly along Gallowtree Gate, from the train station to the city centre; a procession of early- morning commuters and students. There were no umbrellas, they weren't needed today, and some had foregone a coat for a suit jacket or a thick-knit jumper, hanging on to the last remnants of any mild weather for another day.

Rob sat back down after finishing his coffee, having enjoyed a scour of the streets below him. He was back in his office, which already had more of a hum than yesterday. His time in the office had been productive, and he'd had the chance to catch up with Jen, which he'd enjoyed greatly. It had been overdue and he'd been pleased to see her. Jen was already in too, seemingly buoyed by the prospect of an unexplained death.

Nicky and Jack walked in together, shouting their 'good mornings' across the office and waving at anyone who looked up. Nicky dropped a cardboard drinks carrier in the middle of an unoccupied desk and signalled to Rob and Jen that two of the drinks were theirs. Jen wandered towards it, looking for her name. Rob gave a thumbs-up and stayed put.

Rob's coffee was visible when he appeared. He took it, leaving one left in the tray. He had hoped a bag of pastries was obscured from view or being kept warm somewhere. It wasn't and his stomach churned.

The hum had grown amongst a group of friends who hadn't been in the same place at the same time a great deal recently. Work demands, countless cases and an inquiry weren't helping, and that's before life's mix of demands were thrown into the pot. Rob had already farmed his season ticket at Leicester City out more times than he cared to count, and had wondered whether the sizeable investment had been a smart one.

Another fifteen minutes passed before the elegant silhouette of Becky Ryan passed the glass partition leading into the office. She walked in; her smile radiated and the team responded. Her warm demeanour always brought good cheer to the office. She looked taller than usual and was smartly dressed in a dark trouser suit. Neat and crisp with a white blouse, her long black hair was loose and flowing and a smart pair of heels added to her statuesque figure. Her nails were painted in a fresh red and a silver bracelet hung from her left wrist.

"Going somewhere later, Becky?" Jack asked cheekily.

Becky smiled brightly. "Is one of those mine?"

Jack pointed at the solitary coffee on the remaining tray. "It's still too early for those Gingerbread lattes we all like, I'm afraid. Another couple of months," he added with a sad expression.

Becky picked the cup up, which was still warm, and thanked Jack. She took a sip.

It was another ten minutes or so before Becky had set up and hooked her laptop up to a TV screen to show some photographs taken during the post-mortem.

"Everybody ready? So, we've completed the post-mortem on our John Doe—"

"Is it still a John Doe, Becky?" Rob interrupted.

"Well, we found a tooth amongst the debris of the car boot which we've matched DNA to, so technically, no, he isn't," Becky replied.

"So he's definitely a he?"

"He is indeed."

"Name?"

"The DNA from the tooth is a match to sixty-seven-year-old David Cramer. The body was in poor condition, as you'll all have seen. Any exposure to temperatures such as a car fire tends to deteriorate a body considerably. Normally, we can clinically assess the major organs, and we still can in cases like this, but the heat and the fact that the body was effectively baked makes life difficult. The heat breaks all of the proteins down and most of the soft tissue perished, so there's less to work with."

"Could you get much, Becky?" Nicky asked, hopeful for something.

"Not too much, we got a few bits which may offer crumbs of comfort, though."

Nicky sipped her latte and waited.

"There was no smoke in the lining of the lungs, so he was already dead before the fire took hold."

The team sat still. Small mercies were only ever that, but they removed any dark thoughts of a man locked in a car boot, his fists and feet banging in the darkness as flames ravaged the upholstery and the heat became unbearable. Became consuming.

"So he was killed somewhere else, Becky?"

"Yes, I believe he was, and in the last forty-eight to seventy-two hours."

"Cause of death?"

Becky sighed, and paused before sharing the current state of play with a nervous tone.

"For now, the only viable conclusion we have is that he died of natural causes."

"What?" Rob asked, perplexed. The other faces in the room shared his incredulity. "That has to be a mistake," he asserted.

"We don't think it is, I'm afraid," Becky replied, "and although I can understand the quandary, it doesn't just mean I can rustle up a cause of death that suits us all."

The room sat silent for a few seconds as brows furrowed and information was processed. Thoughts began but with few initial answers. Rob broke it with an outburst.

"So why the fuck would you burn a stolen car out with a headless body inside that had died of natural causes?"

The question was directed at nobody in particular and was met with little in the way of a response. With nothing forthcoming, Becky clarified her position: "I'm not saying categorically that he wasn't murdered. You need to bear in mind he's missing a head, so he could have been shot between the eyes and we simply wouldn't know."

"So how do you reach natural causes?" Rob asked.

"In these cases, it's a process of elimination," Becky explained. She went on: "He didn't bleed out, his head, hands and feet were cut off after death, he wasn't strangled or suffocated; otherwise, we'd have clear markers in some of the main arteries and capillary veins, and he wasn't stabbed or shot on any remaining part of his body. There are no puncture marks anywhere on the corpse. He wasn't beaten either, there's no trauma anyway on his body, and although we wouldn't see the bruising literally, we'd see it in the organs if anything had been enough to disrupt the blood flow or have been with enough force to cause death. There was a lot of alcohol in his system, and chronic liver damage, so it appears as if his body reached a natural end."

"But he could have had his skull smashed in or been shot in the head and we wouldn't know?" Rob confirmed.

"I'm afraid not. We'd need the head to confirm that," Becky responded. "There is no trauma to any of the major organs, other than that inflicted by his own lifestyle, and there's no significant damage to the body that would have led to death."

"We've got nothing, have we?" Rob sighed in frustration. "We can't even prove a headless man left to burn in a stolen car was unlawfully killed."

"Are there any tests outstanding, Becky?" Jack asked. "Could he have been poisoned?"

"It's possible, Jack. That's all that's outstanding, but we're not holding out for it. And if he was poisoned, it didn't cause damage to his lungs, heart, kidneys or liver."

Nicky put a different slant on proceedings. "What do we know then?"

"We have a Caucasian male, aged between sixty and seventy years old and in generally poor health. His bone structure is in poor condition and shows a number of deficiencies, and his liver is in particularly poor condition, as I mentioned, with clear signs of alcohol abuse. He's a smoker too, or he was. This was a man in poor health," Becky confirmed, "and there are even some signs of malnutrition."

"How sure are we that the tooth belongs to the body?" Jack asked, smartly. Rob nodded, appreciating the question.

"We're not, but the initial belief is that the tooth does belong to the body. We need to confirm it with DNA from the torso, which we're in the process of doing."

"Well, it's an easy one to start with, guys." Rob got off the desk he was sitting on and arched his back with his hands. He looked in the general direction of Jack and Jen. "We need to find out as much as we can about David Cramer. Background, family, recent or current whereabouts, current financials. That should give us a good idea about who he is and what he's involved in. Let's pull something together and we can decide on next steps, unless this is clean cut, especially as we can't even prove he's been murdered."

"Get an address and get somebody to the house, Jack," Rob instructed. Jack nodded.

The room fell silent again. There was a level of discomfort; the thought of being unable to identify or prosecute a protagonist was palpable. Even if he hadn't been murdered, he'd been beheaded, dismembered and driven into the city, and left to burn publicly on a four-wheeled pyre.

"What's the best we can hope for without anything else to go on?" Jack dared to ask.

"Preventing a lawful and decent burial," Nicky replied, without averting her gaze. It already didn't feel like much to aim for.

"Can we focus on the dismemberment?" Jack asked, trying to think laterally. "Somebody has removed the head, hands and feet of this man. Why?"

"To remove his identity?" Jen offered. "Or to hide or obliterate it. To remove him from existence. That feels quite personal, though. It could be a gang thing, I guess."

"Becky, how easy is it to remove body parts?" Rob asked. "Is it easier to remove feet or hands, or are they equally *tricky*? And I'm assuming cutting a head off is no walk in the park?"

"Have you ever tried it, Inspector?" Becky jibed.

"Not yet, Becky. One day," Rob replied, deadpan.

"Then you should come on the course with me!"

Rob's eyes looked up and met Becky's. She was smiling innocently, as if the conversation was about food, culture or a night on the town.

"There's a course for cutting a head off?"

"It's more to cover general dismemberment, but, yes, there is."

"And you take it?"

"It's a course I helped to write, so yes."

"I might give it a miss, but if the mood ever takes me, I know where to find you."

"Well, I can give you an edited version if you like. I've got a group of four students in the morgue tomorrow who I've invited along. It's timely for them and potentially for you."

"A day in school?"

"A day in school," Becky confirmed.

Rob pondered the benefits of seeing and hearing the details first-hand.

"What time in the morning?"

CHAPTER 12

It was raining outside, and the charcoal hue of the sky, plunging temperature and autumn rain couldn't have been more reflective of the mood in the room. Of some of the attendees at least.

"Has everybody eaten breakfast?" asked Becky, playfully. She already looked like she was enjoying herself. She was in a buoyant mood. Her hair was down; she flicked it to one side before retrieving a hair band from the left pocket of her white lab jacket. She swept it into a long ponytail with both hands and smiled at her assembled crowd.

She addressed the eight people before her, with Rob, Nicky, Jen and Jack introducing themselves before Becky turned to face the four graduates, who introduced themselves in turn. They all looked young, and largely out of place. Rob couldn't help but think they could be plying a trade doing an innocent job in a retail environment. Somewhere easier. Somewhere clean.

Rob was already regretting his decision. An evening with his sister had been a pleasant and welcome distraction for both of them, but already seemed a distant memory. Emily had been happy to wander through the hospice, and they had found a quiet side room with a Nintendo Wii in. Several hours were passed on Mario Kart, with both hammering the characters around their favoured shopping mall circuit. Biscuits were munched and tea was consumed, and for a while, they were carefree, and happy.

Rob snapped back into the room and made a mental note of the names of the two young men and two young women who were here for the educational slant on proceedings; a tall twenty-something who introduced himself as Ash, and a younger-looking guy called Brandon, who had arrived on an electric scooter. The sort that was becoming more prominent in towns and city centres; only he owned his. It wasn't the type you 'borrow' using your phone and then leave when you're done with it. He'd parked it in the corridor with his helmet. It was an incongruous look to Rob, who felt that if he saw him in the street he'd assume he was on the way to school. Two pleasant young women, Lois and Jade, completed the set.

Becky explained to both parties how the morning would unfold, and explained an outline of the ongoing case to the four younger members, which seemed to spark an interest.

"So how easy is it to dismember a body?" asked Rob, impatiently.

"All in good time, Inspector," teased Becky. His face didn't look like a great deal of patience would be afforded this morning. It also had a look that meant any questions from the graduates would go to Nicky, Jen or Jack.

The group found themselves in a side room, just away from the main part of the mortuary, where the post-mortem on the remains had taken place. The room was a smaller lesser-used area of the facility, and the presence of a pig's corpse –

head and other parts of its anatomy – made the setting even more uncomfortable. Becky caught Rob and Nicky looking at it.

"Well, it's not like we could do this in the main body of the mortuary, is it?" She emphasised *body* for the graduates, who laughed, appreciative of the mortuary humour. Rob realised it was he who was out of place. It was an industry line that they'd store away and no doubt use themselves one day.

A flat-screen TV on the wall completed the scene, and Becky used a remote to move it to a diagram of a human neck. It looked like the sort of image from a textbook, with the images painted in white and pink, and with a number of unlabelled arrows on it. Becky began. She stretched out her hand and pointed at the area at the top of the spine. Her fingernails were still immaculate as she tapped twice on the screen.

"So, as we all know, the human neck consists of two dozen interconnected vertebrae which make up the spinal column." She looked at her audience and smiled. "The spinal column protects and houses the spinal cord, which is the long bundle of nervous tissue that transmits neural signals to the brain, and to the rest of the body. It runs from the back of the head to the small of the back." She ran her fingers down the screen to show the bit that wasn't news to anybody.

"To the front of the neck and in the throat we have the laryngeal prominence, which we all know as Adam's apple. It tends to be more prominent in men than in women, and it's this part here, the thyroid cartilage, that makes up the body of the larynx, or voice box, which creates this prominence."

Rob was switched on and absorbing the complexity of the diagram on the screen, which began to move; the image separating at the neck and showing the full extent of the biological system within. Nicky, Jen and Jack were also looking on. Compelled. Becky continued.

"The rest of the system is made up of a series of muscles and tissues. Any takers?" Becky looked immediately at the graduates.

"Scalenus medius and Scalenus anterior," offered Brandon.

"Very good," replied Becky.

"Venter inferior and Venter superior?" asked Lois, not fully sure but she spoke the words well. Clearly.

"Excellent," said Becky, which came with an approving smile. "One more," she said, looking across at the four officers in the room. Nothing was forthcoming. She looked back at the graduates, who were equally non-committal.

"No?" She pointed at it on the screen. "This one? Any takers? No? Okay, this is the Sternocleidomastoideus."

A couple of the graduates nodded as if it was semi-familiar. Rob looked blank.

"The point I'm making here is that the neck is a network of tightly compacted muscles, ligaments and bone. Cutting a head off is not an easy task, trained or otherwise." Becky flicked the image on the screen, which was instantly recognisable. The clean lines and neat diagram replaced with photographs of the headless corpse recovered from the Vauxhall Astra. The screen zoomed in and focused on the part of the neck which had been severed.

"To get started, you need to break the skin and sever the spinal column. That's assuming you go in from the back, but there are two large muscles and two tendons to go through at the same time."

"Does the choice of tool matter?" Jack asked.

"Good question," Becky replied. "It does, but the challenges remain the same. You can use an axe, for example, but that's a brutal job and inaccurate too. You can use something like a petrol saw or a piece of construction equipment. That's *better* from an ease point of view but the blood spatter would be horrific. I mean, *really* bad."

"Do you behead a body from behind then?" Jack asked.

"Well, you don't have to, Jack. It tends to be from the back in all the beheadings I've seen, but there are no rules to it. It's *easier* from behind."

"I'll bear that in mind," Jack replied.

Becky looked at Nicky, who was looking at the images of the burnt corpse. "This looks neat, Becky. Is that fair?"

"Yes. You're right. This shows knowledge. The cut marks are neat but show fine teeth marks on them, as does the spinal column and the very top section of the windpipe, which we found once we'd cleaned away some of the debris and ash. The saw marks show that a fine-toothed hacksaw was used for some, or all, of the dismemberment, which, believe it or not, is the tool of choice for an effective job. It gets through all sorts. Bone, muscle and just the thick gristle that a neck offers."

Becky gesticulated with her hands. Jack winced inside.

"But it's difficult, Becky?" Rob asked. "Even if you're tooled up, it's hard?"

"It's really difficult." She looked at the graduates. "I can't emphasise how difficult it is to behead a body. We'll play later once the officers are done, but it's hard." She looked back at Rob. "Do you remember the jigsaw murders?" she asked. "Nicky, you might too."

They both nodded. "I worked on it," Rob said. The graduates perked up again.

"So did I," Becky replied confidently. "I was a graduate at

the time but I was lucky enough to be involved, so it became the research for my thesis."

Jack mouthed the word 'lucky' to Jen, who smiled.

Becky looked at the graduates, who would have all been in nappies or primary school at the time. She flicked past a few screens on the presentation before arriving at a man cheerfully smiling on the screen. Slightly obese, with short grey hair and rimless glasses. His formal blue shirt was unbuttoned at the collar with his tie pulled down, as if he was at the end of a working day, or had just arrived in the pub.

"Anybody remember this chap?" Becky asked.

"Jeffrey Howe," Rob said, with a tinge of sadness in the pronunciation.

"Correct, Inspector Rhone. This is Jeffrey Howe. He was a fifty-three-year-old kitchen salesman when he was murdered and dismembered in 2003. Parts of his body were scattered across the country in a case that became known as the Jigsaw Murders."

She looked around. Some nods were coming from the graduates, as if they'd read about it in passing. A textbook, or an afternoon lesson before a night in the students' union.

Becky flicked through a few more slides to show some imagery Rob wished he hadn't seen. She continued. "In March, a left leg with the foot attached was found in a lay-by in Cottered, Hertfordshire. It was wrapped in blue plastic bags." She paused. "A week later, a left forearm, which had been dismembered at the elbow and wrist, was found on a grass verge in Wheathampstead. Does anybody other than Inspector Rhone and Detective Sergeant Green recall what was next?"

Jack looked across the room. Nobody. "Head?" he offered.

"Correct, Jack! A couple of days later, March 31st, a head

was discovered by a farmer in a cattle pen in Asfordby, just a few miles up the road from here. It was by the cricket ground on the border with Hoby. The flesh had been removed, as had the eyes, ears and tongue."

Rob breathed hard inside, regretting the two Weetabix and a protein bar he'd had for breakfast. The picture on the screen wasn't helping. The graduates were unmoved.

"I won't go through it all, but other parts were found. A right leg was found in a holdall in Hertfordshire, and a torso, right arm and upper-left arm were discovered in a ditch, also in Hertfordshire, and inside a green suitcase. Interestingly, his hands have never been found, although one of the people convicted has claimed they were buried in Epping Forest."

"It can't be the same person, though, Becky. He's still inside, right?" Jack asked, looking at Rob and Nicky for reassurance.

"Yeah, he's inside, Jack. He's not going anywhere anytime soon," Rob confirmed.

"But the method; are people trained to do this or could it be gangland? We've discussed this being a possible annihilation of an identity, as well as being a warning, but is it more than just a way of preventing an identification?" Jack asked.

"It could be a gang thing, it's not uncommon in parts of South America, but there are examples more recently from Northern Ireland, all from dissident republicans where it's a fear tactic as well as a threat," Becky replied.

"Northern Ireland?" Jack asked, perking up. "David Cramer spent time in Northern Ireland from my initial search, and he served as well. Could it be a revenge killing?"

"We'll take that away," Rob cut in. "The Howe murder was conducted by Detective Superintendent Michael Hanlon from the Bedfordshire and Hertfordshire Major Crime Unit;

codename Operation Abnet. I've already reached out to him in case there is a link or a common factor."

"Who was convicted, Inspector Rhone?" Jade asked. His face had softened considerably and the debate was helpful to all parties, albeit with their different agendas.

Rob looked at Becky, who remained silent. Rob looked at Jade. "Stephen Marshall and his girlfriend, Sarah Bush. They were both convicted, but he was the ringleader. She was twenty-one and went with it, but she went down too, obviously."

Becky flicked on another couple of slides, but Rob carried on.

"It was linked to the Adams crime syndicate. The investigation concluded that Marshall wasn't working for the family by that stage, but he admitted in court to dismembering at least four more bodies."

The room looked shocked. A slide appeared on the screen detailing the allegations, as if it was a planned segment to the session. Becky flicked the slides forward, showing several other parts of the case as she picked up from Rob.

"A review was carried out by the Home Office. The pathologist was Simon Poole, for reference, and he concluded that Marshall had 'skilfully and cleanly' removed Mr Howe's limbs, which he estimated would have taken at least twelve hours."

"Twelve hours?" asked Jack. "And he knew what he was doing?"

Becky nodded. "It is neither a quick nor an easy process. Hands and feet are clearly easier, but again this is not a spontaneous act or a spur-of-the-moment action."

Rob cut back in. "What may be relevant relating to Marshall is that he attacked his first wife in 2003, before he killed Jeffrey Howe, but he was also arrested on suspicion of murdering a guy called Minesh Nagrecha. That was back in 1996 when his charred remains were found, although he was never charged."

"Dismemberment and cremation?" Jen chipped in. "Sounds like a unique MO."

"You're right, Jen, and it's the modus operandi that's interesting." Rob was thinking out loud. "It could be a revenge killing. The Northern Ireland thread looks of clear interest, but it could be gangland too."

Rob decided they'd learnt enough from the session and thanked Becky. He also thanked the graduates and wished them well in their careers. He had got a number of ideas bubbling in his mind that needed following up on, and he wanted the route of the car retracing before it started to get dark.

He'd also decided he'd be skipping lunch today.

CHAPTER 13

It was early afternoon before Nicky, Jen and Jack turned off the main A50 and down the quiet and dilapidated side road that leads onto Soar Lane. Sodden plywood hoardings lined where the demolition remained ongoing, with extensive graffiti and decaying timber edges showing how long the boards had been standing. The slow wheels of progress.

The three had decided that lunch was required and had eaten in the car. Just some sandwiches that had been picked up from a local Londis, along with a few packets of crisps and several bottles of Diet Coke that were now wedged in door pockets. A typical lunch meal that most shops now offered. Nicky had found a vanilla-flavoured Coke and had opted for that as a change. Stomachs were barely ravenous after the session with Becky, but not eating was not an option, and a light lunch on the move had sufficed.

The rain had stopped but the sky remained threatening. The clouds were still dark and a cool wind was carrying them hastily across the Leicester sky. Jen parked her car as close as she could to where the Astra had stood less than forty-eight hours ago, and the three officers stepped out. The scene was still cordoned off, with a uniform presence keeping the perimeter intact. It would soon be gone, and the dog walkers, drug addicts and local youths would reclaim the land, and everything else would be lost.

Warrant cards were briefly flashed to a uniformed officer who was already stepping aside, and they made the short walk up the cobbled incline to the bridge. The Astra was long gone, but the burnt outline on the ground would take longer to fade, if it ever did. An indelible reminder that would remain, and scar the scene for months, if not years, to come. Like a macabre gravestone.

"We're working backwards then?" Jack asked.

"We are indeed," replied Nicky. "There's been a crime committed here, and just because we can't prove it's a murder, or we can't yet, the car was stolen, a man was decapitated and both were left here. We agree they were left to be found?"

"Definitely," Jen nodded. "You don't set a car alight in the city centre and not expect it to be uncovered, so we were meant to find this body."

"Agreed," Nicky added, "only he was left for us to find him, but without knowing who he is."

"Does the tooth bother you, Nicky?" Jack asked.

"Yeah, it does. I can't say why but we'll come on to that. At least it gave us a name."

"Very true. I'm still working on his background now, but it's throwing up some interesting stuff which we'll run through later on. He lives in Norfolk, so they're visiting the house for us."

Jen wanted to get back to the here and now. The three walked past the burnt outline and carried on to the rec, their footsteps becoming hollow and metallic as the solid ground gave way to the surface of the contemporary steel bridge. They crossed the River Soar and walked past another officer on the opposite side of the bridge, into an area of the park that was still cordoned off.

Jen scoured the park, meeting eyes with a number of people watching them from across the rec. Residents of nearby Tudor Road; bike riders and a few youths who were supposed to be in school were dotted around the periphery.

"Where was the car stolen from, Jack?" Jen asked.

"Tournament Road in Glenfield. Two nights ago."

"And that's what? Two miles?"

"Pretty much, yes."

"Any local CCTV?"

"No, nothing. Well, nothing from the theft. The uniforms have been canvassing and we think we've picked the car up travelling down the Groby Road from the direction of Glenfield Hospital about twenty minutes before the call went into the fire brigade."

"Any sight of the driver?"

Jack didn't answer. Jen knew it was a long shot. Her mind had started to wander just before she did, heading further onto the rec. The surface was undulating and two of the hollows in the ground were waterlogged, with deep muddy tyre tracks coming out towards the burnt-out shell.

"It was driven in from Tudor Road then?" Nicky surmised, walking past the tyre marks and following the direction back towards a break in the row of terraces. It was a hundred yards or so before the three were standing in the large gap between the houses. The bases of the four severed bars designed to keep vehicles off the rec had been broken away; the galvanised tubular stumps sticking out of the ground, but only by a few inches.

The three squatted down on their haunches and looked at the metal protruding from the tarmac, with a few stray weeds sneaking out between the metal and the ground.

"This hasn't been done recently, has it?" Jen asked, but again as more of a statement. The access seemed to provide a convenient route to where the car had stood. Nicky walked forward onto the path at the front of the terraces, with people going about their business and with some audible conversations drifting across from some carefree passersby. She looked up, eyeballing the brickwork on houses opposite, on the corner of Paget Road. No shops, no cameras. Nothing.

"Shall we?" Nicky asked, looking towards the north end of the road.

"Yes, we should," Jen replied. She took out a pack of chewing gum and offered it around. Nicky took one; Jack declined. The three walked up the street, surrounded by the bustle of the road, in serious contrast to the sombre scene tucked away behind gardens and everyday lives.

"We've no idea where he was killed, have we? Or where he died if it was natural causes, or at what point he was dismembered and put into the boot of the car?" Jack asked out loud. It was a conversation they'd already had a few times. Debates about possible motives. Why risk driving into town and being caught on CCTV, why risk setting the car on fire? The reasons for the decapitation, and other salient questions, which remained firmly unanswered.

"If he drove the Astra in this way, are we assuming he exited back across the rec and onto Tudor Road?" Jack asked.

"I think it's a safe assumption, much less risky than heading back out towards the A50, especially on foot."

"Are we assuming he was on foot?"

"Are we assuming he's a he?" Nicky asked pointedly.

"No, we're not," Jen replied, "but let's assume that 'he' is a metaphorical 'he' for now, and we'll all keep an open mind."

They continued to walk, reaching a sharp kink in the road which turned to the left. A modern block of flats sat on the corner, breaking the traditional terraces with wrought-iron gates and a plethora of 'To Let' signs from a number of estate agents; their boards vying for space against their competitors and nailed clumsily onto a single wooden post. The kink left a short walk of eighty yards or so, and they headed towards the main thoroughfare of Fosse Road North. The bustle grew as they reached the corner, which had a small community Co-op on one side and a Euro Mini Market on the other, where Jen, Nicky and Jack were standing. A number of shops lined the opposite side; a Betfred, a barber's and a pharmacy were in a short row, with a tattoo parlour and several other local vendors lining the busy main road.

Nicky raised her voice to speak over the traffic. "Have we canvassed these shops, Jack?"

"Yes, we have. They've all been spoken to as to whether they saw anything on the night of the fire. Nobody remembers anything, and nobody saw anyone they would describe as suspicious."

Nicky nodded. "Plenty of CCTV from along here, though?"

"There is," Jack replied. "We've recovered footage from a number of these shops. It's being looked at but we're not expecting a lot. The initial quality looks quite low."

"We don't know who we're looking for, for a start!" said Nicky.

"Agreed," Jack added, "plus, we don't even know if this is the exit route he took."

"It would be worth appealing for witnesses with dash cams. Anyone who used Fosse Road on that day. It's unlikely we'll get many, but anything we do get could be useful."

"Good idea," Jack said, noting it down on his to-do list.

The three stood in silence for a few minutes. Each looking around, looking up and down the road. Thinking.

"What do you think, Jack?" Jen asked.

Jack looked down the hill towards a pedestrian footbridge, and back up in the opposite direction towards one of two main roads out of the city; up towards the A46 and the M1. He looked back at Jen.

"I'm thinking that if I wanted to get a body into the city and onto that park, this wouldn't be a bad way to do it."

CHAPTER 14

It was 4pm before Nicky, Jen and Jack arrived back at Lodge House, entering through the rear entrance and down into the underground car park. It was a dark, tight car park with scraped walls and missing paintwork on the many sharp kinks that formed the one-way system. The roof was low and the lights were temperamental, as were the lifts, which were irrationally small spaces but with the manufacturer's signs claiming a maximum of nine. Jen had often wondered what the nine referred to; it clearly wasn't people. In reality, four was a squeeze, and on many occasions the stairs had been opted for to avoid the awkward proximity or the short-term claustrophobia.

It wasn't befitting of a police station, and looked more like the sort of place where drug deals should go down, or gangland beatings were dished out.

A weak 'ping' sounded as the lift wobbled its way to the tenth floor, and after a second of waiting the doors rumbled open.

Nicky headed to the fridge to see what cans or bottled water were in it, before joining Jen and Jack in the main office.

Rob raised a hand and shouted a greeting out of his open door, before joining them in the main office. The mood was relaxed. Nicky dropped several cans and bottles on the desk between them before cracking open a can of Diet Coke.

"Good afternoon?" asked Rob.

"Not bad," replied Jen, "just not that useful either."

She explained the tracking back of the vehicle across the rec, and although efforts were ongoing with CCTV, nobody was expecting a quick win on the driver. Or the car.

"How was your afternoon, Rob?" Jen asked back.

"It was good, thanks. Nobody died, Mathers is happy, and the CPS are almost certain your rapist is going down for a long time."

"Good times."

"Good times, indeed," Rob replied. He smiled at Jen before changing tack. "David Cramer."

Jen nodded. "David Cramer. What do we know about him?"

Rob picked up a bottle of water from the table and opened it. He took a sip. "He's a little bit of an enigma, or parts of his life seem to be anyway. His birth name isn't Cramer for a start. That's an alias that he started to use after his retirement. He was born in London in 1956 as David Wilson. He's a widower, his wife passed away a few years ago and he's been living the quiet life in a house in Norfolk. He was a military man, and this is where it gets patchy. He served in the forces and the military police in Belfast, but there are some gaps in the timeline of his service, so I'm not entirely sure what he was doing fully during the height of the Troubles."

"How long was he there, Rob?" Nicky asked. She reached over to open the top drawer of her desk and was delighted to see a pack of Frazzles sitting on top of a notebook and a stapler. She grabbed them and opened them slowly, as if she was in a cinema, trying to keep the rustling to a minimum. The air eased out gently, making the slightest of sounds. Nobody batted an eyelid.

"He was there for twelve years, 1985 to 1997, and he was honourably discharged in '97. The records I've got access to show a distinguished career. A ranking officer, a man of honour. He served during some of the darkest days of the Troubles and was reported as a respected, steadfast character. He was a part of the military police for a number of years, and led teams in some of the toughest places, and during some of the worst of the unrest. He was in Belfast for large periods and seemed to have a habit of being in the wrong place at the wrong time. He was in Omagh the day the bomb went off, and he was in Shankill during a number of violent clashes."

Rob paused. There was a silent appreciation for the work David Cramer had done. Being a police officer in 21st-century Britain was no cakewalk, but all four sat quietly, processing the relentless work that would have faced the men on the ground in Northern Ireland during the worst period of violence in modern history. Managing it. Trying to manage it. To react to it, and deal with the fallout. The damage. The injured and the maimed. The dead.

Rob flicked a page of the file and continued. "On the 8th of May 1987, he was working alongside the Royal Ulster Constabulary in Loughgall, County Armagh. The RUC station was attacked by eight members of the IRA who were armed with guns and bombs. The SAS responded and killed all of the terrorists, which represented the most IRA members killed in one single incident." He flicked to another report.

"In November 1987, he was in Enniskillen, in County Fermanagh."

"What happened there?" asked Jack, who was still a toddler at the time. Like many, he knew of the Troubles. He'd learnt about them at school and saw some of the latter stages on the news during his adolescence, but it was always hard to have a full grasp of the level and extent of the violence after a comfy upbringing in middle England. No religious clashes, no daily tension, no night-time reprisals, summary beatings or petrol bombings. Plus, there were simply too many incidents to be aware of them all, and Nicky added that she had no immediate recollection of what happened at Enniskillen either. Jen also nodded to the negative.

"He was at a Remembrance Sunday ceremony for UK Commonwealth war casualties. A Provisional IRA bomb was detonated by the cenotaph, which was at the heart of the parade. David wasn't injured but eleven people, consisting of ten civilians, including one pregnant woman, as well as one serving member of the RUC, were killed. Sixty-three others were injured, some seriously."

"So they killed twelve people that day," Jen added, poignantly. "How unlucky was this guy?"

"He wasn't afraid of being in the thick of it, was he?" Nicky responded.

"He really wasn't," added Rob. He flicked through more pages. The list wasn't exhaustive. He continued. "His career is exemplary. There are parts of his service record which have been redacted, as I mentioned, so I can only imagine what's in there given some of the stuff that's available."

Nicky threw the empty crisp packet into a bin next to her and finished her can. She looked around for the recycling bin, which had been moved. She left the empty can on the desk. "He paid a high price for his service, didn't he?" Nicky asked. The nods from the others were in complete agreement. The mental scars always remained long after any physical ones had faded. "Was he married, Rob? Did he have a family?"

"He had a wife, Mary, who passed away a couple of years ago. They'd retired to a quiet village in Norfolk to live out their retirement, which I imagine was heavenly after twelve years in the thick of it. He also had a son, Chris, who died in Belfast in 1996."

"How did he die?" asked Jack.

"Car bomb. There'd been a demonstration one night. There were a lot of people on the street and Chris was one of them. The force of the blast killed him instantly. He was sixteen years old."

The room fell silent again. The price paid by David Cramer for his service had just increased exponentially. Bullets and bombs were one thing. To lose a child was as incomprehensible as it was incomparable, and all for a career choice.

"At least we all get to clock off and go home," Jen shared. She was right. However hard your occupation was – doctor, nurse, police officer – you got to clock off and go home safely at night, and although you carried the events of that day with you, it was done. To be compartmentalised. To be processed. Nobody had ever shot at Jen on her way home from work. Or tried to bomb her car. Harm her friends, family or loved ones, just for being a police officer.

The mood had dropped. The energy level was on the decline after a busy day, and all were thinking through the information in their own way. Nicky realised she wanted to see her husband and watch some awful TV. Jack could still recall his sixteenth year, the age of Christopher Wilson on that fateful day. All he could recall was his GCSE's, girls and Oasis. And 400 miles between their upbringings that might as well have been a million.

"What happens next, Rob?" Jen asked, rubbing her face with her hands and realising that an end-of-day tiredness was rapidly creeping in. "Are there any other family? Brothers or sisters? Or who's the next of kin?"

"Jack hasn't been able to find any living relatives and his address is outside of our patch, so we've spoken to Norfolk Constabulary. It looks like he's passed intestate. There's no obvious next of kin anyway, so we're unlikely to have anyone to notify, but the local authority and Her Majesty's revenue and customs will need to deal with the estate."

"Shall I notify HMRC in the morning, Rob?" Jack offered.

"I've notified them today, but thanks for offering. Have Norfolk not been to the house yet? If they haven't, can you tell them this is an active murder and to get somebody over there today? There might still be a will, which may give us some insight, and there could be pets to deal with too."

"I'll chase them now," Jack replied.

The session was drawing to a natural conclusion. Nicky sat back in her chair and raised her arms above her head, stretching her back. She asked Jack what his evening consisted of, and got a noncommittal shrug back. Food and sleep was the broad gist. She knew Jen had a date and could sense her getting twitchy. Ready to head home for a shower and a change of clothes before the evening played out.

CHAPTER 15

The early mornings was office time that Jack valued, and was time he used to organise his professional life, as well as his own thoughts. It had been a tiring twenty-four hours, with limited rest and little food other than a Chinese which had been consumed late last night. Chicken fried rice that had filled a hole and then sat heavily whilst he was trying to sleep.

He looked across the office to see Rob concentrating, consumed by whatever was on his desk. He stood up to go and make a tea. His movement didn't attract Rob's attention, so he decided not to knock and headed off to the kitchen to boil the kettle. He sighed to nobody in particular and checked his phone. There was some chatter on the WhatsApp group. All of the earlier stuff had been about the post-mortem, with some images of the stab wounds and some useful information. The few on the screen had now devolved into banter with the sensible text having been replaced with a rake of emojis and several GIFs following a lively Saturday night out in the city last weekend.

The kettle seemed to be taking an age, so Jack used the opportunity to take a short loo break, feeling his phone buzz a couple of times in his pocket as he did so. He ignored it, expecting it to be Nicky, Jen or Becky adding some humour to a WhatsApp group chat.

He arrived back in the kitchen as the kettle had finished boiling and poured the water on top of the teabag and the spoon of sugar, leaving it to stew. He pulled his phone out to see two missed calls, from a 01945 prefix. The voicemail that had been left was from a DC at the station in Wisbech, Vanessa Ryder, who had asked Jack to call her back. It sounded urgent. Jack rang the number back whilst adding a splash of milk to the tea, stirring it as DC Ryder spoke. He listened, intently, clarifying what he was being told before thanking her for the call. He headed immediately to Rob's office, knocking on the door and walking in, with a waved hand granting entry.

"I've just spoken to Norfolk Police. They've been over to David Cramer's house."

"Excellent, and they're dealing with the estate?"

"Not exactly, boss, no – he was in."

Rob looked up with a furrowed brow.

"What the fuck do you mean, he was in?"

"I mean, he was in the house. He answered the door."

"So what have they done?"

"They didn't arrest him, but they didn't know what to do. He was formally asked to accompany the Norfolk officers to the station and they notified us to ask for instructions. What do we want them to do with him, Rob?"

"Ring them back, tell them to make him a coffee and get your coat."

*

Jack was tired, and used another loo break before the

impending journey to splash water onto his face, reset his shirt and make sure that his appearance didn't match the way he was feeling. Being tired was acceptable in any walk of life, and in any occupation, just as long as you didn't look it. Jack had long since learnt to manage his tiredness on the job, and like anybody in a position of authority and responsibility, it was something he had adjusted to. It was never going to be a nine to five, he knew that from day one, but at least, unlike nurses and doctors, he didn't work shifts. Long hours, yes, unsociable hours, often, but on the whole, he spent the darker hours of the night in bed.

He'd learnt the importance of sleep from an early case as a DC. He'd attended a fatality just up the road from the station, one of the first scenes he'd been to with Jen, where a long-distance lorry driver had caused a fatal crash. He'd exited the M1 at Fosse Park in error, after missing the services at Leicester Forest East half a mile earlier, and ploughed into the back of a Ford Focus, killing the three occupants sitting at the traffic lights at the bottom of the slip road. He was found to have fabricated his driving hours and illegally altered his tachograph in order to keep driving. To save himself some time. It ended up costing six years and three lives. The impact on the families was much greater. And for much longer. It had also left an indelible mark on Jack.

Rob had offered to drive, which Jack was grateful for, so he'd made some tea in a couple of travel mugs and grabbed some snack bars and protein bites from his emergency stash. Rob had done the same.

"You ready, Jack?" came the call from outside.

"Coming, boss," Jack replied. He dried his face, looked himself up and down in the mirror and confidently strode out into the corridor. Jack knew King's Lynn was only around seventy miles from the station. It was pretty much a straight line and due east along the A47, the start of which was at the end of the ring road where the police station sat. He was hoping that if they made good time it would take a little over an hour.

Rob knew differently, having spent some time in East Anglia in a previous role. The distance was short, but the A47 was a mix of single and dual carriageway. It was also the only real route from the Midlands into Norfolk, King's Lynn, Great Yarmouth and the areas of outstanding natural beauty that lined the coastline. It was also the county of farming, so Rob knew that if he only spent half of the journey sitting behind a caravan or a tractor towing a trailer full of produce, he'd be doing well.

Jack was admiring the unadulterated countryside as they headed east from Peterborough, and the stunning flatness that made up the fens as they passed the village of March and made good progress towards Wisbech.

The tea had long since gone when they reached a small island with a Starbucks next to an Esso petrol station on one side and what looked like a farm shop opposite. A large sign hung by the island: 'Worzals Café & Bar'. Jack looked at Rob, who half looked back. "On the way back, mate."

It was pretty much two hours dead when they pulled into the car park of King's Lynn Police Station. The frontage was old and authoritarian, with a large copper clock tower shining in iridescent green. The car park to the rear had an entrance to a modern extension which was more glass and steel, which put the dour entrance to Leicester Station to shame. Rob made a mental note to ask Laura Mathers about upgrades and building changes when he was next with her; he hadn't been turned down for a while.

Jack felt more lively and was in the right frame of mind as he signed in and introduced himself to the desk sergeant. It was a few minutes before DC Vanessa Ryder appeared, a dark-haired woman of forty or so, with bright features and cheerful eyes. Her hair was shoulder length, jet black and was offset by the crisp whiteness of her shirt, which looked immaculate despite the time of day.

She offered her hand to Jack, who smiled back. Vanessa's face was warm and congenial, and they quickly started a conversation as if they'd known each other for years. Jack immediately liked her, and felt she'd be Nicky and Jen's cup of tea. He wished she worked in Leicester.

Rob had a similar introduction with Ness, as she'd asked to be addressed, before leading them through to a room. There was a conversation around the circumstances of the ongoing nature of the investigation, with local support still digging into the details offered up by the man sitting in the room next door. Rob was ready to go and headed into the room with Jack, eyeballing the man in the seat as soon as he walked in.

David Cramer raised his head slowly and met Rob's eye. His hair was silver but flowing and well kept. The look he gave Rob was a steely look of defiance, and for a man in his mid sixties, Rob could sense an anger and stubbornness that wouldn't be intimidated by an interview room in a Norfolk police station. Cramer's file had shown an outline of the things that he had seen. Had experienced. Had felt.

Rob introduced himself, as did Jack. Cramer gave Jack a cursory glance then looked straight back at Rob.

"Where were you two days ago, David?" Rob asked.

"I'd rather you address me as Major General Cramer whilst we're being formal, Chief Inspector Rhone," came the emotionless reply. Rob didn't react.

"Where were you last Tuesday?"

"I was at home," came the short reply.

"Can anybody vouch for that?"

"No, they can't. I'm a widower, as you well know."

"So you can't account for your whereabouts?"

"I don't believe I need to."

"I beg to differ."

There was a pause as the two men met each other's eye again. Jack sat still. There was an atmosphere in the room, which he knew Rob would be enjoying, but he also sensed that the man on the opposite side of the table was more than proficient at playing this game.

"We found one of your teeth at a crime scene. It's why you're here, as you well know." Jack pulled it out of his bag and placed it on the table between them in an evidence bag. Rob pointed at it, as if Cramer should recognise it or want it back. Cramer exhaled, which was almost a sigh. As if in some way he was bored.

"Your tooth was found amongst the wreckage of a burnt-out car and with a headless body. We thought it was you, but as you're here and clearly not our victim, it makes us think you may have been involved, Major General." He spoke the rank with tones of disdain. He was tired too. He received a scalding look back and a short silence.

"Was that a question, Chief Inspector?"

"Were you in Leicester on Tuesday of last week, and do you know anything regarding the discovery of a body in a burnt-out car?" The question was more respectful and Cramer sat nodding.

"Tuesday, you say?"

"Tuesday," Rob confirmed.

Cramer sat resolute, which was no doubt a quality ingrained after years spent in Northern Ireland. Rob suspected that if he was allowed to torture David Cramer, they probably wouldn't get any more out of him than they already were.

"I was in Wisbech on Tuesday, Chief Inspector. Depending on what time you're asking me about."

"All day?"

"No, I went to do some food shopping in the afternoon. I visited a bank, the HSBC at Cornhill, and then I got fuel on the way home. I spent an hour in my garden until it was too dark and spent the evening in front of the television. I have told your colleagues this," he remarked, as disdainfully as Rob had been with him a few minutes earlier.

The mood softened as Cramer sipped at the water that had been given to him, in a white plastic water cooler cup.

"How can you explain your tooth being in the car with a dead body in Leicester?"

"I can't. I lost three teeth thirty years ago when I was in Northern Ireland. I don't recall losing any since. I'm wearing dentures now. I can pop them out if you'd like me to?"

Rob waved the offer away with a hand. He knew from the initial conversation with Ness that her team were looking into the CCTV footage, as well as the dental angle. DC Ryder had started to verify with his current dentist the past history relating to David Cramer's teeth. The tooth in question hadn't featured in his records going back over five years, and with his claim that he lost it thirty years ago, there was a time gap of a quarter of a century. There was also the riddle of why it had cropped up now.

The conversation reached a lull. Rob suspended the

interview and walked out with Jack, meeting Ness in the room next door where they'd started. "So how did one of his teeth get into the boot of that car?"

"No idea, guv," came the reply from Jack. Ness looked equally flummoxed but confirmed that she'd just had a call from a colleague who had been to the petrol station on the outskirts of Wisbech. "Cramer's car was on the CCTV, as clear as day, and he's identifiable from the footage. His credit card was used as well, all timestamped at 16:16 in the afternoon, so it matches his story."

"It's in the wrong direction as well," Jack added. "Wisbech is further east than his place, so he was further away from the scene at the time the Astra would have been in Leicester."

Ness agreed. "It's sixty-odd miles from Wisbech to your scene, and he's in his own car when he was on CCTV. We'll check with the supermarket too, but the petrol station was his last stop and he's in the wrong place at the right time."

Rob nodded and agreed. He didn't feel Cramer was responsible for the body in the car. It just wasn't plausible. There was no evidence to suggest he was, and the evidence they did have was very much in his favour. There was also a belligerence about him that could be down to age, but there was an attitude that Rob felt was down to innocence.

"What do you want us to do with him?" Ness asked.

Rob sighed. There was no evidence to suggest Cramer was lying, or was in Leicester on the day the car was driven to the scene at Frog Island. "Let him go home. Take his passport and let him go, but tell him we may need him again. He may not like it but his tooth was at a crime scene, so he's involved."

"I'll get him processed and released," Ness confirmed with a smile.

With formalities wrapped up and with Rob pleased he'd met the man behind the tooth, they walked out into the cool air of an autumn night. Now fully dark and with streetlights on, he breathed in the clear air and felt his stomach rumble.

"What was that place called, Jack?"

"Worzals, Rob. It was called Worzals."

CHAPTER 16

Nicky stood up and stretched as her mobile rang on the desk. On silent but buzzing harshly on the hard laminated surface. She pushed an empty Diet Coke can aside and picked her iPhone up. Bernie Copp's name adorned the screen; an experienced and dependable officer and somebody whom Nicky was keen on. The two had a strong working relationship, which Nicky was comfortable with, especially after his professional relationship with Rob had become strained.

"Hey, Bernie, how are you?" she asked.

"I'm okay, thanks, Nicky. How are you?" came the response. Some small talk ensued before Nicky cut to the chase. "I'm thinking this isn't a social call, is it, Bernie?"

"Afraid not, guv."

"What and where?"

"I'm down at Bouskell Park in Whetstone. A dog walker reported finding a body by some undergrowth about an hour ago. He wasn't sure if it was a rough sleeper or a mannequin to start with. I attended with a rookie and we've confirmed it's very real. He's in shock so we're looking after him. We've got some support, but we need you and forensics down here."

"We'll be straight there, Bernie." She looked at Jack, then to Jen. "Body in Whetstone. Jen, go home." She looked back across to Jack. "Fancy picking a Chinese up with me later?"

*

Evening was starting to settle in when Nicky and Jack drove the final mile down the Welford Road towards the park, past a beautiful row of period red-brick houses, which were set back from the road. The wide pathways were tree lined on both sides, with a mix of large and magnificent English oak, some smaller trees that Nicky thought could be yew trees, and a couple of willows, all of which made the boulevard appear wider. Elegant and tree lined. A picture of suburbia.

"Nice part of town," Jack commented from the passenger seat.

"Very nice part of town," added Nicky, nodding and passing fleeting glances at the properties as they flashed past. It was a side of town she knew to be affluent but had spent very little time in. Serious crime was lower across Blaby, Whetstone and Wigston, and Nicky had little reason, professionally at least, to be familiar with the area. She'd spent much more time in the less salubrious areas of the city. Stocking Farm. Eyres Monsell. New Parks.

The last house on the right gave way to a hedgerow weaved amid a black wrought-iron fence, and as the road eased gently round to the right, the flashing blue lights of Bernie's patrol car became visible. The natural light was dull and she could see the car was parked lengthways across the narrow entrance to a small public car park. Nicky indicated and parked on the pavement to the right-hand side of the entrance, stepping out and smiling as she saw Bernie walking towards her.

"Good evening, Bernie. How are you?"

"I'm good, thanks, Nicky. How are you?"

"I'm really good. How's Greta?"

"She's good. She'll be walking Millie, I imagine, in our local park, which isn't dissimilar to this."

Nicky scanned the immediate area and noticed large gold-painted letters attached to the black wrought-iron railings flanking the perimeter, with a smaller greeting above. 'Welcome to Bouskell Park'. She imagined Bernie's wife walking their golden retriever; enjoyably and carefree across a public park. One that didn't have a dead body lying within its grounds.

A small crowd had started to gather across the road, with most in warm evening clothes with the temperature having dropped as the evening progressed. More than a few hands stuffed firmly into coat pockets. Nicky looked up as a small black Chihuahua sat barking away whilst sitting with his owner. His golden-coloured brother sat patiently alongside him. "Two minutes, Dobby," came the response from the other end of the lead, from a young blonde lady who clearly wasn't feeling the cold. Her t-shirt allowed two American-themed tattoo sleeves to protrude, and Nicky clocked what looked like the word 'California' in red ink. The lady smiled at Nicky, who smiled back.

"Is the scene secure, Bernie?" Jack asked.

"We're pretty much there, Jack. It's a fair-sized park with a number of entrances and pathways. We've secured the immediate scene and cordoned off the body. A couple of other patrols arrived so we worked outwards until we'd secured the outer edges. The other entrances are blocked off and manned, although this is the only car park. We've found several cut-throughs. The main path is circular, so we systematically cleared the park, which took a while but we've blocked off all areas we know of." He pointed at a wooden map within the car park, which was tidy and neatly framed in green-painted timber with a Leicester City Council motif at the top.

"I've informed the local council as well, guv, as it's a suspicious death on public land."

"Great, thanks, Bernie," Nicky replied, whilst starting to look around. The hedging was well kept, the borders well tended and the immediate appearance of the park entrance matched the locale.

"Have you been here before, Bernie?" Nicky asked socially.

"No, I haven't, but it's nice, if you ignore the reason why we're all here," came the dry reply.

"Have we been able to identify those in the park?"

"Yes, we have. We took identification from everybody as we cleared the park. Nobody was acting suspiciously, nobody was difficult, and other than the odd 'tut' where we were cutting a dog walk short, everybody was fully cooperative. No drunks, no druggies and no amorous couples," he added.

"Cracking," Jack replied, nodding appreciatively.

It was a good start. Public areas and dead bodies weren't a good mix, and other than where eyewitnesses and cyclists with handlebar-cams were in play, it could be a difficult scene to process. Plus, the unspoken mood from across the road was almost of disdain; why are *you* closing *our* park? Disrupting our lives in suburbia. Everybody in and around the park had provided identification, and all would be called upon to give a formal statement in the next twenty-four hours.

Nicky had called Becky on the way out of Lodge House

and was starting to wonder after her as her dark grey VW Golf came around the corner and parked behind Nicky's car. Two pathology vans followed and added to the line of vehicles. The crowd across the road was growing and now numbered about two dozen people.

Nicky looked at them, then looked at a small residential road adjacent to where they were standing. Freer Close. The house on the corner was large and the houses neighbouring them looked equally spacious. With more patrol cars arriving and the scene secure, she looked at Bernie.

"Fancy organising some door knocking, Bernie?"

Bernie nodded a 'yes', a job he enjoyed and one he knew was coming his way.

"Excellent. I'd suggest starting at the houses immediately opposite for anybody who saw anything."

"Will do." He nodded then waved a hand at PC Keith Wainwright, beckoning him over before starting to direct the uniformed officers and get the door knocking underway.

"What about the lucky winner?" Jack asked Bernie.

"He was just passing, Jack. It was his usual evening route. We got him home as he only lives round the corner, but he's in shock. He's at home with his wife but we'll get a support crew with him tomorrow for a follow-up and a statement. He wasn't sure it was real, but his dog was."

"Thanks, Bernie," said Jack. He looked at Nicky. "I told you it's always a dog walker."

Bernie started to shout at the uniforms, who were now also growing in number. Nicky had every confidence that the crowd would be quickly dispersed and the early task of information gathering would commence shortly, in an efficient and understated manner.

Becky had suited up and was walking towards Nicky and Jack, her smile growing as she got closer. She greeted them both warmly and with an effervescence in her eyes.

"Good evening, Becky," Jack replied. "How are you?"

"I'm good, thanks. I was midway through a spin session, but that's the nature of the beast in our line of work."

Jack nodded. Becky looked her usual self. Her hair was sleek, black and tied back. Her face and complexion looked fresh. She certainly didn't look like she'd just left the gym.

"It's a shame criminals don't work nine to five. Otherwise, we'd all be somewhere else," he replied.

Three members of Becky's pathology team walked into the small car park, carrying steel briefcases and torches. It wasn't that dark yet but it would be in half an hour or so. Jack was grateful that he'd get to go home at some point. Much sooner than Becky's team would.

Bernie reappeared and greeted Becky, before the group followed him into the park, walking around a hundred yards diagonally to the left, across the grass and towards a tree-lined area towards the periphery on the north-east side, where a taped-off area and a solitary officer met them.

Becky stepped through the tape and crouched down, looking at the body. Nicky and Jack watched from the taped line. The other pathologists joined her, opening one of their steel cases and looking closely at the corpse.

Becky took barely any time at all before addressing Nicky and Jack. "He was murdered, I'm afraid. There's a clear blunt force trauma to the back of his head and other clear injuries where he's been beaten. We'll process the scene and arrange the PM for the morning, but I've no doubt this man was unlawfully killed."

Nicky looked down at the body. Face down. Bloody. The large black coat worn by the victim was in stark contrast to the shorts and stripy socks on the bottom half.

"Big guy," Nicky commented.

"Maybe that's why he was attacked from behind," Becky suggested.

"Coward," Nicky replied. A silence fell as a gentle breeze washed over the scene, becoming slightly stronger as it passed and with a coolness to the cheeks of those not wearing masks. The sound of passing cars was also audible. Nicky looked through the trees ahead of them but couldn't see a road.

"What road is that?" she asked nobody in particular.

"It's Church Street, guv," Bernie offered. "We've got it covered and there's some guys heading around there now."

"Thanks, Bernie," said Nicky.

"Becky…" came from one of the fully suited pathologists who had started to tend to the body.

"Yep," came the response.

A junior pathologist extracted a wallet from the inside jacket pocket of the body. The jacket had flopped open and was lying exposed on the ground. She handed it to Becky, who opened it with her gloved hands and took out a driving licence.

"Martin King. Forty-three years old and local by the looks of it."

"What's his address, Becky?"

"Fifty-one Wigston Road, Blaby."

"Where's that, Bernie?" Nicky asked.

Bernie pointed at the trees, where the noise from passing cars continued to flow. "It's just through there."

Nicky sighed, took a second and addressed Jack. "We'll

go and do it. Bernie, make sure nobody knocks on that door, please. We'll head there now."

"Loud and clear."

"Let's go and see who answers the door."

Jack nodded. It was always the hardest part of the job, especially when you didn't know who was going to be on the other side of the door, if anybody. In this case, it was as likely to be a spouse as it was a parent or a child.

It was a horrible part of the job, and something Jack neither enjoyed nor had gotten used to, but it was an integral part of being a police officer of a certain rank. Jack looked firmly but compassionately at the hard, emotionless man who had opened the door with a scowl. He had an unkind face, several days of stubble and had chuntered under his breath from behind the front door. He'd been defensive as soon as he was presented with two warrant cards. Jack had started the sentence. The death message. The mood had changed immediately. An aggression that became a realisation. He saw the lip quiver slightly, and within seconds there was a glazing in his eyes.

"He was all I had left," was the reaction from a broken-looking man. It wasn't the first time Jack had had that response.

Nicky stood steadfastly and was using the opportunity to consciously but not visibly have a look at the areas of the house they could see, which was the hall, part of the lounge and the kitchen. Priority one was to deliver the bad news, but with an unexplained death, it was useful to quickly see if there was anything obviously amiss in the house. Anything that didn't quite look right. There were no initial signs of impropriety, just the overpowering smell of stale tobacco which Aaron King was already adding to, having learnt of his son's death.

CHAPTER 17

A stranger just nodded at me as I walked past him in the street. I nodded and mouthed a 'hi' back. It just felt odd, as I'd always had the view that Leicester is a bit of a shithole, and I wasn't expecting its residents to be pleasant, let alone chatty. A smile here, a nod there. Maybe I look like I'm local. I can live with that. I'm used to being a chameleon. To blending in to my surroundings, then slipping away like a ghost.

I'm sure I've seen it online in one of those annual 'worst places to live' list. It was low down, admittedly, but definitely made the top one hundred, although compared to places like Rotherham, Oldham and Corby, it's a fucking paradise.

I just wasn't expecting sociable locals. I'm a man who likes to keep his head down. Likes to stay in the shadows.

I stood in a quiet corner of that park and looked down at the dying body of Martin King. He was groaning, there was still air in his lungs, although it was slow. It was heavy. I looked around casually but there wasn't a soul to be seen for a few hundred yards, and if anyone saw me, they saw a coat and some dark trousers. Hardly a smoking gun. So I stayed. I waited. I watched.

It's the benefit of being me. Even without a dog, I blend in. I'm normal. I'm wearing dark blue jeans, a grey hooded top and trainers. I could be local. I just need to work on my accent, but no one will be giving the police my description tonight. I even managed to get out of the park over a wall before the police arrived. Slipped seamlessly away up a side street. Like I was never there.

It was odd that he wasn't as I remembered him. The face, the hair. It just didn't look like him, but it was. It was definitely him. His breathing had slowed, he'd tried to move but that wasn't happening. Just an arm stretching out. Almost crying for help on its own. Begging for it. The fingers reaching for something they were destined never to reach. The blood seeping out onto the ground underneath him as he continued to bleed out. Thick. Treacle-like, and a deep, dark red.

He tried to say something. Tried to draw breath, but the deep knife wounds in his back were doing their job. They had been well placed. At least one had punctured a lung, rendering any screams for help impossible. He was unable to shout. Unable to make a sound.

I watched quietly as he breathed his last breath. The final gentle exhale as the last of the oxygen dissipated into the night sky, and his body became his corpse. And all I felt was the cold. My hands were jammed firmly in my pockets. I'm no spring chicken and the cold was starting to creep in. A nice coffee in a bit will fix that, plus, I can toast the progress.

My brain proclaims, "The King is dead, long live the King!" and I smile at my own macabre humour as I look across the road towards the house Martin King used to call his home.

Tonight was a strange night that might not have happened, or happened very differently. It's all about patience. It's all about biding my time. This is a jigsaw of the most volatile kind, and a plan that could easily fall apart. It's fragile. There are pieces, and they all hinge on one another before I arrive at the end game.

Which is why I'm here. It's the only reason I came. Made the effort. And so far I've met some very pleasant locals, found what surely must be the good part of Leicester, and the added bonus is that I didn't even have to kill him myself.

CHAPTER 18

It had just passed 7am when Nicky parked up in the multi-storey of Leicester Royal Infirmary, with a real sense of déjà vu. It was a brighter morning; the early-morning sun was sitting low in the sky, beaming through the stands of Welford Road Stadium and reflecting brightly off the large glass windows of the Windsor building. Nicky squinted as she walked down a short pathway and felt her eyes adjust as she walked into the dull entrance at the south-east side of the complex. It was a newer part of the hospital, and the signage was providing directions to the other areas, including the Sandringham building and Balmoral. Both named after the residences of Queen Elizabeth II, whose portrait adorned the wall, along with the plaque unveiled during the formal opening of the Windsor building in the spring of 1993. Another sign pointed to the Jarvis building, but Nicky couldn't make a royal connection and had no idea who'd earned the right to have the building named after them.

Nicky hoped today would be a little more normal, not involve any form of cattle and just be a good old-fashioned post-mortem. Simple, a formality, and maybe even provide some evidence. She headed down a long sterile corridor which kinked to the left, and ironically looked like a dead end. The entrance to the mortuary was to the left-hand side and she was buzzed in by one of Becky's team, who cheerily greeted Nicky with a dulcet south-west tone.

They exchanged some small talk before Becky arrived, who was bright and equally smiley. Nicky felt that if she met either of them in the street, she wouldn't have them down as pathologists.

"How are you?" Nicky asked. It had been a while since they'd had a good catch-up, let alone gone out.

"I'm good, thanks. How are you?"

More small talk was exchanged. Dogs, music, rumours. Becky wanted to get cracking so Nicky went to get a coffee. She sat up in the viewing area as Becky and her colleague Mark reappeared in their protective suits and masks to start the post-mortem on the body of Martin King, who'd been found no more than five miles from where his body was now laying.

Nicky was wandering in circles to keep the blood flowing as the post-mortem commenced, with Becky taking time to analyse the clear injuries to the torso as the process continued.

Becky looked up at Nicky. "It looks pretty clear in terms of cause of death, Nicky. There was an initial blow to the back of the head, before the knife wounds were inflicted, also from behind. The body was face down and looked like it had been dumped, but he was attacked on that spot and then just left to die."

"That's callous," Nicky replied, but without any surprise in her voice. Humanity was well past surprising her.

"It's a clean attack, though. With his coat and his rugby kit off, you can see the two stab marks to his back."

"Was he unconscious by that point?"

"Unlikely. The blow was hard but it would have been mildly incapacitating rather than anything else. The blood was thick in his hair, but it looked worse than it was as he's fair-haired. The head wound is relatively minor, especially to a back row forward."

Nicky appreciated the comment. Both women had an appreciation for rugby union.

"So what do you think?"

"I'll show you." Becky asked Mark for his help. Becky was a physically fit woman, a gym-goer and of ample strength, but Martin King was an equally fit forty-three-year-old man, around 6'4" in height and solidly built. He was athletic, and from the physique on the slab was also a gym-goer and clearly didn't miss too many weights sessions.

Becky and Mark respectfully turned the body to show the stab marks Becky was referring to.

"These stab marks are the cause of death. They're symmetrical and well placed."

"How so?"

"Each stab wound entered a lung, one each. It was precise, and they'd have been administered whilst he was either face down, or possibly on his knees after the blow to his head. It's unlikely he saw his attacker."

"So probably not a random killing?"

"I wouldn't have thought so. You said he still had his valuables on him?"

"Yes, he did. He still had his kit bag after his rugby training, and he still had his watch, his phone and his house keys on him. His wallet still had fifty quid in it, so we think he was targeted rather than it being a botched robbery."

"And you've spoken with his next of kin?"

"Yes, Jack and I met his dad last night, who he lived with. We broke the news to him. His dad is divorced, and Martin doesn't see his mum."

"So the killer knew what he was doing, Becky?"

"He did indeed. Both stab wounds were perfectly placed. The knife would only have been five or so inches long, and sharp. Possibly a small-scale hunting knife, but it would have left him in agony. He'd have remained conscious for a while, and because of the wounds, he'd have been unable to scream or call for help."

"Well, that explains why nobody heard anything."

"Yes, and it would have been a painful death as well, I'm afraid. He bled internally into both lungs. The feeling would have been like he was drowning, and it would have taken a while for him to lose consciousness."

"Bastard," Nicky added quietly.

"There is some good news, though. There's some trace DNA on the victim. We've recovered it from around the jaw area, so it's possible he was grabbed from behind. We've sent it to be processed, so it could be an open and shut one, if you're lucky."

"That seems sloppy, especially from somebody who knew what they were doing."

"Agreed, maybe King fought back, or tried to. He was a big lad and would have had some strength as a rugby player. It's easy for anyone to make a mistake in the heat of the moment."

"It could be a possible drug killing if he was involved in that kind of thing. It's too early to reach conclusions, but we're looking at all options. He's a big unit, a rugby player and a gym bunny, and it's entirely possible he liked a few steroids here and there. We're looking into his background and his finances, which should tell us, but it could just have been a dispute. He was just so disrespectfully dumped, it almost seemed symbolic."

"He was," Becky agreed, nodding. Recalling the image of the lifeless body she'd recovered from Bouskell Park with her team. "We'll get his blood and the DNA samples processed. I'll let you know if there are any substances in his blood that shouldn't be, and I'll let you know if we get a match."

CHAPTER 19

Rob was pondering the implications of two dead bodies found in the city. Of a badly burnt and dismembered body, and of the callous execution of Martin King in a public park. The only current lead to the body in the car was a single tooth, which had been identified as belonging to a decorated British soldier.

Two bodies. Two men. From two very different walks of life. A retired man living out the quiet life in Norfolk. A life of gardening, long coffee breaks and afternoons in the sun. And a young man in his prime who until last weekend had been using his physicality to win rugby matches for his local club.

Rob felt like he was missing something. A nagging feeling deep in the pit of his stomach, which he wasn't liking one bit. Martin King's murder could prove to be related to drugs, although for some reason Rob was hoping that it wasn't. Cramer was the real mystery. The tooth. An old tooth. Why was it in that car? And how did it get there? It connected Cramer somehow, but for the time being there was no way that any charges could be brought. There was no definitive proof that the body of the unknown man in the Astra had been murdered; there was proof that Cramer was in Norfolk at the time the car was driven onto the rec.

He pondered, before laying the photographs of both men on his desk.

His phone buzzed in his pocket. He picked it out. Becky Ryan's cheerful features adorned the screen; a fresh profile picture with her jet-black hair framing a perfect smile.

"Hi, Becky."

"Rob, we have a massive problem." There wasn't a greeting, let alone any small talk that usually preceded a conversation with Becky.

"Why? Whose body is it?" Rob asked, pre-empting the response.

"Sorry?" Becky replied, sounding confused.

"The body; whose is it?"

"I don't know." Becky realised that Rob was expecting an identity. One she still didn't have.

"We should have it soon. Really soon. I'll let you know as soon as we do. The samples were low quality but we'll get you a name to work with."

Rob's curiosity got the better of him. "So if you're not calling me with an identity…"

Becky drew breath. "We've matched the DNA that was recovered from the body of Martin King. It's been analysed and it's a match to David Cramer."

"What? Cramer was at the crime scene at Bouskell Park?"

"It looks that way, yes."

"You're sure?"

"Yes, I'm absolutely certain."

"Cross-contamination?" Rob asked. He knew Becky well enough to know the level of competency and professionalism that she worked to, but he needed to ask the question. It's one a defence team would ask if proceedings got to that stage.

"Absolutely not. There is zero chance that either sample was contaminated. Cramer was in the park, and he made physical contact with Martin King."

Rob paused. "The two bodies are connected, and they both have a physical connection to Cramer. We asked him about the wrong fucking murder."

CHAPTER 20

"Jack, grab your coat. We need to revisit our friend Mr King," Nicky hollered.

"You know how to treat me," he replied, with a wry smile. She smiled back, before briefing him on Becky's findings. Findings that had provided an evidential link between the dead body on the rec and the murder of Martin King in Bouskell Park. David Cramer was the connection to both crime scenes.

The two stepped out of the lift and got into Nicky's VW Tiguan, which was parked in the underground car park. Nicky navigated the twisty and narrow exit and merged into traffic on the busy A594, adjacent to the train station, with several Hackney carriages vying for position through a narrow entrance which was neither built for aggressive cabbies nor impatient relatives picking up loved ones. She indicated right. A good Samaritan flashed her. She thanked the driver with her left hand as a blare from a taxi rang out. She made out one of the cabbies gesticulating with his left hand and mouthed the words 'fuck off' slowly in his direction. Jack smiled.

She headed onto Tigers Way, with the Crown and County Court sitting proudly up to the right, along with the Leicester

Museum and Art Gallery. The car headed under a small pedestrian bridge which connected New Walk from east to west as it climbed up towards the entrance to Victoria Park. It was a part of the city Jack had learnt to love; a magnificent tree-lined boulevard perfect for Sunday walks and fresh coffee. The Georgian architecture and neatly kept squares could easily pass for one of London's more affluent areas, and there were several bars, for a more sophisticated Saturday night out than Zanzibar, Krystals or the Fan Club. Less fights as well.

"Aaron King?" Jack asked.

"Aaron King," Nicky replied. "What were your first impressions of him, Jack?"

"I didn't like him. There was a nastiness about him, and he just didn't strike me as somebody I would trust. He came across as quite an aggressive and hateful human being."

Nicky nodded. It was the response she was expecting, but also one she agreed with. He was still bereaved, but in Nicky's eyes he was a suspect. He'd been advised of his son's death by Nicky and Jack, and had reacted in what would be deemed a normal way. But he was also the father of the victim and lived less than 200 yards from where the body was found. He also didn't have an alibi for the time of the murder, something he reacted badly to when pressed for one by Nicky.

"Do you think he's involved, Nicky? Do you really think he killed his son?"

"I'm not sure yet, but if he didn't, he knows our victim better than anybody. He can help us. It's just whether he wants to."

Nicky hadn't warmed to King either. He had opened the door in an aggressive manner, snarling at Jack. He had looked bedraggled, wearing an open shirt with a white vest underneath, and dark hair that was quickly becoming grey, and not in a flattering way. It was unkempt, and a week or so of stubble and a whiff of alcohol gave both the impression that Aaron King was not an accommodating or forgiving man.

Nicky rapped hard on the front door and immediately heard movement, with some chuntering thrown in for good measure. The door opened. King looked upset; the stench of stale tobacco followed his disdain out of the hallway.

"Do you know who killed Martin?" came an abrupt question.

"Not yet, Mr King. May we come in?"

He sighed, thought about it for a second and then stood aside. Nicky walked in. Jack followed, breathing out slowly as he passed close to Aaron King.

Neither was expecting the offer of a drink, which duly didn't happen. They both remained standing in the lounge, observing the dank living conditions that would trouble an RSPCA officer should an animal be unfortunate enough to call this house its home.

"What do you want?" he asked, more calmly than his initial manner.

"Where were you last Tuesday afternoon, Mr King? From around 5pm onwards."

He looked confused, and slightly agitated, which Jack guessed was his stock look. He wasn't sure what the male equivalent of 'resting bitch face' was, but King had it in spades.

"Why?" came the abrupt response. "What's that got to do with Martin?"

"We're not sure yet, Mr King, but we need to verify your whereabouts at that time."

The frown lines in his forehead deepened. He was clearly considering what to say. Nicky and Jack waited.

"Last Tuesday?"

"Last Tuesday," Nicky confirmed.

"I was at work." He looked pissed off.

"Where do you work?"

"I'm a lorry driver. I work for a local timber merchant. I was there until half six that day as we had some goods come in late, and then we went to the pub."

"Can anybody confirm that?"

"Three or four of my colleagues can, there's a camera in my cab and my tacho card will confirm I was at work too. Will that do?" He spat the last three words with more than a hint of fuck you.

"It will, thank you." Nicky smiled back cheerfully.

"Is that it?" he asked.

"One more thing, Mr King, do you know the name David Cramer?"

He looked pensive, and thought hard. Nicky and Jack eyeballed him. Checking the whites of his eyes for any signs of a lie. He replied to the negative.

"Thank you, Mr King. We'll let ourselves out."

*

"How did you get on with King?" Rob asked, sitting himself down next to Nicky's desk, where she and Jack were chewing the fat.

"As we expected. He's withholding something. It's just a case of figuring out what."

"Do you think he did it?"

"His lad? Gut's telling me no, but I've been wrong before."

"Haven't we all?" Rob added. A pause hung in the air.

"We still don't have a decent theory relating to the motive, or a viable suspect for both crimes," Jack added, with all recognising that David Cramer couldn't have driven the body into the city. There was little evidence of Cramer being responsible for the body in the car, and with Becky having confirmed that the tooth couldn't have been extracted within the last five years, there was nothing to tie David Cramer to the death. He was categorically linked to the scene, but for now the cause of death couldn't be proven as unlawful, and Cramer was miles away at the time the car was dumped. He didn't drive it onto the rec either, so his link to the crime was as mysterious as the circumstances surrounding it.

"If these crimes are connected and King's telling the truth, he couldn't have driven the car either, so neither Cramer nor King could have committed both murders," Nicky added. Jack confirmed he'd be checking his alibi for the time the Astra was dumped as soon as the business opened the following morning, and as much as he hadn't warmed to Aaron King, he suspected his employer and the CCTV would support his claim that he was at work.

"Where are we with the rest of the forensics?" Jack asked.

"There's a delay with the lab. We're chasing Becky and she's on it. We'll have answers today."

The team had spent much of the day digging into the backgrounds of Martin and Aaron King. Much of their files and history was redacted, which already stood out as a cause for concern. Rob had immediately escalated a request to Laura Mathers to have their files released, to find what they were hiding. Or hiding from. The records they did have showed Martin King as a law abiding citizen, bar a speeding fine and a single charge for possession of a controlled substance; steroids, which he wasn't prosecuted for. Aaron King had priors for aggravated burglary, assault, GBH and one for assaulting a police officer, which had surprised no one.

The part which had really lit the interest was a birth certificate of Martin King, who had been born in Carrickfergus, Northern Ireland, at the same time David Cramer was based at the barracks on the edge of town. The three men were in the same place, at the same time, and for several years, and although Martin King would have been a juvenile at the time, the suspicions were there. It was too much of a coincidence. Combined with the DNA link connecting Cramer to both scenes, Nicky and Jack had revisited Aaron King, who had given little away but had volunteered an alibi for the time of the car being dumped.

"If he did know Cramer, it would need to be forced out of him," Nicky offered.

"Is it possible they're working together?" Jack asked. "Cramer killing King junior and King senior taking care of our unknown male?"

"It's viable as a theory," Nicky agreed, "but it looks as if neither could have been on Tudor Road Rec, and if Aaron King knew his son was being hit, I'd have expected him to be in a pub with a hundred people to give him an alibi."

"They're linked," Rob stated clearly. "Something happened in Northern Ireland. It may go back thirty years, but there's a link."

CHAPTER 21

Rob hadn't seen his sister in a couple of days, for which he admonished himself. Work was busy, but his sister needed him, and the bond they were rekindling as her illness progressed was strong. It was reminiscent of their childhood bond, only with the memories, and the pride of their achievements in life. She needed him now more than ever, and he'd promised her he'd be with her every step of the way. The time spent with her whilst she was happy and pain-free was enjoyable and precious. So precious.

It was also giving Rob a revised sense of perspective for when things got tough and nights were sleepless.

Jack was retracing his steps with Nicky alongside him, having made the same journey to Norfolk only days before. They'd been tasked to join the search, with Rob hanging back in Leicester and no doubt speaking with either Laura Mathers or Becky Ryan. Or both.

The picturesque and bright vista across the fens from a few days ago had been replaced with a dreary grey horizon, and with Jack now driving he wasn't able to appreciate the view as he had from Rob's passenger seat. He recognised some of the village names as he passed them, knowing there was a view, but with a low mist over the fields he was unable to see it. The village of Thorney was a sure sign they were close, and Jack eyeballed Worzals as he passed it. He knew Nicky would love it, and if time allowed later, he'd drop by for some take-out.

Jack had noted a takeaway service was available during his visit with Rob, and was already considering a toasted sandwich later on. A simple choice, but he'd clocked that they were served on homemade sourdough bread, and with a choice of cheese and ham, bacon, brie and cranberry and tuna mayo, they were well worth dropping in for. The artisan crisps and cakes would also provide a heartier lunch than an average day in the city centre.

Jack could see the familiar row of houses approaching on the right-hand side, and a faint glimmer of blue light from a single patrol car told them he was in the right place. He indicated, pulling into the lengthy driveway that ran off the main road, which was spacious enough for Jack to park behind three other vehicles and a van that were already in attendance.

Jack and Nicky stepped out and took the opportunity to admire the house and the surrounding properties, which were evidence of a retirement being well lived. Nicky commented on how the period of the properties wasn't dissimilar to the properties adjacent to Bouskell Park in Leicester, and what a pleasant break they were from some recent drug raids on properties that were at the opposite end of the social scale.

The Leicestershire team had requested their Norfolk counterparts execute the arrest and search warrant, which was being conducted by Vanessa Ryder's team. It was their jurisdiction, and Rob's team would play a supporting role. Jack and Nicky crunched their way up the gravel drive, with DC

Vanessa Ryder's timely emergence from a side entrance. She was wearing her white coveralls and blue slip-on shoes, after the early raid and with the search and forensics very much ongoing. She smiled and greeted Nicky and Jack, before the conversation quickly turned to the early findings. The main aim had been to arrest David Cramer on suspicion of the murder of Martin King, but Ness' immediate nod had told the team that their man was not at home.

"Empty nest?" Jack asked, pessimistically.

"Yeah, he's in the wind. He's cleared out and gone." Ness replied.

"Any indications as to where?"

Her nod was negative. "Not a clue, I'm afraid."

The team entered the house where a full search remained ongoing. Jack entered an old-fashioned but exceptionally tidy kitchen. The hall was bustling and three members of the Norfolk team were trawling over documents and items being recovered from a study, which overlooked the extensive back garden. A laptop was being placed in a plastic evidence bag.

Nicky looked out onto the neat and well-tended back garden. "It just looks like a retired person lives here. What's caused this? What's the trigger?"

Ness had stayed with Jack to chaperone him through the property.

"We've found a newspaper with Martin King in it. It was on the side in the kitchen. We may not have picked up on it initially but it was open on the sports section, with a beaming picture of Martin King in his full rugby gear."

"So his DNA is on Martin King's body and he has a newspaper with a picture of him on his worktop? That's no coincidence," Nicky stated firmly.

Ryder nodded. "I don't believe in coincidences. The rest of the house just looks normal, though. Very neat, clean and tidy and isn't the sort of place we're used to raiding."

"That makes two of us," came the dry reply.

"So can two murders really be borne from a guy appearing in the sports section of the local rag?" Ness asked Jack. Murder was not a common occurrence in Norfolk. The monthly reports, where the Leicestershire team compared themselves to Northamptonshire, Derbyshire and Nottinghamshire, had consistently shown Norfolk as having the lowest murder rate per head in the UK, as well as being officially recognised as the safest county for all serious crime.

"Who knows. We've got a physical connection between Cramer and Martin King, and a newspaper lying open on a page featuring Martin King."

Ryder nodded. "We've put out his arrest warrant and have every officer in the county looking for him." She reassured Nicky and Jack. "There's no sign of him, though, and there's a safe in the study which is completely empty."

*

It had been a largely fruitless search of the house in Norfolk, which had been left under the supervision of Vanessa Ryder's team. Nicky and Jack had made their way back to Lodge House, having hoped for an arrest or some clear-cut evidence but leaving with very little other than a local newspaper.

Becky Ryan had arrived to go through the forensic findings, and Laura Mathers had unexpectedly joined the team session in the open-plan space outside Rob's office, on the tenth floor of the building.

Rob had greeted Becky on the ground floor; her warm smile was welcome after a hundred- mile round trip had drawn a blank. The team had a brief planned in this afternoon regardless, but he had been hopeful of something. Rob had spoken to Mathers on the phone, so she was fully up to speed and aware that the investigation would continue in Leicester, with the support of DC Ryder and the team in Norfolk.

Teas and coffees were still steaming when Becky kicked the session off. She'd continued to work tirelessly on the evidence recovered from both Tudor Road and Bouskell Park.

"Our work has been ongoing to determine the identity of the human remains found in the Astra at Tudor Road. Microscopic examination of the tooth and DNA analysis from the bones was conducted for confirmation of sex, but it was also that test which confirmed that the tooth and the body were from two different people. A rough assessment of age was made from the skeleton based on anthropological findings, which was found to be a fifty-to- fifty-five-year-old male, and a more definitive result of age estimation was determined utilising dental morphology on the tooth. The dental data, mineral examination and the formulation of microscopic measurements gave us a perfect match on age, but also gave us the identification of David Cramer."

"Good," said Rob, nodding, inviting the continuation.

"The full DNA tests are now back on the bones found, which took time for obvious reasons, but they have now given up their secrets. They belong to Steve Hargreaves, a fifty-four-year-old man who was arrested for possession five years ago but has been off grid recently and is a known face to the guys at one of the homeless shelters across town. They emailed us a picture."

Becky pulled the image from the file and taped it to the

board. The team took a second to look at the first image they had of a man whose end had been violent, savage and inhuman. The image looked sad. A man down on his luck and in need. The room was quiet, appreciating the sadness which often came with these moments. It would allow next of kin to be notified and a burial to take place. A last act of dignity.

Rob broke the momentary silence. "Good work, Becky. Jen, can you follow up with next of kin, please?"

"Of course."

"Are there any military links to Hargreaves from the early work?"

"Nothing obvious," Becky replied, looking at Jack, who had been working with her as the thread had developed.

"Homelessness amongst ex-servicemen is prevalent, so make sure he's not directly linked to Cramer or the other names, please."

Jack gave a thumbs-up. "The Royal British Legion estimate over 6,000 rough sleepers are ex-service, but we'll make sure he's not linked or confirm his background."

"Thank you, both." Rob nodded at Becky and Jack for their efforts. The identification was a solid step but was seemingly of little immediate benefit to the investigation. Steve Hargreaves could well be an innocent party, and although those enquiries would be made, the discussion in the room wasn't optimistic about finding a link between Hargreaves and Cramer. It was likely one didn't exist, and it was equally likely that Hargreaves had simply been in the wrong place at the wrong time and provided the body needed to accompany David Cramer's tooth in the boot of the Vauxhall Astra.

"Why, though?" asked Nicky. It was a question they had all asked. Nobody had a theory, let alone a decent one.

Rob looked at Laura Mathers, who had sat quietly, listening to the discussion without interruption, but Rob suspected she had information on the why, and he was right.

"Your investigation into Martin King raised some red flags, and although you've obtained the records relating to both Martin and Aaron King, large sections are redacted, as you know." She paused, and took a sip of her coffee. "This is above the level of this investigation, so you will all need to sign an NDA, which we'll do later, but Martin King was born Alex Patrick Delaney, and his father, who you know as Aaron, was born Marcus Gerard Delaney. Both men are on the Home Office register, and aren't even known to local government. These guys are serious."

"What's the link, Laura?" Rob asked. "It's Northern Ireland, but what's their link to Cramer?"

"I'm still waiting for full details myself, but Martin King, who was Alex Delaney at the time, was found guilty of conspiracy to commit murder for luring a teenage boy named Christopher Wilson to his death in 1996. They were school friends allegedly, but he used his trust to lure Christopher into a street which had a car bomb located in it. His father, who you've met, and who you know as Aaron King, was convicted with two other men of carrying out the bombing. They were also found guilty of a car bombing at Thiepval Barracks and an attempted bombing at a second barracks."

"Fucking hell." Jen broke the silence. It was abrupt but reflected the thoughts of those in the room. Violent criminals, drug dealers and murderers were sadly commonplace in Leicester. Convicted IRA terrorists were not. Mathers continued: "They were both sent to prison in January 1998 but served less than twelve months inside, and were released under the terms of the Good Friday peace agreement."

"Twelve months?" Jen asked. She sounded angry. "They got twelve months?"

"No, Aaron King was sentenced to life, but he was exceptionally fortunate because of the timing of his conviction in relation to the peace agreement. They were both only inside for ten months."

Jen exhaled loudly. There was an air of incredulity in the room. A man who had been convicted of terror offences, bomb making and several murders had been in prison for less than a year because of a political agreement. He'd walked out in time for Christmas and no doubt spent it with his loved ones, a privilege he had denied to many.

"But how does that tie in?" Jen asked aloud, still not fully certain of how useful the information was.

Rob sat nodding. He knew. Jen looked at him. Mathers had the answer but invited Rob to share the news.

"Chris Wilson was David Cramer's son."

Mathers confirmed it. "Correct, he changed his surname on leaving the army."

"So, Aaron and Martin King were convicted of murdering David Cramer's son? Well, at least now we have a link. And a very strong motive."

CHAPTER 22

I've had some time to reflect on it now, and I'm still not sure how I'm feeling. It felt strange to be walking through that park. Watching. The rugby training session was actually quite enjoyable. It's been a while since I've stood and witnessed any live sport, despite a lifelong love of rugby union. It's the best team game in the world, and the one thing I actually care about. The second, if you count revenge. Plus, they let me have a pint on the touchline. I could get used to that.

For that last half an hour, I actually felt normal. Free. It's been about twenty years since I felt anything approaching normality. Probably longer. It's been a long time to live with the anger. The hatred. It's not healthy. I stopped being me a very long time ago and, if I'm honest with myself, my life has never been the same since. How could it be? I felt nothing watching *him,* though. Literally nothing. Running about with his mates, smashing into those tackle bags. The laughing, the comradery.

I had resigned myself to never being able to exact any form of revenge, but when I first saw that news report, I recognised those features straight away. The mass of black hair, the hint of a monobrow. Even with that false name of his, Martin King. It took me a good while longer to think it through. To decide if I could use it. Whether I should use it. Whether it was right, although I stopped seeing things as right or wrong a very long time ago. The world in black and white, when in reality it's nothing but a sultry myriad of grey.

Getting hold of that newspaper was just too good an opportunity to miss. A seed was sown in my mind and I *wanted* to see what it could start. What it could do. I've felt vindictive for much of the last decade. Spiteful. Seeing his face got me thinking. It shouldn't have done, but it just did. I knew it was him, living out his life. Fit, healthy, and I hated him for it. But I also saw the opportunity. How I could *use* it. To start my campaign of vengeance. Some will say he's an innocent man just living his life. A rugby player. Part of his community. Living with his dad. It sounds idealistic, but it's all a matter of perspective.

I saw something very different. It lit a fire inside me. I saw an opportunity. I thought about who it could draw out. Who it could find. The links, the connections. That's the exciting bit. Not a solitary murder that might not have happened, but the prospect of walking down a path of no return. Down one of redemption.

It's the most exciting thing that's happened to me for a long time and I'm thrilled by it.

We're off and running.

It was even stranger to read the report after the murder. To see Martin King's image in the press again. They even used the picture from the other weekend, the man of the match one. Ironic given that's what gave his whereabouts away. His love of rugby and a stellar performance that day cost him his life, but even though it was something I incited, it gave me very little pleasure. It was nothing more than a means to an end, a starter for ten.

I've thought about how I could get revenge for a very, very long time. The truth is, I've absolutely no idea how all this will pan out. How it will end. But Martin King is dead, and the nature of his death will be provocative.

So far, so good.

CHAPTER 23

The mood was pretty sombre in Lodge House. All had headed home last night with the cold hard facts resonating loudly in their minds. Martin King had been complicit with his dad in order to execute the son of a British military officer, and had seemingly paid for it with his life. It had taken Cramer twenty years to catch up with his son's killer; only in reality, he hadn't. An accomplice at best. A juvenile support act.

The previous evening's session had been adjourned, and Rob and Laura Mathers had proposed reconvening for a morning follow-up, allowing everybody to head home, eat and rest. To process what they now knew. To fall asleep knowing that Martin King, as a teenager, had lured one of his friends to a place where he would be indiscriminately murdered. The simple fact was that Martin King had done the dirty on his friend. Gained his trust and then breached it in the most vile of ways. But he had neither built nor planted the bomb that day. That honour had gone to a man whose house Nicky and Jack had frequented twice in recent days. A man they had both immediately disliked but felt a tinge of sadness for, on breaking the news of his son's death.

On reflection, there was a cyclical nature to the killing;

Martin King had been stabbed and left face down in a park. Dying, yards from his father. A man responsible for causing so much bereavement was now the bereaved.

The small talk was building as the kettle boiled and the toaster popped. Jack trotted across to it, having forgotten he'd dropped a couple of slices in. Seed Sensations. It was slightly burnt and the fragrant smell of warm wholemeal toast drifted across the office.

"Stick us a couple in if there's any left, Jack," shouted Nicky.

"Me too," added Jen.

Jack sighed and slipped four rounds in the toaster for the girls, whilst adding a thick slab of butter to his own freshly toasted rounds. It duly melted into the surface, and a warm pool of liquid butter oozed onto the plate underneath.

"Don't burn mine," hollered Nicky, with a smile and a thumbs-up. He mouthed, *Marmalade?* at her and was met with a nodding head. *Just butter.*

Laura Mathers had sat in a chair; the other chairs which had been abandoned last night still forming a half-circle around her. She was keen to get going. Rob marshalled the troops, with Jack still handing out tea and toast. The butter on Nicky's toast had melted fully and was also dripping onto the plate. She smiled at him.

"Good morning, all," Laura Mathers opened formally. "Following on from last night's session, I wanted to be clear on where we are, expectations and next steps for the investigation. Aaron King is a man of interest to the investigation. There is also the possibility that he could now be at risk given the exposure, and murder, of his son."

"So we assume Cramer is responsible and will also want revenge on Aaron King?" asked Jen.

"It's a reasonable assumption."

"But he could have killed him ten minutes after killing his son, so does he not know where he lives? He could have bumped Martin off in the park, which on the evidence we have, he did, and then popped round to his dad's and taken care of him at the same time."

"David Cramer was a major general in the British Army. I think we should assume he's well informed, well resourced and knows exactly where Aaron King is."

"So he's biding his time?"

"Maybe he doesn't want to kill King," Nicky offered, sipping on her coffee. "Aaron and Martin King murdered Chris Wilson. His dad's been suffering from it for twenty years. Hurting every day. Maybe killing his son was enough, and now he has to live with the pain in the same way he has. Maybe not killing him is a more cruel option."

There were a few nods. Rob chipped in: "We need to speak with Aaron King again. We'll all sign the non-disclosure agreements which Laura needs to file with the Home Office, but we need to notify Aaron King that we believe David Cramer is the man responsible for his son's death, and that he could be at risk. The Home Office will review his case. It's entirely possible he'll be moved and renamed again, but that's out of our hands. We have a duty of care to him."

There was a pause. Nicky and Jen were both biting their tongues. They were both quality officers. Professional, well respected and committed to serving the city to the very best of their abilities. It didn't mean they always had to like it. The notion of having to protect a man found guilty of killing an innocent teenager with a bomb wasn't exactly what they'd signed up for.

Mathers continued: "We know David Cramer served his country in Northern Ireland during a period of significant disruption. I'm continuing to work with the Home Office on this. My contact has raised it at her end as well, as she believes there might be wider implications to the murder of Martin King."

"How?" asked Nicky.

"We don't know, I'm working to have the fully redacted records on the murder of Christopher Wilson released, but for now we've been able to make the initial link between David Cramer, his son and the Kings."

"When did Cramer change his name?" Nicky asked, changing tack and flicking her gaze between Rob and Mathers.

"He changed it on leaving the army," Mathers replied. "It's not totally uncommon for senior military figures to change their names on retirement, particularly those who have been undercover, have been exposed or have been a part of a particular operation, or operations. He was born David Wilson but legally changed his name upon his retirement. I guess he had things he wanted to forget."

It was an opinion but several nods in the room seemed to agree with her logic. He'd served a long and distinguished career. His experience with the military would be worth its weight in gold. Not to mention his knowledge, training, skills and contacts. His service was extensive, but something he'd paid a heavy price for. The heaviest of prices. So had his family. Maybe changing his name had been an easy thing to do. Maybe it had been the hardest. Nicky couldn't decide if changing his name was to protect and distance himself from those who would still wish him harm, or to walk away from a name that he shared with his dead son. One he'd see on every bit of mail, or hear on every trip to the dentist. A new name. One with less pain.

Laura Mathers had spoken to Rob before the session. They'd agreed roles and agreed what needed to be done. Rob assigned Jen and Jack the task of revisiting Aaron King. Of breaking a different type of news to a man they'd now look at very differently. Not in a literal sense. But to look a man in the eye who you knew to be capable of killing another was always a profound experience. Even more so when that person wasn't wearing handcuffs or sitting on the other side of a dock or a visitation table.

Jack and Jen nodded. They'd carry it out professionally and proficiently, Rob had no doubt. They were already gearing themselves up for it mentally. Game faces for when the knock on the door roused a response.

Rob looked across at Nicky. "Do you know where your passport is?"

She smiled. "Yeah, I think so."

"Is it in date?"

"Should be!"

"Great, then head home and pack your bags! I'll meet you back here in an hour."

Nicky had guessed what was happening, but it hadn't been explicitly stated. Like a guessing game, only without the fun.

"Well done, both," Laura Mathers stated, before she stood up, straightened her blouse and thanked everybody for their hard work. Mutters of "Ma'am" followed as she strode up the corridor, her shoes tapping on the hard corridor surface as she went.

Rob looked at Nicky. "I'm sorry I wasn't able to call you earlier. Things have evolved quickly and the arrangements had been made before I'd blinked."

"A surprise trip, exciting! I don't need to guess where you're taking me, do I?"

"Well, you won't need your sunglasses, if that's what you're asking."

CHAPTER 24

It was only a short flight. Less than an hour before the small purple Flybe twin prop descended into George Best International. Rob and Nicky collected their overnight bags and headed through into the arrivals hall, scanning an old-fashioned and cramped area for a contact arranged by Laura Mathers. There was the usual array of taxi drivers holding boards with scrawled surnames on, a small WH Smith to the left and a tacky-looking mobile phone shop next to it. The sort who replaced cracked screens, unlocked old handsets and who still had the odd cover for a Nokia 3210 by the counter. They had no idea what the contact looked like, but those on the job had a way of identifying their fellow officers. The walk. A look, but there was no immediate or obvious sign of him.

Rob was surprised at the size of the airport. For a European capital city, it was tiny, and made East Midlands look like Heathrow. He was also surprised it was still named after an alcoholic footballer. No matter how good Best was, it just didn't seem to fit with modern expectations. Modern standards. He searched his brain for a more suitable Northern Irishman. Gary Moore of Thin Lizzy came to mind, alongside Van Morrison, but neither was an improvement in image terms. He recalled that Sir Kenneth Branagh had been born in Belfast and decided that would be a much better fit.

With Nicky searching for a signal and wandering around the small hall, which reminded her of St Margaret's bus station, Rob walked over to a bank of three chairs and sat down at one end. A man sat at the opposite end, leaving Rob's bag in the middle seat. The two made eye contact, which Rob broke. As he looked away, the man spoke.

"Are you here on official business, DCI Rhone?"

Rob looked slowly to his left, meeting the man's eye again. His Scottish accent was out of place, and Rob half detected some Irish tones amid it. It was an interesting mix, and it made Rob curious. Rob took in the man's features but immediately knew this wasn't the contact Mathers had lined up for them. He was late fifties, maybe a little older, and his hair was predominantly black with slivers of silver streaking through. He was freshly shaven, definitely from this morning, and smartly dressed. Wire-framed glasses, a dark suit with a black overcoat and smart shoes. There was something firmly no nonsense about him. He could be police, but something about him told Rob he wasn't.

"I'm sorry. I didn't catch your name?" Rob asked, tactfully.

"Taylor. Will Taylor," came the almost arrogant reply, as he fed a piece of chewing gum into his mouth, pocketing the wrapper. He coughed, using his left hand to stifle it.

"Are you reinvestigating the murder of Christopher Wilson in '96? And are you reinvestigating the attacks at both Thiepval Barracks and Victoria Barracks?"

Rob's face stayed put. He gave nothing away. He already knew that Aaron King had been one of the men convicted of the bombing at Thiepval, and the attempted bombing at a second barracks, which Will Taylor seemed to know a lot more about than he should do.

"I'm sorry to disappoint you, Will, but I'm just here for the Guinness."

"I think we both know you're in the wrong city for that, Inspector Rhone." He looked Rob in the eye. "Does David Cramer know the investigation into his son's death is being reopened?" He stifled another cough, which came as more of a hack.

Rob waited a second but decided to ignore the question. "Who do you work for, Will?" he asked, with a tinge of annoyance in his voice. Taylor composed himself.

"Irish Associated Press, DCI Rhone. I'm just searching for the truth." There was a steeliness in his eyes that told Rob he wasn't playing games. That he wasn't some two-bit hack who had stumbled across a half-story, or the outline of some facts. The two men sat eye to eye. Neither moved. Neither blinked.

Rob broke the silence and stood up. "I suggest you go and look elsewhere for the truth, Mr Taylor, because I'm not here to visit Thiepval or Victoria."

Taylor remained defiant in his posture. He stood up too. He was slightly shorter than Rob but there was a solidity to his stance and his face was stone cold. Emotionless. He leant closer to Rob, less than a foot away, and with a callousness in his voice, he spat, "Well, maybe you fucking should be." He held his stare for a few seconds, then turned and walked into the crowd, blending in with the businessmen and tourists as he went.

Nicky walked over, asking Rob if he was okay with a perplexed look. She'd seen Taylor walk away but had missed the exchange. "He's just a journalist, Nic, but a very well-informed journalist."

Nicky nodded. "Our ride is running late but he should be outside now. Are you ready?"

"I am, let's get moving."

The two walked outside and were met with a short-ish man in a grey suit with a dark tie. He was older, Rob thought, late fifties, maybe even touching sixty and with a similar hairstyle to Will Taylor but with opposing tones. The grey was dominant with a remaining strain of black that would no doubt continue to fade, and would continue to blend in the coming years. The relentless march of time.

He was pleasant and introduced himself to Nicky and Rob; Inspector Connor Byrne. His accent was thick. A heavy Belfast and Northern Irish accent. It sounded harsh, unlike the softer lilt found south of the border. He apologised for his tardiness, which Rob brushed away, before asking him if he was familiar with a journalist called Will Taylor.

"I don't think so, no. Why do you ask?"

"No reason."

The three walked to Byrne's car and started the short trip into the city centre, exiting the car park near a giant blue IKEA that had been visible as they landed. Almost immediately, the skyline was dominated by two giant industrial yellow cranes with a large black H&W adorning both. Rob was impressed. Sitting dominantly in the old shipyard barely a mile from the airport, and on the estuary of Belfast's main harbour. Connor Byrne caught Rob's eye on the giant machines.

"Do you like Samson and Goliath, Inspector Rhone?"

"I do, they're very impressive."

"Largest working cranes in Europe at one time, so they

were," he explained proudly. The signs were doing a good job, but the tourist advisor in Byrne was well practised. "I'm sure you're aware but this is the docks where the *Titanic* was built alongside *Olympic*, at the Harland and Wolff shipyard in 1910."

Rob nodded. Byrne continued: "It's more of a tourist area now, of course. The *Titanic* museum is worth a visit if you ever come for a social visit, and *Game of Thrones* is filmed in the studios at the end of the dock." He pointed over his shoulder in the general area. Rob and Nicky looked.

Rob was hoping the rest of the visit would prove as informative as the car eased into the city, barely fifteen minutes after leaving the airport. Arriving at the modern police station, with a large PSNI sign outside – Police Service of Northern Ireland – Rob could sense Nicky needed a coffee. He did too.

They were ushered into a smart conference room, which was incomparable to Lodge House. Tea and coffee was brought in without the question being asked, and Connor Byrne appeared, sitting opposite Rob and Nicky and offering a plate of biscuits. He looked relaxed.

"You have an investigation that links to this department, Inspector Rhone." It was a soft opening. Rob knew that Laura Mathers had spoken to Connor Byrne and he had more of a brief than he was alluding to. All had been bound by NDAs, as well as the oaths taken as police officers, with the former being required by the Home Office due to the sensitivity of the case.

"David Cramer is a person of interest in a murder investigation in Leicester. The deceased is a man known to us as Martin King, son of Aaron King."

Byrne nodded. "Car bomb, '96," he stated. He'd prepared some records and had switched on a flat-screen TV to share the information the PSNI had.

"Christopher Wilson was a sixteen-year-old when, on the night of June 6th, he attended a demonstration in the city. It was small scale, to start with, mostly students and a few thugs thrown in. All pretty standard for us. It was a Wednesday, but violence broke out and a number of demonstrators broke away and ended up passing through a narrow residential area."

"Was that common?" Nicky asked.

"Fairly common," Byrne replied. "The numbers in the crowd grew steadily, and the mood deteriorated as the police presence grew in response. The diversion tactic was always deemed safer than blocking the crowd in and inciting a riot. Breaking a crowd up always makes it more manageable, but this one happened naturally. At some point, we believe Chris Wilson became detached from the group, but that he was led or guided towards the Catholic Falls Road, close to the old Gaol. We think he did so as he thought it meant avoiding the area where it was heating up, or that he was heading away from the trouble. He used a cut-through along with a number of other demonstrators, but it bottlenecked, and as he passed a row of cars, a massive car bomb was detonated. He was killed instantly."

There was a pause. It wasn't exactly as Rob had envisaged it. "It doesn't sound as if Chris Wilson was the only target? It seems a bit... random."

"We thought the same to start with. We were able to identify Marcus Delaney, who we all now know as Aaron King, as the bomb maker, and after that we made quick arrests of what was by that point a known terrorist cell to us, which included two other men: John McGrath and Michael O'Callaghan. The four were suspected in several shootings, a stabbing and several other bombings. The bomb killed Chris Wilson, four other students and three police officers. Perversely, the four students were all English and there was little sympathy locally. If anything, the locals supported the bombing."

Rob and Nicky sat back. Shocked, but not. The job had beaten that from both of them, but to hear that the public hadn't taken an issue with a bombing that had taken eight lives was deplorable. Five of the victims were English born, and three were police, so nobody really cared. A sign of the very harsh times. Other than a hard response from the police and the military, there were no reprisals from local gangs, no complaints from either side of the divide, and in some of the well-known dissident areas, the odd party had been held in celebration, complete with effigies wrapped in the Union Jack.

Byrne broke the silence. "Chris Wilson's phone survived the blast. Those Nokias were the best, weren't they?" he asked rhetorically. "We found messages from Martin King, who was questioned, as a witness to start with as they were school friends, but once we'd established that his dad was the bomb maker, he was questioned on a conspiracy to murder charge. He was young too and he coughed to it; to luring Chris Wilson to that spot. He was targeted that night."

"And what about the others who were killed?" Rob asked.

"Wrong place, wrong time," Byrne replied, more casually than he should have given the subject.

"Wouldn't a bullet in the head have sufficed?" Rob wasn't in the habit of condoning any form of violence, but the fact that eight young men had died in an indiscriminate attack seemed egregious beyond belief.

"You need to remember that some men just like chaos, Inspector Rhone." The words came as casually as his last response. Connor Byrne had evidently become desensitised to the appalling violence that had gripped his city for the last three decades. The fact that they were referred to as 'the Troubles' had always stunned Rob. *Trouble*; like a playground dispute or a fight outside a nightclub. Something innocuous. Something that went away quickly. Forgotten about and insignificant.

"Are McGrath and O'Callaghan still alive?" Nicky asked, changing the mood of the conversation. It was information not yet available to the Leicestershire team.

"We believe so. They were both sent to prison for their part in the bombing and were relocated on their release. The information we have shows that both men are still alive."

Nicky nodded. "And the convictions included the attack at Thiepval Barracks?" she asked, knowing the answer.

"Yes, all three were convicted for their part in the attack at Thiepval," he confirmed. "That's in the files you have and on public record," he replied, almost confused.

"What about Victoria Barracks, Connor?" Rob asked.

Byrne's confusion deepened. His brow furrowed. "Yes, that formed a part of the indictment. All three were convicted of the attempted attack at Victoria Barracks. Do you not have sight of those files?" he asked.

"No, we don't."

"Is it relevant?"

"I don't know yet."

"Well, I'll get them for you, but the attack at Victoria was planned to be a bigger version of the successful attack at Thiepval, where the IRA infiltrated the barracks and planted two large car bombs. Victoria Barracks was a large British base back towards the docks where we came in from, and the IRA wanted to make a statement. Marcus Delaney wanted to blow it to bits, but the attack was foiled and the bombs were safely defused."

"Do you know how the attack was foiled?" Rob asked.

"There were suspicions of an inside man but nothing was ever proven."

A natural lull fell in the room as Nicky supped the last of her coffee. "Do you have any dental records for David Cramer?" she asked. It was smart and it threw Byrne, who scrunched his face up once more.

"No, I don't think we do. Why?"

"We're just covering all angles," she lied back.

CHAPTER 25

It was late in the afternoon before Connor Byrne dropped Rob and Nicky off outside the towering facade of the Europa Hotel, in the middle of the city and barely a mile from the police station. The day was still warm and would have been befitting of the weather in Rome, Barcelona or any other continental city. Some locals were still enjoying the late sun on a large grassed area surrounding the town hall, with girls in short skirts and crop tops reading books; basking before heading home, or to a local bar. A number of lads with their t-shirts off were doing much the same thing. The atmosphere was chilled. Relaxed. Convivial. It turned out that bringing a pair of Ray-Bans would have been a good idea.

In this form it didn't look like the sort of place where a riot could kick off in a heartbeat, but both knew as well as the locals that it could. Rob guessed this weather happened about twice a year and decided he'd enjoy it whilst they were here.

Inspector Connor Byrne put his hazard lights on as he pulled into a small drop-off bay near to the entrance, which was lined with flagpoles; their flags hanging limply in the mild and breezeless afternoon. He helped to unload Rob's and Nicky's bags, quipping that the Europa was the most bombed hotel in the world, before casually offering to pick them up later. Rob declined the offer, having spoken to Nicky during a break at the station. Byrne had nodded it away and recommended visiting the Crown, just across the road, as well as reeling off several places of note where good food could be procured. He went back to qualify his earlier statement, stating that a number of British PMs had stayed here, as well as then-President Bill Clinton. As Rob was starting to look forward to a shower, Byrne was pointing at the pavement for no reason in particular, regaling himself with memories of secret service agents looking down drains and removing bins from outside the glass-fronted hotel.

"Meet you at 9am in the morning?" Rob confirmed, which was met with a thumbs-up and a shout of "Enjoy your evening!" as Byrne returned to the driver's seat and eased himself back into traffic.

Rob grabbed his bag, picking Nicky's up with his left hand before the two headed into reception.

"Bar in an hour, guv?" Nicky asked. Rob smiled at the suggestion.

"Yep, then we'll head over the road to the Crown."

*

Nicky had been less than an hour but had spent the time in much the same way as Rob. Bag on the bed, clothes hung up for tomorrow in the slimline and doorless 'wardrobe' that hotels seem to prefer these days, a cursory glance out of the window – both had been placed on the fifteenth floor facing the city. There was time for a shower, and a phone call to home.

As Nicky walked out of the lift and towards the bar, she could see that Rob was already there. She had opted for a pair of black skinny jeans and brown boots, with a black vest top and a printed kimono-style slip. It was all the mild evening needed, and Rob had matched the look with his own skinny jeans and a dark green shirt. Both were firmly in the smart casual camp.

"What do you think?" Rob asked, broadly.

Nicky sipped on a G&T that Rob had taken the courtesy of ordering. The satisfaction on her face told Rob he'd picked the right gin. He smiled back at her.

"I think there's a few strands we need to look into. There are some dangerous people who may, or may not, be connected to this."

"Agreed," Rob replied.

"If this is all down to Cramer, then we just need to find him."

"But you don't think it is?" Rob asked.

"Nicky nodded a 'no' whilst sipping on the G&T. Rob sipped from a bottle of Peroni. She looked back at Rob. "Do you?"

"I don't think so. I wanted to think that we were overthinking it, but I don't think that we are. If it was that simple, I think he'd have already killed Aaron King. Something must have triggered this, but the body in the car seems clumsy, seems out of character from the life he's been living."

"Part of me was surprised that the body in the car didn't belong to O'Callaghan or McGrath."

Rob nodded. It had occurred to him too during the thinking time they'd both had in their rooms.

"I'm just not convinced the body from the car and Martin

King were killed by the same person," Nicky added. "The MO is too *different*. It doesn't fit."

"I'm not either," said Rob, ruefully. "It looks like revenge but somehow this isn't as straightforward as it appears."

"But if it is a revenge mission, we could have O'Callaghan and McGrath in the crosshairs." It was more of a statement, but Rob nodded in agreement whilst taking another large sup of his beer. Aaron King remained a person of interest, but if Cramer had picked now to exact his revenge, there were two other men with blood on their hands, and neither Rob nor Nicky had a clue where either of them were. Something else Mathers would be working on.

"What do you make of Byrne?" Nicky asked, changing the direction of the discussion. She hadn't immediately taken to him and was interested in Rob's view.

"Not sure," he answered, honestly. "For some reason, I'm not sure I trust him. It was almost like he was happy to sit and talk through the investigation, but I felt he was more interested in finding out what we knew than how he could help us."

Nicky nodded. She couldn't put her finger on the reason why, but she felt the same way. Yes, he'd sat with them all day, had worked through the evidence and the details of the investigation, but he'd been more than happy to stay between the tramlines. To stay safe, and to be helpful. Be *seen* to be helpful.

"Do you think he's hiding something?" Nicky asked. "I know he's an inspector here, but he'll have a political persuasion. Do you think he could have any loyalty in this that conflicts with the investigation?" It was an open view, but Nicky and Rob had a lengthy history working together, the relationship was strong, and sharing thoughts, however controversial, inflammatory or inappropriate, were all part of a process that both had stood by. It worked for them and they both respected it.

"God knows. We'll keep an eye on him but for now he's sending us what we've asked for, and we'll need to keep him close."

Nicky agreed, comfortable with their day's work. There was a lull in the conversation as both sat back. A positive day was very much in the latter stages, and both were starting to realise their tiredness after an early start and a day processing information. Nicky stifled a yawn, which triggered Rob to do the same.

"You did that!" he joked. She smiled, not bothering to deny it.

"Do you think he's tying up loose ends?" she asked. "And do you think there's any mileage in either Thiepval or Victoria barracks?"

Rob sighed, polishing off his beer and sliding the empty bottle onto the table between them. "Not sure, we'll see what information Byrne sends us and then get Jack to go digging with it. We don't have any link to Cramer at Victoria Barracks. We know he was at Thiepval on the day of the attack, but does it mean anything?"

"I think we need to consider it."

Rob nodded, knowing Nicky was right. "We should start with Thiepval. We know Cramer was there that day."

Nicky nodded in agreement. "Thiepval remains active, so we can obtain any records they have and see what's in there. Byrne said he may be able to help with that so we'll see if he comes good or whether it was lip service. If it was, we'll get them ourselves." She paused before adding, "What about Victoria?"

"It might not be relevant, so we'll put it on the back burner," Rob said. He rethought his answer. "Did he say Victoria was back near the docks?"

Nicky nodded.

"Maybe we could take a look at it on the way back to the airport. Get an idea of the site and see what it's like now," he suggested.

"I could message our friend and see if we can arrange an impromptu visit?"

"Is it still an active base?" Rob asked.

Nicky shrugged before resorting to Google. "No, it's not, it's gone. Some of the officers' houses are still there, and the sergeants' mess was a social centre, but most of the site was razed. The main building is still standing, though. There are rumours of some new flats, although that looks to have been the case for years, but the rest of it is just abandoned land."

Rob nodded. "I think we'll give it a miss tomorrow. I don't think walking around a derelict site and an old community centre will tell us much."

"Fine by me," Nicky said. "You're right. For now, we have no link between Cramer and the barracks, or nothing that connects any of them to Victoria."

"Have we heard anything from DC Ryder?"

"No, we haven't," said Nicky, "but we still don't know where Cramer is."

There was a lot neither of them knew. Secrets that were buried and convicted murderers who were walking around as freely as Rob and Nicky were right now. They could be the two men behind them joking about the football and enjoying a pint as far as either of them knew, or two other men by the bar who looked like they were locals.

"How's your sister doing?" Nicky asked. She knew it was difficult for Rob. Knew how much it was taking out of him. Police life often demanded more than a family life could give, and with Rob juggling a high-profile murder investigation whilst supporting his sister through palliative care, the emotional weight and lack of sleep was taking its toll.

"She's doing okay, thank you for asking. She's comfortable, she's not in any pain and she's enjoying her food, probably too much!" he joked, but it made him smile. He'd call her again later if time allowed, and he remembered that she'd asked for some Irish biscuits as a souvenir. A big box of shortbread with a shamrock or a leprechaun on would do the trick. The chunky stuff with too much sugar on it would be perfect, and they'd discussed dunking them together in the hospice when he next visited.

The tiredness kicked back in, and with hunger encroaching, action was required. Rob looked at Nicky. "Shall we head over the road to the Crown or are we going straight to that Italian you've found?"

CHAPTER 26

They'd both slept well. Almost too well, and much better than either of them were expecting. The Italian that Nicky had found less than a mile from the hotel had delivered perfectly. A nice vibe, and a quiet corner for Rob and Nicky to continue their discussion; most of which had been social. Plus, the food had been top notch. They'd opted for a pasta dish and a risotto, which had done more than hit the spot, and by the time they'd headed to bed sometime around half past ten, they were both more than ready to go to sleep.

Neither had drunk any more alcohol after leaving the hotel bar, but the travel and the day's exertion had led them beautifully to a state of inertia, and the fresh bedding and soft mattress of the Europa had quickly cradled them into a slumber.

A hotel breakfast was always a welcome start, although the morning's talk of how an IRA gang could be linked to the murder of Martin King and Steve Hargreaves was a stark reminder that this wasn't a relaxing city break. They were both almost certain that the body from the car was a tenuous link rather than a direct one, with Cramer the link to both men.

Connor Byrne arrived as they were finishing up, and

waited in a comfy part of reception with modern sofas and equally modern pieces of art. Rob and Nicky had collected their bags and checked out. Byrne sat patiently and Rob could see that he was cradling a large file which he raised slightly as they approached him, as if they wouldn't notice it, or it was too innocuous for them to see.

"I've brought some information on Victoria Barracks. It will give you some background from around the time of the attempted bombing, and there's some imagery of the site at the time too."

He handed it to Rob, who thanked him.

"Will you need anything else from me this morning, DCI Rhone?"

Rob shook his head. "I don't think so. We'll take this and if we have any more questions, we'll be in touch."

"We're here if you need us," came the reassuring response.

"Thank you. We're only an hour away if we need to come back." He let it hang. Byrne smiled, but it was Rob's way of letting him know that this was far from finished, plus, there was still something about Connor Byrne that he didn't trust; he just couldn't quite put his finger on what it was.

He opened the file and was met with a wedge of paperwork. He flicked through the top few pages; some looked original and there were some photocopies of original pages too. Rob reached some full-page photographs four or five pages in. One large picture was of the entrance to Victoria Barracks, which was in black and white. The photograph was a copy on A4 but it looked old and of its time. Large metal gates, a separate barrier to stop approaching traffic next to a small hut, with the rest of the entrance surrounded by six-foot-high metal fencing covered in hoops of razor wire.

Rob couldn't help but think it reminded him of the entrance to Auschwitz. A large sign, which looked wooden and stood to one side, had 'Welcome to Victoria Barracks' written on it, although the image had no sense of being remotely welcoming.

The regimental crest was pictured on the sign, along with a Latin phrase written underneath: *Esse ultimum hominis stantis.*

"What does it mean?" Rob asked.

Byrne took a look at it. "Is your Latin not up to speed, Rob?"

"I went to a state school in Leicester," came the dry reply.

Byrne looked again, then looked at Rob. "It means 'be the last man standing'."

*

Aaron King had opened the door, begrudgingly letting Jen and Jack in. It was only mid- afternoon but there was more than a hint of alcohol emanating from his breath, which would have been more prominent had the stale smell of tobacco and sweat not been combining so pungently.

Jack winced slightly, his eyes adjusting to the light and his lungs to the air quality. He coughed slightly as the oxygen level deteriorated heavily with every step into the house. Jack noticed a yellow hue to the once-brilliant white architrave around the door, then tried not to look at too much more. He wondered how anything survived in the house, let alone anybody. He also wondered when Aaron King was next due at work.

The cigarette smoke hanging to the upper part of the room was thick. Acrid.

"Do you know who killed Martin?" he asked, leading them into an untidy and dirty- looking lounge.

"We're working on a couple of lines of inquiry, one of which is David Cramer," Jen replied.

Jen placed the name gently in the room and left it there. She watched Aaron King closely. Nothing.

"Do you know David Cramer, Aaron?"

"No," came the blunt reply.

"Are you sure?"

"I'm sure."

"Okay," Jen nodded and met his eye, "although David Cramer would know you as Marcus Delaney. Does that ring any bells?"

King's demeanour changed immediately, like a switch had been flicked and the Jekyll and Hyde element to his personality had been activated. Neither was sure there was much Dr Jekyll in Aaron King, just an angry Mr Hyde.

"Fuck off! Both of you, fuck off!" The outburst came quickly, like a volcano eruption. Violent and sharp.

The anger in him looked pure. It came naturally to men like him. The outburst of aggression followed by a defensive pose. Arms folded at the realisation that he wasn't in Belfast, there was no immediate fight and he was in the company of two police officers. He hated the police. Hated authority, yet here they were, trying to establish who murdered his son less than one hundred yards from where they all stood.

Jen and Jack had expected nothing less. Ferocious anger; attack being the first form of defence. Jack had stood steadfastly with his hands in his pockets, with a formal look about him but ready to defend himself if the need arose.

They allowed King's outburst to fully subside before the afterthought came.

"If Cramer wants to come looking for me, I'll be waiting. Maybe I'll kill him too."

His eyes looked angry; filled with hatred and defiance. Jen could only imagine the ferocity of his nature twenty years previously, with the Troubles still raging and where the escalation of violence was both dreamt up and carried out by men like him. Devising new ways to injure, maim and kill. Devising new ways to retaliate.

"So you do recall Mr Cramer from your past?" It wasn't a question. Jen paused. "We think Martin's murder could have been in response to the murder of his son. Of Christopher Wilson." It was a name Aaron King hadn't heard, or thought about, in a very long time.

"You do, do you? Well, fuck you." His voice was breaking and bubbling under the surface.

"We could do this at the station if you'd prefer, Aaron?"

"I'm not going anywhere," he snapped back. "You think he killed my boy?"

"We're investigating several leads, one of which is that Martin died at the hands of Christopher Wilson's father."

The tension in the room was palpable. The anger had rebuilt inside and was visibly pouring out of Aaron King. He lit a cigarette and took a long drag, buying himself a few seconds and enjoying the feeling as the nicotine reached his brain.

"You think he's crawled out of the woodwork, do you?"

"It's a possibility."

"Do you know where he is?"

Jen assured him they didn't.

He looked her square in the eye. "Well, make sure you find him before I do."

Jen was unmoved. "You don't seem to regret your part in the murder of a teenage boy."

"It was a war. There were casualties." His face was stone

cold, and as violently angry as Jen imagined it would have been three decades ago. There was an ingrained hatred in his eyes that would remain until his dying day.

"Did the people in that street know they were fighting a war? The ones without guns? The ones with kids?" Jen spat it back at him.

"They were *our* streets. They knew the risks." He waved his index finger firmly and angrily at Jen. He was in primal mode, and the cold reply was followed by another long drag on his cigarette. He thought about something as he exhaled the smoke. "Are you telling me this to piss me off or because you think I can help you?"

It was officially the latter but Jen was enjoying the sparring that had become her afternoon's work. She was also taken aback by the question.

"We're here because your son is dead and you may have information that may help us." She paused. "We also needed to make you aware that you may be in danger."

"Well, he hasn't had the bollocks to come here yet, has he?" There was a hint of bravado that came with the statement. An arrogance.

"You could be in danger, Aaron. We wanted to let you know the nature of our investigation, and we will keep you up to speed as things develop."

"You do that," came the calmer reply, which he almost shrugged off without a care in the world. The exchange reached a natural lull, and Jen was happy to wrap it up. They'd notified him of the direction of the investigation, which Rob had asked them to do, and they'd rattled his cage into the bargain.

Jack enjoyed heading back through the hall and feeling the fresh air as daylight greeted them. It was like emerging from a cave, although the smell of cigarette smoke clinging to his clothes would remain. Jack could smell it on himself. The door slammed behind them. Jack was fairly sure Aaron King was chuntering away to himself behind it, probably had another cigarette in his mouth, and maybe even a drink in his hand.

They climbed into Jen's car, a black Audi Q2 that was her new steed. It suited her and matched her stylish elegance.

"Well, at least the focus is clear," Jack stated.

"It is, but we've still got work to do."

"Have you spoken to DC Ryder?"

"No, I need to call her for an update."

"What's next for us, Jen?"

"We need to keep digging into David Cramer and his background. Rob and Nicky should know more when they get back, but we need to know more about him and why he's chosen revenge now, assuming it is him."

"If we are assuming David Cramer killed Martin King for the role he played in his son's death, there's the clear assumption that Aaron King is at risk due to the role he played, but what about O'Callaghan and McGrath?"

"Good questions, Jack. We need to catch up with Rob. We'll focus on Cramer for now and expand as things evolve."

"Do we have a responsibility to protect him? Under the terms of his release."

"I don't think it's our responsibility. I hope it isn't; one for Rob, Mathers and the Home Office."

Her phone rang. She looked at the screen to see Becky Ryan's name writ large across the screen in her car.

"Hey! How are you?"

"I'm good! How was Mr King?"

"As you'd expect, Becky. You can come next time if you'd like?"

"I'm good, thanks. I prefer my clients to be a little colder."

"You won't get a lot colder than Aaron King," came the tongue-in-cheek reply.

"The newspaper that we found from the search of Cramer's house, we thought it was a circular, didn't we?"

"Yes, we did. Why do you ask?"

"We ran it for fingerprints. We were expecting several sets on it as a minimum; which are usually a mix of delivery drivers, newsagents, paper boys, or anyone else who may have handled it, but we only found one set of prints on it, and they were Cramer's."

Jen was perplexed and unsure of the implication. "Is that important, Becky? Or what does it mean?"

"It could be. Newspapers are usually a right old mix of DNA, especially when they've been through a newsagent's or a petrol station. I think it means somebody orchestrated it so that David Cramer saw that newspaper, but was exceptionally careful about how it happened."

CHAPTER 27

It had been a busy few days, which had passed quickly but with no immediate or obvious success. Rob and Nicky had arrived back from Belfast following their meeting with Connor Byrne, Becky had been dissecting information in both the literal and physical sense, and Jen and Jack had been busying themselves, having had a challenging conversation with Aaron King yesterday afternoon.

The office was quiet. Not silent, but everybody was operating in their own bubble. Heads down, working away. Focusing on the workload in front of them, updating in their own minds what they knew, and what they didn't. A jigsaw puzzle that was still short of many pieces.

Jen looked up as Rob gestured 'five minutes' in her direction with a raised palmed hand. She smiled and gave a thumbs-up, passing the message on to the team, which was met with more thumbs-ups and the odd grunt. Enough time to squeeze a loo break or a coffee in for those who hadn't reached their caffeine tolerances for the day.

Jack was the last to sit down, complete with a fresh cup of tea in a funky-looking mug. Jen and Nicky were cradling a can of Diet Coke each, and Rob had a bottle of water. Laura Mathers had joined and looked relaxed. Rob was never sure whether that was something to be grateful for, or fearful of. Her face gave little away, and it wasn't now. He decided that she'd make a good poker player but guessed that she never played, and if she did, it would be for nothing more than pennies or kicks. The thought crossed his mind that she could be a dark horse who spent her evenings on poker platforms hustling cash from gamers and students, but he quickly dismissed it as unlikely.

"Is Becky joining us, Rob?" Jen asked.

"No, she's tied up with another post-mortem, so it's just us. I'm catching up with her later on, though."

"Cool. One more question; did you bring me some rock back?" she asked, with her tongue firmly in her cheek.

Jack looked perplexed. "What the hell is rock?" He was met with an appalled look from the others as the mood climbed and some gentle piss-taking ensued.

"The youth of today, eh? Not a clue," Jen quipped. Mathers was eager to start.

"What did you learn from the visit, Rob?" she asked.

"Firstly, has the name William Taylor cropped up on anybody's radar?" He looked around the room, not expecting a positive response but wanting to test the water. He was met with a bunch of no's, but wrote the name on the investigation whiteboard to one side with a large blue question mark next to it.

"Who is he, Rob?" Jen asked.

"I met him in the airport in Belfast. He's a journalist, or so he claims, and a real bundle of joy. He was too well informed for my liking and he came across as more threatening than

I'd have liked. Byrne said he doesn't know him, but I want to know who he is or if he's connected to any of the other names on the board." He tapped them with the marker he'd just written Taylor's name down with.

Jack was scribbling notes down. "Me and Jen will take a look and see what we can dig up on Mr Taylor," he assured Rob.

"Thanks, Jack."

"So what has your new friend Connor Byrne sent over?" he asked.

Rob raised the thick wedge of paperwork from the desk, which was wrapped in an old manilla brown sleeve. It didn't look official. It resembled something that Rob could have pulled from his loft from his school days. Old homework, a project on road safety or a no-smoking campaign.

"We have this. It's a file on Victoria Barracks, which was a military base near the airport."

"It *was* a military base?" Jack asked.

Rob nodded. "It was. There was an attack at Victoria that bore similar marks to the attack at Thiepval, which David Cramer was present at. The same IRA cell was believed to have carried out the attack at Victoria."

"Relevance?" Mathers asked, challenging the information.

"It may bear no relevance, but we're light on information and this could provide a link between some of the names, or provide fresh information. It could also support or disprove any of the working theories we have."

Mathers nodded but didn't respond, before asking, "And what were the key learnings from Belfast?"

"I don't think we've digested enough to understand it yet, Laura. The attack that killed Christopher Wilson was seemingly more random than it could have been, and killed four other students. We don't have their identities yet, but we'll look into the families of the victims and see if anybody has either the opportunity or the malice to be responsible for these crimes."

Mathers nodded, thinking. "I want you to prioritise the information you have in front of you and establish whether the attacks at Victoria do have any relevance. If not, we need to move on. You also need to run through the four once you know who they are."

Rob agreed. He always enjoyed the irony of how the hierarchy prioritised. It was usually everything at once, and a previous chief constable would often dish out five or six tasks, each followed by the sincere instruction to 'make that your number one priority'. Having five number one priorities was devaluing, but in a murder case there was no room for complacency, and the responsibility to find the killer always focused the mind.

"In simpler tasks, have we heard anything from Norfolk?" Mathers asked Rob, who looked at Jen.

"No, Ma'am, we haven't. I spoke with Vanessa Ryder again this morning, and David Cramer's whereabouts remain unknown. They've now deployed his image on their social media channels to try and flush him out, but the man's a ghost. He's well resourced, and he's a former military major general. He spent years blending in and keeping his head down, and even with his age there's a fight and a defiance in him."

Rob nodded in agreement. "Yeah, there's anger in him."

"So if he's angry and the motive is straight revenge, do we know the whereabouts of John McGrath and Michael O'Callaghan? Are they at risk?" Nicky asked, taking a more simple view of proceedings and with the obvious possibility that the person responsible for the death of Steve Hargreaves was already in their sights. With David Cramer almost certainly being the man responsible for the death of Martin King, the case could be taking a more straightforward direction than the investigation currently was. She looked at Rob.

She'd considered asking about Aaron King, whether he was in danger, and the immediacy of any danger, but decided that was too much of a hot potato with Mathers in the room. She'd spoken with Rob about it a couple of times already, and they both had their views, but neither of them were the chief constable, who was paid to make unpopular decisions.

Mathers assumed that the question had been directed at her and cut across Rob.

"I'm working with the Home Office. There's a formal request to disclose the identity and location of both men. It's possible neither has changed their name. Several senior or former IRA commanders have refused to change their names, and they see it as a badge of honour. Their histories will be protected to avoid anybody without clearance being able to identify them, or carry out any reprisals, but there's an extensive number of people going by the names of John McGrath and Michael O'Callaghan in the country. I don't see any issues with the request, though, given the nature of your investigation."

Rob heard *your* investigation and sighed inside. Ever the politician. If the investigation was wrapped up quickly and showed the Leicestershire force as proficient, especially in front of an official from the Home Office, then he knew full well that *your* investigation would quickly become *our* investigation, or even *my* investigation. *My* officers, at *my* direction. A press photograph showing the swift success of a complex operation would feature full dress uniform, including the hat. Smiling, maybe a choreographed handshake with the Home Office official, and all under a glamorous tabloid headline.

He flicked back into the room and smiled at Mathers. He wasn't sure she'd bought it. Rob wanted to get back to work and decided they'd all be better off getting on with their workstreams. He summarised.

"We'll wait for an update on McGrath and O'Callaghan from you, Laura. Jack and Jen will look into the relatives of the other four victims, as well as continuing to work with Norfolk on the location of David Cramer, and Nicky and I will work through the attacks at Thiepval and Victoria and see what falls out."

He looked at Jen for one final thought. "Don't forget Will Taylor when you have five minutes."

*

It was just before 7pm when Jack and Jen left the office and headed into town to meet Becky. Nicky had left earlier and was due to meet them in the Quay. A beautiful and quaint pub on the banks of the River Soar. It was mostly a student district, but the bar was popular and a nice place to head after a day in the office, especially when the evenings were dry and with a hint of sun. The patio doors were guaranteed to be open and the timber deck overlooking the River Soar was always a nice place to perch.

Nicky was already there when the other three walked in the front door. The pub was quiet, and Nicky had picked a large table near to the bi-fold doors, but still very much inside. There was a breeze that seemed to be growing and had blown a couple of the large umbrellas over outside.

"Are we getting hammered tonight?" Jen asked.

"Shall we see how we go?" Becky replied, with a mischievous smile. Nicky had taken the liberty of ordering a round of drinks, and all took a large sip. Jack loosened his tie and started to settle into the evening, and his thoughts turned to food.

"Is anybody eating?"

"I will if you will," Becky replied. Menus were swiftly procured and all four flicked through the large and diverse selection. It was mostly pub food, but there was a broad spectrum to the quality of pub food, and everyone knew that this menu was decent. Even a simple sandwich would be on fresh thick bread and beautifully presented. Orders were placed with a helpful young woman who seemed jovial and was clearly happy in her work. Her bright tattoos spilled down both arms and suited her, and she smiled as she headed to the kitchen.

Jack asked Jen about a date she'd been on recently, which hadn't gone anywhere. Jen had responded in the same vein, although Jack's love life was now settling well. Him and his partner had just paid a deposit for a new-build house reserved off plan, in one of the nicer villages out of town. His life was growing and he was happy, and Jen's warm smile told him she was happy for him. The mood was good.

"How's it going?" Becky asked broadly.

"It's work in progress," Nicky replied, diplomatically.

"Progress slow?"

She nodded a 'yes' and then qualified it. "It looks like Cramer is responsible for the killing of Martin King, but he almost certainly did not kill Steve Hargreaves."

Becky nodded, looking up as the waitress appeared promptly, with plates of steaming food balancing on her hands and wrists. Becky raised her hand as her meal was the first to be called out. She took a chip as soon as it was placed in front of her, and just before the waitress told her how hot the plates were.

"The tooth just seemed too convenient to start with, as well as a little out of place," Becky said.

"Agreed, it looks to be a red herring to provoke David Cramer and tie him to the investigation."

"Which means there is something, and somebody, behind that has initiated Cramer's involvement."

"The newspaper."

"The newspaper."

"Also very convenient."

"I feel for Cramer," Jen interjected. Jack was getting stuck into a burger, which had been expertly crafted and was far too big to pick up and bite. "It's a sad end to a life well lived, especially if he was enjoying retirement and somebody poked him with a stick."

"Must be a big stick," said Becky, supping on a G&T and tucking into a well- presented lasagne. "So what's the working theory?"

"The current theory is that Hargreaves was in the wrong place at the wrong time, and was used in conjunction with the newspaper to provoke David Cramer. We think that somebody found Martin King and used it to rattle Cramer's cage, which means there is somebody else involved who is driving the agenda."

"Cramer has a lot of questions to answer, though."

"Oh God, yes. He's the prime suspect in the murder of Martin King and still a person of interest in the death of Steve Hargreaves. His tooth was in that car, and that can't be ignored."

"So if there is somebody pulling his strings, who are they and what's their agenda?"

"Could be blackmail, emotional or otherwise."

"It seems unlikely somebody holds enough leverage over Cramer to blackmail him, don't you think?"

"Who knows, Becky. I think there's a debt to be paid, and somebody is out to collect it."

CHAPTER 28

The evening had stayed jovial, drinks had been enjoyed but nobody had crossed the line, and the mood was light as all arrived in Lodge House, ready for another day. Ready to pick up the reins. To continue the investigation into two deaths; two murders. To ask the same questions that had been asked the day before, hoping for a different result. For any result.

All police officers knew their job largely involved breaking Einstein's theory. That of doing the same thing over and over, of asking the same questions over and over, and expecting a different outcome. Murder cases, as with all crime, involved people lying. Initially trying to evade capture, then trying to evade justice.

People had to be pushed, theories had to be broken, and only the level of scrutiny that a murder investigation afforded to the evidence, and to information, would reveal the truths, the mistruths and the out-and-out lies. Keep pushing, keep asking questions. Trust nobody, accept nothing.

Rob was heading out of his office for an 8am meeting with Laura Mathers but took the opportunity to ask Jen the question that he knew was making him sound like a broken record.

"So where are we with David Cramer? Any news?" It was more in hope than expectation.

"No, nothing," Jen replied. She was due to speak with Vanessa Ryder that morning, in what was becoming a twice-daily brief on the investigation in Norfolk. Rob nodded, and didn't ask for any more as he headed towards the lifts.

He straightened his tie in the slim mirror next to the control panel and checked his hair. It was a meeting Rob wasn't looking forward to having. He knew he needed to have it but also knew they were on very different pages. This would no doubt be short, and more of a 'discussion' that he was unlikely to get any change out of. As he entered through the large traditional-looking door, he realised he hadn't been in this office formally since David Parker had 'stepped aside' and Laura Mathers' ascension. He tried to steer clear, truth be known, preferring the down and dirty aura of an investigation room to a wood-panelled office lined with photographs and a Union Jack.

Mathers' PA invited Rob through. There were a few formalities but Rob got to the point. Mathers remained at her desk, with Rob standing before her.

"We think Aaron King is at risk, Laura. There's an obvious motive, and with Cramer at large we think there's a real risk to his welfare."

"What are you asking for, Rob? We've had this discussion, have we not?" Mathers retorted. She didn't bother to look up.

"I think as a minimum we should monitor his house. I don't like it either, but I feel we have a duty of care towards him, given what we know."

"Duty of care? He's a convicted IRA murderer, Rob. There's a resource issue, there's a cost issue, and there's a perception issue. It's not prudent to put men on the street because somebody might want him dead."

Rob exhaled inside. He knew it was a bad position to be in. Protecting a terrorist at taxpayers' expense would never look good in any newspaper, but neither would the same newspapers asking whether enough had been done to protect a man at risk should he be killed on their watch. *He almost certainly wants him dead*, he thought. Rob looked at Mathers but didn't say anything. She lowered her tone.

"I'm not paying to defend a convicted murderer, Rob. I have escalated it, and there is no desire to allocate resources for this part of the inquiry."

Rob nodded, accepting that he'd done as much as he could. He accepted that tough decisions had to be made, and those decisions weren't always his to make.

"Well, if there's nothing else, Rob. Please don't let me keep you." It was dismissive, but it was a conversation Rob needed to have had. He left and headed back to the warmer atmosphere of the investigation room.

Jack and Jen were working away as Rob walked past them. "Have you had the chance to look at Will Taylor yet?"

"Yes, we have," Jack replied.

"So what's his interest in this? Simple truth, revenge mission, or something else?"

"We'll grab Nicky so we can run through it. It won't take long."

Rob waved at Nicky, who was on the phone, and as she finished she slid her chair over and waited. Jen started.

"William Taylor. Born in Glasgow in 1963. He's Associated Press, and he plys his trade as a journalist with the *Belfast Telegraph*. He's not just any journalist, though; he's an award-winning journalist, and he's stepped on a lot of toes. He's written some of the biggest exposés on corrupt politicians, dodgy businessmen and senior IRA figures in recent times. He's a real champion for social justice."

"So he's happy to speak out against people who most people wouldn't dare to speak out against," Rob said. He was processing it. He was surprised. He'd pissed Rob off, he'd caught him off guard, but he was seemingly a social warrior, and no doubt a hero to the man on the street. Those without a voice. Those he spoke for.

"He was entirely responsible for the investigation into corruption at Bombardier, when contracts were awarded based on backhanders, and where directors had become shareholders in the businesses who went on to win the deals. Several directors and their CFOs served serious jail time for that," Jen added.

Jack cut in. "He also exposed an IRA commander in the mid-eighties, who at the time was a prominent community figure. It caused a major reaction locally and the IRA ended up having to part ways. It was too divisive, and once Taylor had exposed him, he became a liability."

"Do we know who the man was?" Rob asked.

Jen nodded. "We do; Jared McGuire. The issue is, he hasn't been seen since."

"He disappeared?"

"They made him disappear."

Rob stroked his stubble with his right hand. "And there's more?"

Jack flicked through several sheets of paper and nodded. "He's like a middle-class *News of the World*. He's a real heavy hitter and it doesn't look like he backs down from a lot. He's a man on a mission. He seems to relish fronting up to people."

"Yeah, I got that from him," Rob offered, dryly.

"What's his interest in our case, Rob?"

"I'm not sure yet. He mentioned Chris Wilson's murder, and he suggested we should be looking at Thiepval and Victoria barracks too."

"What's at Victoria?"

"Nothing anymore. Or so we believe."

"There's something else we found, Rob," Jen added, ominously.

Rob looked up.

"Will Taylor had a son. James. He's missing. Taylor separated from his wife as his career grew and he started to become a target for a number of important, wealthy or dangerous people. Their son was ten years old when he went missing. He's never been found."

"Could it have anything to do with the Kings?"

"It could do, we've found nothing so far to link them, or David Cramer to Taylor. It could be that he's searching for justice for Chris Wilson, but there could be links to the disappearance of his son. It was only three months after he'd exposed Jared McGuire, so it's almost certainly connected."

Rob sat back with his hands behind his head. "What happened to his wife? Do we know?"

"She was in the process of emigrating to Australia with their son. Her sister moved there when she was younger and she wanted to get away from Belfast, get away from the life that Will had brought upon them. Away from the violence. Away from the danger."

"Did she go?"

"She did. She was only here for two months after the disappearance. I can only imagine how hard that must have been, but she must have been too committed to leave, or too resigned to what had happened. Plus, she would have known she was in danger too."

"What's her name?"

"Lucy. She's a photographer." Jen added a smiling picture of Lucy Taylor to the board. Her short blonde hair made her look stylish and carefree. There was a thick camera strap around her neck and the hint of a trail of three star tattoos creeping out from the top of her t-shirt.

"Is she still there now?" Rob asked.

Jen nodded a 'yes'.

There was a lull. Rob pondered. "So Cramer lost his son to the IRA, specifically Martin and Aaron King, and Will Taylor also lost his son, at a similar time, and almost certainly to the IRA."

"Looks that way," Nicky said.

"But we've no links currently between Cramer and Taylor, other than they both lost a son in the eighties?"

Jack said 'no' before adding the final issue from their digging. "We checked his passport too, and you're not going to like this."

"What is it?" asked Rob.

"He's been in the UK recently. He was here for three days."

The penny dropped in Rob's mind. "Was he here when Martin King was killed?"

"Yes," Jack said, "and he flew back to Belfast the day after."

CHAPTER 29

Rob was still chewing the fat over Will Taylor when his office phone rang. Nobody used it anymore so he knew who was calling. Emma Wilson was Laura Mathers' PA, a smart, well-humoured PA whom Rob liked, and she often provided a welcome barrier between him and Mathers.

Emma asked Rob how he was. A few pleasantries were exchanged, and Rob asked Emma if she'd bought tickets to the Isle of Wight festival yet. She was a regular and, as expected, she'd already secured her tickets and was excited about the weekend line-up. The headliners were scheduled to be a diverse mix of Lewis Capaldi, Lionel Richie, Pete Tong and Duran Duran closing on Sunday night.

Rob smiled; he still had 'attend a festival' on his bucket list. One day. With the pleasantries down, it quickly became a summons back upstairs to see Laura Mathers. The bigger issue for Rob was that he had no idea why. He'd been up there earlier in the day, and the only thing Mathers didn't know was the recent findings on Will Taylor.

He told Emma he'd be five minutes and hung up. He sat back and sighed. Thinking. If it was Taylor, why was he going about things this way? Rob could understand the animosity towards McGrath and O'Callaghan. Towards anyone in the IRA who was corrupt, who conflicted with the core values Taylor seemed to hold so closely. But what could he have against Cramer? He was a decent man. He'd served his country, and had lost his son in a similar fashion to Taylor. They had much in common, and from Rob's viewpoint, Taylor had little reason to cause Cramer harm, let alone frame him for murder.

He took the lift for the second time that day, stepping out and smiling at Emma, who told him she was waiting for him. He decided now wasn't the time for a facetious remark, so he swallowed it and knocked on the door.

"Come in, Rob."

Rob still didn't know why he was there but took the opportunity to update Laura Mathers on the day's work. On their findings. Of the fact that Will Taylor had been in the country for three days, which had included the day Martin King had been murdered.

Mathers thought about it. She was standing, in full uniform, and looked as smart and as measured as ever. Her brown hair was straight and neat, her complexion immaculate. She seemed to dismiss what she'd heard and changed the conversation.

"Ask Nicky to look into Taylor, Rob. You've got bigger fish to fry."

Rob didn't like the sound of what he was hearing and was waiting for a gut punch of some description. He didn't speak; waiting for the follow-up.

"Have you ever heard of the ICLVR, Rob?" Mathers asked. She waited for a response.

Rob racked his brain but came up short. Guessing wasn't

his strong point. "No, Ma'am, I haven't," was all he could muster.

"They are the Independent Commission for the Location of Victims' Remains. Based in Belfast, they were set up in 1999 between the British and Irish governments, with the intention of locating those who were believed missing as a result of paramilitary activity. They work in confidence to find the remains of people killed during the Troubles."

"That would be thousands of people, wouldn't it?"

Mathers nodded a 'no'. "The Disappeared, as they are known, are a small group of men and women who were abducted by the IRA and remain 'missing'. They are mostly suspected informants to the police or military, or who were believed to have been disloyal to the IRA in some way."

Rob shook his head. "I'm afraid I've never heard of them, Laura."

"Well, they've heard of you and they want to know why we haven't made contact, or had the decency to flag our investigation with them."

Her voice stayed calm, but from her tone, he knew she'd had a kicking. Maybe a diplomatic one, but a kicking nonetheless.

"Why would we make contact? I didn't know who they are or what they do until you told me just now."

"These things are sensitive, Rob. We need to proceed with caution."

"That's fine, we can do that, but I can't speak to people I don't know exist. And anyway, that's Byrne's world. He needs to be doing these things for us."

"Ah, yes. I'm glad you mentioned your new friend Connor Byrne."

Mathers always seemed to have something that he didn't.

Despite her lofty position, she always had accurate information. She always knew the rumours, and she seemed to enjoy that fact. There was something almost sheepish about her manner, and not for the first time, Rob was struggling to gauge what she knew that he was about to.

"I've had a conversation with the deputy chief constable of the PSNI, who was on leave when my call was taken two weeks ago. Connor Byrne was exceptionally helpful at the time and immediately nominated himself as the lead for this investigation. Everything was done correctly and is above board, but I've now had a conversation with the DCC. He's back from Barbados and I thanked him for the enthusiasm of his office, but he's raised a red flag."

Rob waited. His day wasn't in desperate need of a red flag, let alone one that was blowing into a headwind.

"We believe the reason Connor Byrne was so eager to take this case personally is because he has personal ties to it." She paused, almost for dramatic effect, before adding, "Connor Byrne was Michael O'Callaghan's handler in the nineties. They were based at Thiepval together. Did he mention that over coffee and pastries?"

Rob looked surprised and breathed a deep, hard sigh. "No, he didn't." Then he paused. "His handler?"

"Michael O'Callaghan was a British spy. An exceptionally talented one. He was based at Thiepval and was a popular, efficient soldier. In his early career, he trained as a sniper, and he was deemed to be one of the best long-range shooters in the British Army, but it was his heritage and his efficiency to blend in that made him the ideal candidate as an inside man."

Rob exhaled. He didn't have a great deal to say and waited for Mathers to continue.

"He was the ideal 'type' of soldier too. He was an orphan. He and his twin sister were separated after the death of their parents. His upbringing was hard, and after he left school he found his way into the army, where he excelled. He served tours in Chile, Ethiopia, Iraq, Cambodia and Mozambique. That isn't an inclusive list, and he was handpicked to infiltrate the IRA by the head of the British Army."

"I'm guessing this is classified information, Laura?"

"Yes, it is, even now. His cover is still in place, Rob, he's that good. We can use the information within the confines of our investigation, but Michael O'Callaghan's cover is good. It's less sensitive from a conflict point of view, but if John McGrath finds out that his right- hand man was working against him, he'll kill him."

"Understood," Rob replied, firmly. He envisaged the fallout should this information, which had remained watertight for the last thirty years, be leaked on his watch. On Mathers' watch.

"He's decorated too, Rob. Victoria Cross, Military Cross, Distinguished Service Cross, Conspicuous Gallantry Cross and a Distinguished Service Order."

"So he's not a convicted IRA terrorist. He's the best the British Army has to offer?"

"He's both, Rob. The former helped to maintain the latter."

Rob sighed again. This was significant information that changed the dynamic between the names central to the investigation.

"Is there anything else, Laura?"

"Yes. I have some more records for you. I think you have some of it but from a cursory scan there is some new information surrounding Cramer's records as a bomb disposal expert during the Troubles. He safely detonated a bomb at

Victoria Barracks, which is information you now have – a guy called Francis McIntyre was the head of that unit at the time. I think you have that too, but Connor Byrne and Michael O'Callaghan were both there that day, so it may be relevant."

"We didn't know that. We'll look into it straight away. Anything else?"

"It was Michael O'Callaghan who tried to warn David Cramer that his son was in danger, but it was through Connor Byrne. Cramer did get the message from Byrne but it was too late. The trap was set and Chris Wilson walked into it."

Rob exhaled again. If the information was good, it was providing links between people who may have a motive to either harm or protect other suspects. Other potential victims. Loyalties or divisions that were forged in blood. Loyalties and divisions that don't fade with time.

"So it's possible that Byrne, Cramer or O'Callaghan knew who the inside man at Thiepval was, given their links?" Rob thought out loud.

"I would imagine so."

"And that's assuming the insider wasn't one of them? I don't believe in coincidences," he added. "I think we need to know a lot more about Connor Byrne too – he's clearly got more links to this case than he wanted any of us to know."

Mathers nodded, before showing her final card: "O'Callaghan and McGrath are both available to interview, Rob. I've made arrangements through the Home Office. You have access to both men, at completely separate venues, of course. Both may have a Home Office-appointed solicitor present, and both are aware that they are being interviewed as witnesses, even if McGrath may well prove to be more."

"Does O'Callaghan need a solicitor?"

"There's a reason his cover is still intact, Rob," she replied.

The conversation reached a natural conclusion. She asked him to report back post interviews and gave him authority to share the information within the immediate team, reminding him heavily of the extreme sensitivity of the information. Rob headed back downstairs, his facial expression conflicted and his mind processing the possible implications.

Nicky clocked his expression immediately and asked him if he was okay.

"O'Callaghan is an inside man. Was an inside man. He spent almost all of his life hiding. Pretending. He's one of the good guys and risked his life working inside the IRA."

"Does anyone know?" she asked.

"Mathers, you and me. Oh, and Connor Byrne." Rob went on to explain the complex web of network, deceit and lies that had emerged from his conversation, and with O'Callaghan's cover seemingly still in place, the team would need to decide how to proceed. Carefully.

"It's like he's still undercover," Nicky commented, before adding, "What would McGrath do, even now?"

"I can only imagine," Rob replied. They both pondered the situation. Considering how hatred can fester and manifest itself over time. Like miners still at war forty years after the strikes. Harbouring hatred and anger, seeing it fester and grow. Those were divided communities, like Belfast, but for a very different reason. All belief based; love thy neighbour, unless they disagree with you or your belief system.

Nicky was still considering what this could mean for their investigation, and for the coming day's workload.

"So he's a highly decorated British soldier who spent his life undercover? The man's a hero."

CHAPTER 30

It's a dull, wet Friday. The air is damp and the mood sombre as I stand and watch a funeral cortege leave the site towards the east gate. It's not the one I'm here for. Gilrose is a large cemetery inside the inner ring of Leicester city. Flanked by two main roads and appropriately the Glenfield Hospital, it's a large Victorian cemetery which must be getting close to full by now. Surely, these places have a limit.

Row after row of headstones adorn the flush green grass, with an area close to the main building clearly visible as being more recent. Crisp black headstones with sharp corners and inlaid gold font that I can read through a high-powered camera I've brought along. Fresh, bright flowers and the odd teddy bear. A child.

Older stones to the opposite side are showing the decay and wear brought on by decades of English weather. A gentle hill sits as a cross section of time. Stones visibly age as I swing to my left and my view moves away from the building. Stones with corners eroded into soft edges and with names and dates barely legible. Stones where relatives have long since visited to lay flowers.

Generations have passed since some of these souls were laid to rest. A century or more.

The rain starts to fall more heavily, so I stand the collar of my coat up further and check my watch. It should be next, but it's the lull in between services, and the staff hurry to tidy the remnants from the previous funeral and prepare for the arrival of Martin King.

I put my hands back inside the deep pockets of my coat, hitting the cold metal handle of my Browning 9mm semi-automatic pistol as my right hand reaches the bottom. I'm not planning on using it today but you can't be too careful. Some people are on high alert and I need to protect myself if the need arises.

I check the safety is on with my thumb and pop a stick of chewing gum into my mouth. I realise that it's the same gun as one of the weapons used by Michael Stone all those years ago. On that unforgettable day at Milltown Cemetery in 1988. A day when a funeral turned into a terrorist attack, with three members of the congregation killed and sixty injured by grenades, bullets and shrapnel. Scenes that should have been from a barely believable action film, not something hitting the headlines on the main evening news.

I wasn't there that day. None of us were, but the scenes of total chaos as Stone threw the first grenades before opening fire are vivid. His mop of black hair and equally black beard flowed wild, and as the chaos gripped, a number of mourners chased him from the graveyard. It ended up looking more like a group of football hooligans than a day of sorrow. A day of dignity.

I guess I could have tried to replicate it. I could have launched an attack here, but it would have felt a little bit crude. Maybe too much collateral damage, if there is such a thing.

There's been enough death in the last forty years, so I'll only kill who I need to. Who I plan to, and anybody who gets in my way if the need arises.

I'm about 200 yards from the red-brick building where the congregation will arrive. The view is good, which is why I'm here. On one of a number of slightly elevated banks to the periphery of the site, behind several linear rows of trees. Yew, possibly. I'm behind a worn stone obelisk that was here last century, if not the one before it. There's a real risk I will see an old friend, hence the firearm, but if I'm lucky, I may see an old friend or two from a distance. Gauge who has skin in the game.

Nothing so far. I check my watch again.

A gentle hum from a hearse breaks the silence and leads the funeral cortege into the grounds from the west side. It would have passed the Premier Inn and a cheap chain pub on the Groby Road on its way up the hill, before swinging left through a large pair of black wrought-iron gates that make the entrance typically Victorian.

A number of cars and mourners emerge silently behind, creeping along in line like a colony of ants. The hearse carrying the coffin, adorned with 'Kingo' in white flowers, stops perfectly as the pallbearers approach. It's a smooth, well-practised ritual. The congregation is a mix. I was expecting that. I can see Aaron King for the first time. Black suit. Solemn face.

There's a number of young men. A few of them are wearing blue and white scarves that match the colours of the wreath, and by their build and the odd cauliflower ear are clearly from the rugby club. Interesting that his dad has agreed to bury him under his adopted name. Maybe it's just easier. Maybe he just didn't want to explain why it had been changed by those here to mourn the loss.

There will be those who will remember him as a friend. A colleague. A teammate. Before finding out one day that Martin King was Alex Delaney. Terrorist. Murderer.

I look around the edge of the site, as well as to a row of conifer trees to one side. They are closer and give a clearer view of the cemetery. I did consider placing myself there but the exit would have been much harder, and being blocked in by some of these characters was not an option. I look back at the congregation. It morphs and moves, like a flock of birds in the sky, as people move between themselves and other groups. Circles within circles. Saying hello to Aaron King. Telling him how sorry they are for his loss.

I see a face that may be of interest. I raise my long-lens camera next to the stone I'm standing by and start to click. I swing the lens around and see if I'm the only one here.

It hasn't yet but this should draw some characters from the woodwork. I'll see if anybody else is watching from afar and taking photographs.

I'll see who else's interests have been shaken enough to show up to a murderer's funeral.

CHAPTER 31

The information surrounding Michael O'Callaghan was still sinking in. Jen and Jack were both now 'in the know'.

"Has Will Taylor been formally questioned now, do we know?" Rob asked nobody in particular.

"I'm trying to find out, guv. I think so," came the reply from Nicky.

Jen and Jack were busy combing the fresh set of redacted records that Mathers had provided, which had been cleared by the Home Office for review.

Jack had a stack of detail relating to David Cramer's records as a bomb disposal expert during the Troubles, and was reading out segments that he could scarcely believe had happened.

"'Major General David Cramer safely deactivated a bomb at Ballyshannon power station in County Donegal, which had it gone off would have caused significant death and destruction to the immediate area, including to the power supply to thousands of local properties.' I can only imagine how much that would have infuriated the IRA."

Jen nodded, listening intently whilst thumbing her own pile of documents and papers, relating to murders, attacks and bombings. "It was every day, wasn't it?" she asked rhetorically. "Sometimes two a day. Or three. I remember the odd attack on the news. Every now and again, the odd car bomb, but this is just a relentless campaign of violence."

Jack nodded in agreement. "There were over 10,000 reported bombings during the Troubles. *10,000.* He said it again. He used the calculator on his iPhone to work out that there had been at least one bombing every day for over twenty-five years. He and Jen looked at each other. There was a moment of silence that reflected their shared disbelief.

Jack picked up a file and continued. "Here we go. There was a second bomb that was averted at Victoria Barracks, which is described as a 'very large-scale attack'. Cramer's team deactivated the device minutes prior to detonation, saving countless lives. Frank McIntyre is listed as a key protagonist in averting the attack too. He's painted very well in the segment of the report that we have. He was central to defying the attack, according to this."

"Well, it supports the documents that Connor Byrne shared on Victoria."

"It does, which is interesting," Rob offered. He and Nicky were both listening in whilst having their own discussion around possible suspects and their motives. "Interesting to hear that view on McIntyre too."

With all eyes on Jack and with nobody talking, he carried on.

"'Cramer and his team entered the barracks late on the evening of Wednesday, 10th April, 1996, and quickly made their way to the main mess hall, which was attached to the engineering block.'"

"What happened in there?" asked Jen.

Nicky followed her with another question. "You said team. How many were in his team?"

Jack looked at both as Rob smiled. He read quietly before responding. "'The engineering block housed a large technology and equipment centre. It was where the mechanical guys serviced and repaired equipment, including firearms, vehicles, electrical items,' etc." He read it verbatim as his audience digested it.

"So it would have been well equipped, wouldn't it?" Rob suggested. "Well tooled up, literally."

"Almost certainly," Jack replied. "They were also able to manufacture their own munitions from the block."

"So there would have been gunpowder in some form?"

"I imagine so," he said, before looking at Nicky and addressing her earlier question. "Four. The team was a four-man team, including Cramer."

"Is anybody else named?" Rob asked.

"Negative," replied Jack, showing the page with that section redacted. "It could be relevant," he said.

"I think we should assume anything could be relevant," Rob replied, before writing '4 x redacted names' on the board and making a mental note to ask Mathers if she could have the men identified.

"Is there anything about how the attack was planned, or the perpetrators?" Jen asked.

"No, there is nothing definitive on the perpetrators. The IRA admitted the attack afterwards, but in terms of individuals, nobody was ever arrested. Nobody was ever charged."

Jack flipped the page and looked up. "Aaron King was named as the probable bomber, but there was no evidence to support it and no charges were ever brought."

Rob wrote that on the board too, with a looped arrow to Victoria and another one to David Cramer. There were now three arrows between the two men. A large-scale bombing at a military base and the now almost certain probability that they were responsible for murdering each other's sons was a dark reality.

"Is there anything more specific on how the attack was foiled, Jack?" Rob picked up a chocolate bar and tore the wrapper, taking a large bite from a Wispa and waiting for an answer. Jack continued reading, and as Rob swallowed the first bite, he added, "Or is there anything to suggest there's an IRA man inside the camp?"

"It's possible, isn't it?" said Nicky. "If Michael O'Callaghan had infiltrated the IRA and was working with Connor Byrne, it's entirely plausible to think that an IRA insider could have been working the other way, and helped to plan or even plant the bomb at Victoria."

It was an opinion, but the conversation was healthy as thoughts continued to bounce around the room. Jack rustled some pages.

"Yes, or this report suggests that an IRA insider had almost certainly infiltrated the barracks and was responsible for planning and allowing the attack to go ahead."

"But it doesn't say who, or suggest who?"

"No, it doesn't."

"Would O'Callaghan have been able to use his influence to stop the attack? Do we have any evidence of that?" Nicky continued.

The conversation was breaking up. The possibilities were numerous.

Rob rightly slowed the conversations down and looked at

Jack, who was in possession of the evidence. The team would all go through it in their own time, in their own way, but right now Jack was in the chair.

"There is clear mention of an insider being responsible for reporting the plot, which caused its downfall, so, yes, it could have been him. Cramer and McIntyre are both mentioned very positively, but the details and roles are a bit sketchy."

"That would have been so high risk, though. Given the foiled attack at Ballyshannon, I imagine the senior IRA guys would have kept this very close to their chests."

"They knew somebody was on the inside, they must have done."

"Yet the Victoria attack was still averted."

"McGrath and his like must have been fuming."

"But O'Callaghan is still alive, so if they did believe there was an insider, they clearly didn't at any point think it was him."

"Maybe O'Callaghan had to be fuming too," Jack said.

"Well, at least we have somebody we can ask," Rob said. "Two of them actually."

Nicky nodded. "So we've got a bombing averted by Cramer, at a barracks that connects Michael O'Callaghan and Connor Byrne, and with Aaron King named as a possible suspect."

Jack nodded a 'yes'. "And, two months later, a car bomb claimed the life of Cramer's son."

There was a moment of silence as the team processed the gravity of the investigation. The men involved, and the loyalties and disloyalties that had played out during the worst period of violence in British history.

"Aaron King was implicated in both bombings but was never charged with Victoria. He was convicted in court in

January 1998. He was released ten months later under the terms of the Good Friday peace agreement, as we all know."

The team already knew the length of Aaron King's sentence, but hearing it and realising it again didn't make it any more palatable.

Jack repeated it, trying to believe that the British authorities and a judicial system he believed in had allowed it to happen. "Aaron King murdered a teenage boy and was linked to several other bombings including the failed attack at Victoria, as well as a shooting at a pub. He was convicted, and only served ten months for his crimes."

There was a natural pause. All four officers felt the uncomfortable nature of the investigation, and could only imagine the dismay of the officers who had worked so hard to bring King and his men to justice, only to see them walk before their first Christmas inside had passed.

Nicky used the moment to change the subject. "Have you had any progress with the ICLVR, Rob?"

"Yes, and it's not great."

"What do you mean?"

"I had a useful call with one of their directors. He was quite chipper considering what they do, so we have an ally. We've also papered over any diplomatic cracks, so Mathers is happy, for now at least. They are fully up to speed with where we are and have an open line into me and you whenever they want to."

"That sounds okay?" she replied, a little perplexed. Her frown asking for more.

"We now also have the names of the Disappeared," he explained.

Nicky still didn't see a problem. "Is the list massive?" she asked, making the same incorrect assumption Rob had.

"No, it's not that either."

"Spell it out for me, Rob!"

"The list has thirteen names on it, so it isn't a big list – that's the good news."

"And the bad news?"

"Well, we knew Will Taylor's son was on the list, so one of the names is one we expected; James Taylor. The problem we now have is one of the other names on the list; Sean Byrne."

Nicky frowned further and made the leap. "Relative of Connor?" Her tone was resigned, as if she already knew the answer.

Rob nodded. "Son."

"How did we not know this? How has Byrne not told us, or his senior team not made Mathers aware? They must know!"

"Agreed. It's a question we'll need an answer to, but it also means we now have two men with links to the investigation whose sons were taken, or believed to have been taken, by the IRA."

Nicky pondered. The investigation hadn't been clean-cut from the outset, but it had been made even murkier by men with painful secrets. Men with unfinished business, and fathers with missing children.

"We've gone from having Cramer as the prime suspect to having both Will Taylor and Connor Byrne searching for the truth. Searching for their sons, and maybe something darker."

Two men bound by open grief.

CHAPTER 32

It's been a quiet couple of weeks. There have been no arrests, some feathers have been ruffled and a lot of questions are being asked. The cage has been rattled. I'm just not sure it's the right one.

It feels like a game of chess. How to manipulate those pieces to where I want them. How to get to checkmate. It's a game of patience. A game of nerve.

Having said that, time is a commodity I am not rich on. So I'll need to stoke the fire myself on this one. It's not a fire I was expecting to have to stoke.

Not a murder I thought I'd need to commit.

The park has reopened as I walk in through the same gate that I did a couple of weeks ago. There's little to suggest that a murder happened here recently. The foamex police signs appealing for evidence and witnesses have gone, although ironically I think they've been stolen. There's a small amount of blue and white police tape still tied around a post, which has been clumsily left, no doubt by a young officer desperate to get off shift and go home to a loved one. Pulling the tape harshly and ripping it before disappearing, leaving the tell-tale remnants behind.

It's a good job some of these people are police. They'd make terrible criminals.

There's a few dog walkers, a few runners. Headphones in. Zoned out. Immersed in their own world. Nobody's paying attention or looking at me. Nobody ever does.

It's a cool evening. It's dull. I'm wearing a jacket. I don't particularly like it but it's old, it's practical, and I'll be getting rid of it in the next hour or two anyway.

I'm feeling relaxed but inside I'm angry. Irrationally and massively angry. It's bubbling today. Really bubbling. There's a rage that's bursting to come out. I'm really going to fuck him up tonight.

There's an overwhelming amount of hatred running through me, he's in my way and I'm going to kill him. I want to kill him. He's had his time anyway and this is long overdue.

Game time.

*

I haven't given this much thought considering what I'm about to do. No masterplan here. No deeply thought-out plan, just an end game in mind. What needs to happen. He's in a world of pain, though. I'm feeling vindictive as fuck and I just want to hurt somebody. He's about to be in the wrong place at the wrong time.

You kill some people because you have to. You kill some people because you need to, and you kill some people because you want to.

With Aaron King, I want to. A little bit because he's a step on the journey, but mainly because he's had it coming for fucking years. How somebody hasn't taken him out before now, I'll never know. The man is an oxygen thief of the very highest calibre. He's been clinging to life like a cockroach for years, and his time is up.

With nothing better in mind, I walk up to the red-brick terrace house and knock on the wooden door. I wait. There's no noise, no sound of the TV. Nothing happens. I wait. I consider knocking again, but a light comes on in the hall and he sounds like he's talking to himself. Muttering.

I look up the street, then down. Nobody. I feel relaxed. Maybe that's just the feeling of having nothing to lose. Nothing else anyway.

A bolt clicks. I hear the slide of a chain. I didn't think people used those anymore. There's another click and the door opens.

Even in the dullness of the evening, he squints at me. The minimal fragments of any form of daylight strain his eyes. Then the stench of the house hits me. Then the stench of him.

The waft of stale cigarettes strains my eyes in return. I notice the styrene tiles on the ceiling of the hall have more than a tinge of yellow to them. The staining of nicotine that takes years to build. Maybe Martin smoked too. It's staggering that two people could live like this.

His eyes struggle to meet mine, but not before the smell of alcohol hits me. A horrible bitter smell on his breath. It's mixed with tobacco but it's unmistakable.

He's drunk.

His eyes are mere slits. Several days' worth of stubble litter his chin, which has jowls where his jawline used to be. Life has not been kind to Aaron King, although with his lifestyle being what it was, and so self-inflicted, any sympathy for him is non-existent.

I can see into the lounge. A cigarette burns slowly on an

old glass ashtray. The sort you'd see in a pub in the eighties. Fluted edges and round. It's full of butts and charcoal-coloured ash. I wonder how long it has taken to amass, and when it was last emptied.

"Can I help you?" he offers. He looks down at my hands for a parcel. For a delivery.

I consider my options but say hello. Can't have him thinking I'm rude. I tell him I can help him to find his son's killer. It's technically not a lie.

He very quickly looks on high alert. He asks me who I am. It isn't polite, although it's a fair question. I consider my options again. I turn slightly to one side and then smash him hard in the face with my right fist. His nose immediately starts to bleed. He falls backwards onto his carpet and he struggles for breath as the blood runs down his throat. He tries to stand but coughs blood onto his arm as he falls onto his hands and knees.

I check the street once more and step inside. He hasn't moved. He's still on all fours so I kick him in the ribs. He looks pathetic. I kick him again. And again. And again.

I pick him up by the scruff of his clothing and drag him into the lounge. He starts to fall and half lands on his coffee table. The glass in it breaks.

I close the curtains.

He's already stricken. He may have a decent reputation as a bomb maker, but this is a shell of a man. I can relate to some extent. He barely has his health, there is no strength whatsoever and there is nothing left. Just a corpse of a man and a shitload of anger.

The cigarettes and alcohol have destroyed the rest. And life itself.

There are beer cans everywhere. Has he had a visitor? Two

chairs look like they've been sat in, and surely there are too many cans for one person? I can't believe my luck.

I turn around to look at him. He's still lying on the floor. He's begging. Asking why. His hands are up; there's some blood where shards and slithers of glass have stuck to his palms and sliced into his skin.

"I didn't kill your son, Aaron. Does that make you feel better? I would have done, though. He was a worthless piece of shit. Just like you."

"Get on with it then!" he screams. "You're one of them! Shoot me! Get it over with!"

"Shoot you? In the head? Where's the fun in that? We're not so different, you and I, Aaron. Do you mind if I call you Aaron? I can call you Marcus if you'd prefer."

He looks confused. He looks resigned. He shrugs.

"You know we're both just foot soldiers in a war that can't be won, Aaron."

"That was a long time ago," he replies, spitting blood from his mouth. A string of bright red spittle hangs from his bottom lip as he dabs the back of his hand against his mouth once more.

"Did you get what you were fighting for?" I ask him. "Did you win? Did you lose? Or don't you know?"

He looks beaten. I punch him in the face; he tries to grab my shirt. I brush his hand away and drop a knee into his ribs. He groans loudly.

"Did Martin die in vain?" I ask him.

That strikes a nerve. He forces himself up and onto his knees, still clutching his ribs. His hand trembles as he tries to force himself into a better position.

"You leave him out of this. He was an innocent man!" he

shouts, angrily. He tries to point. Tries to look at me, but his balance denies him.

"He was barely innocent! Maybe by your standards he was, but he wasn't exactly white, was he!" I almost mock him. There are no innocent parties here. Just varying levels of guilt.

He moves to his left towards a side table which is strewn with rubbish. An empty cigarette packet, some tissues, two beer cans. He grabs a lamp and swings it at me. I barely have to move. He misses and it breaks under him as he falls once more. He makes a noise. The broken pieces may have cut into him. He may have stabbed himself. I can't see. He's crawling around, trying to raise himself once more. A lack of balance and the afternoon drinking is not helping him. I pick up the cord from the lamp and wrap it round his neck. I pull him towards me and wrap the ends around my hands. The plug hangs between my fingers. I pull hard and his eyes bulge. His face shines a bright red as the blood flow stops immediately. A vein starts to bulge and pop out of his forehead as I look him square in the eye.

I release the pressure a little and he drops down, gasping for air. His fingers are grabbing at the cord as it slacks off. They're filthy. Dirty and chewed fingernails. His neck is marked where the cord has dug in, even for a period of ten to fifteen seconds. I've never seen that first-hand; I'm not usually this close when I'm taking a life. I let go altogether and he falls to the floor.

There's no fight in him. No life. I'm almost disappointed. I'd geared myself up for a scrap tonight. Thought he'd make me work for it. I was ready for the first fifteen minutes or so being a battle. Thought it'd make me feel alive. But this is a man who is breathing but isn't living. This isn't a life. Aaron King is a man with nothing. Living in a cesspit of a house and with no purpose. No cause.

This is a man ready to die. I'm here to oblige.

CHAPTER 33

"Big day today, Jack!" Rob stated. Not that anybody needed telling. There was a buzz in the office as final preparations were being made. The order and wording of the questions were being tweaked, refined and finalised before the two parties hit the road and headed out in different directions. The aims were the same; to procure information. As much information as possible. It was needed.

Mathers and Rob had agreed on the strategy. Nicky and Jack were en route to meet Michael O'Callaghan. A man who was currently an enigma. A hero. He was also still hiding, and the interview would need conducting delicately. Sensitively. There was a weight of expectation, and Mathers had been very clear about how she expected the interview to be conducted.

Nicky and Jack headed west out of the city, circling Beaumont Leys and meeting the A50 by Glenfield Hospital. Traffic was steady, as it usually was, but eased off as they swept out of the city and over the A46 towards Markfield.

The weather was clear and the journey quick as the small talk flowed between the two, as Coalville came and passed by. Nicky remembered to slow down for the speed cameras as the road headed up from Ashby-de-la-Zouch and into Moira, before they headed down into the town to find Swadlincote's police station tucked in behind a McDonald's.

They got out of the car, looked at the restaurant next door and looked at one another in the shadow of the police station.

"That could be dangerous," Nicky said, dryly.

Jack smiled. "At least we haven't got far to go for lunch."

The two walked into an old-looking building. Dark bricks and blue paint made it look harsher than the average modern police station. Introductions and formalities were had with a middle-aged woman on the front desk who had clearly had a bad morning and who didn't have a face for customer service. Not that Nicky and Jack were customers, but Nicky met her eye with a look that did its best to tell her to cheer the fuck up.

The two were shown along a narrow corridor by the miserable woman who had stepped out from behind her counter. Nicky saw that she was wearing a pair of flat black shoes and walked on her instep. The woman held an arm out to a room. Nicky wondered if she'd been given a reason for the interview, or if she had been given a name for the visitor. She suspected not but wondered what yarn she'd been given for this intrusion. Maybe that explained her face. Maybe it didn't.

Nicky walked in first. The room was bland. She expected it to be. Michael O'Callaghan was sitting on a cheap school-like chair with the standard table in front of him. Two chairs sat opposite him. Dark blue plastic and a black frame, with a hole in the lower back. O'Callaghan stood as Jack walked in and closed the door. The miserable woman disappeared back up the corridor.

He was average height and of slim build. He looked as if he'd lost a little weight in recent times, with his face weathered but rugged. Nicky imagined he'd been a handsome man in his day. He wasn't bad now, with his fair hair neatly kept. He was well heeled too, wearing a navy blue cashmere-type jumper that made him look slim, and a smart pair of skinny black jeans. His watch fell up his wrist as he extended his right hand. Nicky thought it looked like a TAG, but she wasn't sure if it was genuine.

"I'm pleased to meet you," he offered, softly, with a smile and a handshake.

His teeth were neat; his eyes showed some signs of weariness, but given the life he'd been leading for the last thirty years, he could be forgiven for that. Jack asked him if he'd like a coffee and he accepted. Jack disappeared, presumably to find somebody more hospitable than the woman on the front desk.

Nicky sat almost staring. There was something alluring about Michael O'Callaghan. Well dressed but average. Attractive face but not outstanding. A nice smile.

There was something about him, but if Nicky didn't know who he was she'd forget about him in an instant. He was outstanding but forgettable in equal measure. Remarkable but ordinary. Nicky could already see how this chameleon of a man had survived the last three decades. He was everything and nothing.

"Is this interview being recorded, please?" he asked, calmly.

"It will be, but it will only be information accessible by a very small number of people. Those approved by the Home Office acting on your behalf."

"Thank you. That's very reassuring," he replied, as if this was a minor thing for him. Something insignificant.

The interview wasn't being conducted under any form of caution. O'Callaghan was being interviewed as a witness, and Nicky was respectful of a man she could see was cautious. Understandably so. With Jack still on the hunt for drinks, and with O'Callaghan looking ready, Nicky continued the chat.

"You know why we wanted to speak to you, don't you, Michael?"

He nodded.

"I heard Alex Delaney had been murdered."

Nicky checked the notes on her lap. Alex Delaney; Martin King.

"And you think it's connected to historic events," he followed up with.

Nicky waited. She nodded slightly as if to invite him to continue. Jack snuck in with three steaming drinks and put them on the table. O'Callaghan looked at one and mouthed 'thank you' to Jack. He picked it up following a nod and took a sip. He coughed. He coughed again and pulled a tissue from his jeans. He composed himself.

"You think David Cramer was involved, don't you?"

"Why do you ask?" Jack asked, sipping on his tea.

"He's an old man, detectives. And he's angry." He paused. "Time doesn't heal all wounds."

The words were delivered in a profound way.

"They murdered his son. He was a good officer and they killed his son for it. An innocent boy. That's what he was."

"Do you think Marcus Delaney is at risk, Michael?" Jack asked, using the name familiar to O'Callaghan.

"Hopefully," he replied. "It stands to reason, doesn't it?"

"And could McGrath be involved?"

He smirked. Laughed almost. It turned into a smile as he considered his answer.

"John could be involved in anything." It sounded warm.

Using the Christian name of his friend. A man he stood beside. Plotted attacks with. Was convicted with. A man he betrayed frequently. He looked up, at Nicky, then at Jack. "If you need somebody hurting for a cause, or something destroying, you could get John involved very easily. Could he be involved? Yes, of course he could."

He sipped his still-boiling coffee and stifled another cough. Maybe he was an ex-smoker, but Nicky hadn't sensed that on arrival, and his teeth suggested otherwise.

"The main bit that seems to be missing is the reason. Or, more importantly, the time. Why now?" he asked nobody in particular.

"Why now?" Nicky repeated, and then asked of O'Callaghan.

"Revenge is a dish best served cold, is it not?"

"But why wait? Why wait thirty-odd years for it?"

"Maybe the opportunity presented itself." He shrugged, pleased with his suggestion.

Nicky and Jack looked at one another. The newspaper maybe, although they still didn't know how that tied in with the body in the car, or Cramer's tooth for that matter.

"Have you spoken to Frank McIntyre yet?" he asked, which came as more of a surprise.

Nicky considered her response. "Should we speak to Frank McIntyre, Michael?"

O'Callaghan looked confused. "I'd have thought he'd have been the first person you spoke to."

His mentioning of McIntyre hadn't necessarily been anticipated. He was on Nicky's radar and his name was going to be brought up later in the interview, but O'Callaghan had raised it first, and with indifference.

"Why would he be the first person, Michael?"

O'Callaghan looked surprised again.

"He's the one person who connects all of us. I was based at Victoria in the good old days. It was the site we attacked, but it was also foiled because I'd fed the intel to Connor. Delaney. John, me, Cramer, Connor. We were all involved in that attack, in one way or another. I just thought you'd have put that together. You're speaking with me, which means you're speaking with John. I just assumed you'd be speaking to Frank too."

Nicky and Jack sat and waited. Nothing came. Nicky prompted more. "How was your relationship with Frank McIntyre?"

O'Callaghan thought carefully about his response. "He was a difficult man. A *really* difficult man. Arrogant. Nasty. Empowered. I hated him and he was on my side. The British side, to be clear." He paused. "He was meant to be on my side," he added, cuttingly.

"Was he not?" Jack asked. "You both served Queen and country."

"Do you not know anything?" he asked. "McIntyre served himself. He wasn't on our side, he wasn't on your side and he certainly wasn't on my side."

It was an interesting disclosure, and wasn't information Nicky had expected to pick up. For clarity, she looked him square in the eye.

"Was McIntyre corrupt, Michael?"

"Corrupt? Frank McIntyre was the epitome of corrupt. He's a narcissist and I'm certain he had people killed at Victoria. You may struggle to find information to support that, unless you're digging the place up, but that man is responsible for a lot of bad things. Have you not spoken to Will Taylor about him?"

Nicky's response told O'Callaghan that they hadn't.

"You should speak to Taylor," he suggested, "and you should *definitely* speak to Frank McIntyre."

He swigged the last dregs of his still-warm coffee.

"You've got missing people, you've got dead people, and you haven't spoken to Frank McIntyre?"

CHAPTER 34

Rob and Jen headed north out of Leicester on the A6, passing through the leafy frontage of Birstall village, before picking up the A46 at Wanlip and heading east towards Nottingham. The journey was relatively short but always one of reminiscence for Rob. He'd had a great aunty and uncle who had lived in Birstall, in a nice house with a garden backing onto the old Great Central railway line. Days of drinking Nesquik milkshakes in a garden and watching a steam engine roar past felt so normal at the time. Childlike. Carefree. Fun. The strawberry- flavoured powder had always been overdone, and the flavour and the sugar kick were immense. Fuelling longer afternoons as more trains passed by, with families and kids waving out of the carriages whilst bathing in sunlight.

The A46 was a nice road to travel. Roman, bullseye straight and surrounded by greenery as you headed up towards Ragdale. Rob and Jen glided past the junction at Sixhills before hitting the sectional part of the road that triggered a noise under your tyres every hundred metres or so. Like a train clicking over the joins of a track.

The junction soon came as the Nottinghamshire countryside

continued to impress, the A46 was replaced with the A606, and West Bridgford was listed on the signposts for the first time.

Rob and Jen continued to chat. A car journey was also a good time to have a good-quality conversation. About work. About life. About nothing in particular. Jen was in a good place; the rape case she'd worked so hard to secure was progressing well in court and looked likely to secure a conviction. Her career was developing well, and she'd moved into a new house on the edge of town. Life was good, and Rob could see the happiness and the brightness in her eyes.

"How's Emily?" Jen asked.

"She's doing okay," Rob replied. "It's been a difficult few days, but they've got her meds under control and she is up and about again. It's movie night tonight at the hospice so I'm heading over later. I've promised her I'll be on time and with both Minstrels and popcorn!"

Jen nodded. "That'll be nice." She was right, it would be. She could also see the strain in Rob's face. He smiled and glanced at Jen. "It's *Top Gun: Maverick*. We're both very excited!"

"That'll be fab!" Jen remarked. "I still haven't seen the original."

Rob gave Jen a firmer look. "You haven't seen Top Gun!" His tone mocking and appalled in equal measure.

The central police station to the north of Nottingham arrived quickly. Always a sign of an enjoyable conversation and time well spent. Like Leicester, the station was in a heavily populated area, on tight roads and with very limited parking. Neither Rob nor Jen had been here before, despite the proximity of their effective neighbours. The station looked odd. Sitting on a corner, four stories high and with a large black door at the top of three small steps. It looked like it may have been a cinema at some point.

The formalities were official; the station felt cold. Institutional. Rob and Jen were given 'visitor' lanyards and escorted into a large room at the far end of a long corridor. The door closed behind them. A man in a smart blue suit was sitting at the table, his brown satchel-style bag on his lap. He hadn't arrived long ago and was still settling in. He smiled at Rob, but it felt a little awkward.

McGrath was standing by the window. Hands in the pockets of his blue jeans. A white and grey lumberjack-style shirt hung off him, the check pattern woven into the thickness of the fabric. He turned, the shirt was open and a plain white t-shirt sat underneath. His grey hair was longer than the photo Rob had of him, and wild. His beard was also long. McGrath turned and Rob looked him in the eye for the first time. Rob felt a chill run through his body. He instinctively didn't like him.

Jen offered her hand to the man in the suit, who shook it and introduced himself as Graham Hunt. She looked at McGrath, who smiled. His smile was flippant. A smirk.

"We'd like to thank you for your time today, Mr McGrath," Jen opened with, cheerily. She looked at both McGrath and Hunt and smiled. "And we appreciate your support with our investigation."

McGrath was being interviewed as a witness. That much had been made clear to both him and his solicitor, and his attendance was voluntary. It had been entirely possible that he wouldn't show. This interview wasn't compulsory, so to have him in a room already felt like a win.

The plan was to be surprisingly open, considering they were

sitting opposite a convicted murderer. A convicted terrorist. Rob's tone was respectful.

"We're investigating the murder of Alex Delaney, John. And links to David Cramer."

"How is the old boy?" McGrath asked, smiling behind the question. The Northern Irish tone in is voice was still thick, and harsh.

"We're not sure, John, we can't find him," came the honest response.

"So you need my help in finding one of your own?" It sounded a bit perverse when worded in that way.

"We'd like to speak to him following the death of Martin King, who you'd know as Alex Delaney. We think he can help us with our inquiries."

"Help with your inquiries? You mean you're pretty sure he killed him?" The response had an edge to it.

"Don't go sentimental on us, John. Plus, we think there's more to it than simple revenge," Rob replied.

Neither McGrath nor the solicitor knew about the body in the car, or the link to Cramer's tooth. That information was known by a very small group of people.

"Fuck you," came the curt response. The room fell silent and McGrath crossed his arms defensively. The silence held before McGrath reached for a packet of cigarettes and put one in his mouth.

Jen broke his ritual as he fumbled for a lighter, nodding towards the 'no smoking' sign on the wall. He sighed, before resigning himself and replacing the cigarette back in the packet.

Rob repositioned himself. "We believe there is more to the investigation than David Cramer, and we believe the murder may have links to past crimes, and possibly to the attack at Victoria Barracks."

"Well, as a witness, that wasn't our finest hour." He swigged coffee, reengaging with the discussion.

"How many were you hoping to kill, John?" Jen asked. The solicitor raised his hand in John's direction as he drew breath. He took the sign and swallowed his response.

"Somebody blabbed, though, didn't they. Was it one of the Delaneys?" she enquired. "Did Marcus let you down, John? Or was it somebody else?"

The smile vanished. "I don't know." An honest answer, and a reassuring one for Rob, Laura Mathers and especially for Michael O'Callaghan. "But if you ever find out for sure, I'll make it worth your while." He winked. It was still a game.

"All that planning and you don't know?" Jen asked.

He looked across the table. "We had an idea, and we made some enquiries, just like you." His smile was sinister. He'd effectively just confessed to killing people who may have talked. Who may have let the side down.

"But you didn't *know*, did you?" she asked. "So you hedged your bets, so to speak." She gesticulated playfully, as if they were talking about a football match or a horse race, not the witch hunt of a terrorist who couldn't keep his mouth shut. It had already occurred to Jen that men had been taken, and likely tortured and murdered, following the failed attack at Victoria. Men she knew were most probably loyal to the same cause as McGrath, but whose loyalty had been questioned, and for whatever reason, they had failed the test. The ultimate price had been paid.

"I'm a gambling man, Jen. So *maybe* we did."

"Have you ever come across a man named Will Taylor?" Rob asked, changing the direction of the conversation.

McGrath swigged his coffee again, and in waving the empty cup asked for another. Jen asked an officer in the corridor to bring another round.

"I know who he is," McGrath said, nodding knowingly, "and I know some people who would gladly do him some harm, but he never crossed my path." The response seemed genuine. "He seemed to prefer going after people higher up the food chain, if you know what I mean."

"So you've never been asked to acquaint yourself with him?" Rob asked.

The solicitor held his hand up again, but McGrath had nothing to worry about. "No, I didn't. But if I had, I would have done." His face was deadly serious, and all four in the room knew exactly what he meant.

"And anyway, I'm a changed man." He smiled smugly. Rob glared at him. "I earn an honest living these days."

He reached inside his pocket and pulled a business card out. He flattened it and placed it on Rob's notebook. 'John McGrath – Landscaping & Driveways'

Rob tried not to look too unimpressed. His face didn't get the memo. Despite his disdain of the man sitting opposite him, it had struck Rob what a foot soldier McGrath was. He had clearly been trusted by senior members of the IRA, had clearly been involved with the intricate planning of some of the worst atrocities committed during the Troubles, but he was coming across as somebody who needed *telling* what to do. He wasn't a general, not even close.

"You don't seem worried, John," Jen remarked. He shrugged and sat still, sipping the top of his fresh coffee.

"I like your vending machine. The cappuccino is very pleasant."

"Whatever your past holds, John, there's a murder that ties to you. And if there is more to it than straightforward revenge, we'd value any information you could give us." It was a smartly worded statement from Jen. The unsaid part being 'and if somebody is bumping off old terrorists and it isn't you, then you'd be pretty high up their list.'

McGrath shrugged again, seemingly not remotely bothered, and seemingly with little to add. It hadn't been particularly useful so far, although both Rob and Jen seemed content that McGrath had both turned up and been prepared to contribute. He was also clearly a man who couldn't be trusted, and who would revert to violence at the first opportunity.

Rob thanked McGrath and Graham Hunt. It had been a fishing exercise, although Rob wasn't sure if they were the only ones in the room who were fishing.

McGrath stood up. "Say hi to Michael for me," he smirked again, "and Frank. Please be sure to tell him I said hi." There was a real arrogance to the threat.

Rob looked him dead in the eye and replied formally, "As you're now part of an active criminal investigation, you'll need to check in at a local police station every forty-eight hours under the terms of your licence, but your solicitor knows that already."

The smile evaporated. Rob smiled smugly and walked out of the room.

CHAPTER 35

The mood was reasonable in the office. All four officers were in, and there was an element of bustle about the morning's activity. The view from the tenth-floor office was overcast. The clouds were heavy, and there was a drizzle that had caught Jack out as he arrived at Lodge House earlier on.

The printer was buzzing away in the corner. Throwing out a number of A4 pages one after another. Rob still preferred reading and looking at some evidence as a hard copy. The feel of the paper, the sharpness of the ink. Especially with a fresh toner.

He'd never seen the appeal with a Kindle either. He'd received one as a gift a couple of Christmases ago and had thought it was a fad at the time. He could see the benefits, but it just couldn't replace the feel of a book or the crispness of the paper. Plus, Rob was a sucker for a good front cover and would often buy a book if the colour, image or font provided any visual gratification whilst sitting on the shelf.

Nicky and Jen had rigged up a large glass coffee pot, which was plugged into an extension lead and was sitting proudly on top of a filing cabinet, underneath one of the many tall windows of the corner office. The heat from the coffee pot had caused a small mushroom cloud of steam to form on the glass of the poorly insulated window, and the smell of fresh coffee had flooded the airwaves. All four had wandered over to the pot in the last fifteen minutes, pouring mugs of steaming hot coffee and inhaling the freshness of the beans.

Coupled with the bag of croissants Jack had collected from Pret a Manger on Gallowtree Gate, the office had the aroma of a chic coffee shop about it. It was also warm, a rarity which was being enjoyed, although Jen was still wearing a large red knitted scarf.

There was also an awkward feeling in the office. Having to question another officer was always a difficult ask, especially given the team's recent history. Police officers committing serious crime, or involved or complicit in serious crime, was a stain on any force. Two in a year would be problematic, for the team in general but for the wider force. And for Laura Mathers. Her predecessor had fallen on his sword; she would be eager to avoid the same fate.

Connor Byrne had presented a problem to the team. A willing volunteer who had become a stakeholder. One with direct involvement and a personal stake.

People with emotional or family ties were generally bad in any professional situation. It was worse when that person was a police officer.

Rob had wanted to carry this out face to face, but limitations on time as well as budget meant a video interview had been opted for, and agreed between Rob, Laura Mathers and her counterpart in Northern Ireland.

Nobody was sure how long it was likely to last. Jen and Jack had been busying themselves, looking into Connor Byrne's files.

Looking for potential issues. Conflicts of interest, and links to David Cramer, John McGrath and Michael O'Callaghan. Links that weren't already known. Links that might explain two murders.

The team were aware of the positive contributions Connor Byrne had made to the police force. To the security of Northern Ireland as a whole. The risks he took. Firstly just as a police officer, and more prominently as Michael O'Callaghan's handler.

But he was also a grieving father, and a man with a missing son. Sean Byrne was most likely dead, but with neither him nor his body having ever been found, the pain of the loss was still somehow raw. The unfinished nature and the lack of finality was a pain that Rob could only imagine.

Connor Byrne was intimately connected. A fact that couldn't be ignored. Withholding ties to a case was rarely for a positive reason, although Rob was proceeding with an open mind.

The interview was being conducted under caution. Connor Byrne was entitled to a union rep but had declined. Rob and Jen were ready to go, in an interview room with a widescreen TV that Jack had rigged up.

The screen clicked live and Connor Byrne was visible. He was with Liam Boyle. The senior officer Mathers had spoken to and who had disclosed Byrne's position.

The sound wasn't immediately available. Jen pressed a few buttons on the remote before the broad Belfast twang of Liam Boyle came through. Jen adjusted the volume down.

Rob opened with an exchange with Boyle. Introductions were made and Rob thanked them both for their time, as if in some way this was voluntary. It wasn't.

Before Connor Byrne had spoken, there was something resigned, almost confessional about his manner. Slumped shoulders. Hands sitting in his lap. Head slightly bowed forward.

Rob was gentle in his approach, explaining clearly the situation that all four already knew. Reminding Connor of why this was happening. Why it needed to happen, and reading some excerpts of his situation and the 'loss' of his son from a file Rob had in front of him. Times, dates, details.

The mention of his son triggered a wince. It was as if Rob had stuck a knife between his ribs and twisted it. He could see the pain it had caused and he stayed gentle, as Liam Boyle reached across and placed his hand on his colleague's back.

"I wanted to be involved," Byrne offered, without a question being asked. "I saw an opportunity. It was given to me. You gave it to me, and I saw a fresh opportunity to find Sean."

It was already off script. Rob took his glasses off and sat quietly for a few seconds. Jen leant forward.

"We all know how you must feel, Connor, but you've committed misconduct. You don't need me to remind you of that," which was exactly what she was doing, and he knew it. He'd have done the same thing. "But since you answered that call, Martin King has been murdered, and David Cramer remains missing."

Connor Byrne knew full well what the situation was. He had access to pretty much everything and had been fully in the loop until Laura Mathers established his stake in the case.

"One day, he just never came home from school." Byrne looked down, then looked up. Even through the video feed, the small drop of a tear in his eye was visible. It must have been a story he'd recanted a million times, but as he told it again, the raw emotion was plainly visible.

"It was like he just vanished. He obviously had no mobile phone, and there was no CCTV. It was as if he were here one minute and gone the next."

He sighed and sat back. "Do you realise the helplessness? The pain of it. You sign up to protect your own family. Your own children. And I didn't." The tear fell, trickling down his cheek. He left it. Jen had no doubt that Connor Byrne was used to crying for his son. "I don't approve of David Cramer's actions from a legal standpoint, but as a father I'm right behind him. Do you know what it does to you? The anger, knowing he's out there. Knowing that *they* murdered my boy because of what I do."

He drew breath. The pain was etched on his face. In his eyes.

"We've looked. I can't tell you how many hours I've spent looking, but we never found him. He's missing, presumed dead officially, but you know that already. Believed abducted by the IRA and he's listed on the ILCVR list of the Disappeared, but you know that too."

Rob leant in. His tone was very calm. "What we need to establish, Connor, is whether you believe the man, or men, responsible for Sean's disappearance are known to you. Known to us."

It was the entire interview in one question. Rob wasn't sure if he'd get angry and lose it, go straight into denial or rant about whoever he did hold responsible for Sean's disappearance and probable murder. It had occurred to Rob how much time he must have given up thinking about, or physically looking for, his son.

"No. I don't know."

It was all that came. Jen waited and glanced at Rob.

"I don't believe the Delaneys had anything to do with it. They weren't in the area at the time, and Marcus was believed to have been responsible for a shooting at Craigavon at the same time. That's ten miles away."

Jen would double-check the details against the information they already had, but she expected to be able to confirm one way or the other pretty quickly. She also appreciated the incredulity that a murderer's alibi against a child abduction and murder was that he was committing a shooting ten miles away.

Rob waited again but nothing else came. "So after all these years, you don't have a theory or any knowledge at all of who abducted Sean?"

It wasn't meant to be cutting, but it felt as if Connor Byrne's integrity as both a police officer and a father had been shredded. All this time. All these years. Nothing.

Byrne looked at the screen, and in what must have felt like the single biggest failure of his life, muttered the word "No." The tears came shortly afterwards, the pain simply too great to bear.

*

"Do you believe him?" Rob asked Jen. She nodded a 'yes' whilst trying to locate a bag of crisps she thought she'd left on her desk. A big bag of salt and vinegar McCoy's.

"Me too. There are some things that you can't *really* fake."

Both had looked into the eyes of a spouse who had subsequently been proven to have murdered their partners. Parents who had murdered their own children. There was usually something in the reaction of somebody when you asked them a searching question, or told them of the death of a loved one. It was always slightly different when they already knew. A movement of the eye, the tears starting too easily or too late, or a noise forced out to appear genuine but doing exactly the opposite.

"All these years and he's no nearer to knowing what happened to Sean than he was on the day he went missing."

"What does that do to you?" Jen asked, rhetorically.

"Eat you alive, I imagine."

"So let's say we believe Byrne. He doesn't know who abducted or murdered Sean. That means he's just a broken man trying to find the truth about his son, but it may have no bearing at all on our case."

"Hard to see how it doesn't, though."

"If you had a son who was missing and you got a call with resources and a willingness to investigate with you, what would you do?"

Rob didn't answer, but the look on his face told Jen that he fully understood how tempting it must have been for the call to have fallen into his lap, and how easy it would have been to feel the burning pain inside you reignite with hope.

"So where are we with our friend David Cramer? He got a mention in there."

"I need to speak with DC Ryder in Norfolk. I meant to call her yesterday, so I will do it shortly."

"What are we missing? I still don't fully understand the body in the car. If Cramer wasn't involved with that, what was the motivation? Who left that body in that car, and why?"

CHAPTER 36

"How was Mathers, Rob?" Jen asked, after Rob reappeared following a summons from Emma Wilson.

"It was nothing important. Just a bit of police chat and a summary of where we are."

Jen was glad she wasn't yet in the position of being summoned up to explain your team. To explain yourself. Even with her ambitions, she was fairly sure Rob may have just been on the receiving end of Laura Mathers. The case wasn't progressing as quickly as anybody liked. That was policing. Some cases fell into place almost immediately. Some only ever had one suspect and it all came down to solid evidence collection. Some cases were complex and took months or even years. Then there were the cases which were never solved, or, worse, where a wrongful conviction occurred.

Rob's mind often wandered to Suzy Lamplugh. It wasn't one of his, but it was one he knew well. Suzy was an estate agent who vanished in 1986 and hadn't been seen since. There had been suspects, and even recent excavations. And the elusive Mr Kipper.

More parents who have spent decades wondering. Not knowing.

A phone rang and Jack answered it, breaking Rob's train of thought. He rummaged through his pockets, hoping to find some chewing gum but instead pulling out a petrol receipt. He straightened it out to use for his mileage claim from the Nottingham trip. He'd already forgotten to log it on the expenses system and he made a mental note to do so later. There was a sandwich and a bag of crisps from Costa on the receipt folded behind it. He checked the date to see if that needed logging too.

Jack hung up and Nicky and Jen gravitated over to form an impromptu circle.

"Are we all happy with where we are?" Rob asked. It had been a busy forty-eight hours with travel and interviews thrown in, and even with the phone conversations and WhatsApp messages all being positive, little had been learnt and the investigation was showing more signs of stalling than of being wrapped up.

"David Cramer remains missing. The search will be stepped up and Mathers will be speaking with East Anglia and allocating more resources. The evidence suggests Cramer murdered Martin King, so he remains our prime suspect."

Laura Mathers wandered in, looking casual. She sat on a chair behind Nicky and listened. Rob checked her body language. She didn't interrupt, didn't look as if she wanted to interrupt, and she looked relaxed. That was never a bad thing.

"Could this be simpler than we think? Are we overcomplicating it?" Jack asked. It was a brave question with Mathers in the room but Rob respected it and, with a case not going to plan, was always happy to circle back, check the thinking and question the evidence. Question their own logic. Breaking their own circle often held the key. Investigations often stalled when assumptions were made. Assumptions which turned out to be flawed, baseless, or occasionally just totally wrong.

"It's possible," Rob responded, "but with the obvious complication all along."

"The body in the car."

"The body in the car. And the tooth."

Nicky chipped in with her thoughts. "So we all believe that David Cramer murdered Martin King." The room nodded. "But we don't believe he was involved in the disposal of the body in Leicester where his tooth was found, but it's possible he could have been involved with the murder."

Rob nodded. "It's possible."

"And we're all happy that the CCTV and evidence from both his gym and his bank proves Cramer was nowhere near Leicester when the body was dumped."

The nods came. "So there's definitely another party involved with the crimes."

Everybody agreed.

"We didn't get anything from the public dash cam appeal, did we?" Rob asked.

"No, we didn't. The point I was making," Jack clarified, "is whether it could be as simple as Cramer killed Martin King, with somebody else killing Steve Hargreaves independently and leaving his body in the car."

"It's absolutely possible," Rob replied, "but the tooth just complicates everything. It ties the two murders together, with David Cramer the link to both."

The room lulled. Rob changed direction. Still believing firmly that the murders were part of something wider. He was hopeful it wasn't too much wider.

"We believe we're looking for a second party, and we're either looking for a separate murderer who also dumped the car on the rec, or Cramer was involved in the murder but his accomplice dumped the body."

"It seems most likely," Nicky agreed.

"So whoever did dump the body either didn't know Cramer's tooth was within the remains, and Cramer was involved, or that person added Cramer's tooth themselves to implicate him."

"But if it's the latter then somebody had one of David Cramer's teeth."

Laura Mathers chipped in: "I've requested dental records from my contacts in the military, and have asked the Home Office if they have any records on David Cramer losing a tooth, or teeth, during his time in the army."

"Can you tell if a tooth has been recently removed or date it?" Jack asked.

"Yes, you can. Becky has checked with a leading dentist and it's been dated to the early to mid-nineties," Rob replied.

"Which links us back to the names on the board," Jack confirmed.

Rob nodded. He looked at the board that Jack had referred to.

"Connor Byrne. We know he has a missing son, Sean, and we also know he was O'Callaghan's handler in the nineties. In theory, him and Cramer were on the same side, so there's no obvious reason why Byrne would want to harm or implicate Cramer, unless he believed that Cramer was in any way involved with Sean's disappearance."

"Which seems unlikely," Nicky added.

"Will Taylor, who also has a missing son, James. Journalist and a prominent and vocal IRA exposer. He'd have every reason to target John McGrath if he felt he was involved in James' disappearance, and he'll almost certainly have spent time with Connor Byrne, and even David Cramer, as they share the grief of having a missing or murdered child."

Rob paused.

"Taylor, Cramer and Byrne may all have motives on the Kings or McGrath, and we know Will Taylor was in the UK when Martin King was murdered."

"Could he be the link? Could he have planted the newspaper at David Cramer's to provoke him?" Jack asked. It was a smart question.

"Entirely possible," Rob confirmed.

"Should we speak to him?" Jack asked.

"We could, the issue being we have nothing to directly question him on, and no evidence to link him to Hargreaves or Martin King. He remains a clear person of interest," Rob confirmed.

"Aaron King. He's a man with a violent past, and he could be a target as much as a suspect." Rob worded it gently but still noted a raised eyebrow from Mathers. "The big question is whether he has the intelligence and functionality to plan the murders, and again there is no evidence of any recent activity from him.

"John McGrath. Known IRA loyalist, who is clearly still an angry man. He has a clear motive to target or want to implicate David Cramer, but why would he target Martin King? It doesn't make sense. Lastly, we have Michael O'Callaghan; military insider and an IRA man. He was never exposed, as far as we know, and believes that McGrath has the capability and anger to want to harm Cramer now."

"Is he checking in at the station, Rob?" Jen asked.

"Yes, he is, hasn't missed one, so I assume his solicitor convinced him to play ball.

"The conversations we had threw Frank McIntyre's name out several times too," Rob added, mostly for Laura Mathers' benefit. "I definitely think we need to speak to him."

Mathers nodded an 'okay', before asking, "How relevant do you think he is, Rob?"

"His name has been mentioned several times, so I've looked into him as best I can. Major General Francis Montgomery McIntyre, he's a retired general who served a lengthy military career and was discharged with honours, but there isn't a report that doesn't paint him as a piece of shit. A misogynistic, racist bully who ruled with an iron fist and treated recruits badly. It was an era when everybody turned a blind eye, so he may have got the job done, but it was a generation who didn't bother to ask questions over how the job was done."

Mathers nodded again.

"He sounds like a bit of an arsehole," Rob spat. Mathers raised a disapproving eye, although a lack of admonishment told Rob she agreed with him.

Rob continued: "If this was any other investigation and somebody's name came up several times, we'd go and see them."

"We would," Mathers agreed.

"Is he still alive?"

"He is. He's in Yorkshire."

Rob smiled inside. The fact Mathers knew where he was meant that she'd been digging too.

"I think it would be worth speaking to him. I think he knows something, and I think he can help."

Mathers took a breath. A glint in her eye told Rob she'd pulled something off and was pleased with herself for doing so.

"Frank McIntyre is all yours. Just so you know, he was *extremely* difficult to find. In many ways, he doesn't officially exist. National insurance number, electoral register, passport, bank accounts. He's invisible. Oh, and he doesn't exactly want to meet, so you may not get a cup of tea."

"Then why is he meeting me?"

"Let's just say the people who could afford him some protection have opted not to." Mathers was being diplomatic in front of the team.

"So he's pissed somebody off."

"Have a chat with him and see what you think," she replied, dryly.

"Will do."

She stood up and headed for the lift. Rob was feeling pleased. It was progress. It was a new source and it was likely to provide information that could help. McIntyre wasn't in any loop as far as Rob could see. Had nobody to protect, had no loyalties.

He looked at Jen, and in that moment he knew the rug he was standing on was being pulled from underneath his feet.

She looked sheepish. She looked at Rob.

"We've had a call from a member of the public. He's reported what he believes is a body in a house on Wigston Road. It's Aaron King's house."

"At least it wasn't some poor bastard walking a dog," Jack thought out loud.

"Becky has arrived at the scene," Jen confirmed. "It's a bad one."

She paused and looked at Rob, "Are you telling Mathers?"

Rob smiled wryly. "I'll call her in the car."

CHAPTER 37

Rob turned right off Welford Road, having passed the entrance to Bouskell Park, and was immediately met by the police line. An officer started to walk towards him but quickly recognised him, before giving a thumbs-up and leaving him to park. He left his car just off the junction of Welford Road and Wigston Road, where uniform had clearly been on the scene for a while. The scene already looked tightly controlled; there were multiple officers who had set a cordon and were keeping any bystanders at bay. There weren't many, although with the kink in the street, nothing at all was visible from Rob's vantage point behind the police line.

The street looked nice. Quaint. Rob was surprised. He was expecting traditional red-brick terraces, maybe a little run down and with cars parked tightly together. He scanned the street and could see the beautiful stone cottages of the adjoining Church Street, along with a narrow view of the spire atop of All Saints Church.

He was as pleasantly surprised by the area as Nicky and Jack had been when they arrived at the scene of Martin King's murder, around one hundred metres away.

The police line of blue tape was stretched between the post of a residents' car park to one side, which was being marshalled by one of the uniforms, and a lamppost separating a cottage from the Bakers Arms. The pub was old. Really old. Rob looked at it. The gable end was rendered and painted white and adorned with a handwritten 'Ye Olde Bakers Arms', along with an Everard's logo from the local brewery, and a line reading 'Dating from 1485'. Rob assumed it was the oldest pub in the county, if not one of the oldest in the country. He'd Google it later if he remembered. It was closed but he'd need to speak to the landlord at some point.

He walked up the street to the house, having suited up by his car. An officer was guarding the open front door and greeted Rob. It was dry and daylight was good, which always made life easier for the officers and forensic team who would be moving evidence, belongings and the body of Aaron King from his house.

It was modest, and Rob wondered how he'd ended up here. In a leafy end of Blaby, following a life of making bombs for the IRA.

Becky was in the hall and met Rob's eye. She smiled behind her mask and offered a "Hey!"

It was as cheery as ever. The sort of greeting you'd give if you were in the pub back down the road, and for half a second Rob forgot where he was. Then the smell invaded his airwaves and brought him quickly back down to earth. A vile and pungent smell, mixed with the metallic taste of blood and death.

"What are we looking at, Becky?"

"It's not pretty. There's a lot of blood."

"Murdered?"

"Oh, absolutely no doubt about it; shot in both knees from close range, a gunshot wound to the chest and another to his face. He's been beaten too, and there's damage to the furniture, so we'll swab his fingernails for defensive wounds."

"Thanks, Becky. When, do you think?"

"Twenty-four to forty-eight hours. I'll narrow it down when he's on my slab."

Rob nodded. "Was the gunshot to the head the cause of death?" He asked to check more than anything. Two days didn't seem long enough. The smell hitting Rob's gag reflex was telling him he'd been dead for a month.

"I suspect so, it's possible it was post mortem to disfigure him, but if he was still alive after the shots to the knee, I think the neighbours would have heard him scream. There's no sign of a gag of any sort and he wasn't restrained."

Rob nodded again and Becky rejoined her team. He wandered into the lounge behind her and took in the scene. It was a small room, and was full of forensics officers. He scanned. The broken glass, the mess and the smell. It was dark, dank and inhospitable. Jen had described the Kings' house following her visit with Jack last week. Rob had thought she must have overexaggerated the atrocious conditions in which Aaron King had lived, and died. She hadn't.

The body was sitting on the couch. Becky took a close look and one of the photographers was taking pictures alongside her. She was right. It wasn't pretty. Slumped to the left side, with his head gently resting on the back of the sofa. Posture wise, it could easily be confused for a man sleeping if it wasn't for the gaping hole where the left side of his face should be. Rob wasn't going any closer, but it looked as if a large-calibre bullet had entered somewhere near his left eye. It had obliterated his eye and cheek, although his nose still looked remarkably intact. The entry wound was large, and the blood had clotted heavily on his neck, and to the right side of his chest where another bullet had struck.

Jack appeared in the doorway and greeted Rob, telling him that Nicky was upstairs recovering evidence. Phones, laptops, documents. Anything that might help to confirm a link between suspects, a motive, or both.

Rob looked again at the mess. "Do you think he had a visitor?"

"It's possible. We'll bag everything up and swab every can and every cigarette butt."

Rob nodded, feeling sympathy for the young tech whose evening task was to swab the contents of the room.

"Have we spoken to any of the neighbours, Jack?"

"I've got uniform working on it. The pub is shut, as you'll have seen, and there's an old couple in the adjacent cottage." He gesticulated to the left with his head. "Edith and Eric Marshall. Eighty-seven and Eighty-three."

"So they didn't hear anything?"

Jack shook his head. A resounding 'no'. "The pub is closed and there's no obvious sign of CCTV on the outside, but I'll speak to the landlord later on."

"Good stuff, thanks, Jack." Rob's attention was drawn back towards the church. He took the top half of his white suit down, tied it around his waist and started to walk towards the car park. One of the uniforms lifted the tape, which Rob ducked under before heading across the car park towards the far side, weaving between randomly parked cars. There was a simple dry stone wall, but after walking fifty yards or so, the scene was clear. Rob reached the wall and leant on it with his left hand. He tapped his fingers on the cold grey stone and stood thinking. He could see the spot where Martin King's body had been found, just yards over the wall. The trees in front of Rob whistled in the wind, and their smaller branches waved and moved elegantly. Their shadows crossed Rob's face and made him squint in the light. He moved into a shadow.

The spot was marked with a single bunch of flowers, which were mostly dead and still wrapped in cellophane. Rob wondered if they were from his dad, and if not, who would harbour enough emotion to grieve for Martin King? There was no evidence of a girlfriend. The rugby club? Rob would get it checked but wasn't in the mood to climb a dry stone wall in fitted trousers and shoes, especially not as his lower half was still wrapped in a white paper forensic suit.

Had Aaron King had the time to visit his son's grave? Was he the sort to visit the scene and leave flowers? It would have been the smallest act of compassion from a man who had demonstrated very little for his entire life; his bombs and murders were often careless and totally indiscriminate.

Given all that they did know about Aaron King, what sort of a father had he been? Rob feared he knew the answer, although on limited evidence, Martin King held a job, had a group of friends and played rugby to a decent standard. It was something of a miracle given his father's life choices and shortcomings. Plus, the house. How anything had survived in that house, let alone found fitness and successfully compete was beyond Rob, who suspected he already had the smell of tobacco embedded in his clothes. He made the short walk back to the house, where activity was rife. There were already too many cooks buzzing around the small terrace.

Becky appeared at the front of the house and read Rob's body language. "You heading back to the office?"

He nodded a 'yes' and headed for his car.

CHAPTER 38

The office was vibing, and there was a huge amount of energy and intent buzzing across the room. The murder was fresh; the time was rife to work with new evidence and to push the investigation forward. And to step up the search for David Cramer.

Becky was carrying out the post-mortem of Aaron King at Leicester Royal Infirmary, just a few miles across town, but Rob had decided his team would regroup and work from Lodge House. Rethink the motives, re-evaluate those involved, and look to confirm if David Cramer was responsible for the murders of both Aaron and Martin King. That would be the cleanest result. The easiest for the team. It would leave the murder of Steve Hargreaves open, but that would be more politically palatable than news of an IRA terrorist cell committing murders across the city. The investigation was still being conducted secretively, with nothing visible through any news channels. Not even the nosiest of local reporters had a sniff, and Jen was feeding a couple of them updates on the rape trial, which was good press for the team. Nothing inflammatory, just some crumbs that for now was the biggest story being reported on locally.

Rob's team was watertight, which would reflect well on both him and Mathers.

Laura Mathers had gone quiet. Despite the murder, Rob had had nothing more than a message that said *Keep me posted, esp on Cramer*. He'd heard nothing since.

He imagined she was preparing for an internal investigation into the death of Aaron King. One that might not start for months but would look squarely at how Aaron King was murdered when he could very easily have been identified as a high-risk individual. Rob had flagged that fact to Mathers a week or two ago, and he'd-double checked his emails and backed the thread up should the shit ever hit the fan. He was hoping nobody would ever ask him, but if they did, he'd have to choose between accepting his share of the blame or effectively throwing Mathers under the bus. The politics of policing.

He remembered a time when a murderer being murdered was considered tough shit by the police, and was something the British public simply wouldn't have cared about. Now there was a faction of society who would demand to know how, and why, Aaron King had been murdered, and why the police hadn't taken appropriate steps to protect him. He was glad it wasn't his job to answer those questions, and was certain if it was that he wouldn't answer them satisfactorily.

Rob sat back in his chair, stretched his legs and adjusted his watch strap. He sent Emily a WhatsApp telling her what time he'd be with her later, and asked if she needed anything. Cans of Diet Coke, or some chocolate. His mind pondered. The Kings were dead and David Cramer was still missing.

Nicky walked into Rob's office followed by Jen, and Jack dragging a chair. It made a screeching, scraping noise on the floor, and Rob raised an eyebrow in Jack's direction.

"Becky is ongoing with Aaron King's post-mortem," Nicky stated, "but I don't think we'll get much change from it. The key piece we need is whether there is any evidence of David Cramer's presence or involvement, and we could get that at any time."

Rob gestured towards his phone, which was sitting on the desk in front of him.

"We all saw the scene, what do you think?" Rob asked, openly. Nicky jumped in first.

"I know we'll have the PM soon, but I'm not convinced it's the same person, Rob. I appreciate none of us may like that but we had a stabbing in a park, a shooting in a house and a body dumped in Leicester in a burnt-out car. It just seems too inconsistent to be one man."

Jen nodded, and Rob was with them. He'd spent the night throwing the thoughts around in his mind. Over and over. The evidence was clearly pointing to David Cramer having stabbed Martin King, but if he had murdered Aaron King and therefore had a gun, why take the risk of getting so close to a rugby player? Martin King was a big man, strong, and half David Cramer's age. Attacking him with a knife seemed so risky and could easily have gone wrong. It would have taken very little for Martin King to overpower any attacker. Maybe that explained why he was attacked from behind.

"Martin's attack was short, and the knife was skilfully placed. He was practically dead whilst he was still standing up because of how precise the attack was," Jack voiced, "whereas Aaron was beaten, incapacitated and shot in the chest and face."

He was talking himself to the same conclusion that Rob and Nicky had reached, however hard that was to accept. He was already hoping that Becky was about to prove them wrong. Wrap it up nice and tightly with a couple of David Cramer's hairs entwined neatly within Aaron King's blood, and a clean fingerprint to leave the jury in no doubt at all.

Becky's team had completed the wider forensic work from Martin King's murder and had identified traces of David Cramer's DNA on the same stone wall that Rob had leant on. Fibres of clothing which he'd shed on the granite rough surface of the stone. Martin King had bled out slowly, silently and painfully. The team now believed that Cramer may have sat on the wall and watched him die.

Rob checked his phone again. Nothing from Becky. They were trying to get ahead of things, although Cramer's manhunt was being stepped up regardless. Laura Mathers and Vanessa Ryder had agreed additional resources, and a Facebook and wider social media campaign was going to be launched. They needed to find him.

Despite the clear evidence of Cramer's guilt, the intuition of the team was telling them they were looking for another murderer.

Rob paused. He thought, then looked at Jack. "Will Taylor; find out where he is. Or more importantly, find out where he was yesterday."

"Passport wise? I can do that now." Jack headed for his desk and logged onto the database. Punching in his password, he entered it twice, having typed it incorrectly. It was too long and he needed to change it. The system blipped its approval and Jack was in.

As the tap from the keys rattled in the background, the conversation continued.

"What about O'Callaghan and McGrath?" Jen asked.

"Where are they both and are they at risk? And where does Connor Byrne fit in, if at all?"

They were good questions, and all valid points. McGrath's and O'Callaghan's whereabouts would both need checking, and the question of whether either, or both, were at risk was one Rob would take up with Laura Mathers, who would be sensitive to the issue given the murder of Aaron King.

"Connor Byrne should be in Belfast. His passport has been revoked, so he shouldn't have the means to travel," Rob replied.

"I'll double-check that he was in Belfast," Jen said. "Not having the means to travel and not travelling are two very different things."

"Absolutely."

"The newspaper," Rob pondered aloud. "It wasn't a freebie, was it?"

Jen shook her head. "It was a paid paper, so either Cramer bought it for himself and Martin King was unlucky, or somebody bought it to provoke Cramer."

"It ties in with the tooth, doesn't it?"

"I think so. It's possible that Cramer's tooth being left in Leicester and the newspaper were both just a ruse to provoke David Cramer."

Rob played devil's advocate. "But there's no proof of either, is there? It's possible Cramer bought that paper himself and his tooth somehow made its way into that car."

"I'm not comfortable with the tooth," Nicky chipped in, "it's an old tooth and it's entirely possible that Cramer had nothing to do with Steve Hargreaves' death, and why would he?"

"I think that paper was deliberately left at David Cramer's house," Jen offered.

The room lulled. The only evidence they were certain was telling them the truth was David Cramer's DNA in Bouskell Park. Nothing else was telling a reliable tale.

Jack looked up. He made eye contact with Rob and looked pensive. "Will Taylor flew into East Midlands yesterday morning, in the early hours."

The room fell silent.

"Is he still here?"

Jack nodded a 'yes'.

"Issue an arrest warrant, Jack. I want him picking up and I want him downstairs in an interview room."

"On what charge?"

"Conspiracy to murder and obstruction. He flew into the UK the day before the murder of two men he knew to be responsible for acts of terror, and he definitely has information that we need."

Jack tapped away on his keyboard, adding Will Taylor to the database of wanted men, before issuing it to the wider Leicestershire constabulary and the senior leadership and security services teams at East Midlands Airport. Will Taylor would be arrested on sight should he attempt to leave the country.

Rob exhaled loudly. A deep sigh. "There's still way too much of this that doesn't make sense."

He looked at the names that had accumulated on the board. The men whose loyalties, disloyalties and family ties entwined them as men, as suspects and as potential victims. There was a clear motive for anyone still alive to kill at least one of the others.

DAVID CRAMER
JOHN MCGRATH

MICHAEL O'CALLAGHAN

CONNOR BYRNE (SEAN BYRNE – ICLVR)

WILL TAYLOR (JAMES TAYLOR – ICLVR)

FRANK MCINTYRE?

AARON KING – deceased

MARTIN KING – deceased

STEVE HARGREAVES? – deceased

"What's the end game?" Rob asked aloud. "We've got two men who were largely responsible for killing Chris Cramer now dead, but is that the motive?"

"I don't think it can be, Rob," Nicky said. "How can that be the sole motive if the newspaper was planted at his house? And the Hargreaves link is just so tenuous that I don't believe he had anything to do with his death."

Rob nodded, agreeing with the statement. They all felt the same way. Felt somebody was trying to stitch David Cramer up. Trying to provoke him, and they were doing a good job. Nicky continued: "If that is the case, it means somebody else found Martin King first, but for some reason they didn't kill Martin King themself. Instead, they provoked David Cramer into doing it. It just seems so *risky*."

Rob nodded. Nicky was right. "We need to pick that thread up again," he asserted firmly, before writing, 'WHY NOT KILL MARTIN KING DIRECTLY?' in an open white space.

Rob checked his watch. "Let's focus on finding David Cramer and speaking to both Will Taylor and Frank McIntyre. Then we'll regroup. It's going to be a busy few days." The team were energised and ready to go. It felt like a critical point in the investigation. It was.

The phone rang across the room. The landline. Jack picked

the handset up on his desk and pressed a button. He looked up positively and thanked whoever was on the other end.

"Want some good news?" he beamed.

Rob nodded a 'yes'.

"That was Vanessa Ryder. David Cramer has just walked into King's Lynn station and is now in custody."

CHAPTER 39

Rob checked his phone for the fifth time in as many minutes. It was a Thursday morning, but in the context of the investigation, it was massive. Rob had arrived at the office early, energised after the news of David Cramer's submission in King's Lynn. It was still dawn when he'd parked up, the sky a dull mix as the black of the night began to relent into a dark blue of the early morning.

He'd spent an hour with Laura Mathers already, updating her further after an evening phone call to give her the news on Cramer. He'd updated her on Will Taylor's arrest warrant that morning, having saved that card for their face-to-face. Allowing himself to see the satisfaction in her eyes. Satisfaction that didn't make its way to her voice box. It didn't need to. Rob knew she was pleased. Relieved even. Progress had a way of doing that in an investigation, and it was a game Rob was used to playing.

She had also agreed to a plan that Rob had hatched in his mind shortly after Jack had dropped the receiver yesterday afternoon. One he hadn't shared with the team, for a number of reasons. It wasn't one hundred percent above board in the strictest sense, but he was trying to contrive a situation. To make something happen in order to gauge a response. He'd speak with Nicky as soon as she arrived. She'd need to work with him, and he already knew she'd be up for it.

He checked his phone again. Nothing. He headed for the kettle and stood next to it whilst it boiled. He considered coffee over tea before a box of Yorkshire Gold teabags hiding at the back of the cupboard made the decision an easy one. He poured the boiling water into a clean mug, allowing it to brew. His phone pinged. Jack.

Will Taylor has been arrested. ETA in Leicester one hour.

Rob clenched his fist. He went to bang it on the worktop in celebration, but he refrained. His satisfaction, and his relief, palpable. A big day had just got bigger.

*

David Cramer looked tired, but he sat upright in a robust sort of way. His pride, and the military correctness, steadfast. He was wearing a light blue shirt with the top button undone, and the sleeves rolled to just below the elbow. He looked formal. Smart. David Cramer knew how to conduct himself, but he was on the very wrong side of proceedings this morning, and he'd declined a solicitor.

Nicky and Jen sat opposite, in a grey room with a cheap wooden table and even cheaper plastic chairs. It felt institutional, more so than usual. Nicky spoke first.

"You're a hard man to find, David."

"That's because I didn't want to be found, and if I hadn't handed myself in, you'd still be looking for me."

"Then why hand yourself in?"

"I'm too old to be running, DS Green, and my life is over. Everybody I love is dead. Everything I care about is gone."

"Is that why you killed Martin King?"

"I killed Martin King because he's a particularly unpleasant human being. The desire to kill him reared its head. I wanted to kill him, and it felt good."

"Where did the anger come from, David?" Jen asked. No answer. "Did it come from the newspaper? Did seeing his face bring it all back? Did the report bring memories of Chris back?"

Cramer looked agitated at the mention of his son's name. He looked angry.

*

Rob sat opposite Will Taylor, who had been unceremoniously brought in by two uniformed officers. The cuffs had been removed but he was bustling, and confrontational. He was angry, and he looked like he could kick off at any minute. Rob smiled inside.

"Good morning, Will. Would you like a cup of tea?"

"Fuck you."

"Coffee?"

Taylor swallowed the next profanity, before spitting, "Why the fuck am I here? Have you got the faintest fucking clue what you're doing?"

"You flew into the UK the day before Martin King was murdered, and flew back the day after, and now you're in the UK at the exact same time that Aaron King was murdered." Rob leant forward and enunciated very clearly, "I don't believe in coincidences, Will."

"No? How about evidence, do you believe in that?"

He had a point and Rob knew it. "Why were you here? Why are you here?"

"I'm working."

"Define work."

"I'm a journalist, Inspector. As you well know." The annoyance in his voice was crystal clear.

Rob nodded. "And you're a journalist who hunts down and exposes terrorists. People like Martin and Aaron King."

*

"We have your DNA in Bouskell Park, David. We know you killed Martin King."

"Then charge me and stop wasting my time."

"We'll charge you with both murders, David. The Crown Prosecution Service will almost certainly allow both charges to proceed."

Cramer looked uncertain, and it looked genuine. "Both murders?"

"Yes. The murders of Martin and Aaron King."

"I didn't kill Aaron King."

"Didn't you? You found Martin King and killed him. It isn't too much of a stretch to believe that you killed Aaron too. Complete the job."

"I did not kill Aaron King," he enunciated clearly.

"Why wouldn't you? He killed your son. He built and planted the bomb that killed Chris."

Cramer looked firmly at Nicky. "I killed Martin King, and I enjoyed watching him die. But I left Aaron alive so he could suffer. I wanted him to live with the anguish, and the pain. The pain I've carried for twenty-five years. I thought about killing him, for the briefest of seconds, but then I saw him. I saw how completely worthless he is. How worthless his existence is, except for his son. I saw the love he had for his son. The pride. So I took it away from him."

*

"Which fucking side are you on, Rob? You don't think I killed either of those boys any more than I do."

"I think you know who did, and I think you know why."

Taylor shrugged. He'd fronted up to IRA thugs, corporate giants and corrupt political figures. He was hiding whatever he knew, and he wasn't about to break.

"Have you found McIntyre yet?" he asked. Rob drew breath. "Or are you not at liberty to say? You don't have to like me, but you do need to listen to what I'm telling you. You need to look at Frank McIntyre, and you need to look at what happened at Victoria Barracks."

"Is that it?"

"What do you mean, is that it? You asked me what I knew and why this is happening. I fucking told you two weeks ago and you've done fuck all with it. Do you want me to do it for you?"

*

"Where were you two nights ago around 8pm, David?"

He drew breath and spoke matter-of-factly. "I was at the Holiday Inn in Norwich. The one by the football ground."

Nicky raised an eyebrow at Jen. She didn't know how many officers had been trying to find their murder suspect over the past two weeks, but it was more than a few. He hadn't exactly been slumming it, and had possibly even been working on his breaststroke whilst he was on the run.

"We'll need to check that."

"You do that. Room 309, only it was under the name of David Foster." There was more than a hint of irony in his voice. Enjoyment. He'd been at large for more than two weeks, and he hadn't even left the county.

"Did you get into any fights in the nineties?" Jen asked.

He looked, curious. "You'll have seen some of my record, I'm guessing. It's mostly all there."

"Mostly? I wasn't talking about the military stuff, David. I was thinking scraps on barracks. Blue on blue, if you get my meaning." Cramer looked confused.

"We found a body in a burnt-out car in Leicester three weeks ago, just up the road. And we found your tooth in it. The CPA are fifty-fifty currently, but we wondered how one of your molars ended up in a car with a dead body. That's three dead men in less than a month, David, and you're the link to all three."

"I killed Martin King, I didn't kill Aaron. I know nothing about a body in a car, and I have no idea how one of my teeth ended up with it."

"Do you expect us to believe that?" Jen asked, with more than a hint of speculation.

"It's up to you what you believe."

"I believe if I lost a tooth and it wasn't to a dentist, I'd remember."

The room paused.

"And what about Frank McIntyre, do you know him?" Nicky asked. She studied his face intently. It was difficult to read.

"I know Frank. Why do you ask?"

"Do you like him?"

"Well, I haven't seen him in years, but no, not particularly."

"Why not?"

"He's a particularly unpleasant man."

"He was a senior officer, though, and he was on your side."

"Have you met him?"

Nicky shook her head.

"He may have been a British soldier, and he may have been a senior figure, but it doesn't mean he was one of the good guys. It doesn't mean he was on my side either. Don't make that mistake."

"His record looks okay. There's some accusations against his conduct in there, but he got the job done was the gist."

"Not everything gets written down, DS Green." It came out with heavy tones of cynicism. "The times were *very* different. McIntyre did many things, and he did enough good things for the hierarchy to turn a blind eye to the rest of it."

Nicky double-checked her watch and looked at Jen. She closed the interview, stood up, and headed for the door. She opened the door and glanced into the corridor.

"Am I going back to my cell, Detective?"

Jen nodded, and stood. Nicky flickered a finger and Jen tidied some paperwork.

David Cramer stood and Jen moved him slowly into the corridor, turning right and heading back towards the cells. The corridor was brighter than the interview room, and Cramer rubbed his eyes. He looked tired in the interview. He looked even more tired in the harsh light.

A second door opens and Will Taylor walks out of the room. He looks up and stops. Five yards apart. No more. Rob

253

stands behind Taylor. He watches Cramer's face like a hawk. Their eyes meet. Intensely. The corridor falls silent but there is an immediate atmosphere. A mood. Neither man moves. Neither speaks. Neither blinks.

Rob waits. Nicky and Jen wait behind Cramer. There are three cameras in the corridor. Watching.

The stare holds. Neither man moves.

Cramer looks deeply into Will Taylor's eyes and pauses, like he's looking for something. The stare holds, before he turns and walks towards his cell.

*

The day had gone okay. Nothing groundbreaking but not bad either, and David Cramer was about to be charged with murder. It was progress, and Rob was happy with it.

Jack appeared outside Rob's office and caught his eye. He looked sheepish. Rob waved him in and waited.

"We've confirmed that David Cramer was in Norwich at the same time that Becky believes Aaron King was murdered, so he couldn't have killed him."

It was disappointing, but the evidence was clear. He couldn't have killed Aaron King, but the charge of murder against Martin King was as cast iron as it got. David Cramer was going nowhere.

Jack didn't move and continued to look nervous. Rob looked at him and squinted.

"What else?"

Jack paused. Rob waited.

"John McGrath hasn't checked in at Nottingham this evening."

CHAPTER 40

Rob had spent much of the previous evening in the office. Thinking. Considering options, and considering who was responsible for the murder of Steve Hargreaves, and more importantly, why. The 'why' was still bugging him, and although the team all felt that Steve Hargreaves was something of a sacrificial lamb, it still wasn't helping their understanding of why three murders had been committed.

David Cramer had killed Martin King, but not Aaron King. On the evidence they had, he hadn't killed Steve Hargreaves either, but the evidence wasn't ruling him out. The only thing they did know was that Cramer didn't dump the body in Leicester. He couldn't have. It was messy.

Several phone calls had followed. First, to let Mathers know that McGrath had failed to check in after a good few days of compliance. Maybe he'd got bored. Maybe he'd murdered Aaron King and disappeared. But why? Was Aaron King both bomb maker and saboteur at Victoria? Had McGrath figured it out and taken him out? It was possible, and if he could provoke and frame David Cramer along the way, he'd have tied up some loose ends very nicely. For him anyway.

Mathers had taken McGrath's absence nonchalantly, although he was certain she'd be speaking to senior figures as well as the Home Office within minutes of him leaving. After Cramer's two weeks on the run and the murder of Aaron King, the last thing anyone needed was John McGrath on the loose. A fugitive, a terrorist and a loose cannon. McGrath was dangerous. They needed to find him.

Mathers asked Rob to speak to the team in Nottingham to see what they knew. To see what his behaviour was like at his last check-in.

Jack had issued an arrest warrant immediately. Failure to comply with his release licence was an offence in itself, and he would be arrested on sight. He'd need finding first, and Rob was confident that John McGrath wouldn't have the good grace of David Cramer. McGrath also had a stubborn resolve. He'd need finding.

*

Rob's night was sleepless, and the timing was poor. Cats fighting in the street had woken him up. The unmistakable screech. A sound that Rob hated, and one that went straight through him. When he'd awoken for a second time with a full bladder less than an hour later, he'd resigned himself downstairs to the sofa. Settling down with a cup of tea. Lying awake in the small hours.

Thinking.

Had McGrath killed Aaron King, and was he also trying to frame David Cramer? It was entirely possible, but there was still little evidence to support the hypothesis. How was Will Taylor involved? He was in the country for both murders.

Had he provoked one and committed the other himself? Was Michael O'Callaghan in danger? Was Michael O'Callaghan involved? Rob was praying that McGrath hadn't discovered the truth about his friend. They'd need to speak to Michael O'Callaghan. To warn him. Maybe to protect him.

Connor Byrne was a problem. How much did he know? Or was his involvement just a desperate attempt to find his son, and to find closure?

Aaron King was dead, but if he was playing both sides and caused the attack at Victoria to fail, it was possible, if not likely, that Frank McIntyre knew.

And there was Frank McIntyre himself. An enigma of a man. Respected but feared. A leader but a brutalist. The more the team had learnt of Frank McIntyre, the more he was painted in a darker light, seemingly loathed by all. Rob was hours from forming his own impressions.

Rob checked his watch. 4am. He was considering the best way to approach McIntyre, before the tiredness became overpowering.

*

Rob had showered and had two pieces of toast, slathered in butter, before dressing smartly and heading into the office. Another early start. Another long day. Another dark and chilly morning. Tea was needed.

Nicky arrived ten minutes later and gestured at the kettle. Rob held his still-steaming mug of tea up, and she replied with a thumbs-up.

"Fifteen minutes, Nicky?"

"Yep, I'll be ready."

"You okay to drive? I need to sort some emails."

"Of course."

Rob and Nicky got comfy in Nicky's VW before starting the long journey. They headed north up the M1 towards Nottingham, as Rob had done last week, before continuing the long drag towards the M18 junction near Sheffield. It was a journey Rob had made countless times as a child, on family holidays which held fond and precious memories. His dad had always headed east and crossed the magnificent Humber Bridge on the way to Scarborough, but Rob had always been asleep as a child and had repeatedly missed it. He smiled at the memory. Memories of the castle, the beach and ice creams flashed through his mind, along with a photograph of him sitting on a blue painted bench, before he snapped back into the present.

Filey was a popular destination with holiday goers and families. The beach was beautiful and the town sat proudly in the East Riding of Yorkshire. It wasn't a typical town of retirees, Rob had thought, but he could see the appeal. He just wasn't sure how Frank McIntyre would fit in, or whether he even attempted to.

It was exactly three hours before Rob and Nicky arrived, and parked on a lengthy gravel drive. The wooden gate had been left open, which felt in some way hospitable, and the wooden number on the gate had helped them confirm the address. It wouldn't have been the first time Rob and Nicky had knocked on the wrong door.

They walked up the path, the gravel crunching under their feet. Nicky knocked on the door. They both waited.

A hulking figure moved towards the door through a frosted and patterned glass pane. He didn't move freely.

He opened the door with an emotionless expression. He

was wearing dark blue cotton-style trousers with a crease down the middle, brown shoes, which were neatly tied, a shirt and tie and a cardigan over the top. Smart and respectable, if a little dated. His hair was flourishing but exclusively grey. He was clean shaven, which Rob guessed was an army habit that had never gone away. His eyebrows were equally bushy and were bordering on the absurd.

"Detective Chief Inspector Rhone?" he enquired.

"Yes…" Rob replied, and was about to introduce Nicky.

McIntyre looked her up and down. "Are you the secretary?" She hated him already.

"Detective Sergeant Nicola Green." She used her full name and spoke it firmly, in a tone she reserved for those she particularly resented. Rob raised an eyebrow. He rarely heard Nicky refer to herself as Nicola, and he already knew she wanted to punch him in the face.

McIntyre muttered his surprise and turned, gesturing for them to follow.

Nicky looked at Rob, who gestured her in first. She followed McIntyre, boring her stare into the back of his head.

"You know why we're here, Frank." It was a statement rather than a question. Nicky was short and was happy to get down to business. This was far from a social call.

"You have some dead men, DS Green. And, for some reason, you think I can help you."

"We're certain you can help," Rob stated firmly, fixing his gaze. "We have three dead men, two of whom you are aware of, and one of whom was responsible for attacks at both Thiepval and Victoria barracks."

"Well, I hope you don't think I killed them." He chuckled, almost laughing at the absurdity of the conversation.

"When was the last time you saw the men we know as Marcus and Alex Delaney?"

"I've no idea. Maybe twenty-five years ago."

"And David Cramer."

He gave that some more thought, but didn't immediately respond.

"Did you ever fight with David Cramer?" Nicky asked, watching his expression closely.

"We disagreed occasionally." It was a diplomatic response.

"I'll take that as a yes. Did you ever hit him?"

He spoke clearly and defensively. "No, I did not."

"Was it just the recruits then, Frank?" Nicky asked.

He reacted. She'd hit a nerve. "They were the times!" he responded angrily, and with a raised voice. "We don't all get to piss around in a fancy little world of niceties. You have no idea what we had to go through. I built men who survived."

Rob intervened. Nicky was here to rustle his feathers, and she was doing a good job, but they needed information.

"Victoria Barracks, Frank. How did you find out that the attack was happening, and who helped to stop it?"

"It's all in the files. I heard the day of the attack, so we deployed additional resources but kept the gates and front looking normal. We were able to swarm and attack the car when it approached the gates. It was a perfect interception, and we disarmed a device within the grounds too. It was textbook."

Nicky looked unimpressed. "Who did you hear from, Frank? Who warned you?"

He looked at her. "It was an anonymous but credible source."

She looked sceptical. She didn't believe him. "I think you know who it was, Frank."

He looked annoyed again. He looked annoyed that his authority was being questioned, let alone being questioned by a woman.

"David Cramer? Or was it Aaron King? Sorry, Marcus Delaney."

He looked confused. Rob intervened.

"You know we could do this elsewhere, don't you, Frank?" Rob flexed his muscles. Reminded McIntyre of what might happen if they didn't feel he was cooperating. He looked pissed off. Maybe he was scared. Did he feel at risk? Could he be exposed? "A name, please, Frank."

He paused. "It was Cramer." He paused again. "There were people behind him. I think Connor Byrne was one of them, but I'm not sure who found out or who their source was. I didn't ask."

"You didn't ask?" Nicky spoke the words slowly. A rationale that would have been perfectly acceptable in the late nineties. Crisis averted. Head out for a few beers and celebrate a job well done. No investigations. No summary. No learnings. Laura Mathers was still trying to source further records on the foiled attack at Victoria, but nobody was sure exactly what existed, or how helpful they'd be if they did.

"Lives were saved that day," McIntyre replied, justifying his actions. Trying to. "British lives were saved."

"And what about the other days, Frank? What about the lives that were lost at Victoria?"

He replied coldly. "It was a war. Some people died."

"You don't know, do you? Or care?" Nicky was pushing him again, and Rob was happy to let it play out. He ignored the question.

"Do you know Will Taylor?"

He looked at her. There was anger in his eyes but he spoke plainly. Calmly. "I wouldn't listen to Will Taylor. He's a fucking liar, and he's full of shit."

"Is he? His work is responsible for a number of high-profile convictions. He's lauded for his integrity."

He looked at Nicky again. It was more threatening this time. "He's a liar and I wouldn't believe a single word that comes out of his mouth."

"Are you not a fan, Frank? He exposes terrorists and those responsible for corruption. Surely you respected what he did?" His patience was wearing thin. He didn't reply. "I wonder why he doesn't like you." Her tone was unapologetically loaded with cynicism.

He composed himself. His energy was working overtime to stay in control.

"We believe there was an IRA insider at the barracks, Frank. Somebody who was trying to help the attack go ahead from inside. They'd have planned it. They were betraying you."

"We always knew there was an insider, so we were careful," came the monotonous reply. Nicky let it hang.

"Who was it? Who was the insider?" Nicky was pushing him. She picked up on something in his expression. Something in his eyes. "You know, don't you? Who was it, Frank?"

"I think we're done for today, Detectives. I'd like you to leave now."

Nicky stared at him. Her eyes full of contempt. She walked out, leaving Rob to offer any departing niceties. He met her at the car.

"What do you think?" he asked her.

"He's a rude, misogynistic old bastard. He's an arrogant, offensive man who most likely used his position to bully those entrusted in his care. He has zero compassion, and he would have given no empathy to anybody remotely vulnerable. I fucking hate him and everything he represents."

"Get off the fence, why don't you," came the dry reply. Nicky was on a rant.

"Tell me how he's any different to someone like Jimmy Savile."

Rob exhaled, the comparison catching him more than a little off guard.

"He did some good things. He ran a unit that was believed to be successful, or presented in that light. He did enough good things for those in power to turn a blind eye to anything else that happened on that site. The end justified the means. He was accountable to nobody."

Rob understood the point she had made, even if he would have made it differently. He recalled the days when six positive outcomes and one howler was considered a good ratio. When it was accepted that some people died. Prostitutes. Drug addicts. The homeless. Migrants working in sweatshops in the city.

Nicky continued: "The one problem I have with him is that he didn't strike me as somebody with an agenda. Not now anyway."

Rob nodded. That was an issue he'd had throughout. His anger, his hatred, his fight. It was all in the past. Long behind him. It didn't seem plausible that he'd found the Delaneys, or would want to. Let alone instigate their murders. And if David Cramer had averted the attack at Victoria, why would McIntyre want to frame him?

"We need to speak delicately to David Cramer again, see if we can corroborate that he was the insider."

Nicky nodded her agreement, before adding her final cynical thought: "It just worries me that he was one of the good guys."

CHAPTER 41

"So we think Cramer killed Martin King, but not Aaron King, and he couldn't have been involved with the dumping of the body on the rec." Rob opened up. He was sitting in the middle of the office with the team around him. Reaffirming their line of thought. What they knew. What they thought they knew, and what they could prove.

His shirtsleeves were rolled up and he was subconsciously spinning a board marker with his right hand. The nervous energy seeping out through his fingers.

"It doesn't mean he didn't kill the man in the car, though." Jack replied.

"It doesn't but why would he? And if he did, why did he leave one of his own teeth, and get somebody to dump the body?"

Jack shrugged. Nicky and Jen stayed quiet.

Becky walked in. She looked chipper and was wearing a red knitted jumper that looked smart. She was carrying a Starbucks paper cup with her name written on the side.

Rob greeted her warmly and exchanges were made between all in the room.

"Please tell us you have good news, Becky."

She looked apprehensive, waving her right hand as if to suggest the news was mixed.

"I can tell you that Aaron King died as a result of a gunshot wound to his chest."

Rob nodded, although the fact in itself wasn't intrinsically useful.

"We found no DNA on his body, so the perpetrator was careful, but we did find a second DNA profile in the house, and it was concentrated in the lounge. It was abundant, and we found the profile on two beer cans amongst the debris."

"So they had a drink together? He knew his killer?"

"It's a very plausible theory."

Rob perked up. "So whose is it," before adding, "it isn't Martin King's, is it?"

"No, it isn't Martin King's. There are clear traces of his DNA in the house which we'd expect after such a short period post mortem, so we have excluded those, but unfortunately the bit I can't tell you is whose DNA it is. There are no matches in the database."

"But it isn't David Cramer's?" Nicky asked. "Have we got his DNA from his arrest?"

"We have, I've been able to compare it and, no, it isn't David Cramer's DNA."

Rob was processing it. "So whose DNA do we have on file that it hasn't matched to? Who are we ruling out?"

"I can tell you that it wasn't Will Taylor and it wasn't Connor Byrne. We have both of their DNA on file."

"What's on Taylor's record, Jack?" Rob asked.

Jack was already on it. "Harassment, breaking and entering, various public order offences."

"B&E?"

"Yes, he broke into one of the corporations he was exposing for corruption. Ironic that he had to break in to uncover and prove their lawbreaking."

"Indeed. What about John McGrath?" Rob asked.

"Not on file."

"Sorry?"

"His DNA isn't on file."

"He's a convicted murderer, and a terrorist." Rob was exasperated.

Becky explained: "The Criminal Justice and Police Act 2001 made it unlawful to retain samples when an individual was acquitted or where charges were discontinued. It wasn't until 2003, under the Criminal Justice Act of 2003, that we were given the power to take and retain DNA samples, even if somebody was then released without charge or acquitted. Pretty much everything else prior to that would have been incinerated."

"So McGrath could be out there committing all sorts of crimes and we wouldn't be able to match him unless he was lawfully arrested?"

Becky nodded. Rob sighed.

"We've got an arrest warrant out following his failure to report, so as soon as we find him, we'll be able to take one and compare it," Jack confirmed.

"It doesn't look great for him, does it?" Jen asked. "He's checked in for the first four or five days and goes AWOL shortly after one of his old mates is murdered."

"We've got nothing familial we can check either, I'm afraid. No brothers, sisters or parents, either on file or living, that could help us," Becky added.

"Fine, so it's a dead end for now, and finding John McGrath is our absolute priority," Rob affirmed. Everyone in the room was already working to find McGrath, along with various external resources at the request of Laura Mathers. People Rob would never meet or see. People with resources that Rob didn't have.

Becky looked sheepish, before changing the course of the conversation.

"I've also been looking into the murder of Christopher Wilson and have been reviewing the device that was used that night."

Rob looked at Becky. He felt nervous, having no idea what he was about to learn.

"I have a basic knowledge of bomb construction, and it's easy to see why Aaron King and his friends were easily identified and implicated in Belfast. I've also spoken to an old colleague who used to work in bomb disposal, and he's taken a look at our devices."

The room sat in silence. Listening.

"Bombs are like handwriting. They're all similar. They all have similar components, but once you know who has made a bomb, you can very easily identify other devices made by that individual."

"But we know Aaron King was the bomb maker the night Chris Wilson was murdered," Rob stated.

"We do. But we acquired the bomb that failed to detonate at Victoria. It's still in evidence, so we took a look at that too."

Rob rubbed his face, still not knowing, but feeling that the headache that had been manifesting itself for the last ten minutes was about to evolve into a full-blown migraine.

Becky summarised. "It's a different bomb maker to the device that detonated in Belfast."

Rob sat back in his chair, exhaling. "Are we sure? And do we know who did make it?"

Becky nodded. "Yes, we're sure. I can only tell you who it wasn't; it wasn't Aaron King."

The room fell flat once more. "We're sending it away for further tests, but the bomb that killed Chris Wilson was made by a different person to the bomb that was planted at Victoria Barracks."

"So what does that tell us?" Jack asked.

"Both attacks were officially credited to the same terrorist cell. They are both recorded as being made by Aaron King, but I don't believe that it was. It's also unheard-of to have more than one bomb maker in a single terrorist cell."

Rob closed his eyes.

"The second bomb is *similar* to the first, but it's considerably cruder and is definitely from a different hand."

"So we've either got two terrorist cells involved or two bomb makers in play?"

"And based on what we have, there's at least one other person involved in these murders."

"At *least* one."

Rob exhaled loudly and put his hands on the back of his head. A thought crossed his mind and he opened his journal to write it down. He smiled.

"Becky!"

She stopped and looked at him.

"Do you have an evidence bag?" he asked her.

She frowned. "I do." She reached for her backpack and rummaged through the pockets, grabbing one and a pair of gloves. Rob extended his journal out to Becky.

"Can you get DNA from something that a suspect has touched?"

"Of course!" she replied, cheerily.

He pushed his journal across the desk carefully. The shiny white and green business card sitting proudly on the open page. Becky read the name.

"And he gave this to you voluntarily?"

Rob smiled.

CHAPTER 42

Two down. I'm not sure how much the first body threw them off the scent, or got them chasing ghosts, but it seems to be doing something positive so I'll take that.

I do feel bad for the homeless guy, but he was dead anyway, and it seems to have triggered events and got things moving. That was always the plan. I've spent years looking. Years searching, and I just can't find him. The one I want. It's made me bitter. It's made me angry. The time I've given to this. The nights. The travelling. It became an obsession. My mission in life. And I failed. I thought I had anyway.

So here we are. Working towards my final hurrah. There's still a lot to do, but I've got an old friend doing some hard yards with me. A shared pain and a shared goal are focusing the mind.

Killing some of the others is getting me closer to the prize. I'm neck-deep now so there's no going back. I could have stopped after the first one, I guess. There was always the possibility that this may lead to nothing, but it was always just too good an opportunity to pass up on.

Martin King put his head above the parapet, and I found

him. He showed his face and I saw my opportunity. He deserved to die one way or another anyway.

So, on reflection, it's going okay. Trees have been shook, and some autumn leaves are starting to fall. The Kings are dead, things are ramping up and some trustworthy people are asking some beautifully awkward questions. Perfect.

I need to keep provoking the right people. Keep shaking the tree. Somebody needs to fall out; then I can get to the real prize in all of this.

Time is against me.

CHAPTER 43

"I'm going for a Greggs. Anyone want anything?" Rob shouted across the office. Heads were down and Jack had a phone wedged behind his ear but gestured a 'no'. With no takers, Rob grabbed his coat and headed out onto Charles Street, a bustling thoroughfare leading from the train station into the city centre.

He had only got twenty yards from the station when he bumped into a thickset man wearing a black overcoat. Rob was sending a WhatsApp to his son, and started to apologise. He made eye contact with the man. His expression changed immediately.

Will Taylor stood firm and looked back at Rob. "I was hoping to run into you, Inspector."

The mood changed; Rob was angry. Taylor had either been watching him, waiting for him, or both.

"I could arrest you again. I should arrest you."

"What for?"

It was becoming a cantankerous exchange. Rob looked him in the eye. He wanted to hit him, but he was certain that it wouldn't be the first punch Will Taylor had taken. He also had the sort of annoying face that looked like it could take a punch.

"I was just looking for an update, Inspector. I wanted to see if you'd made any progress."

"We would if people told us what they knew."

"You would if you didn't believe what you read or were being told."

"What does that mean?"

"Victoria Barracks, Rob. It's all there. How many times do I need to tell you?"

Rob drew close to Taylor. Aggressively close. People started to look. People across the street slowed down.

"This isn't a fucking game. If you know something, you need to tell me. Stop this smoke and mirrors bollocks."

Taylor chewed his gum and remained steadfast. He waited a couple of seconds. "You've read the Victoria investigation?"

Rob nodded.

"It was botched."

"What makes you say that?"

"It was botched."

"I need more than that, Will. Can you prove it?"

Rob waited for an answer that didn't come.

"You're not helping me, Will, and you're not helping yourself."

"You don't believe that for a second. That investigation was a shitshow, and you know it."

"You don't know that. Have you not read the reports on the bombing?"

"Of course I have. Although you clearly haven't."

Rob frowned.

"You've read the report? And did you see who wrote it?"

Rob's response told Will he didn't. He immediately felt like he'd missed something, or that it wasn't there for him to have seen.

"My god, it's like pulling teeth." He paused before looking at Rob's blank face. "They haven't given you the whole thing, have they? You've got the bits they want you to see. Who wrote that report, Rob? You don't know, do you? For fuck's sake. It was McIntyre. McIntyre wrote that report. The one that paints him as the hero. The one that paints him as the man who foiled it. Well, guess what, he didn't."

"McIntyre wrote his own report? He can't have. How do you know?"

"I've got copies. I'll send you a photo of the front page. The one you haven't got. And the pages that say that the enemy was 'successfully neutralised'. He pretty much admitted what he did and he was celebrated for it. He's a murderer, Rob. He's a fucking murderer."

"Why haven't you come forward with this?"

"You told me not to! Plus, I'd have to admit how I came about it. You must have read enough about me to know that I don't worry about whether evidence is admissible or not. The court of public opinion makes its mind up about my work."

Will Taylor tapped away at his phone, and Rob's iPhone beeped in his pocket.

"How did you get my number?"

"Don't ask me that, Rob. Frank McIntyre. He can help you and he can help me. It's a mutual pursuit of the truth. I know he's corrupt as fuck and I want to take him down. He holds the key to what happened in that barracks, and it's the sole reason that's causing these murders."

"How do you know that?"

Will's tone settled. He looked Rob in the eye and paused.

"I told you, I'm not like you. The paths I tread don't need to be cut and dried. Don't need to convince a jury."

He paused again for effect.

"McIntyre knows why that plot failed, and it had absolutely nothing to do with him. More importantly, he knows who did foil it."

Rob waited. Taylor's gaze held.

"There's a body in the grounds at Victoria. There may even be more than one. If you go looking, you will find your insider. You will find the person who foiled that attack, and they paid for it with their life."

*

Rob was still angry when he walked purposefully back into the office.

"How was the sausage roll?"

Rob stood looking at the board. Thinking.

"Why is he trying to dig out Frank McIntyre?"

Nicky, Jack and Jen looked at one another. Nicky broke the staring. "Why is who still asking?"

"Will Taylor. Why is he going after McIntyre?"

Nicky looked confused. "What are you thinking? Where's this come from?"

"He's outside. He's conveniently bumped into me, and he's sent me this."

Rob waved his mobile phone. Jack and Jen picked up on the conversation and drifted into it. Rob also messaged Laura Mathers, asking her to come down. Formality should dictate that he'd go up to her, but he wanted the whole team to hear this.

He sent the images to Jack via WhatsApp and asked him to print them. Jack nipped off to grab his laptop and run them through the printer. Laura Mathers appeared. She stood with her arms folded. She looked intrigued.

"Will Taylor is still in the city. He's outside, and he just grabbed me for a quick chat."

Jack purposefully headed from the printer, giving Laura Mathers a copy of the report. The pages they hadn't yet seen. He pinned another copy on the whiteboard, with two other pages that the team already had, and drew lines connecting both Will Taylor and Frank McIntyre to the report.

"Why is he still digging? What's his angle?"

Mathers clocked the words 'Major White?' written on the board.

"Why is that up there?"

"It was mentioned within the report, a couple of times," Jack stated. "We're not sure if it's significant or whether it's an alias."

"It's a warning," Mathers replied. "Major White was an IRA codeword used in the nineties to identify a genuine bomb threat, or to identify a bomb attack. There were hoax calls made throughout the period from sick people claiming to have left bombs in towns and cities, and Major White was used so we knew that the threat was a genuine IRA call."

Jack looked shocked. "And that was agreed with the IRA? So it's not a person?"

"No, but if a bomb threat was received from Major White, we'd look to evacuate an area or respond to the threat. If a call came in without the codeword, we'd go after the caller."

"We?" Jack asked.

"I haven't always sat behind a desk, Jack," Mathers replied, dryly.

Jack continued to look shocked. He was also trying to imagine Laura Mathers as the young uniformed officer she once was. Answering calls from cranks. Chasing terrorists.

Mathers wanted to move on. "Is this true?" she asked, "Frank McIntyre wrote this report?"

"It looks that way. And even if he didn't, Will Taylor thinks he did, which means that anybody else could believe the same thing."

"So are Taylor's motives to expose McIntyre? For his corruption?" Mathers asked.

"I think so. It's the reason Taylor has still got the bit between his teeth, and he's saying that McIntyre's actions are the reason that we have three dead bodies on our hands."

Rob walked over to the board and looked at the enlarged version of the report. The one he was reading on his iPhone as he rushed back up to the office.

The threat from the isolated terrorist cell was identified, swift actions were taken and the enemy threat was successfully neutralised.

It was there in black and white, and in McIntyre's own words. Jack had also printed the front cover of the report in full A4. Its edges frayed, the white paper heavily faded to a dull brown, but clearly visible at the bottom was the regimental symbol, and his full title; Major General Francis Arthur McIntyre CB DSO.

"He has a distinguished service order? For what? Don't tell me it's this." Mathers looked annoyed. Like she was being played. She'd had no more information than she'd given to Rob and the team, but the pages before them could prove to be both the break they needed and the reason for the murders.

"'Successfully neutralised,'" Jack read out loud. "It sounds a little... threatening, to say the least."

"Will Taylor is saying this is a clear admission that whoever the insider was at Victoria, whoever was trying to make this attack happen, was identified and killed on sight."

"It's hard to read anything else into it, the language is so inflammatory."

"Would it surprise you?" Nicky asked. "You stood in front of him too. He's no shrinking violet, is he?"

Laura Mathers' brain was working overtime. "So he's a celebrated and decorated officer. A high- ranking British officer. Despite his rumoured behaviour, he has never been close to a disciplinary. There were a number of recorded complaints from junior recruits about bullying behaviour, and notorious treatment of younger recruits, which was particularly brutal around issues of slacking or failure. He was an old school bully, and he was hated. But he was a senior figure, so he was feared too."

The room nodded. Jack agreed. "He literally took the 'Last Man Standing' approach of his regiment, and if they broke, they broke. There was no care, and no thought towards physical health, mental health or welfare."

"And if an IRA insider was identified and brought before him, what do you think he would have done?" Nicky asked aloud.

"It was an eye for an eye with him, wasn't it? He saw it as a war and that reprisals and recriminations were a legitimate part of the game," Jen added.

"So if there was an insider, which we all believe there was, and they were identified and eliminated as the report says, is there likely to be a body in those grounds?" Jack asked, checking the logic of the room. They all nodded.

"That's what Taylor has just told me. At least one, he claims."

"And if there is an IRA insider buried at Victoria, and McIntyre is in play, you've got IRA men who would still be more than happy to settle the debt," Mathers added.

"McGrath," Jack said.

"McGrath," Mathers confirmed. "Any news on him?" she asked Rob.

Rob shook his head. The two would take the conversation upstairs and continue to escalate their findings and their frustrations over the still-missing John McGrath.

"Is there anything else we don't know about that barracks?" Jack asked.

"Probably," Jen added, flippantly.

A quietness emerged as the thinking continued, and as all were drawing a similar conclusion. A difficult one which would have heavy implications, and potentially political ones too.

Mathers summarised. "We *must* find John McGrath. It's critical." She looked at Rob and gestured for him to join her in her office. He stood up.

"We'll also need to look at Victoria. If there is evidence of a crime in those grounds and it's impacting our investigation, then we have a duty to investigate it."

"Ma'am."

"Rob and I will make the arrangements. Keep pushing. We're getting closer to the truth."

CHAPTER 44

It had been a brisk forty-eight hours; several hastily arranged meetings, even more phone calls and a number of online briefings with a small but elite group of people.

Rob and Jen would oversee the investigation at Victoria Barracks and would join a specialised team to search for the truth. For a body.

Laura Mathers had worked tirelessly with the Home Office to make the search possible. She had raised the issue following the emerging allegations of Frank McIntyre's impropriety, and with Rob's friends at the ICLVR. They were keen to support the investigation, and there were surprisingly few obstacles from the Northern Irish Police force, or either government. The operation was being handled discreetly, and would be low key throughout, but anybody who could have blocked the search seemed only too happy to be transparent, or to be seen to be transparent. Times had changed, and the truth was a powerful currency. If Frank McIntyre did oversee violence at Victoria, or even commit murder, then his secrets were on borrowed time. The prospect of finding the remains of an IRA figure in the grounds would have serious consequences for all parties, but that bridge would be crossed as and when the time arose.

Rob and Jen had caught an early flight from Birmingham, which they were hoping would be quiet. It wasn't. A hen party and a large number of business-like travellers had done little to quell Rob's mood, or his need for caffeine.

They were greeted at George Best by Mathers' counterpart, Chief Inspector Liam Boyle, who Rob had spoken to during the investigation with Connor Byrne. Rob recognised him across the arrivals hall, and with the business crew having rushed ahead and the hen party lagging, an air bubble allowed the three to introduce themselves face to face for the first time. Boyle was taller than Rob had expected, and was in plain clothes; blue jeans and a casual hoodie. Totally nondescript and exactly as planned. Rob and Jen were also in jeans and hoodies, and had had to rustle up a pair of steel toe cap boots each.

"Are you with the construction company?" Boyle asked Rob warmly, and with an outstretched hand. He greeted Jen too and seemed much more amiable than he'd been over Teams.

"Yes!" Jen said, as if it was a trick question. In big steel toe boots and in her own grey hoodie, Jen had joked that she felt like a builder to Rob, who had a hi-vis vest tied to the handle on his rucksack. She'd told Rob he looked like a builder, which earned her a stern look back.

The three wandered outside and across to the car park. Rob and Jen followed as Boyle approached a large grey Mercedes Sprinter van. The big model with three seats in the cab. Rob looked at Jen, who smiled back at him. The journey was short, only a few miles. Boyle gave Rob and Jen an outline of what to expect, which was a reiteration of the Teams call from last night, but useful nonetheless. Several contacts from the ILCVR were already on site, and were in addition to a team of six men and women who would be conducting the search.

It had occurred to both that for the team at the ILCVR, this was their job. To look for bodies. For skeletons. For remains. It had also occurred to them that this might not be the first time for Liam Boyle.

Boyle parked the van on the edge of the site, just short of the entrance to Victoria Barracks, and near to a couple of cars. The three got out of the van, feeling the nip in the early-morning air. The sky was sullen and grey. It suited the occasion, and Rob's hoodie was doing little to take the edge off the breeze.

Rob could see three vans within the site. About one hundred yards in and to the left-hand side. Against a wall. He stood and looked at the abandoned entrance. A curved wall on either side with the shadow of the letters that were once fixed to it. 'Welcome to Victoria Barracks'.

A large steel fence rose above it. Eight feet or more, but it had become rusty in places, and the razor wire that adorned the top had become limp. It was loose, and was tapping against the steel fence beneath it. It was the only sound. The site was desolate.

A steel frame hung over the top of the gates and was in serious disrepair. It looked like it could fall at any minute. Rob stood and looked again. It reminded him of Auschwitz. There was a horrible feel to the site. Even now. Despite the rust. Despite the abandonment.

A shiver went through him and he pulled his top up further towards his chin. They walked through the gates and headed towards a building. It was the dominant building, with the rest a mix of concrete-walled structures, temporary outbuildings and some that were now completely gone, with just a concrete floor slab remaining. The whole site had various walls, fences and a mix of buildings surrounded by more walls and fences. It was ramshackle.

Rob had an old map of the site and a hand-drawn scrawl that Connor Byrne had been able to depict. Between the team, they had narrowed the search down to around four acres, with the initial focus on an imposing-looking building that all believed was part of the main officers' block. It was made of dark stone and with the old sash windows still in place. The timber was heavily rotten, and most of the glass panes were broken.

Rob peered in. There was a large room which was empty and had some weeds growing through the floor. Rob and Jen checked a map. This could well have been McIntyre's office. Rob could imagine the fear young recruits would have standing in the room. In front of him.

Jen nudged Rob's arm and pointed at the wall to the left-hand side. It was dirty but still had a green felt notice board with a hardwood frame. Any remnants of paper had gone, but a couple of drawing pins were sticking out, and to the top the words '*Esse ultimum hominis stantis*' were visible. Jen voiced it to Rob – "Be the last man standing."

Two women and a young man came over to Rob. They introduced themselves and exchanged some small talk. Their hi-vis vests bore the name of a construction company that either didn't exist or was a front. There was nobody about to fool. It was quiet. Belfast city centre was only a few miles west, but the morning was still. Silent. Almost haunting. Rob was hoping it was about to give up any secrets it was keeping.

The team were already scanning the site. A small area that had been identified as the initial search area, with two further areas having been agreed, should the search need expanding. There was a walled garden on the team's plans, which would have formed a private area for either McIntyre or any other senior officers to enjoy some outside space. The wall surrounding it was tall, and with a solid wooden gate that was still in place. It was almost an ideal place to bury a body.

Rob tucked his hands deeper into his pockets. He had considered what failure could mean. What might happen next if the search was unsuccessful. Jen clocked Rob's silence and looked at him. "We're following a lead, Rob, they're not always right."

Rob smiled, although his concern was a lot deeper than he wanted to let on. He knew this could prove fruitless. An expensive field trip to an abandoned barracks on the word of some resentful men and an angry journalist. He'd gone on less before, although not all investigations were being watched by the Home Office and two governments.

The equipment looked impressive. An organised and linear search using what looked like a walking frame with some spikes on the bottom. Electric signals being sent down below ground, a beep. Walk forward a metre or so and repeat.

Boyle pointed out to Rob that aerial photographs were also being collected by a topographist. The sort he'd seen on *Time Team* to identify soil displacement on medieval sites. There was also a soil expert within the team. Rob felt in safe hands.

Rob checked his watch and was prepared for a long day ahead.

CHAPTER 45

With the work eight or nine hours underway, and with limited shelter from a cross wind that was building in strength, Jen took a call from Nicky back in Leicester and headed towards the corner of the building. She tucked the phone underneath the collar of her hoodie, and of a coat she had borrowed from Liam Boyle.

Rob had followed suit, taking a call from Laura Mathers, who was asking for an update. Asking for progress.

Jen listened hard to Nicky, the wind whistling around her ears. "Becky has confirmed that the bomb at Victoria was definitely made by another bomb maker. It was extremely crude and might not have detonated if it hadn't been discovered."

"It doesn't sound like an IRA device, does it?" Jen shouted back. Rob looked at her.

"No, it doesn't. Their bombs were almost always effective, and I hate to compliment Aaron King on his craft, but he was a reputable bomb maker, if there is such a thing."

"So it's definitely a second bomb maker. Any suspects?"

"Given the crudeness, it could be any of them. Becky is

certain somebody has tried to replicate King's work but has failed spectacularly."

"A copycat; trying to bomb the site and blame the IRA cell? Blame Aaron King."

"It's possible."

"McGrath?"

*

"Any news on McGrath?" Rob asked Mathers, conscious of his volume, although aware that there was nobody else within a mile, other than those entrusted by him, and the senior figures representing their respective governments.

"There are a lot of people trying to trace him, Rob."

"Well, can you ask them to do it a bit quicker!"

"They're trying! He's not an easy man to find. He knows how to disappear."

Rob sighed, frustrated at the lack of progress. The collective police force had taken two weeks to find David Cramer, who had spent it relaxing in a hotel. Now their ability to find John McGrath was also being questioned.

"The good news is that Becky has confirmed that the DNA we found in Aaron King's house is that of John McGrath, so he was there the night that King was murdered."

"They had a drink together?"

"It looks that way. The DNA was on several of the beer cans and on a couple of the cigarette butts too."

"So they had a catch-up and then something happened, or something was said?"

"Entirely possible. Maybe John McGrath made the bomb at Victoria."

Mathers explained the details that Jen had just learnt from Nicky. Details the team had suspected, which were now known.

"We really need to find him so we can ask him," Rob stated, firmly.

"We do. The other thing you need to know is that Frank McIntyre left Victoria Barracks within two weeks of the failed attack," Mathers confirmed.

"He left the barracks two weeks later? That's quick, isn't it? What reason was given?"

"No reason given, he was shipped out. It looks like he was retired immediately, and he's pretty much been invisible since."

"Until last week."

"Yes."

"McIntyre risked a lot to foil an attack, didn't he?" Rob asked. "The IRA must have known, or at least suspected, it was him. Is that why he left?"

"It could be. The sources who were only too happy to tell us where to find him have gone remarkably quiet now on why he was moved on so quickly. It stinks, so we're pressing hard."

"What have they got to hide? Are they selling him down the river?"

"They allowed him to write his own report, paint himself as the hero and then helped him to disappear."

"So McIntyre officially foiled the attack, although the only version of that being the truth was written by him. He was the commander of that site. Why are we believing him?"

"I don't think we should. If he didn't foil the attack, there could be more to it than him claiming the glory."

"It could also make him a target for McGrath, couldn't it? If McGrath had to make that bomb and for whatever reason has just killed his old mate Aaron King, he could also have reason to want to kill McIntyre."

"If McIntyre did take a call from Cramer, and if he was the contact for Cramer's men, is there not a record of that from either Cramer or Connor Byrne?"

"There are no records at all, all gone. Lost or destroyed, we'll never know which."

"Have you spoken to Cramer again?"

"Yes, we have, and he hasn't spoken well of McIntyre. Not well at all. It doesn't make sense."

"Just because they were both British Army, it doesn't mean they had to get on. They both had a job to do."

"Was he a double agent?"

"Who?"

"Cramer. Or Connor Byrne. Is it possible that Michael O'Callaghan wasn't the only one playing both sides?"

"It's possible. Cramer was a celebrated officer, Rob. I think we need to tread very carefully."

"And Connor Byrne?"

"More possible, but he's been under watch and hasn't left Belfast in the last two weeks."

"And we're certain of that?"

"Certain."

Rob's attention was distracted by Liam Boyle walking towards him. Rob lowered his phone.

"Rob, we think we may have found something."

CHAPTER 46

Rob and Jen had a short exchange. Information they had both just learnt from Nicky and Laura Mathers respectively. They walked back towards the building. Temporary lighting had been set up as dusk started to settle. The temperature hadn't changed all day, and Rob jammed his cold hands deep into his pockets. Searching for refuge from the cold. Searching for warmth, but failing.

He felt his stomach rumble. Food had been sparse, and tea and coffee had been limited to a large tea urn in the back of one of the welfare vehicles, and a solitary Starbucks run from one of the crew.

The lights shone brightly as Rob and Jen walked through a gap in the wall and stood in front of the small team, who looked back. Liam Boyle ushered the two of them towards a small screen covered by a hood. Shielding it from the wind. Jen looked closely; Rob looked over her shoulder. It looked like an X-ray, with several black and white features showing on the screen. Jen couldn't make out what she was looking at. Rob squinted. Neither spoke.

Liam used his finger and ran it down the left-hand side and against a thick white line that looked solid.

"Is that a wall?" Rob asked.

"Yes, it is," Boyle replied, "it's this wall." He gestured to the stone wall behind Jen. He returned his attention to the screen. "And this," he pointed, "we think may be a tibia and a fibula. You see the gap between them?"

Rob couldn't, but had every faith in the men and women who had reached the conclusion that a leg lay beneath them. The team were already retrieving shovels from a van, and one of the women from the ICLVR was taking a significant amount of photography. The clicks and flashes were frequent, and bright.

Rob reached for his phone and realised the ends of his fingers were numb. He turned and realised how close he was to Frank McIntyre's office, and wondered how close he might be to his secrets.

*

The actual digging was relatively straightforward, although Rob and Jen didn't strike a blow between them. A small trench soon emerged and the team congregated around it. The lights were brought over and concentrated in a small area. Rob checked his watch. 10pm.

"Find!"

A man in a blue suit stepped back and was handed a small brush. He gently cleared away some more soil as Rob and Jen craned to get a view of what was in the ground. It reminded Rob of the King Richard III dig. The first trench. Not even that far below the surface. A body. His body. The last Plantagenet king.

The man moved an object in the ground with a gloved hand and then pulled at something. He pulled firmly but gently, before stepping back slightly. He was handed a torch and he shone it. Boyle looked in and made room for Rob and Jen.

He prodded again at the fabric before him but was unable to move it. He turned and asked for something. Rob thought he heard 'knife' but then decided he'd misheard, before a grey steel Stanley knife was produced and passed down to the man.

He made a gentle incision in what looked to be a smooth but tough surface, before gently peeling it open. Nothing still, just another textured surface which immediately looked like an old rug. It's surface thick and knitted with red strains of colour within a pattern.

The gloved man skilfully peeled the fabric back. Woven thick at the edges, and clearly a rug, he opened it like an envelope. Peeling the surface away.

He paused. Rob and Jen looked.

It was unmistakable.

The cover and the rug lay open like a chrysalis. Within the small opening lay a face. A body. The face was totally exposed along with a small part of the upper torso. The body lay at peace, looking up from the grave. Barely two feet down. Defenceless. Vulnerable.

A quiet moment fell over the site as the process stopped and the quiet moment of paying respects began. The first piece of respect shown to this body in years. Decades. The last act having been to dump it thoughtlessly and pitifully in a hole in the ground.

Jen bowed her head. Rob stood quietly.

The team moved in and the photographer got close and continued with her extensive photography. This was now a crime scene.

Jen stepped closer. She wasn't in coveralls so was thoughtful of her proximity, but she'd spotted something and wanted to confirm it with her own eyes. Liam Boyle stood by her and saw her expression.

"Is that hair?" she asked him.

"It looks that way to me."

"Teeth are clearly visible too."

The man digging looked up at Jen and Rob. "The body has been well wrapped in what looks like a heavy duty polythene. It's remarkably well preserved. I'll consult with an expert but it visually looks like the body has mummified, or part mummified, possibly due to a lack of air reaching it."

Jen nodded, before looking back at the skull. There was a hole just above the temple and slightly to one side.

"Gunshot wound?" she asked. It wasn't really a question.

"No doubt about it," came the response.

Rob looked at Jen.

"I'll call Mathers."

CHAPTER 47

The mood in Leicester was buoyant but respectful. Most investigations ebbed and flowed, and developments were generally a positive thing. Finding a body was a development, but for now the identity of the victim remained unknown. The task of identification fell to the ICLVR and the excavation team. Mathers had agreed with both that Becky would travel to Belfast to oversee the work and support the site team. She wanted the work to be as independent and as transparent as possible, and relationships so far had been remarkably clear. Mathers was hopeful that the identity of the body wasn't about to muddy those waters.

She sat with Nicky and Jack in Rob's office. She was in full dress uniform and looked her usual smart and formal self. Black pencil skirt. White blouse with the pips she had earned proudly adorning her shoulders. Mathers was usually health-conscious but had ordered a Domino's for the small team. It had duly arrived courtesy of one of the many two-wheeled couriers, and was sitting on the desk, cardboard lids wide open and the smell of pepperoni wafting across the desks.

"We have a body. The compelling fact is the location."

Mathers referenced several maps and drawings that showed the location of the body in the area that was believed to be the office of Frank McIntyre. "It's pretty damning. The body is in an area of the barracks that he was entirely responsible for, and access to that area was extremely limited. He needs to be brought into custody immediately." It was matter-of-fact. She looked at Jack.

"I've issued his arrest warrant and West Yorks are doing the honours. I spoke with the DCI whose name you gave to me, and he told me it would be handled."

It earned him a "Well done, Jack," for his efforts.

With the discovery of the body, Mathers was keen to go through the interviews and paperwork. To check who told them what, and when. She knew that the body may prove to be a definitive motive, should it prove to be the son of either Will Taylor or Connor Byrne, but with Connor Byrne having been in Belfast for both of the King murders, and with John McGrath's DNA all over Aaron King's house, there was still complexity that would need unravelling.

There was also the unpopular prospect that the body was neither of the two young men listed with the ICLVR.

"What aren't we seeing?" Laura Mathers asked, rhetorically. She was reading through an interview with Connor Byrne whilst guiding the pointy end of a pizza slice into her mouth. She read the excerpt through:

"Connor Byrne (CB) David Cramer helped to avert the attack. O'Callaghan did to.

Rob Rhone (RR) What did Frank McIntyre do?

CB: He sought retribution. And he got it.

RR: An IRA insider at Victoria?

CB: No. Quite the opposite in fact."

Mathers looked confused. "What do you think he meant by that? Quite the opposite."

"Maybe he meant that the IRA man wasn't based at Victoria, or maybe there wasn't an insider at all."

"Will Taylor is convinced that whoever it was helped to avert the attack." Rob added.

"Do you think somebody had bad intentions and came good?" Jack asked.

"I don't know, Taylor speaks of the insider as a hero though. Of somebody who did the right thing."

Mathers pondered. "I think Frank McIntyre has an awful lot to answer for."

Nicky muttered something derogatory, which Mathers chose to ignore. She continued to read.

"*CB: You need to search the site. You'll find the answer in the ground.*

RR: Can you prove any of this?

CB: If I could have done, none of this would be happening. I've been silenced. It's in the past and those in power don't want to acknowledge that mistakes were made, and they let it happen. If you want to solve your case, you need to go to Victoria. You're looking for a body. The body of somebody who did the right thing."

She exhaled. Jack gestured at a pizza box and Nicky slid it across to him. He picked up a large slice and folded it in half, before tipping his head back and taking a bite.

Mathers found another interview with Byrne. This one in reference to the night that Chris Wilson was murdered. The night a bomb claimed his life.

"*CB: That night he called me, he knew it was going down. I tried to get a message to David but it was delayed. It was a night of protests and localised violence. We had old Nokias to keep it simple. There were no smartphones and 4G. No WhatsApp or group chat. We knew it could blow his [O'Callaghan's] cover, but we'd got sight of a number of planned attacks through that cell, and we decided it was worth saving Chris Wilson's life. We could take down the cell and thwart the attacks we knew about.*

RR: But that didn't happen?

CB: No, it didn't. We couldn't get through to him so I spoke to McIntyre. Told him we'd had information about a device. It was a dangerous game of cat and mouse, but it was that or nothing. O'Callaghan did his utmost to save Chris Wilson's life, he was one of us. It was him who managed to get word to us at Victoria Barracks and avert the attack there. Countless lives were saved that night, and it was all down to Michael."

Mathers grabbed a bottle of Diet Coke and poured some into a cup on the desk. Her brain was ticking.

She was searching for the interview with Will Taylor, but she knew the content. She knew what it said.

"Connor Byrne and Will Taylor both *knew* that there was a body at Victoria. They didn't *think* there was a body there, they *knew*."

Nicky grabbed a cheesy dough ball that she'd found in a smaller box, one with a small pot of dip built into the lid. She peeled it back. Garlic butter. "Cramer didn't know, or didn't seem to know. He told us to look at McIntyre, told us to investigate him and painted him as the complete dick that he is."

Mathers ignored Nicky's choice of words once again.

"It isn't his son, though, is it? Cramer's son died and was laid to rest," Jack added, stating the obvious and checking the mood.

"No, but it means that Taylor and Byrne are either in the

same circle or fishing in the same circle. We have no evidence of those two ever formally working together, or any links between them, do we?" Mathers asked.

"Nothing formal," Jack confirmed.

"Yet they both *knew.*"

"Are we ignoring McGrath?" Jack asked. "It seems unlikely that either Taylor or Byrne are in McGrath's circle."

"Agreed. McGrath is still a high priority. He has a clear motive. His DNA was in Aaron King's house on the day he was murdered, and he has a strong motive to kill David Cramer and Michael O'Callaghan should his secret ever be uncovered. He has motive to kill Frank McIntyre too."

Mathers ran her fingers through her hair. She'd taken it out of her usual formal bun. It was long and straight, and it surprised Nicky how long it was. Nicky thought she looked nice. She hadn't thought that before, and realised she'd never seen Mathers out of formal attire. She couldn't picture her in comfy jeans and a hoodie, and then craved her own.

"Why would Cramer be digging all this back up now? What did he have to gain other than to find and kill Aaron and Martin King? All he has is vengeance."

"Is that not enough?"

"I'll tell you what bothers me," Nicky declared, boldly, and with the mood in the room becoming more informal. "If that body is an IRA insider, why would Byrne and Taylor be fighting for 'justice'? They're holding this insider up as a hero. Somebody who defied the attack, not somebody behind it."

"It could be one of their sons, though, Nic," Jack replied, playing devil's advocate.

"But what if it isn't, and what if it isn't an IRA insider either?" Nicky asked nobody in particular.

Mathers looked intrigued. "What do you mean, Nicky?"

"What if McIntyre was the insider and needed to silence somebody who worked him out?"

"The '*opposite*'," Mathers voiced, checking how plausible it sounded out loud. She looked at Nicky. "We really need to identify that body."

CHAPTER 48

Becky had taken an early flight and was travelling light. Travelling anywhere could be tricky as a pathologist, even with the clearance she was afforded by the Home Office, but there was always a nervousness about travelling anywhere with a steel case containing an array of tools. Scalpels and rib splitters never looked good on a scanner, and even with Becky's journey being registered with the authorities, an eye was usually raised by one of the lower paid security team on the front line.

Becky's flight was good, with the Flybe plane starting its descent into George Best before she'd had the chance to order a second latte. A croissant from Pret a Manger had filled a hole before she boarded, and she had some protein bars for what was likely to be a long day.

As she left departures, she felt a cold breeze skim across the airfield. She felt a chill on the back of her neck and was glad that she had opted for a thick knitted red jumper with a black and grey check scarf. She pulled the scarf tighter as she spotted her lift, hoisting her backpack up onto her shoulder and gripping her Samsonite case firmly as she walked.

Becky took in the fringes of Belfast as the car poignantly drove past the innocuous junction leading to Victoria Barracks, where the body had been found less than twenty-four hours ago.

The car moved slowly towards the city centre and past a large institutional building that looked like a prison. Turrets on either end, steep red-brick walls and razor wire covering the length of every peak. Becky asked the question and was told it was a local police station, and needed to be so heavily fortified because of its location to both the Protestant north and the Catholic west of Belfast. It was an area of heavy and violent conflict, and was often a flashpoint in any political tension.

She looked across the road to see a local builders' merchants; JP Corry. The stark contrast of modern-day Belfast was visible in a beautiful landscaping display she'd be happy to have in her own garden, which was sitting directly opposite a police station that looked like it was ready for war. Barbed wire and gun towers at both ends were a reminder of the fragility of the city. Becky eyed a sandstone patio with a raised sleeper bed and decided she'd invest in her own garden in the summer.

The car pulled into Belfast City Hospital, to the south-west. An obscure-looking hospital with a tall concrete chimney to the left-hand side of a stumpy tower block, knitted to a more modern-looking wing of glass and coloured panels. The remains had been brought here several hours earlier under guard, and Becky swiftly found herself within the mortuary, shaking hands and being brought up to speed. The remains had been transferred to a steel gurney, and Becky's arrival was timely. She changed and was ready to go within fifteen minutes, joining one of Ireland's leading pathologists; Eve Strickland, with the ICLVR lead watching on intently.

The body was barely visible amongst the tangle of plastic and fabric. The team had already taken samples of the materials that had held the body for a significant period of time. Both the fabric, which was believed to be a rug, and the heavy duty plastic, which had wrapped the body.

Becky and Eve started to peel back the two heavy duty layers, with Becky feeling the thickness of the plastic for the first time. She was surprised at the feeling and offered her immediate opinion that it was a damp proof membrane, the type used in construction beneath concrete and to provide an effective damp proof course on construction sites.

"It might be worth speaking to the guys at JP Corry. They'll likely have some in stock."

Eve and the dig team had agreed with Becky's view, but Eve seemed surprised at Becky's expertise.

"I spent some time in construction early in my career, plus I had an extension done at one of my old houses. We had to upgrade our DPM. There are two gauges; a 1000 gauge and a 1200 gauge."

Eve nodded, impressed at Becky's knowledge. The two continued to work well in tandem, gently cutting away the material around the body, exposing the full head and upper torso for the first time.

"It's ridiculously well preserved," Becky remarked.

She took in the features of the face. The contours of the body. Eve and the ICLVR had already taken samples and were working hard to process the likely age of the victim, as well as the identity. With the body in this condition, they needed to rule out that the murder had been committed recently. With the site in disrepair and with a state of insecurity, it wouldn't have been difficult to access the site, and it was entirely possible that the victim had been killed since the barracks closed, or even the wrong side of the millennium.

"We should have initial DNA results within the hour," Eve confirmed, "for the identity at least. The ageing process won't take much longer."

The body was extraordinary. Becky had never seen anything like it. She was mesmerised by the appearance, and by the smell. The smell of death was present, and had seemingly been wrapped up and preserved along with the body.

There was limited decay and, even with the testing results outstanding, all felt that the remains had been in the ground for a significant period of time. The rug and the DPM had done much more than carry the victim to their final resting place.

Eve studied a square of plastic that had been removed. "You're right, this is such heavy duty plastic. It looks impregnable, and has protected the body from the earth."

Becky was still studying the body, and the face, of the victim. Hair was visible as Rob and Jen had noted following the excavation, and a full set of teeth was also visible. The face was unique; it seemed to have an expression. The flesh around the face had mummified and was visible. A dull yellow that gave a terrified look, reflective of somebody who had been shot in the head. Becky got closer still and looked at the gunshot wound. It had an odd shape. It was clearly a wound caused by a bullet, but it was more irregular than anything Becky had seen from a standard firearm.

"It's fascinating, isn't it?" Eve remarked. "One of the team has already taken extensive photography and is looking at the shape and pattern of the wound. He thinks he can identify the weapon."

Becky nodded and the work continued. Hours passed. Samples were taken. Eve's team appeared and disappeared from the mortuary, and results started to come in from the early work. Eve had flagged Becky's attention as she reached the abdomen. Becky nodded and the two worked hard to establish everything they'd both need to identify the victim, but as more of the body was revealed, more secrets began to reveal themselves.

*

Twelve hours passed in a heartbeat, and with Becky taking a break from proceedings, she messaged Rob, asking if he was available. She jumped on a Teams call from a conference room, and was happy to see the friendly faces of Rob, Nicky, Jen, Jack and Laura Mathers. All were hard at work in Leicester, and all were keen to get an update from Becky. She smiled, taking a sip from a can of Coke. Mathers got straight down to business.

"Have we matched any DNA, Becky?"

"Unfortunately not. And that's against the national database and against the family- held database used by the ICLVR, so it isn't one of the Disappeared as far as they are concerned."

"Does that mean it isn't the son of either Will Taylor or Connor Byrne?"

"Exactly that. For the benefit of all of us, both men will be notified of the find and of the DNA comparison, which is in line with the ICLVR's internal policies."

"Taylor's going to know we've been digging," Mathers remarked, cynically.

Jack had spent the day working hard, processing and cross-referencing old documentation. He was keen to give Becky some positive news.

"Frank McIntyre had some building work done on his offices at Victoria around the time of the attack. There was a small extension to a wing which housed his office."

"Great work, Jack! That's such good news. We haven't aged the material itself yet, but we can. He's in a world of shit, isn't he!" Becky remarked.

It was an outburst but the relief across the team was palpable. The recovery of the body was significant, and although it wasn't a blood relative of Will Taylor or Connor Byrne, it was clearly significant to the case.

"We believe the deceased was around twenty-five to thirty-five years of age at the time of death, and there is damage to the skull, which was caused by a single gunshot to the front temple. One of the team thinks he can identify the gun. There's a lot going on here."

Becky ran her hand through her hair. She looked energised yet tired. She had enjoyed the day thoroughly, including her time spent with Eve, as well as the unique nature of what lay in a room back down the corridor.

"Have we identified him yet?" Nicky asked.

"Her."

"Sorry?"

"Identify *her*. And not yet but we're still working hard on her identity."

"It's a woman?"

"Yes, it's a woman. And you need to know that she was pregnant at the time of her murder."

CHAPTER 49

Rob and Nicky had spent an hour or more in Rob's office with Laura Mathers. Deep and critical conversations ahead of another busy day.

Rob had the relatively simple task of an online interview with Connor Byrne. Byrne would be under caution, and would once again be accompanied by Liam Boyle, who Rob had found to be a warm and credible character.

Nicky had the more pressing task of interviewing a tired and almost certainly aggravated Frank McIntyre. He'd been transported overnight and would be woken as early this morning, as procedure allowed. The days of interviewing somebody after three hours' sleep were long gone, but Nicky wanted him off guard. She wanted to push his buttons. It was also likely that any sleep he had got was low quality, but the box would have been ticked and McIntyre would be fair game. A two-inch rubber mattress was unlikely to do much for the posture of a man drawing a pension, but Nicky's mood was anything but sympathetic.

With Rob's time approaching, Nicky left Rob and Laura Mathers in his office and headed downstairs with a sly grin on her face.

"Have you heard from Becky?" Mathers asked.

"Nothing critical, just a few updates, but there's a lot to process," Rob replied.

"How do you think Byrne will go?"

"I'm not sure. I think he's hiding something still, I'm just not sure what."

"He made several requests to search that site, and all turned down either due to a lack of credible evidence, or with the court ruling that it wasn't in the public interest to pursue it."

"He knew something was there, same as Taylor."

"How many times did he try to access the site?"

"Three."

"He was persistent."

"Do you think it was easier to not investigate what was there?" Rob asked. It wasn't the sort of question he usually asked of Laura Mathers, but the frustration and the ignorance of the past was something Rob was struggling to comprehend.

"I think that if Connor Byrne and Will Taylor knew something was there, they weren't alone," came the diplomatic reply. "You've done a good job with the ILCVR too, Rob. They've been complimentary about our operation, which reflects well on us all."

"Did they not have any suspicions of impropriety at Victoria?" came another brave question.

"Their official line was that they couldn't be supportive at the time as there was no evidence that any of the final victims recognised as the Disappeared could be at Victoria. In their view, it was a police matter."

As the conversation lulled, the screen kicked in and a cheery-looking Liam Boyle appeared, wishing Rob a good morning. Laura Mathers made her excuses, and Connor

Byrne was reminded that he was under caution. He looked relaxed.

"Who did you think was at Victoria, Connor? Your son? Will's son?" Rob asked a blunt opening question, but he asked it compassionately. He was eager to explore what Connor Byrne knew and, more importantly, what he knew and was yet to disclose.

"No," he said reticently, "I didn't think you'd find my son." He looked calm but there was emotion in his voice.

"We've searched the site, Connor. You know we have. You wanted to, and we have. Tell me what you know. It may save us a lot of time."

Byrne took a sip from a plastic vending machine cup of water. He took his time. Rob noticed a gentle tremor in his right hand. If it was nerves, what, or who, was he nervous about?

"Frank McIntyre wasn't a hero," he offered quietly, "quite the opposite, in fact. I tried so hard to nail that bastard. So hard. They wouldn't listen. They didn't listen." He looked squarely at the screen. He looked strained. Emotion. Anger. Pain.

"It didn't suit the narrative. Their narrative. It was easier to let him retire. Move on, Enjoy his life. But she didn't. She was dispensable. She served her purpose and it was easier to turn a blind eye."

Rob couldn't see a tear in Connor Byrne's eye, but he suspected that one was there. His voice had the same tremor as his hand, but he felt that Connor Byrne was in a chatting mood and was ready to share what he knew.

"But you wouldn't, would you?"

"Why should I! He murdered a defenceless young woman and was allowed to get away with it."

The anger was there. In his words. In his body language. Connor Byrne had tried to stand up for a murder victim. Had tried to investigate a site where he believed a murder had been committed. He was ostracised, demoted and ridiculed. He was denied the right to search for the truth, which in turn had denied a family the right to know what had happened to their daughter, mother or sister.

There was a tension, and Rob met Boyle's eye. He gave Byrne a minute to compose himself and noticed the half-smile thank you from Boyle.

"So who was she, Connor?" came another compassionate question. "Was she one of McGrath's stooges, or what was her link to the IRA?"

Byrne looked confused, his face contorted.

"What? No, you misunderstand. She was one of us. She found the bomb at Victoria three days before we averted the attack. She told Cramer there was a bomb on the site. He told me and we mobilised the response."

"What am I missing, Connor?"

"We got eyes on it. It was poorly constructed, she knew that. She knew what she was looking for and she told us it was duff. We deemed that the risk was low so we sat back and kept watch. The only person that went to that device in the days before the attack was McIntyre. Frank McIntyre built that bomb, and when he realised it had been rumbled, he murdered the one person he knew must have spilled the beans. She paid for it with her life."

Rob was astonished at the claim. His brain was racing. Was it true? Could he prove it? Did others think McIntyre was playing both sides? The implications were massive. He paused, before responding with a rational question.

"Do you have any evidence that Frank McIntyre built that bomb, Connor?"

"I did have. It was taken away from me, and I'm certain it disappeared when Frank McIntyre did. It was like he didn't exist. Like nobody wanted to acknowledge what he'd done. He's a murderer. He's a liar, and he's a traitor. He tried to attack his own barracks with John McGrath, and he fucked it up."

A silence hung across the room. McGrath and McIntyre. An IRA henchman and a British general. It was a scandalous accusation, but in Rob's mind it already had some sense to it.

"I had the bomb, and there was evidence that McIntyre built it. Prints, sweat, the usual stuff. They took it away and I haven't seen it since. But if it still exists, you might be able to get evidence from it. Believe me, don't believe me, but I'm telling you that Frank McIntyre built that device. They couldn't get one of Aaron King's devices in, so McIntyre replicated it under McGrath and King's instructions."

Rob sat back. Liam Boyle nodded his head gently. The time on the Teams meeting had barely ticked past fifteen minutes, but Connor Byrne had blown the investigation wide open. Rob needed to speak to Laura Mathers urgently, and Nicky just as urgently. She needed to know that her interview could be with a man who had tried to bomb his own barracks, and he needed to decide whether raising that this morning was a sensible strategy. With no evidence. With no corroboration. He already knew that Frank McIntyre wasn't going anywhere anytime soon.

"Why are you telling me this now, Connor?"

He paused. He looked tired. Drained.

"I've been silenced for a long time. Trying to investigate her murder cost me everything. My credibility, dignity. My marriage. Even now, this will cause problems for some people. People with power. People with something to lose. But I haven't. Not anymore. They've taken everything away from me, but I believe in you. I believe you want to find the truth."

Another pause hung. Even over a video call, Connor Byrne looked mentally exhausted.

"Maura Kelly." He sat slumped in his chair with his head down. Sadness. Tiredness. Pain. "Her name was Maura Kelly. She was a member of the auxiliary staff. We thought we had a problem at the barracks but didn't realise it was McIntyre, so we recruited her and she reported what she saw and what she experienced back to Cramer and me. She was a fantastic young woman. A real people person. Bright, bubbly, intelligent. She was almost perfect as an insider. Innocuous and observant in equal measure. She was such a bright young woman. Somebody with a bright future. I wanted to find her and lay her to rest. I wanted to find him and I wanted to prosecute him. You have to believe me."

Rob gratefully ended the meeting and immediately called Becky. He wanted to know where she'd acquired the bomb from, and whether the chain of custody on it was intact. If it was, there was still a chance that they could physically connect Frank McIntyre with the device.

CHAPTER 50

Nicky had worked herself into the right frame of mind to interview Frank McIntyre. To look him in the eye. She was confident the interview would be straightforward, and relatively easy from a professional point of view. She was also confident that McIntyre would only go one way. His arrogance would take care of that.

She'd spoken to Becky, who knew when McIntyre was being interviewed and had asked for any updates as they became available. Nothing. Becky and the team in Ireland had been able to provide estimates on dates and periods that would not be good news for McIntyre. Nicky was well armed, and looking forward to the confrontation.

She paused and composed herself. She remained hopeful that there would still be a piece of physical evidence that connected Frank McIntyre to Maura Kelly, the young woman who Connor Byrne had just put a name to, but for now that evidence remained elusive. She checked her phone one last time and slid it into her pocket.

Jack and Jen were now frantically working away in the office, and would feed in any live updates should anything change, and should any new evidence come to light. Rob had disappeared upstairs to speak with Laura Mathers, and Nicky had left them both just a few minutes ago. It had been agreed that the information relating to the bomb wouldn't be fully disclosed at this stage. There were far too many variables, so Nicky was to focus on the discovery of the body and the murder for which Frank McIntyre had been arrested. He'd also been arrested for prevention of the lawful and decent burial of a dead body, to give the team some more leverage should the murder charge not stick.

Nicky entered the room. She ignored his solicitor, a smarmy-looking man in a waistcoat who reminded Frank McIntyre that he was being interviewed under caution. He looked furious. There was a look of contempt in his eyes, which Nicky met. Then she smiled.

"We've been up to Victoria with a ground team." She looked him square in the eye. "Whose body is it, Frank?"

"Major General McIntyre," he corrected.

"I'll address you however you want, Major General, but I'm more interested in the body we found."

"I don't know what you mean," came the deadpan reply.

"You should do. It's right by your old office, Frank. But you know that already."

The solicitor objected heavily. Nicky continued to ignore him.

"Nothing to say for yourself, Frank? You must have been expecting this for years, or did you pass the point of thinking you'd ever get caught?"

"My client denies any involvement in this discovery and—"

"Weren't you in charge of the site, Frank? The highest-ranking officer. The top dog. It was your name above the door, and you ruled with an iron fist from what we've been told."

"There is no evidence that my client had any involvement with any impropriety, let alone a murder."

Nicky looked at the solicitor for the first time. She already hated him nearly as much as she hated McIntyre. "You believe what you want to to get paid. I'm investigating the murder of somebody who was thrown mercilessly into a hole."

"I know nothing about it. It was a Victorian site, as you know, so maybe it predated my time there," came the weak attempt at an answer.

"Oh, you're going to need to do a little better than that. We've been working on the body. Working on that site. On *your* site. Analysing soil and tissue samples which have dated the body extremely accurately, to within a few weeks of the date of death. Have a guess when it was, Frank."

The solicitor looked rattled; he rustled papers. "We haven't had sight of those documents, DS Green."

"You protected the barracks, Frank. You did what was necessary." Nicky referred to her notes from an earlier interview. "You were faced with a threat from the IRA, according to this anyway." She almost had a mocking smile on her face. "Should we thank you for your service?"

"I had nothing to do with the death of anybody at my barracks, and you won't prove differently," he stated. The arrogance had started.

"Will we not? Tell me about the building works you had done. We've found the plans, lovely little extension to the officers' wing, particularly your office."

"And?"

"The body was wrapped in a DPM, Frank. It was from the construction, which means we can link the body to the construction works, and to you. You authorised those works, and you buried that body right outside. In your little garden."

"Think what you like, I didn't kill her."

Nicky looked at him hard. She bit her lip and felt the pain.

"We believe that as well as the DPM, the body was wrapped in a rug, Frank. *Your* rug." Nicky removed an old photograph from a file and slid it across the desk. "We've taken this from your house, Frank. This is you," she tapped, "and this is the rug in your office. You're standing on the rug we believe the body was buried in."

The solicitor went to speak but McIntyre cut him off. "You've got nothing. This is circumstantial at best and doesn't link to me. It doesn't prove anything."

Nicky looked at him.

"You said you didn't kill her, Frank."

"I didn't kill her."

Nicky paused. "Then how did you know the victim is female?"

"You said so."

"No, Frank, I didn't. So I'll ask again. How did you know the body is female?"

His solicitor put a hand on McIntyre's arm. He looked rattled. His face had patches of pink, and the broken veins in his cheeks became visible. A maze of red lines that was down to more than red wine and good living.

"It was a barracks, Sergeant Green, during a time of war. I dare say if you continue to dig, you might find other things that you might not like."

His solicitor closed his eyes. It was blasé. It was bold. It was the answer of a man who felt bulletproof and didn't seem to care about a death that happened under his command.

"The military is not for the weak. We trained those men to

be the best they could be. To fight. To continue to fight, and *always* to be the last man standing."

"What does that mean, Frank? Be the last man standing? Or woman, of course. Although you're not keen on women, are you?"

McIntyre seemed to be ignoring the use of his Christian name but shot Nicky a hard and disapproving look anyway. He was under pressure. He wasn't used to having his authority questioned, and Nicky was revelling in doing so.

He looked resolute. His military rhetoric kicked in. "It means to keep going no matter what. To not relent. To not yield. Fight through pain, through injury, and to stay on your feet. Put the other man down. Kill him if required and to leave the battlefield the victor at all costs. There is no greater feeling than victory."

McIntyre spoke the words with true conviction. With belief. Nicky realised in that moment that he'd do anything to win. To be the victor. Maybe even more so now.

"So whose body is it, Frank?" Nicky asked abruptly. "You know she was a female, she was outside your office and her body was wrapped in your rug. You killed her, Frank."

McIntyre took a sip of water and stayed cool. Emotionless. He chose to not respond.

"You know we're searching your house. You're an old school military man, and I *know* that you would been issued with a service revolver, do you still have it?"

He chose to stay silent again.

"You don't strike me as the quiet type. Especially when she clearly did something that made you angry. Did she defy you, Frank? Or did she work you out? See you for what you *really* are." Nicky was venomous with her accusation. Enough to not draw the wrath of the solicitor, but more than enough to have McIntyre know what she might be speaking about.

He looked angry. The veins bled from red to purple. There was doubt in his eyes. Real doubt.

Nicky saw it and was revelling in his discomfort. "Maybe she knew something about the bomb. Maybe she knew who *really* built it."

The solicitor had nothing on the Victoria attack. Had nothing on the bombing. He was here to defend against a murder charge, and on a charge of preventing a lawful burial. Nicky looped back.

"So who was she, Frank? What's her name?"

"I don't know," came the ice-cold reply. The 'I don't care either' was implied.

Nicky looked him in the eye and categorically knew he was lying. Frank McIntyre had slipped up. He knew exactly who Maura Kelly was.

Nicky stood up and started to leave the room.

"Can I go home?" he asked, pathetically.

"No, and if I have it my way, you will *never* go home." Nicky was angry and was way past caring about McIntyre.

"Where are you going?" he asked, weakly.

"I'm going to prove that you murdered Maura Kelly because she saw you for exactly who you are. And when I've done that, I'm going to tell the fucking world."

CHAPTER 51

Becky had been working hard with the Belfast team, and the ICLVR had continued to offer valuable support despite their period of official involvement having ended. They were well funded, and had access to equipment that Becky had only read about or seen at trade shows. Their ability to extract and find the most molecular level of DNA was mind-blowing, and was something she hoped would trickle down to her unit in due course. It was the height of technology, and equipment that she, on a general basis, didn't have access to.

The work had been painstaking. Arduous. But two key lines of enquiry had been relentlessly pursued despite the clear possibility that nothing would be found. That nothing could be proven beyond all reasonable doubt.

The lab was buzzing, samples had been extracted and both elements of the investigation were close to bearing fruit. Becky could feel it. She was pushing hard, desperate to provide information. Desperate to provide a breakthrough.

In some ways, she felt powerless. Her small but proficient team were working as hard as ever, but with multi-party involvement, Becky's role was to manage and direct the technicians temporarily under her supervision. They were talented, motivated and competent. It was a good vibe, and gave Becky increased ambitions for her unit.

The first element reached a stage which could allow it to be processed, using procedures Becky had only read about and with the absolute certainty that the evidence would be admissible. The staunch eyes of the broader team had been meticulous.

Becky checked on the second evidence stream. It was at a similar stage and would be run concurrently. Within twenty minutes or so, the team would have the information and the evidence they craved.

*

Becky had called Nicky on Teams from her office. She was sitting within her smart glass-walled office, at a desk that she had only seen in the high-end section of John Lewis.

"Rob asked me to review the remains of the explosive device from Victoria. We have and we've managed to find and extract DNA evidence from within the bomb."

Nicky perked up; progress was happening in live time and she could feel it. The invigoration.

"There were some skin cells and a partial print, although the print is degraded to the point that I'm pretty sure it would be inadmissible, but the DNA looks good."

A wave rushed through Nicky. "Whose is it?"

"It's Frank McIntyre's."

Nicky exploded inside. Cold, hard evidence that McIntyre had betrayed the army. Betrayed his recruits. Betrayed his country.

Becky wasn't done. Nicky looked at her, already elated.

"You remember how I said that the bullet wound to the skull is pretty unique as far as gunshot wounds go? We now believe that the injury was caused by a .45 calibre bullet."

"Is that significant?"

"Yes, we believe it is. The nature of a bullet causes a pattern, so we've been able to identify the revolver that fired the bullet from the damage to the skull. The ICLVR guys have been a revelation. Their knowledge is extensive, particularly on explosive devices and firearms."

Nicky's already heightened adrenaline spiked again. The feeling flooded through her. McIntyre was in a world of trouble. His arrogance and his feeling of untouchability were crashing down. She smirked inside. Becky continued.

"The injury came from a Ballester-Molina. It's an Argentine-made firearm which was only issued to British servicemen during a three-year period, and to servicemen who fought in the Falklands in 1982."

"That's quite a narrow period," Nicky remarked.

"It is, and there is only one man still alive who served during that period, and who was issued with a Ballester-Molina: Francis McIntyre."

Nicky looked delighted, even though they hadn't found the gun in his house. It was possible, if not likely, that he'd long since disposed of it, although men of his arrogance very often held on to their relics. It was circumstantial, but combined with the ongoing work on the rug, the location of the remains, the weapon used and the physical evidence connecting McIntyre to the failed bomb attack, Nicky felt confident that a strong enough case was being built. Strong enough to take McIntyre down.

"I'll speak to the CPS and progress with a murder charge. We might even be able to get him on a terror charge too."

Nicky was buzzing. It was the most physical evidence they'd had. It explained who was responsible either in full, or in part, for the failed attack at Victoria. McIntyre was a traitor; Nicky and the team would now need to reassess if his disloyalty had led to the deaths of Steve Hargreaves, and Martin and Aaron King. Nicky felt content.

"There's a little more if you're interested." Becky teased. "We were able to extract DNA from the remains of her womb. It's a technique I've never seen before, and until recently we wouldn't have thought it remotely possible, but there we go."

Nicky looked genuinely intrigued and waited.

"The upshot is that we've got a DNA match on the unborn child. It's Will Taylor. The baby was Will Taylor's unborn son."

CHAPTER 52

Jack and Jen were working frantically. They had been for hours. Old documents, interviews, reports Laura Mathers had acquired, and dates. Checking them. Cross-referencing them. Trying to find the piece of information that would identify the why, and then the who.

With Becky's guidance, Jack had been able to locate several invoices relating to the building works, proving that the DPM had been delivered to the barracks a month before the failed bomb attack. A family-run business and some relics for archives had been an unexpected godsend for the team. Becky herself was still working to provide physical evidence that connected the rug and Maura Kelly's body to Frank McIntyre.

"You look tired," Jen remarked. Jack had pulled his tie down and opened his top button. Several coffee cups and some bottles of Diet Coke had provided the morning's fuel, and the hours and lack of air were taking their toll.

The office phone rang and Jack answered it. It was the desk sergeant, Ellie Sharpe.

"Hi, Jack, I've got a call from an old boy in Anstey. He wants to speak to a detective."

"Can't you deal with him?"

"I'm not a detective, I'm afraid, so I'll put him through! You're welcome!"

Jack took the call; his brain started to switch off as the old man on the end of the phone started to tell him that he'd been in Marbella for the last three weeks. Jack felt envious. The prospect of some sunshine and some time off was more than appealing.

As his brain wandered back to the conversation, the old man was talking about a T-bone steak and a restaurant overlooking the beach. Jack rubbed his face with his spare hand.

"Can I help you with something, Mr..."

"Jacobs. Eric Jacobs."

Jack waited.

"Oh, I saw your appeal for dash cam footage. I remember the date as we were in town that day. We had an appointment for my wife and it's also our daughter's birthday..."

"Do you have something that you think might help, Mr Jacobs?" Jack asked, as patiently as he could muster.

"Sorry, yes. I've had a look on my laptop, and I've found some footage of a silver Vauxhall Astra. It's quite clear actually."

Jack immediately perked up.

"Where are you, please, Mr Jacobs?"

It was a short drive up the A50 towards Anstey. Jack arrived in the quiet cul-de-sac, which did plenty to indicate to Jack that he was surrounded by the retired community. Perfectly manicured front gardens and the sound of a lawnmower buzzing at 10am on a Tuesday morning. Awnings and ramps to front doors to afford wheelchair access. The odd gnome.

Jack checked the house number on his phone, before walking up the neat pathway to the immaculate front door and ringing the bell. The volume reverberated down the hall and the small figure of Eric Jacobs opened the door and welcomed Jack in. Jack clocked his hearing aid and saw that his wife was in the sitting room. Waiting for him. The decor was floral and fanciful and there was a hardwood serving hatch in the wall. Jack had never seen one and looked through it into the old kitchen.

"We've been in Marbella for three weeks, you see. We're retired and we like the sun, although we have to come home for Lily."

"Is she your daughter?"

"No, she's the cat."

It was timely but a Bengal with a stunning coat sauntered past before shouting at her master, presumably for food.

"Would you like some Battenberg?" offered a very polite and neatly dressed Julie Jacobs.

Jack declined politely, and regretted it immediately when the large homemade cake appeared along with a pot of tea.

"It was on the rec, wasn't it?" Eric Jacobs asked politely, whilst firing up a large old laptop.

"It was," Jack replied, "but we're looking for footage along Fosse Road." He was nervous his time was being wasted.

"Excellent!" he said, taking a bite from his Battenberg, before clocking forward. "Here we are."

The image loaded. Jack recognised a corner shop at the bottom end of Glenfield Road as the footage moved slowly along the tarmac and towards Fosse Road. Jack waited. The picture quality was excellent, much better than he was expecting.

The camera swept to the left and met Fosse Road, past a Tesco Metro on the left-hand side. It was crystal clear. Jack checked the timestamp. It looked about right.

There were surprisingly few people walking the usually busy pavement, and the road looked quieter than Jack had ever seen it. Maybe why the response to the appeal had been poor. The car headed down the hill at a leisurely 25mph, and past the site of the old Empire pub. As the old steel footbridge veered into sight, Jack saw it. His eyes opened. He perked up.

A silver Astra.

He felt it in the pit of his stomach. The twinge. He checked the time again. The car grew closer. How many of that model could there be? Closer still. Jack saw the number plate and felt the excitement start to bubble, although the reflection on the windscreen protected the driver. Closer still.

As the Tudor Road junction appeared, the car being driven by Eric Jacobs slowed as the Astra indicated.

The flash of light sparkled across the screen as Eric Jacobs flicked his headlights to give way to the car, and as the Astra turned, the driver gave a raised hand by way of a thank you. He looked squarely at Jacobs. It was crystal clear. It was unmistakable.

Jack felt the emotion pour through him. He frantically pulled his phone out and continued to watch the screen of the small laptop. Jacobs followed the Astra along Tudor Road before the brake lights appeared and the car indicated left. Jack checked the timestamp again. Nine minutes before the first 999 call was made to the fire service.

"Mr Jacobs, this is critical information – thank you. Can I download this onto a USB drive, please?"

"I'm glad it's useful. You can borrow the laptop if you'd like."

He'd got it all. The car being driven. His face in near-perfect resolution. The hand thanking Jacobs for giving way, showing the signet ring on his little finger. The car being driven towards, and then directly onto, the rec.

Jack stayed cool despite his heightened emotions and headed slowly out of the front door. He dialled Rob. Voicemail. He dialled him again. Rob answered.

"We've got him, Rob! Footage of the Astra being driven onto the rec just before the fire was lit. It's crystal clear. It's perfect!"

"Who is it? Who was driving?"

"It was Will Taylor."

CHAPTER 53

Rob was absolutely buzzing. He'd frantically waved his hands at Jen, who was busy working away in the office. She was on the phone but hung up, promising whoever was on the other end that she'd call back, before heading swiftly into Rob's office.

Laura Mathers was also heading purposefully across the office. Rob had summoned her once more on the promise of a major development, and with Jack on his way back from Anstey with a laptop, Rob started to share what the team now knew.

Before he could speak, Nicky dashed into the office at speed, smashing the office door open and crashing it against the wall. The hole where the handle hit the plasterboard grew, and white fragments of gypsum fell on the floor. Rob drew breath and stared at Nicky. She raised a hand as an apology.

Rob cut to the chase.

"Will Taylor dumped the body of Steve Hargreaves on the rec. Jack is on his way back with clear footage."

Laura Mathers looked elated. She also looked relieved.

"Have you seen it?" she asked Rob.

"No, but Jack has and he says it's crystal clear."

"It was Taylor all along?" Nicky asked, with just a hint of surprise. It wasn't who the money had been on, but on Jack's promise the imagery was irrefutable.

"Arrest warrant?" Mathers asked.

"Already issued," Rob replied. "He's in the UK. We believe he's in the county, and we have every officer in Leicestershire looking for him."

Laura Mathers' brain was already working on overtime. Rob's had been doing exactly the same since the call from Jack ended.

"Why? Why did he do it?"

"Justice? For Maura? For his son? I can't think of a reason why he'd want to frame Cramer, but by implicating Cramer, he's forced his hand to the point that he's murdered Martin King."

"But why?"

"Two terrorists are dead, and Frank McIntyre has been discredited and disgraced. For a man like Will Taylor, I'd think that was a reasonable result."

"So we're saying he left a dead body in the middle of Leicester with Cramer's tooth in it?" Jen asked.

"Provocation, it has to be. He wanted to provoke Cramer, and it worked. Cramer murdered Martin King after seeing him in the newspaper. Taylor must have been the one to put it through his door."

"Why didn't he just kill Martin King himself?"

"And then what? It would just look like a single murder and not draw everybody out of the woodwork."

"How did McGrath get involved?"

"We got him involved. We found him. We spoke to him."

The room fell quiet.

"We were dragged into this by Taylor. He's provoked all of this by using that body, and three men are dead because of it?" It was already a hard pill to swallow.

"Why would Taylor do this and risk waking up McGrath? He's spent his life doing good, one way or another. He told us about the body," Jen exclaimed. There were still many unanswered questions.

"Steve Hargreaves?" she asked.

"Collateral. Somehow, he had one of David Cramer's teeth and used it to draw him out. Finding Martin King seemed to be the first step."

"So is he done? What about John McGrath? We need him for Aaron King's murder and he's failed to check in. We all know what McGrath is capable of. Surely, he's the sort of man Will Taylor would like to take care of?"

"It's possible, we have a warrant out for both; Taylor for Hargreaves and McGrath for Aaron King. With McIntyre in custody, that should clear it up."

"What's the warrant for, Rob?"

"Preventing the lawful burial of a body and desecration of a corpse."

"Make sure the video footage is watertight. Those charges tell a solicitor that we don't know whether Steve Hargreaves was already dead or not."

"True, but he drove that car there and left that body to burn."

"What about O'Callaghan?" Mathers wanted certainty that his anonymity was intact.

"Taylor has no reason to harm O'Callaghan. They both tried to bring McIntyre down, they both fought for justice. So did Connor Byrne."

"What about McGrath? He knows that Cramer killed Martin King. Is it possible he knows O'Callaghan isn't the friend he once knew?"

"That's the risk. We need to find McGrath. He's dangerous, and he may feel threatened. His network is falling and he'll feel exposed. I don't know how he'll react if he feels cornered."

"So where is he?" Mathers asked. She knew Rob didn't know any more than she did. It was a problem that was about to grow. Mounting pressure and the political implications would become significant.

"He's in the country. His passport was handed in by his solicitor so theoretically he's in the UK. He's here. His photo is with every force in the country – we will find him."

Rob spoke confidently, before confirming, and reminding Laura Mathers, that John McGrath last checked in on Tuesday morning of last week and had now been missing for a week. Her face looked sceptical. She had serious concerns over the fight-or-flight mentality of John McGrath.

The investigation had accelerated forward. The team had now identified three murderers; David Cramer was in custody, Frank McIntyre was also in custody and John McGrath was being hunted down.

John McGrath was the final link. The outstanding piece of the jigsaw that would cap the investigation off. Really close things down and reflect well on the force, and on Laura Mathers.

She thanked the team and headed back upstairs to her office. To make a number of phone calls. To escalate the search further still, and to remind those above her that her team were performing exceptionally well despite the lack of support from those searching for, and failing to find, John McGrath.

CHAPTER 54

Rob splashed some water on his face and looked in the mirror. He was feeling it, but the progress had provided a much-needed injection of life into the morale of the team. The workload had been relentless, and the progression had been a relief. Laura Mathers was putting Rob under pressure. Pressure to find John McGrath, even though the responsibility only partially fell with him, and pressure to close the investigation. He felt good. There was some clarity, and there was now some sense where there had been none. Motives and the actions of the guilty had started to bleed from the surface.

Will Taylor had been located quickly from a credit card receipt and apprehended at a hotel on the edge of town. Another Holiday Inn. There'd been no fuss, no resistance, and he was already sitting in an interview room downstairs. He was the third man to be arrested, and having reviewed the CCTV footage with Jack and the wider team, Rob was feeling surprisingly relaxed. Taylor had refused a solicitor as well, either deciding to fight his own battle, or accepting that his number was well and truly up.

It was just after midday when Rob walked into the

interview room. Taylor was sitting down and didn't look up. His glare fixed. He looked tired, resigned almost. There was still defiance, though. It was there. A lifelong trait that would always be an ingrained part of a fiery character.

"Good afternoon, Will. Can I get you anything?"

He looked angry. Powerless. "A coffee would be great," was all he could muster.

Rob sat upright and looked directly across the table.

"Why did you leave Steve Hargreaves' body on the rec, Will? Why did you kill him?"

"I didn't kill him," he replied firmly.

"So you just decapitated him, set his body on fire and left him to burn?"

Taylor sighed. There was an air of resignation in his manner. "Whatever else you think of me, I didn't take his life. It's important that you know that. He wasn't murdered."

"So he was just unfortunate, was he? In the wrong place, and his body made for a good prop?"

Taylor ignored the question. Rob waited, before continuing.

"I thought David Cramer would have been an ally of yours. Courage, bravery, dignity. Right up your street. Stitched him up a treat, didn't you?"

"This isn't about Cramer. Why aren't you fucking listening? You've not listened to me all along! McIntyre is the key to all of this and you're not doing shit!"

"You don't know who we're speaking to, Will," came the frustrated and robust response.

"I know you've had a team in Belfast, and I know McIntyre isn't in custody."

"You know that, do you? Maybe you don't know as much as you think you do." Rob was angry. Taylor had been toying with people's lives, and defying the law throughout. He was also acutely aware of the investigation, and of the search at Victoria. He was a real force of nature, and considering that he was also fighting for justice, albeit in his own way, he had been a major pain in Rob's arse from the moment he landed in Belfast.

"Isn't prison where you normally put terrorists and murderers?" Taylor asked, sarcastically.

"That's why you're here," Rob spat back.

"You haven't got there yet, have you? Spin you some yarn, did he? Cantankerous old bastard." He leant over the table and whispered ominously, "Get me access to Frank McIntyre for fifteen minutes and I'll get you the proof that you so desperately need."

It was a clear threat, and one that came maliciously. Taylor was visibly shaking. The fire of his anger, the emotion and tears clearly visible in his eyes. It was all there, bubbling away behind his eyes and on the brink of boiling over.

"I know you have a body. I knew it wasn't my boy, but it was somebody I cared about. She was the insider. You need to know that." He jabbed his finger on the table. "And he killed her."

Taylor sat back and the room paused, changing the tone slightly. Rob placed the stills from Eric Jacobs' laptop on the table. Timestamped and crystal clear. Jack hadn't needed to clean the image up; it wasn't necessary. It was there for all to see. Will Taylor had no plausible deniability. He was bang to rights.

Taylor looked at it, then looked away. He looked up. Rob looped back to Will's reference to their female victim.

"Who was she to you, Will?" Rob asked delicately. He

knew what Will Taylor was capable of, and despite their clear differences, Rob felt the pain of his loss. Even now. "You loved her, didn't you? You loved her and she was taken away from you."

Taylor bit hard on his lip but said nothing.

"What was her name, Will?" It was a rhetorical question of sorts. The team had a name from Connor Byrne, although so far Jack's search for Maura Kelly had drawn a blank. Nobody listed under either of those names on either the military or auxiliary staff, as Connor Byrne had claimed.

Taylor sat silently. He checked his watch. He looked up, then looked away. He tried to hold on. But he'd gone. The lump in his throat was there. The first tear glided softly down his cheek, followed by another. The tears streamed down his face. The emotions began to overwhelm him.

Rob had to continue. "I need to ask you something, Will. I need to ask you if you knew that she was pregnant at the time of her murder."

The shock was real. The horror writ large in his eyes. The emotions flooded through his face and the pain looked excruciating. His face contorted, his head collapsed into his arms, and Will Taylor sobbed uncontrollably.

CHAPTER 55

It had been a swift twenty-four hours. Will Taylor had been charged with preventing a lawful burial and desecration of a corpse. With no clear proof that he had killed Steve Hargreaves, the CPS had refused to allow any murder or manslaughter charges to progress.

It was disappointing, but Taylor would be remanded, and the evidence against him was simple but compelling. The dash cam footage would be played across large screens in court, and only the softest of juries would have no issue in deciding quite clearly that Will Taylor was the man behind the wheel of the Astra. The man driving a car that was alight less than fifteen minutes after Will Taylor had been caught on camera driving it. There was no reasonable defence, no plausible way he could deny that Steve Hargreaves' body was in the boot of the car at the time.

The thin ice that Will Taylor was skating on had cracked.

The Home Office and the security services were still frantically searching for John McGrath. Mathers had assured Rob that McGrath was very much their problem, and the hunt was not something that would reflect badly on him, her, or the force. Whether John McGrath was found quickly, or at all, would always reflect badly on the authorities once the press got involved, but with politics in play, Laura Mathers was very capable of making sure the hot potato was being held by somebody else. She smiled at Rob. It didn't happen often.

David Cramer had also been remanded and was no longer cooperating. He had declined to elaborate on any incident surrounding the loss of one or more of his teeth, and was flatly refusing to discuss any issues, personal or otherwise, that existed between him and Will Taylor. The team could only speculate about whether a disagreement, pub fight, a game of rugby or some other reason caused David Cramer to lose a tooth, and there was even more speculation about how it came to be in Will Taylor's possession. There was absolutely no doubt that Taylor had gone about setting David Cramer up. Enticing him, luring him, and framing him. His entrapment had led to David Cramer committing the murder of Martin King.

Frank McIntyre had also been charged. Nicky had taken the greatest of pleasures in standing before him with a smirk on her face. She'd worn one of her finer tops and trouser suit combos. Wanted to really feel the part, and to look the part, before reading out charges of murder and preventing a lawful burial, and, to top it off, the CPS had authorised a charge under the 1940 Churchill Act of Terrorism.

"Smug bastard, you should have seen his face." Nicky smiled contentedly at a job well done. Charging some people was hard. Pensioners, the vulnerable, domestic abuse victims who finally snapped and retaliated. But McIntyre was as good as it got. The cream of the cream. A misogynist. An arrogant man of honour who had disgraced his country and betrayed the values of Queen and country. Nicky was also in the process of having him stripped of all of his military titles, both actual and honorary. It was a move that would see Frank McIntyre buried as a civilian, when that day came.

She had also taken great privilege in recording his name on the charge sheet as *Mr* Francis McIntyre. A final insult. A final slap to a man who had abused his position, and abused his authority. Taking him down felt monumental. If only Maura Kelly, or whoever the young female victim really was, had a family to notify. Somebody to bury her. Somebody to finally grieve for her.

"What was it Connor Byrne said, Jen? Quite the opposite?" Nicky asked. "He knew, didn't he? Byrne knew that McIntyre was rotten too. Do you think they all knew?"

"It looks that way. Yet even with their combined authority, they couldn't expose him."

"It's worrying to believe that there were greater forces at play."

"It really is. Cramer was a well-respected senior figure, Connor Byrne was mid level but had huge trust placed in him, and Will Taylor was just a complete firebrand. A law unto himself, and even with his access and capability, he couldn't take McIntyre down."

"I'm not sure why Taylor seems so guarded now. He clearly had feelings for her, they were clearly very close, but he seems to be holding something back at a time when he could give her and her family the closure he knows they deserve."

"You're not wrong. We've pushed him and he won't say, but he seems close to breaking. It's like he wants to give it up, but it almost feels like he's waiting for something."

CHAPTER 56

Becky and Jack had been working closely, if from very different ends of the investigative spectrum. Becky was working tirelessly to process DNA and dental records, and to look to confirm or refute the true identity of Maura Kelly.

Jack was doing the same but as a paper chase. Records, old photographs and fragmented files provided throughout the investigation. Records that were clearly incomplete. Whoever the victim of Frank McIntyre's murder was, she'd seemingly been able to gain access to Victoria Barracks, and to work and operate across the site without existing. No payroll. No service record. It was a foreign concept to Jack. It was practically impossible to exist in the modern world without leaving a trail.

There was no birth record registered under the name of Maura Kelly, and thousands of births had been registered in the name of Maura from around the time Becky believed the young woman would have been born.

The preservation of her body, due to the conditions in which her body had been both wrapped and buried, had allowed the team to accurately age her, to between the ages of twenty-five and thirty-five. The clear condition of the skull had also allowed

Becky to state that the probable cause of death was the single gunshot wound to the head. One of many strands of evidence that had led to Frank McIntyre's almighty fall from grace.

Becky exhaled. "We know she was pregnant with the child of Will Taylor, but we still don't have a confirmed identity for our victim. We just have the name Maura Kelly, which was given to us by Connor Byrne."

Jack nodded. He'd taken to working out of the mortuary offices. They were somehow nicer than the police headquarters back at Lodge House, and the proximity to Becky made aligning their workstreams easier. Jack sighed loudly; Becky looked at him and invited the conversation.

"I can't find or account for a single female soldier of any rank on the whole site. There's nothing. It's like she didn't exist. Whoever she is, and whatever she was there for, it doesn't look legit."

"Could she have been one of McIntyre's stooges?"

"It's possible, but he's saying nothing. She might have been one of his, or an IRA implant, and he killed her when she crossed him. It's what Connor Byrne and Will Taylor are both saying."

"And you've checked all of the records for the cleaning, clerical and catering staff?"

"I have, or the records I have anyway. There's no Maura."

Rob walked in through the slick glass doors. Becky had spotted him and released the doors. The air in the mechanism hissed softly as they slid open. He could see the conversation was flowing and raised a hand to say 'hi', before swinging left towards the small kitchenette, which was also considerably nicer than the one at the station. Plus, the kettle was a Smeg. It was small but showroom-esque.

"So she's not under her own name," Rob confirmed,

holding a scarlet Welsh rugby union mug full of steaming hot tea. "I really do need to get you some decent mugs."

Becky glared at Rob playfully.

"And there are no female names on the ICLVR list?" she asked Jack.

"No. Well, there are, but they are one hundred per cent certain that none are Maura, and that's based on extensive DNA and dental records."

Becky nodded. Rob looked at Jack.

"The Irish authorities are working hard on missing cases, and the ICLVR have thanked us for our service and have formally ended their involvement. The good news, if there is any, is that I have one of the women there working on birth records for me. She'll keep me posted."

"Make a good impression, did you?" Rob smiled at Jack.

"Have you ruled out Connor Byrne?" Becky asked. "He has a missing son, so are you assuming that the young woman isn't connected to him?"

Rob rubbed his chin and sipped his tea. "Maybe not biologically, but the same was true of Will Taylor until we found that she was carrying his baby. Taylor is neck-deep in this, and it's still possible that Connor Byrne has more invested here than a simple miscarriage of justice."

"What about McGrath?" Becky asked. It was a little bit of a touchy subject. A convicted IRA terrorist who would be at the edgier end of his mood was out there. Plotting. Planning. Or deciding what to do following the murders of Martin and Aaron King.

"Good question," Rob replied. "Have you been able to find anything to connect McGrath to the murders as opposed to just placing him at the scene?"

Becky shook her head.

"Does McGrath have a sister?" she asked.

"I can't find one," Jack replied, "although that doesn't mean that it can't have been related to him. It's more than possible, though. He murders Aaron King just before a dead IRA insider turns up at a barracks. If it is his sister, then there is the possibility that she was involved in the bombing."

"But if she is McGrath's sister, I'm pretty sure that Byrne and Taylor wouldn't be crying over her."

"She was carrying Taylor's baby, so if it is McGrath's sister, then it would have been a very messy situation given what he was doing at the time."

"Maybe that's why Will Taylor isn't corroborating her name. An IRA insider and an anti-corruption journalist," Jack suggested.

"It could be. He clearly had feelings for her, or loved her. You'd think he'd want her family to have closure. You'd think he'd want the opportunity to lay her properly to rest. Give her back some dignity."

"Can you imagine the funeral? Taylor and McGrath weeping side by side."

Becky waited. "Maybe we're getting ahead of ourselves, gents. The good news is that her teeth are fully intact and we have a crystal-clear DNA profile waiting to be matched, so when we have something to compare it to, we'll know."

Rob's mind wandered. A thought leapt into his mind.

"Have we run her DNA against the suspect base as opposed to the criminal database?" Rob asked.

"No," Becky looked perplexed, "it's negative against the criminal database. It wouldn't match for McGrath anyway as we don't have his DNA on file."

Rob looked at her. She waited.

"Business card."

She smiled. "Can we check against that sample? Is that legitimate?"

"Mathers says so. Run it. It's better to ask for forgiveness than permission. We need to know who this young woman is, who she's related to, and we need to know quickly."

CHAPTER 57

The mood in the office was as calm as it had been in months. Relaxed almost. Nicky was munching on a bag of crisps and was starting to think about some time off. Indulging herself with thoughts of sunnier climes and days on the beach. Cocktails and afternoon naps by the pool. The conversation was buoyant, with Jen and Jack continuing to work studiously and with an array of chocolate bars to keep them company.

Jen had made the teas and had brought in a tin of Quality Street that she'd found left over from last Christmas. Stashed in a cupboard but perfect for an office day stacked with paperwork. The soft centres were taking a hammering, and by the time Rob emerged from his office, there was a disappointing mix of toffee pennies and fudge sticks left over. He found a solitary coconut eclair and peeled back the blue foil wrapper.

The team felt as comfortable as modern policing ever should. David Cramer had been charged with murder. Frank McIntyre had also been charged with murder, as well as a terrorism offence and preventing a lawful burial, and Will Taylor had been charged with preventing a lawful burial.

Nicky was also working on charges relating to abuse of a body following discussions with Mathers and the CPS, but Taylor would almost certainly be remanded and would be going nowhere.

Three murder charges was a good result, and even the inevitable inquiry into whether Aaron King should have, or could have been protected was something Rob was giving very little thought to. Mathers would be fighting that battle, and the collection of charges against the three men was reflecting well on him and his team.

Jen was in a good mood, having secured a conviction against the rapist. Against *him*. Her mood was bright and only tempered by the tiredness brought on by an investigation which was taking so much.

Rob had taken a phone call and looked agitated, before heading out of his office at speed. Jen and Jack waited.

"Will Taylor, he's not being remanded. He's being transferred to a hospital facility."

"Sorry?" muttered Jack.

"He's being moved…"

"No, I heard you. Why?"

"It's on health grounds. He's ill. Really ill." Rob looked exasperated. Shocked. "He hasn't said a word. Not a word. His solicitor has made an application for compassion to the CPS. They've provided his medical records. He has an advanced stage cancer. It's inoperable and he'll be treated by a palliative care team. They think he's got four months, tops."

"How did we not know that?" Jack asked.

"Why would we?" came the blunt response.

The mood flattened and Jen laid the pile of papers she was working through on the desk.

"Nothing is ever clean, is it?" she asked. Her frustration echoed in Rob and Jack. "Does anyone still think we've missed something?" she added. "Nothing has been as it seems, has it?"

"It feels that way," Jack agreed, his frustration clear. There was always an element of sympathy. Jen and Jack were both brilliant with people. They had healthy levels of compassion and cynicism that made them both fantastic with people. The empathy was there, but Will Taylor had been responsible for the desecration of Steve Hargreaves' body on the rec, and now he wouldn't face justice for his crimes.

"Fancy a beer?" she asked.

They opted for a local pub. The Royal Standard. It was an old-fashioned pub, lost somewhere in the late eighties to early nineties. An old man's pub, although the atmosphere was usually decent. It was a short walk along Charles Street from the office, and the drinks were cheap.

Jack was delighted to see a fridge behind the bar housing numerous bottles of Peroni. He ordered one and a couple of pints for Rob and Jen. He saw some nuts on a cardboard dispenser hanging up and ordered one for posterity.

He sat down. There was a low key 'cheers' and he split the bag of nuts open, laying it on the dark hardwood table in front of him to share. Jack sighed and took a swig of his beer. Rob's phone vibrated in his pocket. He sighed and answered it. It was Becky.

"We're in the Standard if you're local," he joked. His smiling face turned stone dead. "Where?"

Jen and Jack waited. He checked his watch and mentally calculated a time.

"We'll be an hour." He hung up.

"Fuck!" he muttered angrily. A number of men at the bar glanced over.

Rob looked at Jack before sharing the news. "John McGrath has been found dead in Nottingham."

CHAPTER 58

The office was quiet but with a dull undertone. Rob had spent the last couple of hours with Mathers, who would no doubt be managing the fallout following the discovery of John McGrath's murdered body last night. She would now be managing the situation with her peers, and people with a political stake who Rob had absolutely no interest in talking to. He had checked his shirt in the mirror on the way down and adjusted his waistline. He was warm but his dark shirt was hiding any physical signs of sweat, and he grabbed a bottle of water from the fridge to cool down and to rehydrate.

He checked his phone for messages. Nothing from Nicky and Jen, who had travelled the hour north and were working the scene along with their Nottingham counterparts. Jack was in the office and was digging frantically into the invisible background of Maura Kelly, trying to identify whoever Maura Kelly was. McGrath's body had been found inside a commercial waste bin. A bright red Biffa bin with a sliding black lid from the images Rob had seen, behind a Travelodge and close to the M1. It was a brutal end to a life, but one that John McGrath may have envisaged at some point. It was also possible that he'd been responsible for other men and women winding up behind cheap hotels in bins. It was a cold circle of life, and it had caught up with John McGrath.

The relative calm of yesterday had become a brand-new storm. A big one. The weather outside was matching the mood. A gloom had descended over Leicester and the grey concrete buildings to the north were blending into the charcoal sky. It was monotone and full of rain, whipping oversized raindrops into the poorly glazed windows of Lodge House.

Becky was across town, and was due to relay information from a post-mortem that had been expedited and carried out overnight. Becky and her team had worked diligently and through the small hours, following the processing of a messy scene in Nottingham. The authorities had approved his body to be transported to the bowels of Leicester Royal Infirmary; they all needed to know what secrets his body held, how he was killed and when.

McGrath had been the prime suspect and a major loose end. The team had needed to find him, and they had, but Rob had envisaged seeing John McGrath in handcuffs. He'd imagined his defiance at being hauled into a police station, and then hauled into court to be branded a murderer. Again. Finding him dead was somehow bad news. A final loose end, one that was unclean and left more questions unanswered.

Becky looked remarkably bright as she appeared on the flat TV screen in Rob's office. She was no doubt energised by the adrenaline and the demand to find the truth, but she'd had limited sleep and Rob knew she probably felt as shitty as he did. Rob was optimistic. Becky was the best pathologist he'd worked with, and he knew that if anybody could detect the truth, it would be her. The truth from a man full of anger and lies.

Becky greeted Rob and smiled. Her hair was tied back and she was in the zone.

"It's all pretty clear is the good news. He was beaten to death, but there was a knife wound to the back too, which I suspect was inflicted first. There were a number of blows to the head with something hard and with a round end; almost certainly a hammer."

"That's the cause of death?"

"Yep. There were several blows pre mortem, one from behind that would have put him down, and then a number from the front. There's a large injury to the frontal area of the skull, just above the left eye, which would have been fatal, and then there are a number of injuries inflicted post mortem."

"How many post mortem?"

"A dozen or more."

"And it would have been obvious that he was dead?"

"No doubt at all."

"And the knife wound wasn't fatal?"

"No, which is interesting. The wound is almost identical to that inflicted on Martin King, but it's just not as precise. Not as accurate."

"So it's only similar to Martin King's murder?"

"Yes, it's definitely a different knife. We're certain that David Cramer murdered Martin King from the DNA?"

"Are you asking? Yes, we are, we've absolutely no doubt that Cramer killed Martin King."

"Cramer was in custody for this murder, though?"

"Depends on the time of death."

"Sorry, yes, of course. This is the tricky bit. From his lividity, I'd say he's been dead for seventy-two to ninety-six hours. So he died in very close proximity to Aaron King. *Very close proximity.*"

"Shit. Cramer was in custody." Rob pondered. "Taylor?" he asked aloud, before adding, "you're certain?"

Becky nodded a 'yes'. "He was either killed on the same night as Aaron King or within a short period afterwards."

Rob sighed a deep sigh.

"I'm not liking the timing of this. I'm really not."

CHAPTER 59

Will Taylor was being held and would be transferred to hospital for ongoing treatment when a suitable facility had been agreed between the CPS and his solicitor. Within twenty-four hours or so, according to the paperwork Rob had seen.

"He's been relaxed, almost chatty in custody. He's still not giving up anything on her, though, it doesn't make sense. He just seems so relaxed."

"He's dying and he's getting away with murder, no wonder he's relaxed. This probably feels like a win to him. I'm going to speak to him, see if he'll give anything up."

Rob headed down to the cells. The custody sergeant opened the cell door, and on Rob's authority left the door open. Taylor was ill, and although his illness wasn't overly showing physically, Rob knew that inside he was hurting. In more ways than one. There was no strength left to offer, and although Will Taylor had all the bravado of a man in his prime, he was weak. Physically impaired. Dying.

Rob stood with his hands in his pockets.

"You could have told me, Will."

"To what end? What good would it have done? Would you have felt sorry for me? Disliked me any less?"

"I don't dislike you, Will."

"Yes, you do. You think I'm a pain in the arse. Same as everybody else."

Rob smiled at him.

"Why did Steve Hargreaves have to die? What did he do wrong?"

"Nothing." He looked up. "He was dead already. He wasn't murdered, Rob. There was no need to. He died in a sleeping bag in an old factory. No violence. Nothing. If his family are feeling sad, you can tell them he didn't die violently. No pain. He died alone, I believe, which is more tragic in my book."

"From what you believe? You weren't there?"

"No, I wasn't. Not that that matters now."

"No violence?" Rob asked, with a perplexed face.

"I didn't know that was the plan. I didn't know, I promise."

"You didn't dismember him either?"

Taylor winced and avoided the question. Rob pondered. Still trying to understand Will Taylor. "Then why him?"

"He was just a means to an end." He realised how cold it sounded as he said it. "It drew Cramer out once you'd been to see him, though. That tooth did the job, and once you'd been to see Aaron King, all of the people who needed to be in play were there. It was just like old times." He smiled fondly.

"What aren't you telling me, Will?"

"All men have secrets." He smiled again, before looking at Rob. "I'll make you a deal, DCI Rhone." His mood seemed almost too bright for Rob's liking.

"I'll confirm the name of the female victim in exchange for a phone call."

Rob looked at him, but Taylor continued. "How's my boy Frank doing?"

Rob was still trying to work out what his angle was, but decided honesty was appropriate.

"He's appearing in court this morning. Anytime now. He's been charged with murder, Will. You got him."

"No, you got him, and look at what it's cost me. I don't care what happens to me, you need to know that, but he deserves to die in prison. Leicester Crown, isn't it?" he asked, casually.

"It is," Rob confirmed.

"Good." He checked his watch again. "Then I'd like to put on record that I was only too happy to help. I've got nothing left to give, you see." He seemed reflective. Emotional even. "We exchanged information for years. He helped me to bring some of them down. McIntyre was untouchable, that was the problem. Nobody could pin anything on him. Me, Cramer, Byrne. And we tried. Oh, we tried. I'd have given anything to have found that man twenty years ago. Anything. And we couldn't find him."

"Who's *we*, Will? McGrath? I could never see you in bed with the IRA."

"Judge me however you wish to. I don't give a fuck anymore. You make your assumptions."

Rob paused. He was still standing. Leaning against the door frame and looking down at Taylor, who was sitting on his bed with his head down. There was no audio recording of any of this, and other than the CCTV, there was nothing formal to the conversation. Rob asked him anyway and looked at him closely.

"Where were you on Tuesday night into Wednesday morning, Will?"

Taylor looked perplexed, and decided to not give an answer.

"Did you kill John McGrath?"

Taylor paused. His head stayed low. Almost lifeless.

"He's dead, is he? I can't say I'll shed a tear tonight. He was a murderer. He was a sick human. He's had that coming for years."

"Are you saying you didn't kill him?"

"I didn't kill him, not that it matters anymore. All you need to understand is that *he* brought that newspaper to me and told me what he was thinking. Why not? I thought. One last chance. One last dance."

"McGrath? Who's *he*, Will?"

Taylor paused. Rob waited.

"I was in hospital overnight on Tuesday," Taylor offered, "you can check, and I've no doubt you will. John Radcliffe at Oxford."

Rob made a mental note, but it seemed genuine. Something so easy to check would be a poor lie, and it wasn't the sort of sloppy excuse that Taylor would dream up.

He checked his watch again, before casually dropping the bomb. "Her name was Maeve Kennedy, and I loved her. She changed her name when she was a wee girl. Had to. Part of the adoption process, and that's when she became Maura Kelly."

Rob sat and nodded. "You could have told me that sooner, Will." It was dry and Taylor almost appreciated the sentiment. "Maura Kennedy," Rob repeated, "I'm sure her family will appreciate the chance to lay her to rest, properly this time."

"I'm sure they will. Please could you give them my regards when you speak to them?" Rob nodded, but in a non-committal way.

"Can I have my phone call now?" Taylor asked.

"You can. It'll be monitored by the custody sergeant, but you're entitled to make a call."

"That's fine, thank you." It was the most contrition Will Taylor had shown since Rob had met him several weeks ago. In the arrivals lounge of Belfast Airport. When he was cocksure, aggressive and arrogant. In the light of the cells, Taylor looked pale. His skin looked pitted, and Rob could see the effect the last few weeks had had on Will Taylor. His eyes were bloodshot and he looked weak as he stood. He followed Rob along the corridor.

Rob gestured to the custody sergeant, before looking sternly at him. All calls were monitored and recorded, but the strong look told the custody sergeant very firmly to keep both an eye and an ear on Will Taylor.

Rob left Will with the custody sergeant and headed upstairs to speak to Jack and start the formal process of confirming the identity of whoever Maeve Kennedy had been.

CHAPTER 60

Rob pushed the door open and walked through the main office. He made a beeline for Jack, who was still neck-deep in paperwork. Still trying to find a crumb that would narrow the field.

"Kennedy!" Rob shouted. "Maeve Kennedy; have you got her on your list?"

Jack looked flustered and started to flick through several files, and then through a large number of A4 pages that had been white at one point in time.

"That rings a bell, I think. Why?"

"Taylor's given it up. Says the body is Maeve Kennedy."

Rob waited. He checked his watch and retrieved his phone from his pocket. He looked at Jack, who was still searching for a document. For a record to say who Maeve Kennedy is, or was. Nicky had messaged Rob earlier to confirm she would be in court that morning. She'd had a busy twenty-four hours but was adamant that she wanted to sit in court and see Frank McIntyre start to answer to his crimes.

Jack pulled a solitary document from a file and looked it over. "'Maeve Kennedy,'" he read aloud.

"So who is she?" Rob asked.

A mile away, in the magistrates' court, Frank McIntyre's remand hearing was getting underway. It was expected that he wouldn't be remanded into custody; the CPS had advised that was likely. It was disappointing, but a combination of his age, his reputation and the expensive lawyer eating into McIntyre's extortionate army pension was combining, and could well work in his favour. It was probable that he would be bailed to appear at a later date, but either way he would be facing a murder trial. Nicky was particularly disappointed that he wouldn't be remanded. He deserved to be in prison, and the judge assigned was known for being particularly harsh on men who had committed violence against women. Nicky knew her well enough and had highlighted to her the extent to which McIntyre's misogyny had shown no bounds, reminding her of the brutal murder of the young woman found in a shallow grave in Belfast, but to no avail.

Jen had joined Nicky. There were no formal requirements from either to attend, but Nicky and Jen would both take some joy from seeing McIntyre in the dock. Jen knew which courtroom was being used, and had sat and faced *him* during his trial. She had told Nicky exactly where she could sit in order to get in McIntyre's eyeline. To let him know exactly what she thought of him without saying a thing. A look that could convey a million words and tell him to go and fuck himself in the same breath.

Back in Lodge House, Jack was accessing a birth record. His fingers tapped nervously on the keyboard as it loaded. Rob was pacing up and down. He'd had a WhatsApp message from Nicky telling them they were in court. He'd replied but the one grey tick was telling him that Nicky's phone was now off.

Jack was working through the birth records, before casually commenting, "Is it me or does it feel like all we've really done is flush out Frank McIntyre?"

Rob looked at him and frowned. "What did you say?"

"Some of the deaths only happened because of the newspaper. Cramer wouldn't have killed Martin King otherwise, and that led to Aaron King's death. We've charged Taylor and Cramer, but McIntyre was the big dog who we had to root out."

Rob was thinking it through when Jack's screen returned some files. The text was large and abundant across the screen. He looked at Jack, who immediately started to scroll.

"Maeve Kennedy..." he skim read "...her date of birth would have put her in her early thirties, which matches. Her date of birth looks familiar," he commented. He continued to look through the record, muttering parts of the text before reaching her birth name. One that had been changed on adoption, following the death of her parents. "Fuck. Holy fuck."

Rob waited but couldn't read the text on the screen.

"What? What is it?"

Jack checked another record. "She was born Maeve O'Callaghan." He checked her date of birth again. "She's Michael O'Callaghan's twin sister."

Rob froze. There was panic in his face. Blind panic.

"Shit." His brain was racing, his eyes wide. The adrenaline was pumping, the blood in his veins coursing.

"Call Nicky. Call the court!"

"And tell them what?"

Rob picked up the phone on Jack's desk and called down to the custody sergeant.

"Who did he call?" he shouted.

"Sorry, who?" The desk sergeant was flustered. He rustled his paperwork.

"Will Taylor; who did he call?" Rob shouted again.

"Erm, it was nobody important, it was only a short call. Erm, it looks like it's just one of his old army buddies, I think. Hold on… he called a Major White."

CHAPTER 61

Across town, Nicky had bagged the spot that Jen had assured her was prime viewing. Jen was perched next to her, with the two of them wearing their best power suits. Nicky was ready to see Frank McIntyre enter the court. She was ready to watch him standing before the system he was entrusted to defend, and to have to start to answer for his crimes.

It was only a remand hearing, but he emerged with a shuffle. He wore a grey suit that was ten years old and too big for him, and he had clearly lost weight. He looked haggard, with bags under his eyes. A shadow of the arrogant misogynist that Nicky had met in Yorkshire, and if his brief was looking to present McIntyre as an old man battling old age, he was already doing a good job.

He looked at Nicky briefly, who fired daggers right through him. He looked immediately down at the floor before being helped to his seat. Nicky glared into the side of his head and urged him to look up again, but he didn't. She knew he'd seen her. He knew she was there.

The judge entered the court and the formalities were read. Nicky looked around the old-fashioned courtroom. Timber-panelled walls and a grubby off-white paint screamed outdated. It was also quieter than she'd expected, which Mathers had told her would be a good thing. There were one or two local journalists, whom Nicky recognised, but for today at least it was low-profile hearing. Mathers was doing her best to delay the inevitable carnival when the red tops eventually got wind of a major scandal.

The formalities were concluded without Nicky hearing them. McIntyre was still looking down and had to be nudged to confirm his name, which he did with a mutter, before his brief stood. He drew breath and launched into what an honourable man Francis McIntyre was, and was immediately told to hold the character defence for the trial. Nicky smiled. She had an intense dislike for most defence solicitors, and already held an irrational hatred for the man who had been tasked to defend McIntyre.

He apologised and changed his tone, before an alarm sounded. The courtroom fell silent and everybody looked at the judge. She paused, waiting for it to stop. It didn't.

A clerk entered and whispered something to the judge. She stood and immediately ordered the court to be evacuated. More clerks entered, several holding radios, and started to usher those in attendance towards the large double doors, which had been pegged open.

Nicky looked at Jen, before looking at McIntyre. His expression was blank, and if anything he looked surprised too. His brief held his arm and started to move him towards the door. As a free man attending a preliminary hearing, McIntyre was allowed to leave the court and was being helped towards the main exit by his solicitor, who held his arm throughout.

Nicky pulled alongside him, and with her adrenaline coursing was desperate to get in his ear. His solicitor caught her eye and she gave him a look, a filthy look, and one that told him exactly what she thought of him defending McIntyre.

Jen had disappeared, and had reappeared with her phone. She passed it to Nicky, who looked at the screen. Eight missed calls from Rob, all in the last few minutes. She hit redial before realising that the call would be blocked whilst still within the confines of the courthouse. She tried again anyway.

"Shit."

A number of people were being ushered to the front of the building, and Nicky saw a clerk she knew well.

"What's happening?" she asked him.

"I'm honestly not sure, but it isn't a fire alarm and it isn't a drill."

She rushed through the open doors to the front and saw McIntyre just in front of her. Daylight hit her eyes and brought the inevitable squint as the brightness funnelled its way along New Walk, shining brightly on the frontage of the building. She raised her hand to block the light.

She gestured to Jen and headed in McIntyre's direction. She didn't trust him. Didn't trust his supposed frailties, and was keeping an eagle eye on him. She increased her pace and was a few yards behind him when her phone rang. It was Rob. She slid the bar and answered. It was garbled and she checked her signal. One bar. He was shouting, but it was unclear.

Nicky skipped down two of the dozen or more steps and shouted "What?" back down the phone. The broken signal left Rob largely inaudible.

"McInt… sister… targ…"

Nicky looked up and got closer to McIntyre, a yard behind him to the left. Still on the front steps. Still with his solicitor.

"I can't hear you!" she shouted, frustrated.

Two bars. Then three.

"McIntyre is the target!" shouted Rob. Loudly and clearly.

"What!" Nicky shouted back. It was pandemonium around her as dozens of people headed away from the court.

"Shit. Jen!" she screamed, before rushing towards McIntyre. His solicitor turned and looked ready to defend him.

Then it came. The noise. The unmistakable noise. One Nicky had heard infrequently, but it was unmistakable. It was more of a pop than a bang. She looked up; it was like everything had paused. Somebody screamed. Several people fell to the floor.

The bullet ripped into Frank McIntyre's head like a bomb had gone off. His head kicked back violently. The side of his skull exploded. Blood and fragments of his brain sprayed behind him. Nicky closed her eyes but felt it hit her face. She opened her eyes to see Frank McIntyre's body slump to its knees. Head half gone. Face half open. People realised. People were screaming. Another woman was covered in brain matter and was screaming hysterically. A vile and ear-piercing scream.

The solicitor looked like he had no idea what to do. He looked up, looked towards a building on New Walk. He realised that wherever the sniper was, he was exposed too. He froze, and Nicky clocked the terrified look on his blood-spattered face. His white shirt was splashed in crimson red and there was sheer terror on his face.

Another pop. More screams. The second bullet smashed into McIntyre's chest, and his body collapsed into a pile of blood on the floor. Surrounded by pieces of his own brain. His own shattered skull.

Nicky looked up and stayed close to the solicitor. They were exposed. There was no point running. The sniper could pick a dozen or more off if they wanted to. Jen had taken the opposite view and had run up towards the entrance to the court and was trying to make a call. Maybe Rob had got her, or Jack.

Nicky waited. Waited for the next bullet. Ten seconds passed. Then twenty. The screaming carried on and those lying down were staying put. Terrified. Playing dead, or too paralysed with fear to move.

Nicky looked up and saw a figure. She squinted in the light and saw his silhouette. Screams erupted from those at the front as the man holding the rifle walked towards but then past them. People kicked themselves backwards on the floor. Some begged for their lives but he ignored them. He walked into the shadows and towards Nicky. She felt totally exposed. She had no baton, no pepper spray, no taser. Nothing. It wouldn't help to defend her against a highly trained killer, but she still felt bare.

She swallowed hard, and nervously as an armed Michael O'Callaghan strolled casually closer to her, like he was in the park, or on a day out. He seemed oblivious to the carnage around him, and as he reached Nicky and stood in front of the broken and shattered corpse of Frank McIntyre, he looked Nicky squarely in the eye.

Nicky swallowed hard and stood perfectly still.

O'Callaghan paused, then laid his rifle down before her and saluted.

"Sergeant Michael O'Callaghan, reporting for duty."

Nicky waited and took a step towards him, before he calmly surrendered himself to her.

CHAPTER 62

It had been a difficult and sleepless night. Nicky had been taken to hospital, not from any physical injuries, but she was being treated for shock. Jen had spent it with her, sleeping in a plastic chair in a corridor and listening to nurses chattering at their station in between blood tests on various patients, which had woken her up almost hourly.

Rob had been in the office with Laura Mathers. The political games had started, and although they were both as happy as they could be that the right man was now in custody, questions would be asked. Mathers would no doubt come under pressure, and she wanted to get their ducks in a row.

Michael O'Callaghan had been arrested for the murder of Frank McIntyre. It had been a cold-blooded assassination in the end. The area around the court had been cordoned off and there had been a heavy police presence overnight, including a considerable number of armed officers. The national press had descended and a temporary screen had been erected whilst the investigation continued and the forensic work was completed.

Becky and her team had been responsible for removing the remains of Frank McIntyre and for carrying out the post-mortem. It was an unenviable job, and her team would have collected every last piece of Frank McIntyre from the sandstone steps.

Michael O'Callaghan had spent the night soundly asleep in his cell. He had been due to be interviewed but was refusing to leave his cell and was refusing to be interviewed. Rob had spoken to Laura Mathers and had decided to try a different tact, albeit an inadmissible one. He nodded at the custody sergeant, who opened the cell door, and nonchalantly walked in carrying two cups of tea. He sat down near O'Callaghan's feet, and put the second cup of tea near to his right hand. Rob sipped the red-hot liquid but looked at the now-closed cell door.

"You murdered or provoked the murders of four people so you could find and execute Frank McIntyre?"

Rob asked the question rhetorically, and O'Callaghan double-checked that he wasn't being recorded, verbally at least.

"I can sense that you disapprove of my methods." He yawned, and almost seemed bored.

Rob looked at the heavy figure of Michael O'Callaghan, who was still clearly waking from a deep slumber.

"Sleep okay?"

"Best night's sleep for years."

Rob paused. "Why did you do it?"

O'Callaghan smiled wryly. "Do you have a sister, Rob?"

Rob swallowed hard but didn't answer. He thought about his sister. Her illness, and the precious time that he had left with her. Time that was ebbing away.

"I'll take that as a yes." O'Callaghan could see it. He didn't need the response. "Would you do everything in your power to protect her, Rob? Would you kill for her?"

Rob felt a wave of emotion wash over him and he swallowed

hard. He wanted to see his sister. Wanted to hold her. Wanted to tell her how much he loved her. He'd leave work and spend some time with his sister later on. Precious time. Time that he knew was running out.

"I'd almost given up trying to find him, you know. Me and Will have spent years looking for that man. Spent years trying to get justice for Maeve. We knew he could be dead, but we never stopped looking. All these years. Then Will called me and told me about his diagnosis. It was devastating. He's lost so much."

O'Callaghan looked Rob in the eye for the first time. He sipped his tea and winced slightly when the boiling water glanced against his lip.

"But then I saw the photograph in the paper and it all came flooding back. The emotion. The anger. I felt excited for the first time in years, and then one Friday night it just came to me."

"You sold David Cramer down the river."

"No, I didn't." His tone was calm. His voice was emotionless. "Nobody forced Cramer to kill Martin King. He wanted to. The thing you need to know about men like us is that we do what needs to be done. Things that normal men can't, or won't."

Rob listened intently.

"I was in the park that day. So was Will. I was there to kill Martin King. I wanted to kill him, but then I saw David and I knew why he was there. It was perfect. It was just so perfect, like a piece of art."

"You killed John McGrath." It wasn't a question.

"It needed to happen, it was overdue and he knew that."

"But you were friends."

"Were we? He was a terrorist, I was a British soldier."

He sipped some more of his tea.

"I've been working towards this for weeks. It was my final chance for justice. My final chance to find and execute McIntyre. I got justice for my sister yesterday. It's just different from your justice."

He lay his head back down and still looked tired. His eyes were deep and heavy in his face.

"Did you know where Maeve was, Michael?"

O'Callaghan raised his head and stared at Rob.

"No," it looked painful, "we were certain she was at Victoria, but between me, Will and Connor, we could never get close to finding her. We couldn't find anything that told us where he'd put her. He was the only one who knew where she was, and we found him, and we found her. Maeve can be laid to rest at home now. Properly. That gives me so much peace, I can't tell you. And he's obliterated. This is a win."

Rob pushed himself from the hard surface of the bed and wondered how O'Callaghan had slept so well.

"You'll face justice for your crimes, Michael. You may be a decorated soldier, but you'll stand trial for what you've done."

"Will I?" O'Callaghan smiled, which became more of a smirk. Rob waited for the gut punch.

"I have a tumour." He patted the right side of his temple. "It's inoperable. Like it or like it not, this is what winning looks like for me. Thirty years. It's taken me thirty years to get justice for Maeve, justice for Chris, and justice for all of the others."

Rob waited. He looked deep into Michael O'Callaghan's eyes. Into his soul.

"Men like me and Will, we were on a mission. Will was dangerous. He was dangerous years ago when he had everything to lose, and now he has absolutely nothing left he's a complete psychopath. I just channelled that energy. That anger. And we found him, we found him guilty and we executed him. We beat him, Rob. We won."

"You think this is winning?" Rob asked, looking at the sterile surroundings of the ten-by-eight cell.

"Oh, this is winning, make no mistake. This is my swansong. My crowning moment. It may not be for long but look around you, Inspector. Look at the *others*. Even McIntyre would appreciate what I've achieved given his ethos. Given his fucked-up mentality. Can't you see it? I'm the last man standing."

AUTHOR BIOGRAPHY

Born in Melton Mowbray, Leicestershire in 1980, Richard graduated from the Open University in Milton Keynes and has worked within the building materials industry for over 22 years. His first crime novel, Killing Time, was published in December 2020 with Troubador, after Richard was furloughed from work.

His second novel, Last Man Standing was published in 2024. Richard continues to work on new writing projects, including both fiction and non-fiction as well as a series of children's books.

Richard is married to his wife Nicola and has a teenage son Dominic from a previous marriage. His eldest son Alexander passed away in 2022 following a long battle with illness, and shortly after completing his GCSE exams. He smashed them.

Richard likes to keep fit; he has run two London Marathons (2020 and 2022), as well as the London Triathlon and the Windsor Triathlon. In September 2023 he cycled over 400 miles from Loughborough to the Eiffel Tower to raise funds for Rainbows Children's Hospice, and in September 2024 he will run the Great North Run, also for Rainbow's.

This book is printed on paper from sustainable sources managed under the Forest Stewardship Council (FSC) scheme.

It has been printed in the UK to reduce transportation miles and their impact upon the environment.

For every new title that Troubador publishes, we plant a tree to offset CO_2, partnering with the More Trees scheme.

For more about how Troubador offsets its environmental impact, see www.troubador.co.uk/sustainability-and-community